The Girl
WHO
SAID

Yes

Audrey Dillon

The Girl Who Said Yes
Copyright © 2016 by Audrey Dillon

Published by Piscataqua Press
An imprint of RiverRun Bookstore, Inc.
142 Fleet Street | Portsmouth, NH | 03801
www.riverrunbookstore.com
www.piscataquapress.com

ISBN: 978-1-944393-27-4

Printed in the United States of America

Part One

Chapter 1

"Wahoo! Happy birthday to me, baby!" Tess cheered, feeling the world at her fingertips. And what a feeling it was. Now that she could add purchasing alcohol to her list of attractive qualities, she knew this year was her year. Once and for all, her biggest dream was going to come true, not that she had any idea how exactly, but that didn't matter because something deep in her core told it was true. She simply felt it as she stood at her favorite bar, ordering the next round of drinks, in the multifarious Boston neighborhood of Allston-Brighton.

"And how are you, good-lookin'?" Tess said to a hunk passing by, too quietly for him to hear, and took the first swig of her fourth beer. He kept on walking. Watching him saunter all the way back to his seat, Tess felt disappointed.

A few moments later another cutie walked by. "Hey, stud. I'm single, and it's my birthday," Tess said louder. The guy paused and looked her up and down. While she stared back with hope and anticipation, he gave her a dismissive smirk.

"That'll be twenty-four bucks," the bartender said, placing the final beer on the tray. The gruff saltiness in his voice drew her toward him, away from the other guy.

"I have a tab going, don't you know?" Tess said with a drunken smile.

"Birthday girls shouldn't be buying drinks," he replied, but he didn't ask for her name. She stood there, baffled. She had never considered such a rule.

With a smile, she said, "Ryan, Tess Ryan," and paused, hoping he would compliment her on the way she said her name. When he didn't, she explained, "Well, how else am I going to get a group of girls out on a Monday night?"

After a piercingly long look and a soft smile, the bartender tapped the bar top and walked away. Tess began to follow him to explain herself, but Aimee Babineaux, her best friend, intercepted her.

"There you are!" Aimee, a smart, kind, and patient soul, said. She was a good three inches taller than Tess, with blonde hair, green eyes, and an hourglass figure. "I thought you fell—wait, what's this?" she asked, noticing the round of beers. "Tess, you don't buy! You're the birthday girl!"

"I know, but it's a Monday night, and you guys…"

"It's your twenty-first! Who cares what night of the week it is? We're here to celebrate!"

Embarrassed by Aimee's kind scolding, Tess forced the feeling away, and put a smile on her face. Aimee sent Tess and the drinks back to the table and asked the bartender to transfer Tess's round to her tab, adding strict instructions to not let Tess pay for a thing.

Upon her return to the table, Aimee said, "To the silliest, spit-fieriest, lovingest redhead I know!" She raised her glass.

"To finally being twenty-one!" Brie chimed in.

"It's about damn time," Sarah added.

"Let the shenanigans begin!" Zoe exclaimed.

"To having the best, crazy, fun year in life, love, and school!" Nora cheered.

"To Tess," Cecily said. And with that the seven girls clinked glasses, toasting the birthday girl.

Tess couldn't remember the last time she felt so loved. The sensation was amazing, yet foreign. She was more familiar with subdued gestures—birthday cards with a hundred bucks signed *Love, Mom*, text messages saying *Happy Birthday!* from her little sister, Eve, a belated voicemail from Dad. Aimee always went out of her way—balloons, flowers, singing, a cake, the whole nine yards—but it was usually just the two of them celebrating.

Aimee must have noticed Tess's discomfort when she grabbed her hand under the table and whispered in her ear, "You so deserve this, Tess! Enjoy it! I know we are."

"Damn right! To me!" Tess took another swig, instantly taking Aimee's message to heart. "And to having the best senior year in the history of UMass!"

The girls all whooped. Then they began to share their hopes and goals for the upcoming year. Most of them simply prayed to end the year with a job lined up or to pass all their classes. Tess, however, revealed an entirely different plan.

"I'm going to meet the man I'll marry this year. I swear it.

Come hell or high water."

Silence arrested the table. The girls looked at each other, clearly wondering if Tess was serious.

Tess snorted into her beer. "Gimme a break! Like you guys can honestly tell me you don't think about marriage or boyfriends. Well except for you Sarah. You have one! But to the rest of you, how can you not want to be swept off your feet by some handsome devil, for all the world to see? Like meeting someone in the worst possible circumstances, maybe on the day before you graduate and move to Africa, or in a hospital after one of you has been in a terrible accident. But despite it all, you fall madly in love…"

Caught up in her fantasy, Tess gazed at the silent and pensive faces around the table. She struggled to understand their lack of understanding. *Doesn't every girl want a man who will make her feel absolutely, undeniably loved? What is wrong with them?*

"Whatever. This is my year. Starting right now, I'm counting down the days until I meet the man who is going to take my breath away."

After another round of awkward shared glances, Tess said, "Ha ha! You guys should see your faces right now! You all look petrified. Come on, I know that stuff isn't real. I'm just hoping he's wicked hot and pays for dinner."

Everyone but Aimee burst out laughing.

"Oh, how about that one over there? See? With the blue shirt and nice hair?" Tess giggled, pointing. She quickly glanced at Aimee who was glaring at her. Knowing what the harsh look meant and not willing to let it dampen the evening, Tess ignored her.

"You mean the married guy with the nice hair and blue shirt?" Brie asked, noticing his left hand.

"Damn it. Okay. Hmm. Oh, what about that one? He'd make a stellar boyfriend. Love his long hair and that scruff. I bet he's got lots of tattoos!"

Tess stood, preparing to walk toward the rocker guy, but Aimee grabbed her shirt and pulled her back. "Not tonight. I think it's time to get you some water."

"Boo, Aimee! What if that guy's my soul mate? Now you're going to win that bet!"

"Oh, there's a bet? What's that all about?" Brie asked.

"Nothing. It's really nothing," Aimee replied.

"How dare you!" Tess squealed, half mad, half joking. "That bet is everything! How can you say that?" Her sloppy-drunk thoughts raced back to the summer before eighth grade, when she and Aimee had watched endless reruns of *Beverly Hills 90210*. Tess had bet Aimee that she would meet a bad boy like Dylan McKay and turn him into a tender-loving husband.

"Tess, you're drunk. You don't know what you're talking about," Aimee said.

"Hey, I'm only a little drunk." Tess stood up. She quickly felt the room spin and her stomach drop, as if she were on a carnival ride. "Okay, whoa. So I might be a *lot* drunk, but it's my birthday, so *meh*." She stuck out her tongue and backed away from the table, slowly, holding Aimee's gaze.

"Excuse me," Tess said, bumping into some one.

"Sorry," the handsome stranger said.

"Oops."

"Here, I'll go this…"

"Way, and I'll go…"

Curt smiles dropped from both faces as they swerved with audible, annoyed gasps of frustration they did not stifle.

"Look," the serious fellow finally said, taking Tess by the shoulders. "You go this way, and I'll go that way."

Tess gave a quick smile and did the opposite of what he said. She crashed into him yet again.

"Okay, Tess, follow me." Aimee appeared, taking Tess by the arm, and led her away. Tess sent the guy a timorous smile, indicating her desire for his forgiveness, but he shrugged, rolled his eyes, and ignored her.

Moments later Tess was outside on the sidewalk surrounded by fresh air. Aimee was watching traffic, her arm outstretched for a cab.

"Do you think that guy was secretly a Calvin Klein model? Should I have given him my number?" Tess bit her lower lip.

"I think it's time to call it a night."

Tess began to sway. Aimee put an arm around her shoulders.

"You're right. I'm glad I didn't give him my number. He's probably some uptight doctor-lawyer guy. Oh, but those eyes. Mmm, they were so, so, so…"

"Serious?"

"Sexy."

"See, Tess you don't really want to get married. You just want to have fun, like the rest of us. Oh look, here comes a cab!" Aimee stuffed Tess into it and gave the driver directions and a twenty-dollar bill.

"But, but what if Sexy Eyes is my soul mate? And now he's gone forever. Poof! Into the night sky."

"Don't you worry about Sexy Eyes. I'm sure you'll see him again."

With a warm smile, Aimee shut the door and sent Tess on her way.

Chapter 2

The following day, noon arrived all too soon. If it weren't for her five-star hangover and the loud crashing sounds coming from the kitchen, Tess would have slept until next Tuesday.

Staggering into the kitchen with her hand on her head, Tess asked, "Hey, Lori, can you put off dismantling the kitchen until tomorrow?", prepared to see her father's longtime on-and-off girlfriend.

"Who the fuck's Lori?" demanded the scantily clad stranger standing next to the kitchen sink full of pots and pans. Her South Boston accent was strong and her bleached blonde hair greasy, with stringy ends.

The appearance of an unfamiliar half-naked angry woman in her dad's apartment should have surprised Tess, but it didn't. Random women were the norm. What did catch her off guard was that this one couldn't have been more than five minutes older than her. "And who are you?" the girl asked.

"Hugh's daughter."

Relaxing a bit, the girl looked her up and down, then said, "Nice getup."

Smoothing her dress, the one she'd slept in despite wearing it the night before, Tess asked, "And who are you?"

"Hugh's girlfriend."

Translation: Just another flavor of the week, Tess thought. The girl would be gone within the hour. "Right."

A familiar awkward pause ushered in. After waiting a couple of moments in silence for the girl to say something else, which of course didn't happen, Tess shuffled to the bathroom in search of headache medicine.

From the bathroom, Tess heard her father's conversation loud and clear.

"A daughter, Hugh? What the hell?" The girl's agitated voice grew louder. "Great, don't say anything. I'd think having a daughter who is practically the same age as me isn't something you just leave out." Again, no response. "I swear to God, Hugh. This is the last time I ever come to this sad excuse for an apartment!"

Tess smiled to herself, thinking, *wait for it...*

BOOM! was the next thing she heard as the front door slammed. Again not surprising.

Just as encountering a random woman in the apartment was not a surprise, neither were the usual one-sided screaming matches, followed by the woman storming out amid promises to never come back. Tess cringed in pain from the noise and reached for ibuprofen.

With the medicine in her system, Tess found her father sitting on the couch in his desolate unkempt living room. She took a seat next to him.

"Tess? You're here?" Hugh asked in his thick Irish brogue. Even seated, it was apparent that Hugh was a very tall, slender man. His rumpled hair was deep red, complementing his freckled porcelain skin. His baby-blue eyes were captivating. She'd seen many people hold his gaze just a little longer than usual when they first met. Tess was his clone in every way but gender, height, and girth. She carried a few extra pounds around her middle.

"Like I have been all summer, Dad," Tess replied, a little hurt but used to it.

"Oh, yeah. So what have you been up to?"

"Well, yesterday was my twenty-first birthday."

"How about that? Happy birthday, kid."

"Thanks, Dad," Tess said, feeling like an afterthought.

"So how about you take your old man out for a drink tonight? I'll show you off to all me friends down at the Silhouette."

"Really?" Tess said, beaming. From afterthought to centerpiece, just like that. Tess's imagination began dancing with classy outfits and behaviors that would make her father proud.

"Yeah, really. When was the last time this guy turned down a free drink?"

Tess smiled and thought about her bank balance. Her father's hopeful face silenced her doubts. Then her cell phone rang. Tess stood and lifted a hand to her dad before she headed back to her room.

"Mom, hi."

"You sound congested. Are you okay? Are you coming down with something?" Grace replied.

"Nope, not sick. I'm fine."

"Oh. Okay. So tell me. How was last night? Did you go out?"

"It was nice. Aimee and Brie and a couple other friends took me out."

"Good. I'm so glad you had some people to celebrate with. I remember when I turned twenty-one like it was yesterday. Well, it was eighteen in my day. God, I'm old—"

"Stop, Mom. You're not old."

"I am, baby, but it's okay. I've earned it. Anyway, I just wanted to see how your first night as a full-fledged adult went."

"It was fun. You know, just had only a few drinks. Nothing too crazy."

"I see. That's why you sound stuffy and are still wearing what you had on last night."

Tess scanned the room for a camera. How did her mother know that? "No! I'm still in my pajamas."

"At a quarter past noon?"

Tess frowned. *How does she always know when I'm lying?*

"I miss you so much. I still don't understand why you didn't come home for the summer."

"Because I am home, Mom. Boston is it."

"I know, but so is Santa Fe. I wish you had come home, at least for your birthday. I would so have loved to buy you your first drink."

"Aw, thanks, Mom, but I'm still not flying out there. It may be your home, but it's not mine."

Halfway through her sophomore year of high school, Grace had packed up herself and her two daughters and moved to New Mexico from Boston. Santa Fe was not the Land of Enchantment, as all the license plates said. To Tess, it was the Land of Entrapment. The dry, empty landscape and sing-songy Spanish accents drove her nuts. Everyone sounded stoned or stupid and on occasion both, especially at her new school. At least the city had an ice rink. At least she could continue figure skating, her beloved sport since she was seven years old.

"I was at the grocery store the other day with your sister Eve. You remember her, of course—the one who is about to start her senior year of high school and misses her big sister and could seriously use some guidance."

"Geez, Mom, of course I remember Eve!"

Grace's normally thick Boston accent momentarily shifted into the droning New Mexican one. "Anyway, while we were at Albertson's, we ran into some of your old skating friends—you know, from the ice rink. They all asked about you and wanted to know when you were coming back to town."

"Okay, Mom. I appreciate what you're doing here, and I say this with love, but it's not going to work. I'm happy here with Dad. Boston is where I belong."

"How is your father, by the way? Seeing that Lori woman still?"

"Yeah, I guess," Tess said. Just then an arrow of pain pierced her head, and her stomach churned.

"That's good. I hope she's giving him the stability he needs."

Just as Tess opened her mouth to respond, the call waiting beep came through.

"Hey, Mom, Aimee's on the other line. I gotta go."

"Right. Happy birthday again, my twenty-one-year-old. Remember to drink lots of water and take two aspirin. Hello to Aimee, my best to your father. Love you, baby."

"Got it. Love you too. Bye, Mom," Tess said, clicking over to Aimee before quite finishing. "Aimee! Oh my God! I am so hung over I think death by skin peeling would feel better."

"Thanks for the reminder to not get on your bad side."

"What?"

"Nothing. So, champ, you ready for Moogy's Dizzy Pig?"

"Sure. A heart attack on a plate sounds pretty good right about now."

"Cool. See you there in twenty minutes?"

"Twenty minutes! Dude, I need like an hour."

"Seriously?"

"No, but pick me up anyway?"

"Fine. But please brush your teeth. I can smell your breath from here."

"Shut up! No you can't."

"I'll be there in ten."

Tess checked her breath and then did as she was told. Ten minutes later, she was wearing a fresh pair of jeans, a clean T-shirt, and baseball hat, and yes, her teeth were brushed.

Half an hour later at Moogy's and staring down at the pockets of bubbling grease on her plate, Tess felt her stomach gurgle. After just a few bites, her mind-numbing hangover would be a relic of the past. Hot grease was usually Aimee's cure as well, but for some reason she had ordered a Greek salad. Tess couldn't figure out how Aimee drank at least as much as she did but somehow looked rejuvenated instead of haggard, like her.

"There is no way you drank as much as me and feel only half as bad," Tess said, shoveling bacon into her mouth.

"Actually, there is," Aimee replied. "I don't have time to waste being hung over, so I started looking around for things that actually work."

Tess slowed her chewing.

"And I think I finally found the trick."

"Yeah? What's that?" Tess swallowed hard.

"Before I went to bed last night, I took two aspirin, chugged a ton of water and a bottle of Gatorade, and now I feel perfectly fine."

"How were you not up all night in the bathroom?"

"That's the thing. Alcohol dehydrates you. I wasn't in the bathroom because I replaced the hydration I lost."

"And look at you! Beautiful and perfect as ever," Tess said, contemplating her next bite.

"Try it next time. Then you won't have to ingest *that* mess," Aimee said, waving her hand over Tess's plate.

Tess raised her eyebrow. She understood where her best friend was coming from. She really was just trying to help, but despite the fact that this was only her second day being twenty-one, this was definitely not the first time Tess had been hung over. She knew what worked for her and wasn't about to go changing that.

"Ah, yes, that's the stuff," Tess said, feeling her anguish dissipate as her stomach gratefully received the food. "Tell me, what are we doing today?"

"Seeing it's past one, I think we should talk about your life plan."

"Life plan?"

"Last night, you said your goal for this year is to get married."

Tess took a long, deep breath, trying to remember what she'd said. It wasn't as clear to her as it seemed to be to Aimee.

"It's kind of limiting, don't you think?" Aimee looked Tess in the eyes. "What about your love of reading? History? Don't you still want to be a history teacher?"

"Married! Ha! No. I'm too young to be married this year."

Aimee looked like an unsatisfied customer.

"All I meant was I want to be dating the guy I'm going to marry someday. Geez, Aimee, what kind of idiot do you take me for?"

"Every other day you're in love with someone new. Just last night, you nearly asked out three guys. One of them was married."

"Like that even counts, Aimee. I was drunk. And so what if I'm a romantic?"

Just then she pictured her perfect guy. He'd be tall, like her father, with warm eyes and an equally tender touch. At a moment's notice he'd play a musical instrument, like a guitar or piano. He'd be both well-spoken and well-read, but not in an uppity way because of his natural gentle nature. Though gentle, he'd be assertive when the situation called for it and happy-go-lucky, with a great sense of humor. But most important, he would be attentive and affectionate, placing Tess above all others.

"How is that even possible?"

"Excuse me? What do you mean?"

Aimee spoke carefully. "It's not like your parents lived happily ever after."

Tess became silent. Talking about her parents' failed marriage made her uncomfortable and angry. Had her parents worked harder to stay together, Tess never would have been forced to move her sophomore year of high school. "Whatever. I'll prove to you that I can find romantic, happily-ever-after love," Tess said, breaking her silence.

"I'm sorry, Tess. I didn't mean to upset you. I just don't want you to get your heart broken so much."

"Please. You never let that happen anyway." Tess quickly looked at Aimee then said, "Okay. Well not, like, *really bad* heartbreak."

Aimee rolled her eyes, sparking Tess to remember the day they made another bet, so much more powerful than the one from eighth grade, that it had become Tess's reason for being.

It was the evening of Monday, September 3, 2001. She and

Aimee had just walked from their new college dorm rooms in Orchard Hill to the idyllic campus pond. "So what do you think it's going to be like, college and stuff?" Tess had asked, staring at a particularly svelte brunette wearing short Daisy Dukes, a white halter top, and bright shade of red lipstick and helplessly comparing herself to the stranger.

"Well, if my brother, Asher the Thrasher, is any indication, it'll be one big party that earns us a permanent spot in my parents' basement," Aimee said. "Promise me you won't turn into one of those girls," she said, looking in the same direction as Tess.

"Oh, we'll party…but not like Asher. We're here to get an education. We could've just rented some cheap apartment in Allston with ten roommates if we wanted just to party."

"Thanks for the reminder, *Mom*."

"Whatever—you know what I mean." Tess paused, selecting the spot to claim as *their* sitting spot. Settling on the slope in front of the Old Chapel, Tess continued. "But most of all, I think I will—well, I hope I will—fall in love. You know, the classic romance. The kind where we see each other across the room but never exchange names. Then neither of us stops searching for the other until we meet again. Then we fall madly in love and live happily ever after."

"Ha! That only happens in the movies." Aimee's tone was sharp.

"What? No, it's totally possible."

"Yeah, if you live in TV la-la land. How can you, of all people, believe in that stuff?"

"Because I just do, okay?" Tess said, signaling silence by turning her face away. A dark cloud then entered the conversation. As Aimee reminded her of her parents' messy breakup, Tess felt like she wasn't allowed to believe in happily ever after anymore. But she did. In fact, she clung to it. Her parents' failure only made her want to find true love even more.

Suddenly, a swan, from out of nowhere, came barreling toward them, flapping its wings, squawking stridently. Without a word, the girls got up and ran as fast as they could toward the Du Bois Library.

"Holy shit! What was that?" Tess said, gasping, when they stopped.

"Asher told me that the swans here were nuts. Super territorial. I thought it was just a joke his stoner friends told him. Guess not," Aimee replied, also out of breath. "Hey, I'm sorry. I didn't mean anything by it. Really."

Tess looked at her long and hard. She knew deep down Aimee didn't mean to hurt her feelings. She was just being Aimee, a fierce pragmatist. Resigned, Aimee said, "Okay, fine. All love stories on TV and in the movies are real. You happy now?"

"Almost," Tess paused. "Let's make another bet. I'll bet you, starting today I *will* meet and fall madly in love with a guy here at UMass, and I will be with that very same guy until the day I die."

"That's nuts! You're only eighteen."

"Yeah, and?"

"You can't just say when you're going to meet the one. It has to happen…naturally."

"So—is it a bet or not?"

"And what if you *don't* fall madly in love by the time we graduate?"

"I don't know! I'll just get a bunch of cats and name each one after every guy I thought I ever loved."

"If you say so, but I just want to state, for the record, you're crazy. And, that as little as I want to, I will start a special Ben and Jerry's savings account. You know, just in case."

"Your faith in me is overwhelming," Tess said as they shook on it.

"Tess, you're beautiful. You don't need to make some silly bet to find love. It's out there for you just as much as it is for me or anyone else."

"Said the buxom blonde with a killer rack and ass to match."

Aimee gave her a look.

"Yeah, come talk to me after the first question out of every guy's mouth is 'Fire-crotch?'" Tess said, referring to her red hair. "See, I win."

Aimee shrugged and the bet was made. That bet drove Tess. Always, she was ready. Hair done, clothes perfect, makeup flawless. Never would Tess miss the chance at meeting her perfect match. Every guy was a contender—even the guy working the pumps at the gas station. Who knew? What if he was a closet lover of literature or some gadget inventor sitting on a wad of cash? For Tess, every minute of every day and every guy she encountered every day had the potential to be the one.

"And we need to do something about those swans. Look, there're two more. They're chasing those people over there," Tess said, looking back toward their former seats.

"Definitely."

Back in the booth at Moogy's, Tess heard everything Aimee was saying, but acknowledging that would lead Aimee to think she was right and Tess was wrong and Tess wasn't ready to hand her that victory just yet. She signaled her desire to leave by asking, "Hey, can I borrow twenty bucks?"

"For what?"

"I have a date tonight."

"No, you don't. You would've told me way before today."

"Can I borrow it or not? I probably won't even need it. I'll give it back tomorrow."

"Fine," Aimee said, taking the cash out of her wallet. "Tomorrow. I want it back tomorrow."

"Don't worry about it."

"So what's his name?"

"Hugh."

"Hugh?" Aimee paused. "Damn, Tess! Give me my money back."

"But my dad wants me to take him out for my birthday."

"Tess, daughters aren't supposed to pay for their birthday dinners."

"I know, but my dad is a little strapped right now."

"I have never known him not to be."

"Well, he's old. I'm young. It's my turn now."

Aimee knew well that there was no changing Tess's mind once it was made up. "Fine. I hope you have a good time."

"We will, don't worry," Tess replied, clearing both of their plates. When she got back to the table, Aimee was ready to leave as well.

Returning home a few hours later, after an unsuccessful trip to TJMaxx, Tess found the apartment empty. As this often happened, she figured her father was out getting her a belated gift. *Better late than never*, she thought with a smile. Hugh had his flaws, but it wasn't his fault he had a terrible memory when it came to dates. The important thing was he was most likely thinking of her birthday now. In the meantime, she took the opportunity to take a luxuriously long shower. It was the least she could do to get over the fact that she wasn't able to find something new to wear out that night.

Now seven o'clock, Tess was fresh and looking divine, well divine-ish. She wasn't thrilled that she had to wear an old sun dress rather than a new one, but it was her best sun dress with its waist cinching cut and billowy skirt. Tess even did up her eyes and coated her lips with a generous amount of clear gloss.

After admiring herself in the mirror, Tess realized there was still no sign or word from Hugh. *Not a problem*, thought Tess. He most likely just lost track of time. No need to worry. It was only seven after all. Hardly late in terms of getting a drink. Confident that her father would show up at any moment, Tess turned on the TV and patiently waited for what she thought would be fifteen or twenty minutes at most.

Finally, at ten o'clock Tess had had enough. There were only so many *TBS* movies a girl could take in one night, especially when she had plans – even if they were with dear old Dad.

Naturally, her first reaction would have been to call him, but she knew that was a futile endeavor. Hugh almost always had that damn thing switched off and never bothered to set up the voicemail. What was the point of even having a cell phone if it was always off and no one could leave a message?

Unable to call, Tess had only two other options: one, call Lori or two, check the Silhouette and see if he somehow thought she said to meet him there. She chose the latter. Lori was nice and all, but if she and her father were in the midst of a fight, Tess along with the rest of Boston would hear about it.

"Tess, how are ya kid?" Marlene, the veteran waitress called out as soon as Tess walked into the Silhouette.

"Marlene, how are you?"

"Can't complain, love. You're looking beautiful as ever."

"Gee. Thanks Marlene. That's very kind of you." Tess blushed as she looked down at her strappy sandals with studded rhinestones around her ankles.

"What brings you in tonight? Not a date I hope. This isn't

your kind of place. We both know that," Marlene paused. "Looking for your father are you?"

"Indeed I am. Have you seen him?"

"Yeah, hun. He was in here about an hour ago. Left with some cheeky young thing. Looked as if they wanted something more private, if you know what I mean?"

Tess cringed at the mental image Marlene had just painted at the same time her heart broke. While this was by far not the first time Hugh had let her down, it still hurt. She could barely count the number of times he'd forgotten her skating shows or to even pick her up from school. And yet, there she was all dressed up in a grimy, poorly lit excuse of a bar thinking her father would have been there, excited for his daughter to officially buy him a drink for the first time. She felt utterly awful and she could tell she was letting it show on her face by the way Marlene was looking at her.

"Sorry, Tess. I didn't mean to upset you. You know how your father is. Got the attention span of a fruit fly. I'm sure he didn't mean to not be here."

Giving a well rehearsed hundred-watt smile Tess said, "That means a lot Marlene. Thank you, but it's fine. I'm sure wherever he is, it's something important," and turned to leave.

"Fair enough, but what was it that got you all dressed up then?"

"My twenty-first birthday," Tess said and slipped out the door.

Walking home and feeling rather low, but in all honesty, not that surprised, Tess admitted to herself that deep down she knew her father was going to be a no show. She just knew because this certainly wasn't the first time another woman stole her father's attention.

Then her phone rang, catching her by surprise.

"Aimee, hi! What are you doing up so late? Don't you have to work tomorrow?"

"I can't sleep."

"Watched another episode of *Outer Limits*?"

"I wish. I don't know what it is. Just can't sleep. How's your night?"

"Pretty great, actually. My dad and I are having an awesome time." Tess lied. She couldn't bring herself to be honest. It would only get her a, "I told you so," from Aimee.

"That's good."

A long pause followed.

"And hey, don't worry about that twenty bucks," Tess said. "I'll give you back the exact same one you gave me earlier. Turns out my dad was kidding about the whole birthday-girl-pays thing."

"Seriously?"

"Told you there was nothing to worry about."

"Well then, I'm—" A yawn interrupted her voice. "Glad to hear it."

"Wow, Aimee. Is the sound of my voice really that boring?"

"Whatever. I was just calling to check on you." Aimee yawned again. "Now that I know you're fine, I'm going to go to bed. I'll call you tomorrow."

Yup, Tess was fine. She was always fine. She and her dad were having a great time, just not together. *It's cool. He'll come home. He'll say how sorry he is and promise never to do it again. Then we'll just stay up late watching movies or something,* Tess reasoned, as she neared the apartment. Who was she kidding? It was more likely that he would come strolling in at some ungodly hour and wake up with no memory of his promise to go out for a drink.

Had Tess known any other way, like a father who kept his word, she surely would have never agreed to take her father out in the first place, but this was the only way she knew. On the bright side, her father's unreliability made her more independent and self-sufficient, as well as driven to find her Prince Charming and cancel out all of her father's non-Prince Charming qualities. On the even brighter side, only seven more weeks until she was back at school. Only seven more weeks.

Chapter 3

"Good day," a Mr. Magoo look-alike professor bellowed through the hallowed lecture hall on the first day of History 140, one of the easy classes Tess had deliberately saved for her senior year. "This is European History, 1500 to 1815. This course consists of two lectures and one discussion section per week..."

She'd heard it all before. Watching the lost freshmen straggle in and clamor for seats, Tess sat comfortably, listening to the professor, waiting for the introduction to be over. What she really wanted to see was the syllabus. *Is this really going to be an easy class?* she wondered. Half the class was late, it seemed, and she quickly realized they were only late because the professor had started early. That was never a good sign.

"Hello," mouthed a tall, dark, and handsome graduate student towering over her while he passed her the syllabus. She looked down at her fingers resting on his. The entire room fell silent. All she could hear was her teeth clench. Sweat moistened her forehead. Chills raced over her body.

He was maybe five foot eleven, with slightly rounded shoulders, she guessed from poring over loads of books. His face was square, with deep-set almond eyes and thick eyebrows that made him look pensive and curious. His thick, dark-brown hair looked luxuriously soft. She fantasized about running her fingers through it. She even liked the thin chinstraps that gave him an Abe Lincoln kind of look. His body was firm and slender. *He can't be more than twenty-five,* she thought. While he continued to pass out the syllabus, Tess caught him looking back at her. The chills came rushing back.

After class, Tess bolted from Herter Hall, home of the history department, and found Aimee in one of her usual spots, one of the cubbies in the southeast corner of the library on the fifteenth floor.

"Aimee! Aimee! Aimee! I have to tell you something!" Tess professed breathlessly, at a volume far too loud for a library.

Aimee, with her back to her friend, almost jumped out of her seat. "Jesus, Tess!"

"Sorry, sorry," Tess said, insincerely. "I think—no, I *know*— I've just won the bet!"

Aimee's left eyebrow popped up. Just last week, Tess had said the same thing about the guy standing in line in front of them at Target.

"So I'm sitting in Herter Hall for History 140. The syllabus is going around—no big deal, right? Then, when the syllabus touched my hand, out of nowhere I was covered in chills! I mean, it was, like, totally random. A sign!"

"Yeah, so random…Anyway, so what does he look like?"

"He's the perfect height. Well, I assume he is. I was sitting, so I'm not exactly sure, but based on the distance to his warm chocolaty eyes, I figure he's tall. Oh, and he has the perfect body, slim and muscled." Tess stopped for a minute, picturing his hot body shirtless. "You know, he kind of looks like Abraham Lincoln, now that I think about it."

"Gross."

"Well, okay, fine. So he doesn't look like Lincoln. He's still mega hot."

"If you say so." Aimee shrugged her shoulders. "What's his name?"

"Oh, ah, I dunno…"

"Ah, Tess, that's Dating 101."

Tess chuckled. "Whatever. I've got loads of time to learn his name."

Aimee rolled her eyes. "Just promise me you'll learn his name before you run away with him."

"I promise. It's not like I'm going to be all crazy excited around him like I am now. He'd think I'm a nut job!"

Aimee chuckled at Tess's rare moment of self-awareness and proceeded to let her friend share the play-by-play of what happened.

"Good Morning, I'm Nick Donovan." Tess didn't need to look at the person connected to the voice; it was *him*. His voice alone sent chills all over her body. "I'll be leading this discussion section for History 140." His overly professional tone sounded like he was trying to hide his nervousness. He fussed with some papers and began calling names without looking up from the roster. "Beverly Adams…Shane Cunningham…Kai Donnell…Tessalie Ryan." He paused, looking around the room. When he met Tess's eyes, he looked at her for several seconds longer than he had anyone else before he continued calling names.

…And that was it. After that one look, she was in love. Tess took a one-way ticket to dreamland. The only other passenger on that train was Nick Donovan. Just as the lovebirds rounded a corner in la-la land, Nick called on Tess to introduce herself.

Panic set in. She had nothing prepared. She couldn't risk embarrassing herself in front of this perfect specimen of a man. *What to say? Say where I'm from, grade, major. Crap, why can't we just skip all these formalities and get married and live happily ever after?* Then her mind went blank.

"Tessalie, tell us about yourself," Nick encouraged her again. His hotness was all she thought about.

"I'm Tess."

The silence in her head soon filled the classroom.

"Okay, Tess. Anything else you want to share? Hometown? Favorite color?"

Silence.

Forty eyes descended on her, waiting for an answer.

Nick gave a confused smile and moved on to the next person. Tess could have kicked herself. She officially had no game; there were twenty witnesses to prove it. She searched the room for a rock to crawl under. *So much for impressing the hot TA.* At least she told him to call her the name she went by.

Feeling defeated, Tess called her mother as soon as the class was over.

"So...what do you think? Do you think he likes me too?" Tess shared every little look, glance, and word between her and Nick.

"Slow down. Let me get this right. You didn't actually say anything to him?"

"Yes."

"Okay, then what are you asking me again?"

"The way he looked at me longer than everyone else in the room—what does that mean?"

"It could mean anything, honey. Maybe he has a family member named Tessalie."

Tess groaned. *I'm the only one with such a ridiculous name*, she thought. "But you're an experienced woman. You're supposed to know these things."

"Tess, I wasn't there. I can't say one way or the other," Grace paused. "Give it some time. See how things go. Once you know him better, you'll have a better idea of what he's thinking."

"Fine."

"Oh, Tess, you're so dramatic. You'll find someone. He's out there."

"I know, I know, but why can't he just be here already!"

Grace laughed. "Tess, you're only twenty-one. You've got time. There's a guy out there with your name on him. Now, get off the phone and go study."

Yeah, and his name is Nick Donovan.

"Yes, Mother."

As usual, Grace had a point. Deep down, Tess knew it was nearly impossible to tell if a person was interested from just a few looks, but she had a feeling in the pit of her stomach that even without words, something was there; he was her man.

"All right, guys—first quiz of the semester. If you did the reading, you'll be fine. If you didn't, well, I guess I will see you in my office next week," Nick said, passing out the quizzes a week later. Tess didn't miss Nick winking at her when he said, "See you in my office." *Is he suggesting that I am an idiot?* Great, she'd done more damage than she thought. *No, he couldn't mean that—he doesn't even know me. I read, I studied, I attended all of the lectures. I am ready for this quiz...*

But she wasn't. The following week she learned that she scored 60 percent, a big fat D-. *What the hell went wrong?* She answered all the questions right when the class discussed them after the quiz. Now the molehill she'd created the week before was quickly becoming a mountain.

"Hey, Nick, can I talk to you for minute?" Tess asked, nervously, at the end of the discussion.

Nick looked her up and down before responding, "Ah, yes, Tessalie," and then turned back to putting his belongings in his backpack.

"Tess, it's just Tess." *God, he's hot.* She mentally kicked herself. *Come on, Tess! Stay focused. And try not to sound so stupid.* "Right, I was just wonder—"

"I totally get it, but I can't talk right now." A smirk crossed his face as he checked her out again. "Come by during my office hours next week. We'll discuss it then," he said as he left the classroom. Alone, Tess let out a soft squeal. *Twice. He checked me out twice!*

Chapter 4

Riding up the elevator to the seventh floor felt like an eternity. Tess had time to humor a fun thought. *Maybe I really scored a 100 percent, but Nick marked some of the questions wrong to get me in his office. He did openly check me out twice.*

When she found the right office, she was arrested by the number she saw on the door: 712. *July 12th is my birthday. This has got to be sign.* She braced herself and knocked; the slightly open door swung wide open. Three large, green metal desks ran along three of the four walls, making everything else in the room look green and small. Nick sat at a desk on the right side of the office. He turned around right away.

"Hey, Tess." His tone was the warmest sound she had ever heard. She instantly felt weak in the knees. Their eyes locked. Tess felt the hairs on the back of her neck stand up. Nick performed a full-body inspection with his eyes. *That's three!* She felt herself begin to smile and tried to hide it. *Tess, you're embarrassing yourself. Pull it together.* He smiled too.

"I bet I know why you're here."

"You do? Sorry. Duh, you graded it. But, yeah, I wanted to know what I did wrong."

"First of all, it's not you; it was your answers." His response assuaged her fears. *He knows just what to say,* she thought. *How could I have been so stupid on that quiz?*

She couldn't pull her eyes away from his mouth. It looked so soft. When words came out, she imagined each word being carefully sent off with a gentle push. She wondered what his lips felt like just as she felt herself falling toward him. Thankfully, she caught herself before she landed somewhere awkward, like his lap.

"Let me ask you something," he began. "Are you worried that this quiz is going to bring down your entire grade?"

Tess looked out the window.

"It's okay. It's only one D out of the hundreds of grades you will earn in the next four years."

"Four years? What are you talking about?" Her face twisted with offense.

"I'm kidding. You're a senior," Nick paused. "Yeah, a senior. Why is that? This is usually a freshman class."

Tess's stomach tightened. "Naïve freshmen," she said, buying some time as she thought up some better response than the truth.

"Come again?"

"Hey, I read the fine print when I signed those papers to become a history major. The massive internship only for seniors…I knew I didn't want anything to distract me from that, so I saved a couple of easy classes for my last year."

"Hey, all right, cool—a history major. So wouldn't that mean you know History 140 is a prerequisite for precisely everything else?"

"What can I say? I have a way with advisors."

Nick cleared his throat and shifted in his seat. "History then. Why did you pick history?"

"That's easy. I often wonder what life was like before we all got here and made a mess of things. And yes, I'm aware that life in general is messy, but the past just seems simpler. They had simple messes, unlike today."

"Interesting."

"But what I really love about history is all the stories. I simply cannot resist a good story. Take the love letters of Heloise and Abelard. Their story is so complicated, yet sweet and heartbreaking, all the while honest."

"Heloise and Abelard?"

"Twelfth-century Heloise was one of France's first feminists, whose disdain for marriage and the prescribed life of a woman made her love affair with Abelard complicated and scandalous, especially after the birth of their son. Her uncle and guardian, Fulbert, forced the new parents to marry in secret, which of course angered Heloise, but she was so madly in love with Abelard she went through with it anyway. It's all so complicated and romantic. I love it!"

"I'm impressed. Not many undergrads know such detailed French history. How did you come across that story anyway?" Now, Tess noticed, Nick began leaning closer into her.

"I love to read. When I was old enough to go by myself, I would hop on the T and go down to the main Boston Library branch, the one with the lions out front, and spend the entire day there just reading."

"Nerd."

"Excuse me?" Tess felt her nostrils flare a bit.

"It's okay. I'm a nerd too. My parents weren't rich, so I spent some time with books too."

"Well, good. At least I know where you stand and...just how hard this class will be."

Nick paused, then said, "So you think this class is going to be easy?"

"What? Like you're going to make it hard." Her eyes twinkled.

The air suddenly became much warmer.

Scratching the left side of his head with his index finger, Nick said, "Okay, look. The D is because, while your answers weren't wrong per se, they just didn't articulate what they needed to say in order to get credit."

"You can't be serious." Tess had never heard such a ridiculous answer about her work. "Before you even graded it, you heard me give all the correct answers verbally."

"True, but I can only grade what I have on record, which is what you wrote down."

Tess gave him a disappointed look.

Nick flashed a lascivious grin, and in that moment Tess became seriously hooked. Feeling more confident, she was about to ask him another question when a female walked in.

The girl instantly changed the mood. Nick sat up straighter, and his face went stern. The student had a mixed look of disgust and curiosity. Tess chuckled silently at Nick's sudden change. For a moment, he even looked a little guilty. The girl's eyes darted back and forth between the two. Tess gave away nothing and proceeded to gather her backpack.

Moments after leaving his office, she heard Nick pardon himself.

"Tess, wait up a second. If you want any help, don't hesitate to see me. We can go over the material before each quiz."

Tess was overcome with excitement. *Is he asking me or telling me to come back and see him?*

Seizing the moment, Tess said, "By the way, you should stop by the activities fair on the sixteenth. I'm founder of the Save the People, Save the Swans Club. We're trying to get the swans moved safely and humanely off campus for good."

"Swans?"

Tess shared her swan attack story from her first night on campus as a freshman.

"Oh, really? You know, you could save the students and your time by just shooting them."

"Hey! Mean creatures or not, they have a right to live too. We advocate for the permanent removal of the animals. That way everyone's happy."

"I see."

"And we can always use more grad student support, so come on by," she said enthusiastically. Nick smiled again and returned to his office.

Feeling like a kid in a candy store, Tess strolled across campus and ran into Aimee studying at the student union building. Tess wasted no time telling her every little detail. She even mentioned that his office number matched her birth date.

Aimee paused before responding. It looked like she was considering what she was going to say. "So you got his name, right?"

"Nick Donovan."

"Yeah, okay, that's a hot name," Aimee said finally. "I liked a TA, quite like this TA of yours, once." She paused again, her brow wrinkled in thought.

"So what did you do?" Tess's mouth went dry with anticipation.

"Nothing."

"What do you mean, nothing?"

"I decided that if he wanted me, he would ask me."

"What you're saying then is that Nick will ask me out?"

"Yeah, sure, if he wants to."

Tess's heart fluttered momentarily.

"Slow down there, rookie. I'm not saying he will or he won't."

"Well, how will I know if he wants to or not?"

"You'll just know. And you'll know for sure when he asks you." Tess, lost in thoughts about Nick asking her out, didn't pick up on Aimee's sarcasm. Aimee looked at her with a funny expression. "You know, Tess, don't you think you should cool it a bit? He is a TA."

Tess's head jerked. "What does that have to do with anything?"

"His being a TA has to do with everything. He's grading your papers, isn't he? Don't you think it's a bit of a conflict of interest if you sleep together? It's in the student code of conduct. No TAs can date the students in the classes they grade."

In disbelief, Tess said, "No, it's not. You're making that up. And if that is true, why didn't you tell me that sooner?"

"Because you know how you are with crushes. You're madly in love with a guy on a Tuesday and by the next day you have no memory of him. Forgive me for thinking this is any different." Aimee paused. "And I wish I was making it up. It's the whole reason that TA I liked never did anything. He was also a total chickenshit, but that's beside the point."

"Nick's definitely not a chickenshit," Tess said. "Definitely not, based on the way he checked me out like ten times."

"Tess, I'm serious. It could be a huge problem. You could be flunked out of the class, and he could be kicked out of school. It's like a dishonorable discharge in academia."

"Oh, well then I probably shouldn't tell you that I invited him to come by our booth at the activities fair, should I?"

Aimee rolled her eyes with a half-smile and went back to her books.

Tess thought about what Aimee said. *How does she even know? Does she have the code of conduct memorized or something?* Not wanting to face it, Tess ignored Aimee's advice and let her fantasies about her hot TA run wild. Just because she couldn't touch didn't mean she couldn't look.

Chapter 5

September sixteenth arrived faster than either Tess or Aimee thought it would. They bickered cordially as they assembled the booth for the activities fair and finished just in time for the doors to open. "I think our booth looks really good," Tess remarked proudly. She was eager to sign up new members. At the moment, the group consisted of Tess, Aimee, and a few sophomores. Clearly they needed more members if they were ever going to be taken seriously.

"This booth would look so much better if someone else had put it together," Aimee said.

"Come on, you're not even a little proud of yourself?"

"It really is a shame that you and that guy Miles from last semester broke up. He would have had this thing up in ten minutes."

"That's low, Aimee, even for you. You know I'm still not ready to talk about it."

"Tess, you're nuts. You dated him for like two weeks. It's been four months. You weren't even a *real* couple."

Tess sent Aimee a death stare, though she knew Aimee was right.

"At least if he'd put it together it wouldn't be crooked, like it is right now," Aimee said, pointing out the flaw. "I'm sorry, but you know how much I hate this kind of stuff."

"Because you've always had Mumsie and Dadsie to pay for someone else to do it for you." Tess did her best fake stuffy English accent.

"That's not fair! Just because my dad does well in real estate doesn't mean I'm a spoiled brat."

They worked the booth for a few hours and talked to a handful of people. They'd collected only one e-mail address. At that pace, the remaining hour there was going to be very long. Tess yawned and stretched her arms above her head.

"Oh my God! There he is!" she squealed, noticing Nick meandering through the crowd.

"Who?" Aimee asked, scanning the crowd.

"Nick! Nick came! Oh, wait--nope, not him. Sorry."

"Bummer."

"Totally. God, I hope he comes. How great would that be if he joined our club? Not only could we all hang out all the time, but he could persuade the other grad students. You know what? We might just get somewhere this year! Oh my God, Aimee, this will be our legacy!"

Aimee laughed and picked up a magazine she'd already read three times. Half an hour passed. One person stopped but didn't leave an e-mail address. Bored, Tess constantly searched the area for Nick. Sending him to her booth was the least the universe could do in return for her sitting through all these interminable hours.

"Wait a minute! I think I see him. I think it's really him! Oh, no—someone else."

"I have to pee. If it is him, keep him here until I get back. I want to meet this guy."

"Ha! Like you have to ask!"

With Aimee away, Tess fluffed her hair, freshened her lip gloss, and watched the crowd intensely, pleading, praying, for Nick to show up.

"You weren't kidding about saving swans," Nick said, sidling up to Tess's booth several minutes later.

"Nick! Hey, you made it! Sign up for anything?"

He chuckled. "Me? No. Grad students have their own clubs."

"Oh, really? Then what are you doing here?"

"Had to see for myself just how devoted you are to swans."

Where the hell is Aimee? Tess wondered. *She has to see how hard he's flirting with me.* "I never said I was devoted to swans. I want everyone to be able to enjoy the campus pond without fear or terror, human- or swan-inflicted."

Looking over the paltry signatures on the sign-up list for new recruits, Nick said, "I can see there's an overwhelming amount of support for your cause."

Tess's cheeks instantly flushed. "Well, why don't you sign up? I'm sure you've got clout with all your grad school club friends."

"Perhaps I do. Perhaps I do," he said, writing on the e-mail address clipboard. Tess felt her toes curl with excitement as she watched him. "There you go. Hope it helps."

"I'm sure it will. So where are you headed next?" she asked, stalling on Aimee's behalf.

"What time is it? Do you happen to know?"

Reading the clock behind his head, Tess said, "Four ten. Why?"

"Oh, damn, I've got be somewhere. But, hey, good luck! Hope you can save some students *and* some swans."

Before she could beg him to stay, he was gone. Watching him walk away was disappointing. She hated to see him go.

Naturally, Aimee returned moments later.

"You won't believe how long the bathroom line is! I think I heard someone say there's something wrong with the free chili they're serving over at the culinary club booth," Aimee said, taking her seat.

"Thanks for the warning."

"So…did I miss anything?"

"Oh my God, yes! Nick was here. He signed up!"

"No way! Really?"

"He sure did," Tess said, grabbing the clipboard. "See? It says, 'Nick Donovan, e-mail: *Justshoot@them.com.*' Oh."

"Ha ha! That's funny! I just might like this guy."

"No, it's not, Aimee. He thinks this is all a stupid joke!"

"Calm down. Read it again. Trust me, it's funny."

Tess read it again. It was a little funnier the second time, but not by much. "Aimee, why are we even doing this? No one takes us seriously. We're never going to accomplish our goal."

"I think it's time we really think about that. Swans are wild animals. They kind of live wherever they want. I don't think there's anything we, as in humans, can do to stop them from living here." Aimee paused. "Unless, of course, we do shoot them." Aimee did her best to keep a straight face but failed immediately.

"Damn it, Aimee!" Tess said, half mad, half smiling. "How long have you felt this way?"

"A while. Really, after sophomore year, when I found out the biology department uses the pond for all kinds of experiments. I thought, well, the swans may die anyway because of all the weird stuff the biologists were doing to the water."

"Hmm, no wonder we're strongly discouraged from swimming in there."

"Right, might lose limbs or something."

Tess gave a disgusted faced. "So what do we do?"

"I say screw it. Let's just take this booth down right now, get some beers, and pretend like all our hard work was just a bad dream."

And that's what they did. Tess drank to Nick making the effort to sign up, and Aimee drank to the end of the club. For different reasons both girls felt victorious thanks to a TA named Nick Donovan.

Chapter 6

A few days later, when Nick's sting wasn't so sore, Tess decided it was time to give him the update. His e-mail address was a major player in the death of Save the People, Save the Swans. Perhaps if he knew how much he'd hurt her feelings, he would come around and apologize, or better yet, ask her out to make it up to her.

"Well, well, well, so we meet again," Nick said when Tess entered his office. "What can I do for you today?"

"I just have some questions about this week's topics."

"Go ahead, shoot," he said with a welcoming grin.

Tess took a deep breath. "I understand the whole progression toward the revolt, but what I don't understand is how it took the common folk so long to rebel when the abuses were so obvious."

"I think that's a question you could ask about anything. Why do people take so long to do anything, really?"

Although he didn't give her the answer she was looking for, he did give her the opportunity to begin a rather spirited debate about human nature, which temporarily distracted her from her original reason for being there. But when they got to the topic of what it meant to be human, of good versus evil, right versus wrong, Tess was reminded of his *just shoot them* e-mail address.

"Wow, so based on your belief in humans over animals, you must've shot some swans this weekend," Tess said, shifting the tone in the room a bit.

"Didn't find the e-mail address funny, I take it?" Nick leaned back in his chair.

"How could I? There's nothing funny about killing innocent animals, even if humans are above them on the food chain." She repositioned herself in her seat, ready to fight.

"Tess, they're not innocent animals. They've been terrorizing UMass since I was here the first time."

"But they're still living creatures. They probably think humans are terrorists." Tess paused, embarrassed, realizing a bit late that the 9/11 attack anniversary had just passed. "Right. Anyway, so your first time here was…?" Tess asked, abandoning the terrorist angle.

"I did my undergrad work here. Class of 2002."

"So that makes you…twenty-four/twenty-five?"

"Quick math. Sure you're a history major?"

"I can name all forty-two US presidents and recite the whole preamble to the Constitution."

Nick started laughing. "That's impressive. What do you plan to do with such knowledge?"

"Definitely going to be a teacher. I've wanted to be one since I gave my first skating lesson when I was twelve."

Nick cocked his head. "Skating lesson? As in skateboarding?"

Tess laughed at her mental image of herself on a skateboard. "No, definitely not. Figure skating."

"Hmm. Figure skating. How long have you been doing that?"

"Fourteen years." She noticed his eyes narrow. "Minus one, for when I was forced against my will to move to New Mexico."

"Fourteen years! Wow, you must be pretty good then. And flexible," he added. "But New Mexico—that's a hike. Where did you move from?"

"Boston. So really, I'm just a local girl. Where are you from?" she asked, loving his personal questions.

"Connecticut."

"Cool. Wait—east of I-91 or west of I-91? I can't be associated with any of those West 91ers and their love for the Yankees."

Nick chuckled. "East, and yes, I'm a Red Sox fan."

"Phew. So that means yes to Celtics, Bruins, and the Patriots?"

"Yes, yes, and not a chance!"

"How can you not like the Patriots? There isn't a single better team in the league."

"Yes, there is. The New York Jets."

"Oh, gross. The Jets are terrible, and Rex Ryan is a joke!" Tess gave him a skeptical look, which he responded to with a charismatic smile. "Anyway, any plans for what you're going to do when you finish?"

"None, as a matter of fact. I took a year off before I started this program to find out what I wanted to do. I worked at a law office thinking I'd want do that. Turns out the law sucks. Now, I'm not sure. Last year, I took some public history courses. Might take more and become a museum curator."

"That sounds so cool. I'd love to be a museum curator!"

"Those jobs are scarce and hard to find and with all the TAing since last year, I've been kind of thinking of teaching high school history too."

Tess lit up when she heard him say he also wanted to be a teacher.

"I know everyone says teenagers are just so awful. They're already set in their ways and you can't reach them, but I disagree. Anybody can be reached at any age."

Tess bit her lower lip. Her heart rate ramped up. This guy was speaking her language.

"You know that moment after you've been explaining something to someone and the proverbial lightbulb goes off? The moment when they finally get it? Their faces light up with sheer joy and accomplishment. I love that look. It's such a rush. I think that's why I want to become a teacher," Nick said.

"Stop it! Really? I feel the exact same way." Tess smiled and stared at Nick for several moments. When she tucked some hair behind her ear, he glanced at the clock. They had been talking for nearly an hour and a half.

"Right. Well, Tess, I hate to cut things short, but considering the time, I have class in about twenty minutes. Anything else you need?"

Thrown off by his sudden change in tone, no longer informal and flirtatious, Tess replied, "One last thing. Any chance you like hockey? Do you go to the games?"

"Sure, I like hockey. Why?"

"It's not until December, but the skating team is doing a fundraiser for kids with cancer at the UMass-UConn hockey game. We're putting on a show before the game."

"Hmm, that's random. I'm not making the connection. Are you skating in the show?"

"Yes," she said, nervously. "But I'm telling everyone! If you go to the show, you get a free ticket to the hockey game. And now that I know you're from Connecticut, I thought you might be interested."

After a brief pause Nick said, "Yeah, figure skating is lame."

"Oh...but it's for a really good cause. I can promise you there will be some *very* short skirts," she said, remembering the look on his face when he'd called her flexible. "I know, because my best friend is the head designer for all the costumes. It's a final project for her fashion merchandising major."

"Like you said, it's far off. Remind me when it gets closer."

With a big smile, Tess said, "I will definitely do that. Thanks again for your help! See you in class tomorrow."

It definitely hadn't felt like an hour and a half. He was so easy to talk to, minus the whole "kill the swans" thing. She wished he'd at least acknowledged that what he said wasn't the nicest thing. But then after second thoughts she realized he was a man of principal. Damn, that was hot too. And he flirted with her constantly. *TAs just don't flirt with their students.* Tess was definitely getting the sense that Nick Donovan was not simply a TA.

Chapter 7

By the end of October, Nick was all Tess talked or thought about. She had an unofficial standing appointment in his office every week to "make sure" she was ready for the quiz, which was a total sham. After the first few, she'd figured out the quiz formula, which meant she didn't actually need any extra help.

"Well, why not use all those Humerus bones as ice skates to get around?" Tess asked during a morbid discussion on post plague Europe. The topic seemed fitting enough, at least to Tess, with Halloween just around the corner.

"You know that funny bones are not real bones, right?"

"No, the *Humerus*. The bone in your arm that connects to your shoulder."

Nick looked at her blankly. She pointed to her own arm.

"Oh. So here." Nick touched the top of her shoulder. "And here," he said, ever so lightly running his fingers down to her elbow.

Tess gasped and swallowed hard. Noticing that she'd choked up, Nick placed his hand on her knee and asked, "You okay there?"

Definitely not anymore, she thought. His warm hand resting on her knee sent her mind racing, her thoughts blank. Things were beginning to throb. *What should I do? Shimmy forward so his hand moves up my leg and our lips meet?*

"Fine. Me? Yeah, I'm fine," she mumbled.

Nick gave her a smug look and then removed his hand. "Right. So…the Humerus as an ice skate?"

Tess needed more time to recover. *Nick. Donovan. Just. Touched. My. Knee. NickDonovanjusttouchedmyknee,* she screamed inside. *Some policy,* she thought, thinking of Aimee.

Regaining her self-control, she remarked, "Yeah. I mean, it's what cavemen did during the Ice Age. It's not like they had cars back then."

"Ha. No, they definitely did not have cars back then."

Sensing a lull coming on Tess asked, "Got any plans for Halloween?"

"Nothing of note. Most likely going to just stay in and watch horror movies."

"You're such an old man! Halloween is the *best* night to go out. Everyone is all dressed up, inhibitions are that much lower…"

"Sounds like a perfect recipe for disaster, if you ask me."

"You say that like it's a bad thing," Tess said, hoping Nick would find an excuse to touch her again.

"And on that note, I've got to get to class."

"Oh, right. Not good to be late."

"I'm sorry, I don't ever mean to kick you out."

Tess stopped in the hallway and turned around. "Hey, no

worries. I've got some work to do on my costume. Can't lose out on winning best costume at all the parties." Eyebrows raised, she waited for him to ask her which parties she was attending.

"Good luck," Nick said with a smile. "I'll see you next time."

In the days that followed, Tess focused completely on Halloween. She didn't buy it that Nick was just going to stay in. There was not a single student—grad, undergrad, or otherwise—who would not be out that night. "It's against the law of college partying," Tess always said. The more she fantasized about crossing Nick's path, the more she saw it happening. She was bound to run into him at some point. And being in costume created the ideal opportunity to find out how he truly felt. If he felt the same way about her that she felt about him, success! Reveal true identity. If not, true identity remains a secret. Tess giggled with hope.

Halloween was also a big deal because Tess and Aimee competed for best costume every year. Aimee usually won, but with the possibility of running into Nick that night, Tess made her biggest effort ever to win. Five-foot-four, hundred-and-thirty-pound Tess attached foam breasts, each the size of a beach ball, to her chest under a see-through shirt, and donned skintight zebra leggings with a Mötley Crüe wig, as if straight out of a Poison concert circa 1985.

"Holy hell, Tess! What are you wearing?" Aimee howled with

laughter from the driver's seat of her car.

"I'm a wet-T-shirt-contest-winning trailer park queen. See, that's what my sash says," Tess replied, digging the buried sash out from her cleavage and snapping her gum. "Don't I look fabulous?"

There was no question who would win. Aimee's mermaid costume paled in comparison. The girls laughed so hard they nearly wet their pants. Ten minutes later, the girls picked up their other friend, Brie, who had a long laugh as well.

Jackpot, thought Tess. Now all she had to do was run into Nick.

When they entered the off-campus apartment of the boyfriend of a friend of a friend of Brie's sister's ex-boyfriend, the room fell silent. Tess had never turned so many heads. Aimee was normally the one heads turned for. But with a rack like hers that night, how could anyone not stare? Feeling awkward as the focus of attention, Tess made a beeline for the beer, while scanning the crowd for Nick. *Nope.*

As disappointment set in, Tess figured her best option was to drink it away. At first, she kept a normal pace. As the alcohol did its job, her interest in the party expanded, as did her hope of running into Nick.

"Hey, Brie, do you think there're any grad students here?" Tess asked, waiting in line for a refill.

"I dunno. Why?"

"I know what you're thinking and no, *he's* not here," Aimee said.

"There're like three hundred people here," Tess said, exaggerating.

"Tess, grad students don't party with undergrads."

"They don't?" Brie asked.

Aimee rolled her eyes. "Grad students are, like, forty. Why would they ever hang with twenty-one-year-olds?"

"Nick's not forty."

"Whatever, Tess. A lot of them are. But in any case, Nick's not here."

"Way harsh, Aimee," Brie said and then gave Tess a reassuring look as she said, "Aimee's just mad that Brad guy she likes never confirmed whether he was coming or not. Now stop worrying and have some fun."

Brie's words were well received but they didn't completely stop Tess from hoping to find Nick.

When Tess was drunk, everything was a delightful surprise and super funny. No one would ever know her heart was longing for someone. Having armed herself with liquid confidence, she became the life of the party. While seemingly happy, she endlessly scanned the faces around her. At the same time Tess grew tired of looking, she realized she was rather drunk and needed a break.

"You win, Nick. I get it. You're not here," she told the mirror after a trip to the bathroom. Begrudgingly, she gave up and figured it was time to follow Brie's advice.

When the clock struck midnight, Tess wasn't sure if it was her imagination, or the beer, but she saw the band ZZ Top walk in. She thought it was weird. They hadn't been popular for at least a decade. But college kids were notorious for bringing obscure trends back, calling them retro.

"Why are they here? Last time they had a hit was like 1986," she observed out loud. *Whatever. It's a costume party, and apparently being old school is cool.* The only thing that concerned her was whether or not they increased the competition for best costume.

After several cups of water forced upon her by Aimee, Tess noticed that one of the members of ZZ Top kept staring at her. He was tall and slender, with slightly rounded shoulders. A pair of dark sunglasses hid his face with a long gold-colored beard dropping down to his stomach. Completing the costume, the guy wore a cowboy hat and a beat-up trench coat.

His gaze was like a lasso. It totally wrapped around Tess. As flattering as his interest was, she reminded herself he wasn't Nick, so there was no reason to pay him any attention. Yet the closer he came, the more she thought there was something about him she couldn't ignore.

"Tess, there are cupcakes! You have got to try these cupcakes!" Aimee said, totally inebriated. Tess, a sugar junkie, jumped at the chance to stuff her face—well, she stumbled at the chance.

Aimee was right. The cupcakes were amazing.

In their drunken silliness, the girls looked at Tess's enlarged breasts and then each other.

"Are you thinking what I'm thinking?" Tess asked.

"How badly you want to eat that cupcake?"

"If I can eat it off my breasts with no hands?"

"Same thing."

Mr. ZZ Top played witness to this exchange. After following Tess into the kitchen, his stare became intense. Tess didn't need to look at him to know that. She simply felt it. She felt his eyes locked on her face and then on the cupcake on her foam breasts.

"Nice cupcakes," Mr. ZZ Top said, leaning against the refrigerator. His voice stopped her dead in her tracks. It was familiar, but the fizziness in her brain made it difficult to place. *Mike from sociology? No. Rob from the bagel shop? Hmm. No. Adam from History 141? No, no, no. Nick? No. Nick wouldn't pick such a gross costume.* Tess cycled through each guy who came to mind. *Dave from anthro? No. Who the hell is this guy?*

Too drunk to sort it all out, she turned her focus back to the cupcake. But she had a nagging feeling. There was something very familiar about the guy. Tension began to mount between Tess and the bearded man. Aimee, with half a cupcake in her mouth, looked back and forth between Tess and Mr. ZZ Top. She carefully finished the cupcake and slowly backed away.

"Dusty Hill," Mr. ZZ Top said boldly, offering his hand for

Tess to shake.

"You look it."

"Of ZZ Top?"

She didn't respond. She wasn't a fan of ZZ Top, and she wasn't about to pretend she was.

"Okay then," Dusty said. He paused. "So tell me, how are you going to eat that there cupcake?"

Tess had momentarily forgotten about it. The cupcake hadn't moved. "Oh, just you watch, baby!" she slurred.

Tess clumsily tried to unwrap a cupcake for her first attempt. She was too enthusiastic and smashed the bottom so it couldn't stand up on its own. The next cupcake worked out a bit better, but only because Dusty held it in place.

"Ta-da!"

"Was that the big show?" Dusty laughed. She had only licked it.

"Eh, sugar, check it," she retorted, nearly incomprehensible. She tried to munch the cupcake, but it was always too far away. She pushed her neck as forward as she could, but it wasn't far enough. *I should have been a giraffe,* she thought.

With a snort of frustration, she gave up, used her fingers, and consumed the sweet treat the old-fashioned way. Tess rocked on her feet, a bit stupefied, before she realized Dusty was still standing in front of her. "Didn't I tell this creep to take a hike?" she asked herself softly. She was suddenly overwhelmed by the all-too-familiar scent of his cologne. *No, that's not what I think it is...is it?* Tess thought. She she tried to conceal a smile. Then

Dusty began asking her questions. She could not have been less interested in small talk with a guy who she told herself wasn't Nick and made a dash for the dance floor.

The living room was a sea of bump and grind. Everyone she saw was either getting it on with someone's leg or chugging booze. The real aficionados somehow managed a combination of the two. Aimee happened to be one such aficionado; she shimmied between a slick radio DJ and a brawny fisherman.

Spotting Aimee, Tess immediately jumped in next to her. Dancing, Tess finally felt free of Dusty and his creepy gaze. But her freedom did not last long.

Only a few minutes later, Dusty found her yet again. With her back to him, he made his presence known by brazenly placing his hands on her hips and danced behind her back-to-chest.

"Okay, dude, what's your problem?" Tess asked, spinning around without restraint.

"Can't a guy get a dance with a…" Dusty paused, retrieving the sash from her cleavage. "Excuse me, *the* wet T-shirt contest winner?"

Tess, though offended by his disregard of her lack of consent to be touched, liked the feel of his hand on her synthetic chest. It was heavy and strong, yet light and exciting.

"Okay, fine. I'll dance with you, but just one."

As their bodies touched, thoughts of Nick crept in. She felt like she was cheating on him. Crazy idea, she knew. She and Nick were in no way together, but she felt as though she was doing something she shouldn't. She would have been devastated if Nick were out doing the same thing with some other wet T-shirt-contest-winning floozy. Overwhelmed with boozy guilt, she turned back to Aimee, giving Dusty the cold shoulder.

She was suddenly overwhelmed by the combination of too much booze, sugar, and guilt. Feeling dizzy, Tess tried to calm her stomach with deep breaths. It wasn't working. She needed more air—and fast. Everyone around her kept right on gyrating and chugging. *Why doesn't anyone notice me?* She began to panic. She desperately needed to get out of there as soon as possible if she was going to avoid a mess. Too many people were between her and the door when chunks rose in her throat. Just in time, Dusty wrapped an arm around her shoulders and led her outside.

"I promise to never drink like this again, I swear," were the first words out of her mouth, about ten minutes later, after she'd regained her composure and was certain that the chunks weren't going anywhere.

"Sure," Dusty said with a skeptical chuckle.

She took several deep breaths. The cool outdoor air worked wonders. She had no memory of how she got outside, but it was such a relief to be there that she didn't care about the details.

"You going to be all right there, tiger?" He handed her a bottle of water.

"Course I will, and so what if I'm not? You don't know me." Tess stopped. "Sorry, that was rude." Tess gave Dusty an apologetic smile and invited him to sit down next to her on a long lawn chair. He obliged.

"Nice costume," Dusty said softly, barely above a whisper.

"What? I didn't hear that." Tess leaned closer to him. Dusty repeated what he had said even more softly than the first time.

Tess, again, leaned closer. "Okay, one more time."

The warm whispered breath on her ear gave her the chills. His sunglasses rubbed against her head.

"Thanks," she said delicately, in a daze.

All was quiet, except for the unavoidable creaking of the plastic lawn chair they were sitting on. A creak followed each breath. Out of nowhere, a befuddled laugh broke the silence. "Goddamn, am I drunk!" Dusty snorted with a chuckle.

Tess cocked her head like a confused dog. She could have sworn he was stone-cold sober, but after all the beer she'd consumed everyone seemed sober to her.

"Ha!" He paused. "Yeah, it's funny how it can sneak up on you." Tess wasn't sure if he was talking to her or himself. He continued without clarifying. "Guess day drinking will do that to ya. Ha. Ha ha ha!"

Around them, the air thickened and began to imitate a hot summer night instead of the last night of October. They sat there in a goofy, silly, drunkenly comfortable silence. Mindlessly swaying from side to side, Tess made the distance between them smaller and smaller. Suddenly aware of this, Tess looked deeply into Dusty's eyes while they sat fixed should to shoulder. At the same time, they swallowed hard. Feeling her body tingle with anticipation, Tess smiled. Soon low panting grew from barely audible to heavy and deep, as their faces inched closer. Tess licked her lips and took in that ever so familiar scent. The moment she closed her eyes, Dusty pulled down his beard, chucked off his sunglasses, and placed his lips on hers.

"Nick!" Tess gasped upon opening her eyes. "I wondered if it was you."

"Hi, Tess." He grinned and finished removing the dangling beard.

Tess couldn't believe her senses. *Am I really kissing Nick Donovan?* Elated with excitement, Tess began asking a million questions. "Is this really happening? Why didn't you say anyth—"

"Shhhh." He silenced her with another kiss. "You're just so damn cute. The way you ask all those questions…" He kissed her again. "That we both know you know the answers to." Nick wrapped his arms about her waist and pulled her closer. "I can still taste the sugar on your lips from that cupcake."

"Well, then stop kissing me so hard." Tess's smile was rather randy.

"I think about you all the time. I actually look forward to my office hours because I know you'll be there."

"Really?"

He scoffed. "Like you don't notice how I much I stare at you during discussion."

"That's because I'm the only one who talks!"

"The only cute one. You taste so good," Nick said, kissing her neck. "This is so wrong. We shouldn't be doing this."

"How is this wrong?" She didn't stop him as his kisses wandered farther and farther down her chest. "We're both adults."

"True, but you're my student." Nick kissed her skin harder and faster. "Now tell me how you want me to kiss you. Tell me this is right and not wrong."

"Oh, Nick, I want you to kiss me all over! There is no way this could be wrong," Tess said, surrendering.

With a smile, Nick pulled away for a minute without breaking eye contact. He repositioned himself so that he was lying down and invited Tess into his arms. He closed his eyes while Tess settled into him.

It was not easy to figure out where to rest her huge foam accessories. She couldn't lie comfortably next to him on her back. With the beach balls between them, their lips would be too far apart. Not wanting to waste this moment, she decided the best thing to do was take them off.

She hesitated for a moment. The only shirt she had was the see-through white top that was part of the costume. Her lacy purple bra beneath it would be on display for all the world to see. *Whatever, it's dark,* Tess reasoned. *Nick's bound to see it anyway* and proceeded to liberate the enhancements.

Once settled into the lounge chair, she pulled Nick's arm around her. Tess could not have been happier. There she was, Tess Ryan, snug in Nick Donovan's arms, ready to kiss him all night...

"Nick?" He didn't move a muscle. "Nick, are you awake?"

She tried kissing his cheek. Nothing. She tried kissing his lips. Still nothing. He was out cold. "Aww *shucks.*" Making the most of situation, she burrowed deeper next to him and soon fell asleep with her head on his chest.

The next morning, feeling the tingle of sunlight on her cheeks, Tess began to stir. Seeing Nick still beside her, she felt a sense of triumph rush over her. Unfortunately, it did not last long. As soon as she wiggled her back, her whole body writhed in pain from the awful combination of drinking too much and sleeping in an awkward position. But it only took one look at Nick to make all the pain go away.

It must have been Tess's squirming that caused Nick to open his eyes a few moments later. His eyes went from squinty to bulging.

"No, no, no," he said, awkwardly trying to stand.

"Are you okay? Do you want some help?"

Tess offered her hand, but he didn't take it. Tess accepted his rejection like it was a surface scratch on her knee. There was no need to worry. Everything would get better on its own. He probably just wasn't a morning person.

"This can never happen again. No one can find out about this."

"Excuse me?"

"This." Nick waved his right hand between the two of them.

He then suddenly paused with a distant look on his face. "Please tell me we used protection."

"Protection? For what?"

Nick looked like he was struggling to find words. Watching, Tess realized what he meant.

"Oh, wow. No! Nothing like that happened."

"Are you sure?" he asked, staring at her sheer shirt.

"Geez, Nick! What kind of girl do you think I am?" The doubt in his question throbbed like a scratch deepening into a cut. It stung pretty badly, but she *was* wearing a see-through shirt and sitting next to a large pair of foam breasts.

"I'm sorry. You're my student. I can't even think right now about how many ethics violations I just made. I could lose my job and my spot in the program." Nick paused. "God, what have I done?"

"Do you really not remember?" Tess glared at him. The need to ask such a question made the symbolic cut on her knee feel fine compared to the way her chest began to ache. Just then the chill of the crisp first-morning-of-November air struck, and Tess shivered. She crossed her arms for warmth. Nick jetted his eyes away from her now-concealed chest.

Nick shook his head, his puppy-dog eyes desperate.

Tess chose her words carefully. "I was about to faint, but then you saved me by bringing me out here. We sat on this chair. You kept saying something that I couldn't hear, so I leaned in closer to you, and that's when you kissed me."

Nick cocked his head to the side and asked, "I kissed you?" in disbelief.

Ouch! Oh my God, ouch!

"And you told me you think about me a lot. You look forward to me coming to your office." Tess paused to check Nick's reaction. His face appeared blank. "And you said I was really cute." She purposefully left out the part about how kissing her was wrong because of their teacher-student status. She didn't want to help him remember that part.

Nick's face remained blank, as if he really had no memory of what had happened. Looking at his blank expression made Tess's chest tighten even more. *It's okay, Tess. He admitted that he was totally wasted. Of course he wouldn't remember. But why would he have said all of those things if he didn't mean them?*

"Tess, I'm sorry. This was a mistake. I can't do this with students. Promise me you won't say anything to anyone about it. If you do, I cannot even begin to think about the consequences."

"A mistake? You're calling a kiss a mistake? It was just a kiss!" Tess's heart felt like a knife had been stuck through it. She couldn't understand how the sweet guy from office 712, the one who told her mere hours ago how much he liked her, was the same guy calling her a mistake. It took every resource she had not to cry.

Looking at her watering eyes, he said, "But it wasn't just a kiss."

"What?"

Nick's eyes jetted into the distance as he took a deep breath and said, "The truth is, I'm not allowed to feel that way about you."

"But you do?" Hope began to replace fear in Tess's eyes.

Nick was quiet for a moment. "I do." He paused, looking straight into Tess's eyes. "No. I *did*. Tess, I..." Then Nick's eyes darted from left to right, as if they couldn't stay still. Tess had never seen him look at her like that. It made her feel like there was something he wasn't telling her, that something was stopping him from telling her. *If only I knew what he was thinking.*

Just then another gust of cold air whisked by, sending shivers all over her body. Noticing her shaking shoulders, Nick took off his trench coat and wrapped it around her. She accepted it hesitantly before she saw that he had a long-sleeve shirt under the green flannel one.

"Thank you," Tess said softly. The kind gesture made her both happy and confused. Then the smell of his cologne surrounded her, temporarily putting her in a daze.

"No problem."

An awkward distance expanded between them. After several moments of them both hemming and hawing, Nick shrugged his shoulders and let out a large sigh. "I'm sorry, Tess. If only you weren't my student," and he quickly searched for his hat, sunglasses, and beard. He gathered them and left.

"What about your coat?" Tess called.

"Don't worry about it," Nick said, without turning around.

Once he was out of sight, with her face in her hands she began to cry. He said so many things that she had no defenses against. She couldn't live with herself if she became the reason he lost his job and place at school. It would ruin his life. But one thing kept gnawing at her. "If only you weren't my student" repeated through her mind, over and over. *What did he mean by that?* She began to look at it as his way of telling her that it wasn't that they could never be together, but it couldn't be so right now. The realization dried her tears and put a smile back on her face. She may have been down, but she definitely wasn't out. Plus, she had his coat.

Chapter 8

Crawling into bed after the seemingly endless 1.7 mile walk back to her dorm, Tess's aim was to shut out the world. She told herself everything would be much easier to sort out once she had some good rest. She fell quickly asleep, but was rudely awakened a few minutes later to the shrill ring of her phone.

"Hello," she said, irritated.

"Where the hell are you?" an angry voice asked. Tess's head screamed for silence. "Tess? Hello?"

"Hey. Yeah, I'm here, sort of."

"Oh my God, Tess, are you still drunk?"

Yeah, probably.

"Brie and I have been worried sick. You just wandered off last night. Where the hell did you go? We couldn't find you anywhere!"

Tess said nothing. The shrill voice, that she realized was Aimee's, finally went silent.

"Hmm, yeah—I guess I drank too much, eh?" Tess chuckled.

"Hardy har har. Glad you think it's funny. Tess, I needed you last night, but you were off God only knows where. I needed you—"

Tess stopped listening. She couldn't focus on anything besides her present ordeal.

"—and that's when Brad showed up. I'm telling you, it was phenomenal! Oh, if only you were there. Your mind would've been blown. I swear!"

Tess had no idea what she was talking about, but it sounded important. *Great.*

"Dude? Hello? You sound like crap. Brie's still with me. We're coming over."

Tess agreed but didn't promise to actually get out of bed and answer the door. She hung up and caught sight of a bottle of aspirin on her dresser. *Hallelujah!* She forced herself up and got two pills down the hatch with the assistance of a bottle of water from her roommate's stash.

Aimee and Brie arrived an hour later. Tess was happy she'd had a full hour of sleep. More would have been sweet, but motivated by the irritation in Aimee's voice and her own excitement to talk about Nick, Tess forced herself out of bed.

"Well, don't *you* look like you've had one hell of a bender," Aimee said, entering the room before Brie.

"I made out with Nick last night."

"You *what* last night?" Brie asked.

"I kissed Nick. That's where I was." The smile on Tess's face was beaming.

"You're making that up. Nick wasn't even there," Aimee said.

"But he was. He dressed up as one of the members of ZZ Top." Tess paused and then pointed at Nick's trench coat. "See that coat over there? Nick gave me that this morning."

Brie and Aimee's eyes zeroed in on the trench coat. They remained fixed on it as Tess continued her story. Eventually, Aimee went over to it, touching it, inspecting it.

"And then he confessed how he thinks about me all the time, how hot he thinks I am."

"You really did make out with him. I remember a guy following you around wearing this," Aimee concluded.

"I am so happy, I could cry!"

"The important thing is how things were left. Are you going to switch into the other discussion section now?" Brie asked.

The smile on Tess's face vanished.

"You did talk about what happens next, didn't you?" Aimee asked.

Tess was silent. The sad truth brought back the painful side of what she thought should've remained a sweet memory.

"Tess, are you okay?" Brie asked.

"He begged me not to tell anyone and called what happened a mistake." Tess was unable to look directly at her friends, too afraid of their reactions.

"He really called what happened a mistake?" Aimee asked, much to Tess's surprise. Aimee's reaction was far tamer than she'd thought it would be.

"But only because I'm his student and he's not allowed to feel that way."

"What an asshole!"

"He's not an asshole, Aimee. Come on, we were both drunk. I mean, now that I think about it, yeah, it kind of was a mistake. I don't want the beginning of our relationship to be because of altered mental states."

"Beginning of your relationship?"

"You know," Brie said suddenly, "I think it's kind of romantic."

"On what planet is that romantic?" Aimee asked. "He totally took advantage of her and then made it look like his bad decision was her fault."

"Brie's right," Tess said, feeling suddenly less doomed.

Brie smiled. Aimee shrugged.

"Think about it. He also told me how much he's attracted to me. We can't be together because he's my TA. He said, 'If only you weren't my student,' which means he wants to be with me too. This totally has the makings of a great love story!" Tess paused to take in as much oxygen as her body could hold. "Oh my God! I found him. He's the guy I've been waiting to meet since freshman year!"

Brie and Aimee shared an apprehensive look.

"Tess, you're not hearing what I'm saying. He took advantage of you. He treated you terribly."

"I hear you just fine, Aimee, but I think you're wrong. It's not as simple as you're making it out to be."

"Aimee has a point," Brie said. "He didn't exactly handle it like a gentleman."

"But you just said it was romantic!"

Brie folded her arms across her chest and said carefully, "Yeah, in a Hallmark movie kind of way, but that stuff never happens in reality."

"Whatever. You're both wrong, and I'll prove it to you."

"Really? How?"

"I'll call Eve. If she thinks he was a jerk, then it's true."

"Right. Like Eve would know. She's seventeen. What does she know about guys?"

"Hey, my little sister knows a lot more than we think."

Aimee's eyes momentarily bulged out of their sockets. "She's in high school, Tess! We're in college. Relationships are totally different."

Tess stared at Aimee and searched for a response. She couldn't find one.

After a long silence Aimee asked, "Well, are you going to call her or not?"

"I am, but it's only eight in New Mexico. I guarantee you she's still sleeping."

"Right. Well, you should get some sleep too. You look awful. Maybe with some rest you'll see things more clearly."

Tess was hurt by Aimee's jab, but loved the idea of getting back into bed for a few hours.

Aimee turned to Brie. "Come on. Let's get some food. Tess, I'll call you later."

"Sounds good," Brie responded. She turned to Tess.

"Remember, we love you. We only want good things for you."

Tess smiled, said good-bye, and crawled into bed. She tried her best to forget about what Aimee had said. *Nick didn't take advantage of me. He wouldn't do that. He isn't that kind of guy...or is he?* She was determined to snuff out the seed of doubt Aimee had planted. Nick was the one for her. They were meant to be. They just had to be, after all that had happened so far. In a few hours when she called her sister, all doubt would be gone. Eve would prove Tess right and Aimee wrong.

Chapter 9

Tess slept well past noon and woke up feeling refreshed and even more set on talking to her sister.

"Eve! Hey, it's me. What's up?" Tess said as soon as she heard her sister's voice on the other end of the phone.

"Hey. What's up?" Eve's voice was calm and cool, just the way Tess expected it to be. Eve was always the level-headed one. Any time disaster struck, like losing a crucial homework project, Tess was an emotional wreck, while Eve simply took it in stride. Sometimes when they were younger, Tess would check Eve's pulse to make sure she was actually living.

"Not a whole lot. You know, the usual. Went to a Halloween party last night. Got a little drunk. No big deal." Tess did her best to sound nonchalant.

"Cool."

"Yeah, it was cool." Tess suddenly felt nervous about asking Eve for advice. She was the older sister—she should be giving advice, not asking for it.

"So is that what you called to tell me?"

"Right. No, sorry."

"It's okay, Tess. You can tell me. I'm not Mom. I'm not going to lecture you."

"You know that guy Nick I've been telling you about? And *promise* you won't tell Mom."

"I promise not to tell Mom. Now just tell me already."

"We made out last night."

"Is Nick the one that's your teacher or something?"

"Yeah. Why?"

"That's just weird." Eve's words killed Tess's excitement.

"It's not weird, Eve. He's, like, only twenty-five. I'm twenty-one. It's really no big deal." Tess began to wish she'd never called her sister.

"But he's your teacher."

"Teaching assistant, actually. He only does the grading."

"Well, whatever. He still has power over your grade."

"Come on, Eve. I thought you would be happy for me." Tess's voice was whiny.

"I guess. I mean, if you're cool with letting him take advantage of the situation, then hey, more power to you." The familiarity of her words felt like shards of glass cutting at Tess's heart. In an effort to get Eve to see things the way she did, Tess retold the evening's events in precise detail.

"Did you guys at least exchange numbers or anything?"

Tess chuckled. "Of course not. We can't date yet. I'm still in his class."

"Sounds like you gave him—what is it that Mom says all the time? 'The milk for free'?"

"God, stop saying he took advantage of me!"

"Whoa. Calm down. Based on what you've told me about him, it doesn't sound like he had your best interests in mind."

"But he does. That's why we can't be together yet. I'm sure he'll ask me out as soon as the semester is over."

"I hope he does too, for your sake."

"What's that supposed to mean?"

"You just need to make sure he treats you right. Don't settle just because you think he's hot or super cool."

"Trust me, Eve, he does treat me right." *At least, as far as I can tell*, Tess thought. "He's always polite in our discussions and hospitable in his office. In fact, this was the first time he has been a little off, but how can I blame him? If just a kiss could jeopardize his whole career and education, I think allowing him to be a little upset about it is the least I can do. We have the rest of our lives to figure it out. I can wait a couple of months."

"Whatever you say. Hey, I'm just waking up, and I want to go watch cartoons."

Upon hanging up, Tess considered all the great love stories that started off with some kind of challenge. *Romeo and Juliet*, the ultimate love story, was surrounded by challenges that in part made their love story so compelling. From that moment on, Tess resolved to ignore Aimee and Eve's advice and stay the course. Just because they'd kissed but couldn't kiss again right away didn't mean they would never kiss again. All Tess had to do was wait for the semester to end. She knew it would be tough, but, as she told herself, good things come to those who wait.

Meeting up at the dining hall for dinner, Tess recapped her conversation with Eve to Aimee and Brie. Brie, with her head bobs and sounds of agreement, was definitely more understanding than Aimee. Aimee listened more rigidly. At one point Tess wondered if Aimee was maintaining a stiff expression on purpose.

"Since even your little sister agrees with me, you believe me now?" Aimee asked when Tess finished.

"What you think, what Eve thinks, doesn't matter. This is America. I'm allowed to disagree with whoever I want."

"Well, that's awfully bold of you," Brie said. "What brought on this turn of events?"

"I know you guys think I'm just hopeless when it comes to guys, and for the most part that's been true. But Nick's different. I may not be able to explain it to you, but whenever I'm around him I feel the most alive I've ever felt. My whole body tingles, and I can't stop smiling."

"You're nuts," Aimee said.

"Maybe, but I owe it to myself to at least wait until the semester is over. Plus, when was the last time I was this interested in one guy?"

"You have a point," Brie said.

"See, Aimee? There is something special about him."

While Brie and Tess carried on talking, Aimee shuffled her leftover peas around her plate. She looked vacant, like she was no longer listening.

"What are you going to do about his coat?" Aimee suddenly asked. "It's not like you can keep it. That's perfect evidence to get him fired."

"Keep your voice down, Aimee!" Tess said. "People could be listening."

Aimee flashed an uneasy look at Brie.

"Well?" Her volume stayed the same.

"I don't know. I'll just bring it back to him during office hours later this week. It's no big deal."

"Won't it be awkward to see him in his office alone?" Brie asked.

Tess thought about Brie's question for a moment. "At first maybe, but then when he sees that I'm cool about everything, it'll be like nothing happened."

"I don't think you realize the magnitude of what happened," Aimee said.

"I don't think *you* realize the magnitude of what happened, Aimee. No one is going to find out. We're both going to be mature about it. The semester will be over before we know it, and then the fun will really begin."

"Fine, but, Tess, you do realize that Brie and I both know," Aimee said in a hushed voice. "Because you, Tess, told us."

"Damn, Aimee," Brie said. "Now you're just being ridiculous. No one is going to say anything. Wouldn't you want Tess to support you if you liked a guy this much?"

Aimee didn't respond right away. She shoveled more peas

around her plate. "You're right, Brie. Tess, I'm sorry. I just don't want you to get hurt. I see how much you like this guy. I fear it could be really bad."

"Aww, Aimee. I love how you're my fierce little mama bear, but there's no need. Nick and I are meant to be together."

Aimee gave Tess a faint smile, putting the argument to rest. Tess responded with a wide-mouthed smile that lit up her entire face. Knowing that her best friend was in her corner gave her the confidence boost she needed to face Nick in a few days.

Chapter 10

In the days that followed, when the reality of seeing Nick alone in his office loomed, Tess became secretly terrified. It was one thing to see him in a lecture amid a sea of other students but a completely different situation to be alone with him. There'd be no buffer—just him and her. With her friends she tried to play it cool and didn't really talk about it. But beneath the surface she was in knots. The same questions ran through her mind over and over. What if he remained cold and distant, the way he was the morning after Halloween? What if he really did look at what happened as a mistake and now wanted nothing more to do with her? *Was* it a mistake?

"No, Tess, it was not a mistake," she said to herself as she applied the finishing touches to her makeup before heading to Nick's office. "He just has a lot on his shoulders right now, and you don't want to mess that up, do you?" Tess shook her head. She fluffed her hair and gave herself a last once-over, confirming that everything was where it should be.

Wearing a flattering pair of relaxed-fit jeans and a snug hunter green sweater, Tess was ready to go. Her eyes were highlighted with mascara, her lips polished with clear gloss. She didn't want to wear too much makeup and look like she was trying to impress him, but she didn't want to go au naturel either and let him think she didn't care about her appearance. Just before leaving, Tess rolled up his trench coat and stuffed it into her backpack.

Alone in the elevator, Tess rehearsed just what she would say. She put the reflective metal to good use and practiced her facial expressions. By the time she reached the seventh floor, she felt ready to march right into his office, but noticing the empty hallway, her nerves got the better of her. After several deep breaths she marched over to Nick's door.

Her footsteps, the only sound in the empty hallway, were loud. The sound pushed through Nick's closed door and should have given him ample warning. However, he looked totally surprised when she burst into his office.

"Tess. What are you doing here?" He quickly stood and closed the door. This was not the greeting she had expected, but she forced herself to remain confident.

"It's okay. I come in peace." She let her words sink in as she removed her backpack to reveal her tight sweater. She watched Nick's eyes scan her whole body.

"I think you shouldn't be here."

"Really, I'm not here because of the other night. Well, not for anything bad." Tess felt herself blush. Her palms became clammy. Feeling shy, she took a seat. She unzipped her backpack and handed him the coat "This is yours."

"No, it's okay. Keep it." His tone was cautious but soft.

"What am I going to do with it?" She opened it up and held it against her chest, demonstrating how oversized it was on her. Nick watched with wide but quiet eyes.

"Look, our secret is safe," Tess said, breaking the silence with perfect delivery, just as she had practiced. What she was about to say next would not be so easy. The simple fact was that she didn't agree with it at all, but she thought if she appeared to agree with him, it would put him more at ease with the situation. "We were both a little drunk, and my costume...well, it was pretty suggestive, so you're right. It was a mistake. It won't happen again." Tess choked a little on the last sentence, but she got it out, and that was all that mattered. And she was grateful that she did.

Tess noticed that Nick's shoulders dropped in response. He appeared to be letting his guard down. He even smiled a little. Her words were working. Tess felt her heart skip a small beat.

"And as much as you may or may not believe my questions about the reading are genuine, I ask because I really don't know the answers. I hope that we can put this behind us so that I can still ask." Tess paused. "I would hate to start failing now, especially since I do have some more questions."

Nick let out a gasp. Tess met his gaze as he took a seat. He sat in the chair right next to hers.

At first they sat in silence just staring at each other. It felt like Nick was testing her determination not to make a move. Despite wanting to kiss him, Tess meant to keep her promise and let the silence grow louder and louder.

He looked her up and down, his eyes stopping on the low v-neckline of her sweater. Watching him look at her made her heart beat into her ears. She felt her breathing quicken. Suddenly, Tess's body propelled her to turn away and get the textbook out of her backpack.

When she sat up she noticed that the space between them had shrunk. She looked down, pretending to be shy. Without breaking her gaze, Nick slipped the book out of her hands and laid it between them. His boldness made her smile and nip her lower lip. His gaze dropped to her mouth.

"My question…" Her voice shook as she opened the book.

Nick didn't move. She thought he would at least sit back a little bit. He didn't budge, except for the glint that floated into his eyes.

"Yes…your question," he said. "Please, do ask me your question."

Oh God, I can't do this. Tess panicked. "Yes. Ah, Machiavelli." She swallowed hard. "He…he wrote in *The Prince* that using fortresses, ah, works, yet not always." She paused. *Come on, Tess, get it together. You can do this. You've got to do this.* While she was internally cheering herself on, the scent of his cologne swirled around her. She quivered, losing all focus.

"And?"

"And…and all of his subjects will hate him if he puts a wall between them, rendering him totally inaccessible to his people," she said with more ease. Thinking about something other than what his lips felt like steadied her voice.

"Uh-huh."

"I don't understand why Machiavelli writes that it's better to be feared than loved."

Nick moved closer again and in hushed tones said, "How did I know you were going to ask me that?"

Tess smiled and unconsciously licked her lips. She had no idea what he had just said. His gorgeous face was all she saw.

"In his writing, Machiavelli is only giving suggestions based on his theories, which thereby negates any responsibility for his recommendations."

Wait, what? She began to feel like they were no longer talking about Machiavelli. Rather than kiss him, she wanted to slap him.

"But Machiavelli should take responsibility because ultimately he is guiding a prince in caring for his people. In so many ways, Machiavelli holds the fate of the innocent in his hands." Her confidence kicked into high gear.

Nick had no response. His office became still. All that could be heard was the pounding of their hearts. Like magnets, they seemed to be drawing closer to one another. She felt Nick's breath on her lips. *Oh my God! Is this really happening again?* Tess silently squealed.

"Tess, I can't do this," Nick muttered faintly under his breath. "It's simply not fair to anyone."

"I'm sorry?"

"This is all so complicated and messed up on its own. Making everything worse is that, and I don't know how to tell you this, but I have a girlfriend."

"You what? You have a girlfriend?"

"Her name is—"

"I don't want to know her name," Tess interrupted, avoiding eye contact. "I need go. Now."

"Tess, wait. Don't leave like this."

"Here," Tess said, handing him the coat. "Thanks for letting me borrow it."

He refused to take it. "No. Keep it. I already have a coat and no way of getting another home."

Tess gave him a half smile and draped the coat over the chair she was sitting in. With one last look, she slipped out of his office. Her heart shattered into a million pieces. She knew there had been the possibility he would break her heart, but she had no idea it would actually happen. She fought back tears all the way back to her dorm.

Once she was safe inside her room, Tess crawled into bed and cried herself to sleep. She didn't bother setting her alarm. There was no way she could see him in the discussion group the next day. Instead she would give herself a few days to recover and then beg him to give her a makeup quiz. It would be the least he could do for her.

Chapter 11

After his near kiss with Tess, Nick went straight to McMurphy's Tavern. It was just after four. Having just opened, the place was empty, which suited him perfectly.

Shit. What the hell were you thinking? Oh, that's right, you weren't, Nick thought to himself as he stared down the mouth of his beer bottle.

"So what's got you all bent out of shape?" Will, his roommate and a fellow TA, asked, taking a seat next to him. He was slender, a six-foot guy's guy with blond hair and green eyes. Like Nick, he was working on a graduate degree in history. "And why meet at the bar when I just stocked the fridge?" Will turned to the bartender, "I'll take a Guinness. Thanks."

"What do you think of the idea of dating an undergrad?" Nick asked.

"You had me rush down here for that?"

"Humor me. What do you think? Would you do it?"

"I don't see why not. If she's hot, can buy me a beer, and isn't empty between the ears, it could be cool." Will took a drink just as it arrived. "Why? You into an undergrad or something?"

Nick didn't respond. He took a slow drink from his beer and

waited for Will to say something.

"Wait, what about Liz?"

"Yeah, what about her?"

"You're not thinking of cheating on her, are you?"

Nick glared at Will. "It's complicated. She's in Connecticut. I'm here. She comes up; she doesn't come up. I never know until she's on my doorstep. If she does come up, she's only here long enough to drain my bank account and get her rocks off. Then she's gone by morning."

Will started laughing.

"How's that funny?"

"So what are you asking me about an undergrad for? Sounds to me like you can do as you please."

"How do you mean?"

"Girls these days aren't as innocent as they like you to think. They know the deal. If Liz is coming up for what sounds like a no-strings-attached roll in the hay, I'm sure you're not the only one on her list."

"No. Liz's not like that. She's just busy. She's going to school and taking care of her mom, who isn't doing well. She wouldn't do that to me without saying anything."

"You guys have been together a while right? You met her over the summer? You must've had the 'what are we' conversation by now?"

Nick had to think. *We've had that conversation. I'm sure of it.* But he wasn't really. He had no memory of directly deciding to call each other boyfriend and girlfriend. He figured after a while it was just assumed that they were a proper couple. "You say that like it's mandatory."

Will looked at Nick as if to say, "You do know how girls think, right?" Instead he said, "Yeah, man. You're a booty call."

"Shut up! No, I'm not." *Am I?*

"All right, whatever. So why do you care about my opinion on dating undergrads?"

Nick's stomach tightened with worry about what his friend's reaction might be. He felt his heart beat a little faster and then shared only part of the story. "I almost kissed a student during my office hours today."

"You what?" Will asked, choking.

Nick took a swig of beer and repeated himself.

Will ordered another Guinness despite being only half way through his first.

"Crap, dude. How does that even happen?" Will held the bottle to his mouth before taking a sip. "You, of all people, know how fast you'd get kicked out of the program for something like that. You remember Peter?"

Nick tensed up. Images of the Halloween party filtered through his mind along with images of his old roommate. "Peter. Yeah. That was pretty awful," Nick agreed. "So stupid on his part." Nick quickly glanced at Will. He wondered if his friend noticed his nervousness.

"So true."

Peter had a student who visited his office often, just like Tess. She was cute. Peter developed a crush on her. Then one day he gave into his urges, thinking the girl was equally interested in him, and kissed her in his office. It turned out that she wasn't. She went straight to the dean. Within two weeks Peter had become a cautionary tale to all the other graduate students. Nick began wishing he had thought about Peter before he went out on Halloween.

After a moment of silence, Will asked, "So what happened?"

"From what I could tell, it was business as usual. My student shows up right at 3:10. Asks some obvious question that I know she knows the answer to. I'm about to answer it, as if I think it's some great question, and then all of sudden I feel her breath in my face and all I can think about is how soft her lips are." Nick's voice trailed off. "How much I want to feel them."

"Wait. Is this the redhead you mentioned a while back?" Will asked. Nick nodded and took a drink. "Well, thank your lucky stars nothing actually happened."

Nick, lost in his own thoughts, continued. "She's got these bright blue eyes, freckles on her nose—and I bet in other places I can't see—porcelain skin, curves in all the right places. She smells like sandalwood and lilies of the valley." Nick paused. His faraway look made it seem like he was picturing Tess doing to him things only married people were allowed to do.

"How do you know what she smells like?" Will's question catapulted Nick back to the present. He swallowed hard and suddenly looked faint. "Hey, man. You okay? You look like you've just seen your life flash before your eyes."

"Who, me? I'm good."

Will looked Nick up and down. "There's something you're not telling me. You're doing that thing again. Your eyes are twitching."

Nick took a deep breath. "Okay, I kissed her."

"Your student?" Will's eyes were as wide open as his mouth.

"Yeah, my student," Nick said. "Her name's—"

"Don't tell me that shit!"

"Hey, keep your voice down."

"What did she do? I thought you said you almost kissed her?"

"Yeah, *today* I almost kissed her."

"What the hell? This wasn't the first time?"

Nick took another glug of beer. "We kind of made out at a Halloween party."

"Holy shit, man. Is she still in your class?"

"This girl is different. I don't know what it is. Whenever I'm around her it's like I can't get enough of her."

"And when you're not?"

"What does that have to do with anything?"

"If you feel that way about her when she's not around, then I'd say switch her into Jed's section and marry the girl. But if it's out of sight, out of mind, well, then you need to get over that shit A-sap."

Nick sneered.

Will gave him a look of pity. "Well, you've gotten yourself into one hell of a mess."

"Promise you won't say anything."

"Trust me. I won't say a thing. I don't even want to know, but

I can't unknow it now can I?"

"Thanks, man."

"Out of curiosity, how did you leave it with the girl?"

"I told her I can't do anything with her because of my job and Liz."

"You told her about Liz?"

"Yeah. How is that bad?"

"You think this girl has a thing for you?"

"I think so. She seemed pretty upset when I told her I have a girlfriend."

"What are you doing then, man? The girl clearly likes you. You can't go around kissing her and then telling her you can't be with her because of your job and then, 'Oh, and by the way I have a girlfriend'. You're totally jerking her around."

"But I don't mean to," Nick said. "I was just being honest. You know what's at stake. What was I supposed to do?"

"Do you like the girl?"

"Of course I like her. I wouldn't have kissed her if I didn't."

"You like your job? Want to finish your master's?"

"What are you getting at?" The questioning was getting on his nerves as Nick had a pretty good idea of where his friend was going. He drank his beer and gave Will a dismissive look.

"I can't tell you how to run your love life, but getting with a student whose work you're grading is some serious stuff. So figure out whatever it is you need to figure out, and no matter what else you do, don't mess around with that girl. Your career depends on it."

"Okay. Whoa. Ease up."

"Promise? I'm not going to let a second fishing buddy of mine go off the deep end because he can't keep it in his pants."

"Overreaction much?"

"Promise me."

"Will, I promise I won't mess around with Te—" He caught himself. "The redhead."

Will smiled and patted Nick on the back.

If only figuring out his feelings were as easy as promising to do nothing about them. Now his attraction was out there in the open; it was real. This was not something Nick thought would happen. Until Halloween, Tess was just a flirtation, nothing more, nothing less. But he couldn't stop thinking about her now. He began to wonder what she was doing, where she was, whom she was with. Will was right. He needed to figure out his feelings, and quick. He couldn't juggle his career, degree, girlfriend, err ladyfriend, *and* feelings for Tess for much longer without something crashing and burning.

Chapter 12

"Well, you look like crap," Aimee said as she and Brie walked into Tess's dorm room the next day just after 11 a.m. Neither Brie nor Aimee had heard from Tess, which was cause for concern. It was not like her to have a meeting with Nick and then not tell them every little detail about it within an hour of seeing him.

"You know, you keep saying that," Tess said from her bed, face down and half-awake.

"Come on, sleepyhead, get out of bed," Brie said, pulling the covers from Tess. Tess growled and rolled away, trying to pull the covers over her head.

"Tess, it's been two days since we've heard from you. We know something is wrong," Aimee said.

"Go away. I'm dead."

"Tess, sit up. You're being ridiculous."

"No, I'm not!" Tess's anger at Aimee's insensitivity forced her upright. "He has a girlfriend."

"What do you mean he has a girlfriend?"

"I went to his office, you know, as planned. It was tense at first, but then he relaxed. He even sat so close to me our shoulders were touching." She stopped to brush tears away.

"Then we got into this stupid argument about taking responsibility. The next thing I know we are so close to each other that I felt his breath on my lips." Tess noticed Aimee's right eyebrow peak with interest. "Then *boom!* Out of nowhere he tells me he has a girlfriend!"

Brie put her arm around Tess as she cried. Aimee was calculatingly quiet.

"He was even going to tell me her name!" Tess continued. "I'm such an idiot, such a frickin' idiot! How could I think I actually had a chance with him? He's a TA, for God's sake."

All of a sudden Aimee said, "He's a liar."

Brie and Tess shared looks of confusion.

"Look. I don't know what his problem is," Aimee said. "Obviously he has a thing for you, but something also tells me he's a liar."

Instead of hearing Aimee's concerns about Nick's morality, Tess heard a message of hope when she said 'he has a thing for you.' The more she thought about Nick's reactions to the Halloween kiss, the more they made sense. Tess began to smile. *He was doing the right thing, being honest.*

Brie and Aimee quietly watched Tess transform from a mopey mess to a revitalized woman on a mission.

"You guys! I've got it! Aimee, like you said he is attracted to me but totally confused about it. So all I have to do is make his choice crystal clear. Instead of sitting around feeling sorry for myself, I need to sex it up. Then all I have to do is wait it out until the end of the semester. By then he'll be so turned on, the first thing he'll do after he turns in his grades is ask me out."

A lull fell over the conversation. The three girls sat in silence for a couple of minutes.

"I'm not saying I'll go all Pamela Anderson or anything, but I definitely need to be a little more J-Lo. When he sees me looking all crazy hot and whatnot, he'll be begging for my number. Girlfriend, schmirlfriend." Tess cackled. She couldn't stop picturing Nick on his knees, begging for her number. "Whoa, I'm so gross. I need to shower," Tess said after a glimpse of her hair in the mirror. "Okay, it's totally cool if you want to hang here while I get dressed and stuff, or I can just meet you at Aimee's. Then we'll all go to the mall, okay?"

"Tess, I'm not going to the mall," Aimee said. "I'm certainly not aiding and abetting this fantasy."

"Oh, come on. Please?"

"No. Tess, I can't. My dad called me just yesterday to yell at me for spending too much on the credit card again."

Brie muttered to herself, "Now that's a problem I'd like to have."

"Fine. Just let the most amazing guy I've ever met just slip through my fingers."

"Tess, now you're just being dramatic."

"Am I, Brie? What about the chills the day we met? The endless conversations? How he confessed what he felt and then was brutally honest? What about the fact that his office number is the same as my birthday? Neither of you can deny that there's something between us, even if the timing isn't the best right now."

Brie and Aimee said nothing.

"So come on, let's all go to the mall. I'll pick out a few things, you'll give me the thumbs up or down, and I'll have another chance at true love." Tess gave them both her biggest, saddest, most pathetic puppy eyes she could.

Aimee and Brie shared another look.

"Damn it, Tess!" Aimee said.

"So you'll take me?"

"We'll wait here. You've got twenty minutes."

"Thank you, thank you." Tess sprang up and hugged Aimee.

"All righty, ladies, all set to go to the real mall?" Tess said exactly nineteen minutes later, dressed and raring to go.

"Wait a minute! You didn't say you wanted to go all the way to Holyoke!" Aimee said.

"I'm sorry, but the last time I checked, the best JC Penny can offer is sexy grandma, and kitten sweaters and muumuus aren't exactly the look I'm going for."

Brie looked down at her own butterfly print shirt. It was from JC Penny.

"Holyoke it is then," Aimee said. Tess threw a fist in the air with a heartfelt "Yeah!" Aimee took a deep breath and projected a fake smile.

Chapter 13

"This is ridiculous," Aimee mumbled to herself while riding the elevator. Of course it was just her luck to get stuck with a bunch of people who needed every floor when she needed the top. It was the day after what she considered a disastrous shopping trip. All Tess picked out were tarty little outfits that screamed for the wrong kind of attention. No matter how much she pleaded for her to pick something more appropriate to her goals, the more Tess resisted. "Finally." Eager to get to where she was going, Aimee gave the elevator doors an assistive push.

"Nick Donovan?" Aimee said, barging into his office.

He was the only one in the room with his back facing the door. He looked to be packing his things to leave.

Turning around he said, "The one and only. And you are?"

Aimee noticed Nick's eyes survey her body. He smiled when his gaze returned to hers. By God, Tess was right. Nick was hot. Tall. Kind smile with devilish eyes. This was bad, very bad. Aimee felt her resolve weaken as she couldn't help but admire the sight before her.

"Aimee Babineaux."

"Okay Aimee Babineaux, is there something I can help you with?"

"One of your students is a very, *very*, good friend of mine." She swallowed hard. It was distressing to find words when she couldn't stop undressing him with her eyes. "And…"

Nick looked at her as if he were reading her mind, further distracting her. He placed a gentle hand on her forearm and looked deep into her eyes. Fiery tingles ran ablaze up her arm. Her cheeks involuntarily flushed with desire. She was supposed to be yelling at him. Telling him what a complete ass he is and that he needs to stop stringing Tess along.

"Say no more. I can see this is something very important. The thing is, I really need to get to this, ah, last minute meeting." Aimee was distracted by the way he nervously tapped an unopened letter against his hip. "I want to give this all the attention it deserves. Why don't we talk about it tonight? Say seven o'clock, at the Moan and Dove? I'll give you my undivided attention then."

Aimee's jaw practically hit the floor. Did he really just ask her out? Shoot, was she flirting back? This was a bad idea, a really bad idea. Just as Aimee was about to respond, he deftly flung his backpack onto his right shoulder, winked, and left before she could say no.

Even though she was overwhelmed with guilt, Aimee ultimately decided to go. She promised herself to not flirt with him. She was only talking to him to stick up for Tess. In reality, it would be a five-minute conversation anyway.

Delighted to see the place was dimly lit, Aimee felt a wave of relief. Dark bars always made it easier to hide. The last thing in the world she wanted to happen was for anyone she knew to see her with Nick. God, what was she doing here? How would she feel if Tess were out doing the same with the guy she liked?

Aimee reminded herself that it was in fact for Tess that any of this even happened. Why did Nick have to be so hot? Have a touch that was so electrifying? Aimee was beginning to see what Tess saw in him. Gulp. Right. It was time to focus. She had a job to do and that was it. No flirting. Or at least she wouldn't flirt back, well at least so he couldn't tell.

"Great you came," Nick said, taking the last free seat at the bar. "This place is packed. I've never seen it so full this early."

"I was hoping to get a booth."

"A booth eh? So private. This really is serious." Aimee attempted to respond, but wasn't given the opportunity. "You'll have to excuse me. I've had a hell of day." He then tucked something deeper into his back pocket. Aimee recognized it as the same envelope from earlier. Only now it had been opened. "While I'm all for resolving whatever this is, I really need a drink first. Do you mind? First round is on me. Just need a breather before I jump back into it."

Nick seemed so confident and cool. He made Aimee feel like she was a freshman back in high school falling for the senior quarterback of the football team. All she could do was smile and nod. She was also dying to know what was in that letter. Hopefully the beer would loosen him up.

"And what'll it be for you Miss?" the bartender asked.

"Raison d'Etre please."

"The Raison d'Etre, wow. Looks like this is going to be one hell of night," Nick said.

"What's that supposed to mean?"

With a sporting glint in his eyes he replied, "Just can't wait to hear what all this is about, but first some good beer and light conversation."

Aimee felt her body temperature jump several degrees higher. This guy was such a smooth operator. No wonder Tess was crazy about him. If she wasn't careful, Aimee would create a messy love triangle that would undoubtedly end badly for everyone.

Upon delivery, Nick raised his bottle of Midas Touch. "To helping a friend."

"To helping a friend." Aimee clanked her bottle thinking, *And to not falling for the guy of her dreams.*

Three and a half Raison d'Etres later, Aimee felt good. So good in fact, she had nearly forgotten all about the real reason she was there in the first place and the letter. The light conversation had easily slipped into flirting. Always a girl with a man on her arm or at least waiting in the wings, Aimee didn't realize until that moment just how dry her recent spell with men had been. She began to feel sick. Comfortable with men she may have been, but a man-stealing best friend she was not.

"And to think I thought spoiled rich girls couldn't hold their alcohol," Nick said, embarking on his fourth Midas Touch. "I just may have found my match."

"Rich yes, spoiled no. The real estate business may be kind to my father, who in turn is kind to me, but I have to work for things."

"Oh please. A gorgeous girl like you with your blonde hair, banging body, and amazing taste in beer has never had to work for anything in her life."

"Excuse me? You didn't just say—"

"Don't play dumb. You heard me just fine."

"Don't call me dumb." Aimee's face twisted with irritation.

"Bossy. I like it." Then before Aimee could protest further, Nick pulled her stool up to his. Her legs had no other place to go than between his. Sitting so close to him caused sparks of electricity to buzz all over her body.

Aimee suddenly froze. *Oh God. Oh. God. Is he about to do what I think he's about to do? Stop. No. This can't happen.* But then it did. Nick kissed her directly on the mouth. At least he tried. Rather than lips meeting lips, Nick's lips met Aimee's palm, which then slapped his cheek. Hard.

"*Ouch!* What was that for?"

"Me coming to my senses." Aimee slapped him again.

"*Jesus!* What the hell?"

"And that's for Tess."

Rubbing his face Nick said, "Wait. Tess Ryan?" He looked as if he had just seen a ghost.

"Now is not the time to suddenly have a moral compass."

Looking like he was putting the pieces together Nick asked, "Hold on. She didn't—"

"Chill out. She hasn't done anything...yet." Aimee's smile was smug. "Now mark my words. Stop leading her on. Otherwise, well you know what I'll do."

Now it was her turn to wink and walk away before Nick could say anything and that's just what she did. She also vowed to never speak a word of this to Tess.

The following Tuesday around three in the afternoon, Tess headed to Nick's office wearing a sinful shade of ruby-red lipstick and a pair of dark wash jeans so snug that they demanded a thong or nothing at all. Her semitransparent black halter top left little to the imagination, revealing her smooth skin and belly button. Because it was November in Massachusetts, Tess was forced to wear a cardigan under her fleece jacket. "Hot damn, I look good," Tess said to herself before leaving her dorm.

Nick's office door was tightly shut; a sight she'd never seen before. His door was always open, or at the very least ajar. She took a moment to double-check that she had the right office. *Yup, office 712.* It was still weird to see her birth date on his door. *It has to mean something,* she thought. With a deep breath, she placed her hand on the doorknob. But before she could turn the knob, another TA interrupted her.

"He just left," the new TA said in a thick Southern accent. When she turned to face him, his eyes went straight to her midsection. "Nick Donovan your TA?"

"How'd you know which one was mine?" she asked, checking him out. He was a little shorter than Nick, with a strong jawline and sandy-blond hair. His facial scruff and rimless glasses contributed to his unusual look, a rare combination of athlete and intellectual. A faint yelp escaped her when her eyes met his. She couldn't deny that she thought he was a stud, but she had a plan, and as cute as he may have been, he was not a part of it.

The TA smiled and checked her out again instead of answering her question. "You literally just missed him. I can call him if you like. He can't be too far away."

"Sure. That'd be great." Tess noticed how deliciously smooth and charming his Southern accent was.

The TA ducked into his office a couple of doors away, leaving the door open. With no other distractions in the empty hallway, Tess watched as he stared at her through the doorframe. While on the phone, she noticed a smug look spread across his face.

"Nick'll be right over. He's downstairs with Professor Midge. So about five minutes."

"Hey, great. Thanks."

"Any time," he paused. "Mind if I wait with you until he gets here? Answer some questions?" The overconfidence in his voice was intriguing, yet mildly annoying.

"Thanks for the offer, but I'm all set."

He looked right at her belly button, then her face.

"Really, I'm fine."

"Hey, you never know—you may be surprised by what you get with us *other* TAs."

"Yup, got it." *Where the hell is Nick?* This TA's tenacity was making it harder to resist him.

"I'm Drew, by the way. Come by some time. I'm sure I could answer your questions and more."

"I'm Tess." She blushed. *Damn, he got me.* Just as she was about to launch a flirtatious comeback, Nick arrived. The atmosphere was instantly awkward.

"I'll see you around, Tess," Drew said, walking away. Tess watched Nick as Drew headed to the elevators, Nick's eyes locked on him. She smiled when she noticed Nick's fists clench, along with his jaw.

"Hi, Nick."

"What are you doing here?" He was jumpy, like he wanted her gone.

"I missed the quiz on Friday, and I was hoping I could take it now?"

"Everything okay? Have any interesting conversations lately?" His tone suggested that he wasn't asking in general terms but that he was really asking about the last time they were in his office.

"Everything's good. Thanks for asking." Tess felt uneasy, but she smiled and took her normal seat. "So can I take the quiz?"

Without a word, Nick grabbed his backpack and dug out the quiz.

From time to time, Tess would check his reflection in the oversized glass window to see if he was looking at her. Each time his eyes were focused on something else. Her heart sank. It was weird to see Nick like that. Feeling totally ignored, she began to second-guess her makeover. *It's too much. He doesn't like it,* she thought.

Nick cleared his throat without looking her. She took it as a reminder to get back on task.

"Done," she said a few minutes later.

"Any questions?"

"Nope."

"All right then." He took the quiz from her hands and returned to whatever he was doing. His body language screamed it was time for her to leave. Taking the hint, she gave him a long, hard stare before storming out. Although Nick's snub felt like a knife in her heart, it drove her to want to change his mind even more.

Chapter 14

As the semester went on, Tess eased off on appearing for Nick's office hours but continued vamping up her outfits for class in an attempt to make Nick want her. The few times he was within view, Tess made sure he locked eyes with her and didn't let go. She was determined to draw him in, make him pay attention to her. She forced him to watch younger, beefier guys get a shot at what he couldn't have.

On the surface, Tess relished all the attention, but truthfully her confidence and flirting with other guys was just for show. Deep down, she hurt more than she ever had. She observed the way Nick looked at her, how his eyes lit up at first and then went blank, as if he didn't know her. *It must be guilt mixed with his continuing desire for me,* she reasoned.

If only they weren't so awkward with each other in discussion, she might have felt braver about trotting up to his office and prancing around like she had before Halloween, but now the situation was just too delicate. "Just wait for the semester to end. He'll have broken up with his girlfriend by then, and he'll ask me out as soon as he sees me," she told herself and her friends.

She thought about him all the time. It didn't matter whether

she was studying, eating, sleeping, or skating. She missed the way
he inhaled and stopped midexhale when she asked him a new
question before he finished answering her first. She missed
laughing at his nerdy jokes, which they both knew were not *that*
funny. She even missed his off-color jokes that could easily be
misconstrued as insults. She missed everything about him.

By early December her sadness began to affect her skating,
which couldn't have happened at a worse time. She began to wish
she hadn't committed to the rapidly approaching charity skating
show several months before. Despite spending as many as three
or four hours a day practicing for the show, she just wasn't in the
right frame of mind.

"Come on, Tess! What's with you?" Stephanie, the captain of
the skating team, said the day before the show. She stood in the
middle of the arena watching Tess struggle through her solo
program. "Where's your head? I can't have you skating like this
in the show!"

Stephanie's forceful tone pushed Tess to go into her next
jump, a double toe loop, with as much speed as she possibly
could, which, it turned out, was not a good idea. Tess had never
been comfortable with speed. She preferred grace and style over
speed and height in all of her moves, but with the captain of the
team riding her to do better, she forced herself to go as fast as
possible. Then, as she knew might happen but desperately hoped
wouldn't, Tess overrotated and came down on the wrong side of
the blade, which drove her straight into a hard fall.

"That's just great, Tess! Now you've gone and injured

yourself. Can you even get up? How am I going to fill your spot? It's tomorrow."

Tess struggled to get up. It was a painful fall but appeared to be nothing she couldn't skate off. Once she was finally up, she skated over to Stephanie so she didn't have to yell.

"If this is because of that guy you're always going on and on about," Stephanie said before Tess had a chance to start, "I have no sympathy for you."

"Stephanie, this isn't about Nick," Tess said, defiantly. "Maybe I'm coming down with something."

Stephanie stared at Tess. "Your friend Aimee? She still on track to finish all the alterations on the costumes on time?"

Tess nodded. "They all look really great. She's going to have her own fashion line someday, you know."

Stephanie rolled her eyes. "You better be on point tomorrow, Tess. I'm not messing around." Stephanie reversed and skated to a group of skaters huddling in a corner at the other end of the arena.

"And you wonder why I don't hang out with the team more often," Tess muttered after letting out a sigh.

Tess could have kicked herself, but her butt was already throbbing. She knew she had been distracted, but she hadn't thought it was noticeable to anyone else. She also knew that if she wasn't focused, she risked not only embarrassing herself but the whole skating team, and the charity organizers too.

Remembering she hadn't reminded Nick about the show as she'd said she would, she decided to go ahead and do so. It would be short and sweet. She would just say hello, hand him the flyer, tell him when to arrive, and then leave. There was no reason to linger. The plan was perfect. She would not only relieve her longing to see him, which would bring her focus back, but she would also make another ticket sale.

Tess left practice without a word to anyone, especially Stephanie. She was too excited. She didn't bother changing back into her jeans. She left wearing her black leggings and figure-hugging wrap sweater, only exchanging her skates for sneakers. On her way out the door, she grabbed a flyer.

She marched over to Nick's office. As the entrance to the concrete history building came into view ahead of her, a voice called her name.

"Tess! Hey, Tess!"

"Ah, hi," she responded, trying to recognize who was calling her.

"How's it going?" the guy asked as he approached her. Tess didn't respond. "Drew, from the history department?" Tess noticed him staring at her backside.

"Drew. Yeah, hey. How's it going?" Her response seriously lacked enthusiasm.

"Good. Good, thanks. Yourself?" Drew's response, on the other hand, was full of excitement.

"Fine."

They stood three hundred feet from the entrance to Herter Hall. "All right. Well, if that's all, I'm going to go now." She looked up at Nick's office window.

"Sure is nippy out here, wouldn't you say?" He tapped her elbow before she got too far away. "Come get a coffee with me?"

Tess hesitated. A vision of Nick sitting in his office curled up with a book all alone, waiting for someone, anyone, to show up— *me, maybe*—filled the movie screen behind her eyes. When the vision vanished, she looked back at Drew.

He is pretty hot, she thought. There was something different about him too. She tried to zero in on what it was. *The smile? No...Well, kind of. Eyes? No. Is it the fact that he is actually asking me out? Yes. Yes! That is the difference between him and Nick.*

Drew's cunning smile told Tess that he was nothing but temptation and bad decisions. Yet it gave her a bit of a rush. Had she seen Drew first, she might not have ever noticed Nick. *What the hell,* she figured. *It's just coffee.* Plus, if she worked it just right, she would have an excuse to spend more time in the history department and be closer to Nick without going to see him directly.

"I take it that's a yes?"

No, she said to herself. *I can't just give up on Nick.* "Yes, but I'll be right back. I just have to drop something off." With a quick turn on her heels, she sped away toward Herter Hall. Drew, several steps behind, followed her into the building.

Once inside, Tess turned to him and said, "Hey, do you mind waiting here? It'll be really quick. Don't want you to have to go all the way up to the seventh floor."

"Uh, yeah. I guess so."

"Great! Be right back."

In front of Nick's door, Tess smiled from ear to ear. Simply standing near his office she felt better. She knocked softly and waited for a response. But there was none. Tess figured no one was there. Then the door opened. Tess's heart skipped a beat.

"Nick, hi! I..." Tess stopped. The person who opened the door was definitely not Nick.

"Nick's not here," the very studious-looking female wearing glasses said. She was short, with a thick waist. "Are you a student of his?"

"Actually, I'm a member of the skating team. I'm handing out flyers to get the word out about our fundraiser tomorrow. All the proceeds go to a great cause. Kids with cancer." Tess frowned when she realized how stupid she must have just sounded. Quickly, she reached into her shoulder bag and handed the girl the flyer.

"Thanks." She didn't even look at the flyer.

"So you'll make sure Nick gets it?"

The girl gave her a funny look. "Sure."

Tess smiled and took a deep breath. "Thank you so much. I really appreciate it. The whole skating team thanks you. We hope to see you all there!"

The girl smiled and politely closed the door.

Tess took a moment in front of his closed door to release her disappointment. When she was ready, she sighed, touched the door, and ventured down to meet Drew.

"Coffee? How about hot chocolate?" Tess asked Drew with a flirtatious smile as she got off the elevator.

Walking through campus, the pair decided to go to the Blue Wall in the Campus Center. It was easy and welcoming, and at four in the afternoon they figured it wouldn't be too busy.

"I get a little uncomfortable in large crowds," Drew said as he and Tess settled into their seats at a table in the corner with their drinks. "I appreciate you sitting at a corner table with me."

Tess raised her eyebrows. "And yet you're at a school with twenty-two thousand students."

"When was the last time you saw all twenty-two thousand students in the same area?"

Tess took a sip of hot chocolate to hide her smile. "Tell me what brought you up to UMass all the way from Georgia. Had you ever seen snow before you got here?"

Drew chuckled. "I'd seen snow before." He sipped his café mocha. "Now how do I put this so I don't sound...you know, spoiled?"

"Oh, come on. Like you're about to tell me you're some heir to a massive fortune the moment your big paw-paw dies."

Drew smirked. "You see, both my parents descend from long lines of plantation owners—"

Tess swallowed hard. "Wait—does that mean your family used to own slaves?"

"Which means I've had—what do you northerners call it?—a

silver-spoon upbringing."

Tess took a deep breath and lowered her chin to her chest. His accent was smooth and delicious and made her momentarily weak in the knees.

"And so, for as many Christmases as I can remember, I've gone someplace like Switzerland or Aspen, Colorado. So yeah, I've seen snow."

"I see." Tess felt totally insignificant and a little awkward. *Did his family own slaves or not?* She really wanted to know. The answer could be a huge deal breaker. She began wishing she could have been holed up with Nick in his office instead of having had accepted Drew's offer.

"Go on, it's no big deal. I think it's kind of nice that I got to tell you about where I come from so early on. Usually, the girls I date either know who I am and only want my money or find out I've got some and then only stay with me for the money."

"Date?"

Drew smiled. "I can't believe a girl as attractive as you would have to ask such an obvious question."

Tess's face turned bright red. She was instantly flattered. She began to wonder more about who this guy Drew sitting across from her was. "Why, thank you. No one has ever said such a nice thing to me."

"You can't be serious." Suddenly his cell phone rang. He pulled it out of his pocket to check who was calling. "I am so sorry, but will you please excuse me? I must take this." Drew rose from the table before Tess had time to respond.

She tried to listen to his conversation, but he had walked out of earshot. She watched as he paced back and forth, looking annoyed. She began to imagine who Drew could be talking to just as he came back to the table.

"Everything all right?"

With a sigh Drew said, "Looks like I won't be mending any fences tonight."

"What does that mean?"

"Oh, right. It means my plans for later got canceled." He paused, holding his gaze on Tess. "Hey, you want to get dinner?"

Tess quickly looked around the dining room. "You want to get dinner?"

"Why not? I'm hungry. I'm sure you could use a good meal. We'll have some drinks. You are twenty-one, right?"

Tess nodded.

"Great. It'll be fun."

"But I'm still wearing my skating clothes."

Drew's eyes narrowed and grew dark. "That's not a problem." His eyes roved over Tess's body. She felt him try to look through her clothes.

"I need to change. Meet you back here in half an hour?"

"I could just go with you?"

Tess hesitated for a moment but then came to her senses. "I had no idea Southern boys had such crude manners."

Scoffing, Drew said, "Forgive me. I forgot how prudish New England girls can be." He grinned with a rueful look.

Standing, Tess said, "I'll be back in half an hour."

"By the time I finish my coffee and get to my car, it'll be half an hour. How about I meet you at your dorm?"

"That would give me a few extra minutes," she said. "Dickinson in Orchard Hill."

"Great. I'll see you soon."

Walking briskly, Tess's head began to spin. How had her little plan for distraction from Nick so quickly turn into a full-blown date with a small-time—or maybe big-time—aristocrat from the South? He was certainly cute, rather charming even. She loved his foreign yet familiar accent. It made her feel safe and taken care of. It was such a rush each time he complimented her looks with his kind words and devilish eyes. Much to her surprise, Tess actually was having a good time with this guy who was so clearly not Nick. *Oh, but Nick!*

Tess pictured him all alone in a dark, cold room with only a book to keep him company. She envisioned him longing for her company, longing to pick up where they left off with soft kisses and warm hugs. Her heart yearned to be wrapped in Nick's arms. Knowing her feelings for Nick were still so strong, she couldn't imagine going out with someone else.

"I should cancel," Tess said aloud, but she didn't have his number. "No, Tess, it'll be fun. Who knows, you might actually have a good time. And it's not like you can't have a little fun while you wait for Nick," she told herself, opening the door to her room. *True.* So it was settled. Tess would have dinner with Drew. If she had a good time, wonderful. If she didn't—well, at least she would get a free meal out of it.

Not about to discourage Drew from doling out more compliments, Tess wore a sleek pair of jeans that made her backside dazzle and a low-cut sweater that left just enough to the imagination.

Precisely thirty minutes later, Drew was at the main door of Tess's building. He boasted a confident smile and whisked her off to dinner at Fitzwilly's, a fun, lighthearted place where the food was good and the drinks were strong. Tess was delightfully surprised by Drew's decision to take her there. Fitzwilly's was rarely a first-date kind of place for college students. Perhaps a slightly larger distraction from Nick than she originally planned was just what she needed.

Chapter 15

The hot chocolate that evolved into dinner ultimately led to breakfast, sort of. When Tess woke, Drew was snoring heavily on top of her. From what she could see, her roommate was not home. *Thank God,* she thought and began nudging Drew awake.

"Hmm, it's sure been a while since I've slept next to someone in a dorm twin," Drew said, waking up. "Can't imagine what would a happened if we'd done more than sleep."

Tess smiled and wondered what he meant by that.

"What time is it?"

She looked at her alarm clock. "Crap. Time for me to head to the rink."

"Want me to come with you?"

"Nah, I have to be there most of the day. It would be pretty boring for you."

"That's okay. I wouldn't mind watching you twirl around in those little skater outfits."

"Very funny, but really, I've got to get going." She was out of bed, brushing her hair. Seeing her become mobile, Drew got himself up and put his shirt back on. She chuckled at how uncomfortable it must have been to sleep in his jeans.

"Show starts at five, right?"

"Hey, you remembered!" His thoughtfulness made her blush.

"So I'll see you then? And after you shake your little thang, we can see about getting drinks."

"And there you have it, folks—how America really feels about figure skating."

"Go on now. I didn't mean nothin' by it."

"It's fine. I'm used to it. Even Nick—" She stopped before saying something she'd regret. "My cousin Nick hates it, and he used to skate."

Drew chuckled. "I'll see you later," he said and left Tess to get on with her day. She pulled her hair up in a ponytail, tugged on her leggings, and went to the rink, full of anticipation, for a multitude of reasons.

Her biggest worry was about her ability to skate a clean program as her bum was still pretty sore. She also feared how Stephanie would treat her if something went wrong. She also worried about what her date with Drew meant. Was this flirtation about to become something serious? But most stressful of all was not knowing whether or not Nick got the flyer and whether he would actually show up at the arena. If he showed up, it would mean he meant everything he said about how much he liked her back. If he didn't? Well, Tess couldn't think about that.

Four hours later, Tess was in her costume giving Aimee the play-by-play of her date. Aimee said, "How about that?" with a mouth full of pins as she made last-minute adjustments to Tess's costume. "Sounds like you and Drew had a great time."

"How could I not with that Southern accent? I melt every time he says 'y'all' or 'darling.' It's that Georgia-boy charm."

"Does this mean Nick's out of the picture?" Aimee had a huge smile on her face.

Why did Aimee have to mention him? Tess was already working overtime not letting thoughts of him interfere with the day more than they already were. Tess gave Aimee a look full of overwhelming indecision.

"Crap, Tess. Really? How can you be with Drew and still be pining for Nick?"

"I don't know. First it was just for coffee, and then he offered to buy me dinner. I was hungry. I may have had one too many drinks with dinner, and, well, he walked me to my door. He buttered me up with that accent, and the rest is history. It's not like we did much. Just second-base stuff."

"You're playing with fire."

"How so?"

"The history department can't be that big, and people talk. You can't be with Drew if your heart is with someone else. If you ask me, Drew sounds really amazing."

"Right. So I decided today is the final test with Nick. Yesterday I dropped off a flyer for the show and told myself if he shows up, he's interested. If not—well, then I'm done and I will give Drew my undivided attention."

Aimee sighed. "But Drew is free and clear. You don't have to worry about the ethics, or his morals, of him grading your work."

Tess half smiled at Aimee's assertion, wondering if there was a hidden message, but quickly refocused on her plan. Though simple, Tess knew it was anything but. Unbeknown to Nick, he was under a lot of pressure.

Now warming up on the ice as people were taking their seats, Tess found herself scanning the Mullins Center for Nick. It was a futile endeavor as gliding on ice made everyone in the crowd a blur. Two minutes later the whistle blew, indicating it was time for the skaters to take their places. Tess promptly skated off the ice until it was her turn.

Lost in fantasies about Nick showing up with a huge smile on his face and flowers at the end of her program, Tess jumped when the stage manager told her she was up next, which sent her tumbling onto the ice. She looked like someone who had never been on skates before. Without fail she heard the crowd gasp. *Oh God, I hope Nick didn't see that!* Then all of a sudden Tess had an idea. One that would definitely get the crowd going – especially Stephanie.

When the spoken lyrics of the song "Do You Love Me?" by the Contours began, Tess on purpose, tripped again. She felt crowd cringe. She deliberately looked clumsy. Each twist and hand gesture was ever so slightly off from the lyrics. She felt the audience hold its breath. She knowingly took her first jump, a single toe loop, slowly, cautiously, like a beginner. Then with a flawless landing, the crowd gave an encouraging clap. As the music picked up, Tess ditched her novice demeanor and made each move more daring than the last. The crowd was loving it with their clapping and whooping. Feeding off the crowd, Tess skated harder, turned sharper. She became defiant even. *Eat your heart out Nick*, she thought. Then came time for the big jump— the one where she had to land right as the music came back after a brief silence.

Axels were her hardest jump. She had mastered her single, and her double was decent. Her triple...well, landing a triple axel was about as likely to happen as pigs flying, which was why, in this moment, where she was laying it all on the line, she just had to switch it from a single to a triple...

Tess gained more speed than she ever had before a jump. Realizing this, she got nervous, really nervous. *Okay, maybe this isn't such a good idea*, she thought. The audience was one stream of blurriness. As she tensed up, she felt the audience tense up with her. There was no backing out now. *Well here goes...*

And she nailed it! The crowd roared to their feet. Hearing all the support around her, Tess was truly proud of herself. She had only actually landed a triple axel a handful of times. Her hand didn't even touch the ice this time. *Please God, Nick better have seen that*, she thought as she skated the last forty seconds of her program.

Drew came to congratulate her right after her program. "You had me going there for a minute. I thought definitely, you were going to fall. That was amazing."

Tess was flattered but continued to scan the crowd for Nick even though she had that horrible feeling in the pit of her stomach that said he most definitely was not there.

Giving her a hug, Aimee said, "Tess, a triple axel! A holy frickin'-A axel! And I couldn't be more thankful that I tucked in that extra piece to make the bodice tighter. You looked so hot!"

"Aimee, stop!"

"She's right," Drew said. "Hi, I'm Drew, by the way," he said, putting his hand out to Aimee.

"Great. Now you two can get to know each other while I go change. Who's up for a beer when I get back?"

"Are you not going to stay for final bow?"

"After what I pulled, I want to stay as far away from Stephanie as I can."

Aimee chuckled. "Screw her. It was awesome. Anyway, I can't leave until the show's over. I'll catch up with you later."

In the dressing room, Tess took her time. Her heart cracked over not seeing Nick. She'd adamantly believed he would show up. But who was she kidding? She'd tried to remind him only the day before the event. He probably didn't receive the flyer. With a shared office, maybe one of the other TAs saw it first and threw it away. The TA she spoke to might very well have tossed it straight into the trash. Whatever the case, Tess had to accept that his absence meant what she'd feared the most: he really wasn't interested.

"There you are," Drew said. "I was thinking of sending out a search party."

"Sorry, just wanted to do a little stretching. Don't want to get stiff, you know."

"Don't I know it, darling," he said with a wink.

Tess smiled back a little weakly, reminding herself he was a good guy. He was polite, he'd paid for dinner, he minded his manners—for the most part—and he had a seductive attitude that made her feel desired. Yes, he was a good guy who was actually interested in her.

During the week and a half that followed and despite the end of the semester being underway, Tess and Drew achieved full-fledged boyfriend-girlfriend status. It was fast, it was fun, and it was just what Tess needed, she realized. For the first time in a long time, she wasn't thinking about Nick.

Tess went back to Santa Fe over the January break, which Aimee, admitted later, feared would kill the newfound relationship, but it turned out to be no problem at all. Drew called her every day and even offered a place for her in his apartment should she want to return early. As tempting as the offer might have been, Tess didn't take it. The warmer Santa Fe sun felt far too good to exchange for the gray bone-numbing cold of Amherst.

"I know. I miss you too," Tess replied during one of their late-night phone calls.

"I still can't believe you chose New Mexico over me. You know, it's just as warm up here."

"Oh, is that so? Where?"

"My bed."

Tess stifled a giggle. "Of course you'd say that."

"Because you know how hot this body is when it's working to keep yours warm." She couldn't deny that. The ultimate Frisbee he played had sculpted his body in all the right places.

"Right. And I'm going to let you go now."

"Wait, wait—what? I thought we were going to, you know…"

"I know, but it's late and my parents are still up. I can't handle another awkward lecture from my stepdad. It's just too weird hearing him talk about 'sex in my mother's house' and 'the universe is always watching.'"

The phone went silent, but Tess could hear Drew pouting.

"Come on. I'll be back in three days. And you know that I can't wait for you to do that thing you do."

"Yeah, and what thing is that?" Hope had returned to his voice.

"Oh, you know." Tess's voice dropped to a soft whisper.

"When you run your—" Tess heard a noise and suddenly stopped.

"Hello? Tess?"

"I heard something is all."

Drew waited for a moment but returned right back to it. "Okay. Now, where were we?"

"Yeah, I'm going to call it a night."

"Hey, that's not fair. You can't just leave me hanging here."

"Drew, you'll be fine. I'll be back in a few days and then you can have your way with me, okay?"

"Really? My way?"

"Goodnight, Andrew," Tess said before hanging up the phone. She crawled into bed, her mind whizzing with excitement. In three days, she would be back in Drew's arms and moving to an off-campus apartment with Aimee. While the New Mexican warmth was nice, having to abide by rules like she was sixteen again made her antsy to get back.

Chapter 16

Meanwhile, Nick spent his January break finally having a long overdue think about the choices he was making in his life since receiving that letter. It had been two months. He hadn't bothered to respond because even after nearly two years, he still couldn't bring himself to even say *her* name, so how could he ever write a response? More importantly there was no way she was right. Yet, it got him thinking.

That slap from Tess's best friend was a wake up call. Despite how complicated and unclear his feelings were for Tess, there was no way he wanted to hurt her by trifling with other women, especially her best friend. It was time to quit messing about and end whatever it was he had with Liz. This left him open to focus on defining whatever it was that he had with Tess.

Once the new semester started, Nick felt confident in his decisions. He excitedly waited for Tess to come sweeping into his office like she always did. After a week of no Tess, Nick turned to Will for some perspective.

"No one can look that devastated and not be willing to wait it out," Nick said to Will the first Saturday afternoon of the semester. They were in the living room watching a Celtics game having a couple of beers.

"I still wouldn't touch that girl with a fifty-foot pole, if I were you," Will said. "Thank your lucky stars she hasn't said anything…yet."

"Yet? What do you mean *yet*? There's nothing for her to tell. I guarantee she wanted me to kiss her. There's no way she would turn me in when she might still want me."

"Oh, don't you sound like the stud. You're starting to sound like that Southern con artist, Drew."

"That guy's such a sleaze, isn't he? Fun to drink with, though."

Will nodded in agreement.

"But anyway, I know she'll come back to my office. I'll tell her I'm single. She'll get all girly excited, I'll ask her out, and the rest will be history."

Will gave his roommate a sideways glare.

"Whatever, man." Nick took a drink. "She'll come around. I can count on that."

At the same time that Nick was planning his move on Tess, word was spreading through the history department that Drew had yet again made another conquest. Hearing the news, Nick was not that surprised or interested. He knew of at least three other girls Drew had gotten together with last fall alone, only to break their hearts a few weeks later. In any case, there was nothing about this new fling that told Nick it would be any different, so he didn't bother listening to the gossip long enough to learn who the unaware victim was this time. More importantly, he was focused on preparing for the first time Tess came prancing through his office door.

But she never went to Nick's office. From the moment she got off the plane, things with Drew became hot and heavy and utterly consuming. After she and Aimee moved into their off-campus apartment, it was as if Drew moved in with them. Legitimately not thinking about Nick, Tess was rather content with Drew. Her initial impression of him—that he was bad news—turned out to be nothing but her nerves over preferring someone over Nick.

At the beginning of March, Drew's thesis proposal was finally approved after more years than he liked to admit, and Tess was busy trying to survive midterms. She spent forty-eight sleepless hours striving to complete two take-home midterms by 8:00 a.m.—one for Iranian history, the other for Tudor England, which she submitted in the nick of time.

Brain-dead, she failed to double-check which paper she was actually handing to each professor, leading her to mix them up. Desperate for sleep, Tess headed back to her dorm not realizing her mistake until six hours later. She woke up to the sound of two urgent e-mails from her professors asking what had happened. By the grace of God, Tess was able to go back and make the switch before the professors took out their red pens.

Already in the history department, with some time to kill before her shift at the video store—a job she had been forced to pick up to support the rust-bucket of a car she'd bought to get to and from campus—Tess decided to make an unannounced visit to her man. "Hey there, hot stuff," she said, barging into Drew's office with darkening eyes and pouty lips.

"Tess, hi. What are you doing here?" he asked from his seat at his desk. He turned around to stand. Her expression told him what she needed: a "come take me now" kiss. Instead, all she got was a peck on the cheek. Mildly annoyed, she went over to the couch and made herself comfortable. As a PhD candidate, Drew had managed to score a single office, unlike Nick, a mere master's candidate.

"Today could not get any worse," she said.

"Hey, it's not that bad." Tess had already filled him in when she called him to make sure both professors were still in the building. "At least they gave you the chance to fix it."

"You're right. Thank God for that." Taking a breath, Tess looked out the window and was saddened by what she saw. Gray sky and narrow sidewalks from all the snow. "Man, is it ever going to warm up? I can't take this awful, dreary weather anymore."

"It's only March, Tess. I thought you were a hearty New England girl. New Mexico softened you."

"Well, then come over here and warm me up."

Drew quickly looked at the open door and looked as if he was listening for signs of anyone in the hall. When it seemed clear, he moved to shut it. Just then, Nick walked by.

"Drew, man. Hey, how are ya?"

"Good, man." Drew proceeded to shut the door.

"Hey, I haven't seen you in, like, forever." Nick pushed his way into the office. "I heard the good news and—" The sight of Tess on Drew's couch stopped him. He stood there, frozen.

Tess's stomach dropped.

"Tess," Nick stammered. There was an awkward silence. Nick's eyes darted between Drew and Tess. "I didn't know Drew was TAing this semester," he said to her.

"I'm not," Drew answered.

It seemed to take Nick a minute to fully understand what was happening. When it looked like he finally did, he let out a big "Oh" and nodded. "Well, then, I'll be on my way. Nice seeing you, man. And good job on finally getting that approval. Hopefully, you can get the thesis done in the next ten years," he said with a smug smile and then slipped out the door without looking back.

Drew cocked his head to the side. "What the hell was that?"

"I don't know. Maybe some girlfriend dumped him?" Tess tried her hardest to sound impartial.

"Oh, yeah, that's right. Poor guy. She accused him of cheating on her."

Tess swallowed hard. "Do you think he really did?"

"Nick? I don't know. Maybe. I remember he kinda had this thing for someone else last semester, but I'm pretty sure it was just talk. I heard she was an undergrad. I really can't see him going for an undergrad."

Noticing her sudden shivers, Drew sat next to her and wrapped his arm around her. She gave him a smile that he took to be an invitation. He began kissing her neck. At first she liked it, but when she noticed the door was still ajar she shot upright.

"I think we should change things up and actually go out tonight. After my shift at the video store, let's go to the Harp."

Drew dropped his head and shrugged.

"Come on! The weather sucks, and we always stay in," Tess said, which was true. They primarily hung out at her place.

Tess sat back down, and Drew attempted to pick up where he left off, but Tess pushed him off. "Come on, Drew. It'll be fun."

"But, babe, I'm really busy."

Tess was annoyed by his rejection and gave into thoughts about Nick. *Was he talking about me? What did he say? I wonder how he's doing. Did the girlfriend call it quits or did he?*

"Fine!" Tess said and decided to abruptly leave his office.

Alone in the elevator, Tess said to herself, "Holy hell." For a moment, she breathed heavily and felt sweat bead on her brow. Seeing Nick again brought a rush of all her old feelings. *What the hell is happening?* She really believed she only had eyes for Drew. She hadn't *seriously* fantasized about Nick since she returned from New Mexico. But to find out that he may have had told people about having a thing for her made her stomach flip-flop.

"If I didn't know better, Miss Ryan, I would think you were following me," Nick said, surprising her when the elevator doors opened on the first floor. *Crap,* Tess thought. *Play it cool, Tess. Play it cool.*

"And if I were?"

As she left the elevator, Nick walked in, bumping into her

shoulder. He stared at her for a moment with a cocky smile and then pressed the button for his floor. "You're trouble, Miss Ryan. Trouble, trouble, trouble."

"What? No, I'm not!" she said, but it was too late. The elevator doors closed and Nick was gone. Tess stamped her feet and let out a frustrated squeal. Feeling like she'd had enough excitement for one day, she shrugged it off and began the trip to work via the supermarket, to stock up on work snacks.

Always hating the size of grocery stores, she was in and out in five minutes flat. Safely back in her car, Tess took a minute to compose herself. *I'm fine. Everything is fine.* It was just a bad this-too-shall-pass kind of day, as her mother always said. It was time to move on and clear her head for her mind-numbing job. All she had to do was make sure a movie was playing and customers were paying. Feeling better and silently praying for nothing else bad to happen, she backed out of the parking space. And then she felt a sickening thud as she backed into something.

"Oh no! Oh no! What did I just hit?"

A little old lady lay on the pavement behind her car.

"Holy shit! Oh my God! Ma'am, are you okay? I. Am. So. Sorry! Please, please let me help you." Tears involuntarily streamed down her face. The woman looked at least eighty-five. She had wild white hair, pearl earrings so heavy they tugged against her earlobes, and, of course, bright red lipstick. She wore white polyester pants, a long, tan trench coat, and leopard-print orthotic platform sneakers. *Really? Leopard print?* Tess thought, momentarily distracted.

"Eh, fuck you," the old woman crowed as she rose and dusted herself off. "Fuckin' kids." Tess reached for her arm to make sure she was okay. "Don't touch me!" the old woman screeched, blocking Tess's attempt. "I told them not to put a university here," she muttered to herself.

How old is this woman? "Ma'am, I am so sorry. Are you all right? Does anything hurt?"

"Just the kitty cat I slew to make these beautiful, beautiful shoes." The woman gave a maniacal snicker as she lifted each foot, showing them off.

"Okay, well...can I give you my number and insurance info, so you have it? I am so, so, sorry."

"Eh, fuck you, kid. Get out of my way." The old woman squawked, rapping Tess on the shins with her cane.

Tess's face writhed with pain after the woman's assault. She decided helping her was a lost cause. The woman was clearly bonkers. Back in her car Tess waited for the old bat to pass behind her. Oddly, as she observed her in the review mirror, the woman suddenly looked like a pleasant little grandma, a sweet smile affixed to her face.

"Holy mother of Christ, what was that?" Tess said as she turned onto the street. She breathed fast and shook her left leg. Her nerves were too rattled to go directly to work. She needed to talk to someone. *Call out?* she wondered. *Crap, I need the money. Call Aimee?* But it was three thirty. Aimee was in class. *Drew.* His apartment was only two minutes away. He would have finished his office hours by now. *Perfect.*

Having only been to Drew's apartment once, Tess hoped she remembered exactly which unit was his. They all looked the same. Thankfully, she found it without much trouble. The main door to Drew's building was unlocked, allowing her to walk right up to his unit. Likewise, his front door was unlocked. *Small stuff, I know, but finally, something is going right today*, Tess thought, as she cruised into Drew's apartment unannounced.

From the living room Tess heard muffled noises coming from one of the bedrooms. She wasn't clear which room it was, Drew's or his roommate's. As she got closer to Drew's room the noises became louder, though still muffled. She wondered if a dog was whining to be let out. *Wait. Drew doesn't have a dog.*

Then the noises became clearer—human voices, one male, one female. The female voice panted between moans. The male voice was making low grunting sounds. *What the hell? Is there actually another woman with him?* Tess pushed the door open a crack.

"Aww, yeah, that's it. Fuck! Yeah! Oh, shit!" Drew panted, out of breath and half-naked, clearly enjoying the moving images of orgiastic bodies splayed across his computer screen.

"Drew!" Tess experienced a sudden mixture of relief, disgust, and intrigue as she pushed into his room.

"Shit! Tess, you can't be here!" He clamored to hide his little—well, rather enlarged—mini him. Tess froze in his bedroom doorway. Deep moans from the computer filled the room.

"Seriously, Tess. What the hell are you doing here? I've told you, it's not a good idea for you to be here. Did anyone see you?"

"I ran over an old lady."

"You what?"

"I...ran over...an old lady."

"Oh my God. Really?" Drew buttoned up his pants, still shirtless but now one hundred percent focused on Tess. He stood and gave her a hug. The skin flick still played at full volume. "Is she okay? Are you okay? What the hell happened?"

Tess struggled to wrap her mind around what was happening. *Where do I begin? Did I die and no one told me? This day is just too much. And that damn porno is really distracting.* She tried to block it out and answer the questions. "Yeah, um, I have no idea what you just asked. Could you maybe turn that off?"

"Yes. Sorry about that." Drew broke their embrace and turned it off.

"And could you put a shirt on?" she asked, carefully. Not that she didn't like what she was looking at, but she needed to get the image of her boyfriend pleasuring himself, without her, out of her mind as soon as possible if she was ever going to be able to go to work. *Work—right.* "I'll be right back," Tess said, excusing herself and going to the living room to make a phone call.

"Hey, Kenny…yeah, it's Tess."

"What are you doing?"

"I'm calling you," Tess said, annoyed at the obvious question.

"It's so nice to hear your voice. I hope you're well today." Kenny's voice was soft and lazy-sounding, like a hippie high on drugs.

"Oh, that's nice of you to say. But hey, I'm really sorry to call so last minute, but I can't come in today."

"That's so sad. Is everything all right?"

Tess needed a good story, because at this point no one would believe the truth anyway. "I've got my period, and I'm bleeding so bad I can't leave the bathroom."

"No way, Tessie. That sounds serious. You need to go to the doctor toot sweet, man." The concern in his voice was kind. Kenny had such a gentle soul. She hated taking advantage of it, but she knew if she went in, her day would only get worse. She had had enough.

"Okay, yes, I'll call the doctor right away. Yup. Uh-huh. Okay, bye, Kenny," she said and hung up the phone.

Fully clothed, Drew joined her in the living room. Tess noticed he quickly scanned the room, as if someone else might be there. "So, ah, what you just said. Is that ah…"

"What? My period? Gross. No. I'm fine. I just didn't think he would believe the truth."

"So you going to jail and all that now?"

"Ironically, no. The old lady, turns out, is crazy. She told me to eff off…several times, and smacked my shins with her cane.

Then she just walked off, not even limping—nothing—with this sweet-grandma smile on her face."

"You kidding me?"

"She refused to take my information. She didn't even look at my license plate."

"You're so damn lucky." Drew paused. "So you okay? 'Cause if you are, I really need to get back to work."

Silence took over the room as Tess thought about his weird answer. *Why is he rushing me out? I just ran over someone! Am I really that bad in bed that he would rather watch porn?* Instead of calming down a bit, she began to tense up. The image of walking in on him wouldn't leave her mind.

"So are we going to talk about the whole, ah, movie thing?"

Drew shot her a quick look before he turned away and said, "Nope."

"Got it. Okay then. You are, for sure, taking me out for a drink tonight."

Tensing up, Drew replied, "Babe, I can't. I really can't. I've got too much work to do."

Tess rolled her eyes, making sure he saw. "You know what, you're right. I shouldn't have come here. I'm sorry." Tess turned to leave.

"Hey, come on, babe. Don't be like that. I care. I'm sorry you had a bad day. It's just, well, you know, being a grad student is a lot harder than being an undergrad. I can't, like, just blow stuff off to have a drink."

Tess wasn't buying it. If anything, graduate school was easier than undergrad. Grad students didn't have to take a bunch of random classes outside their number-one interest, like math of distant/nonexistent galaxies, or biology of the grass seed, as was the case for Tess. They only took two classes a semester, TAed a class or two, and studied what they wanted.

"Whatever. I'll be at the Harp, with Aimee," she said and walked through the door, leaving Drew in her dust. She'd blown off work, and now she needed to blow off Drew. Instead of comforting her, he'd only made her feel worse. Surely a vodka cranberry would be more soothing.

Chapter 17

The floors of the Harp were always sticky. Nothing was served on or in anything but plastic, and the wood-paneled walls were covered in Guinness posters and pictures of Ireland. As a good Irish girl from Brighton, the moment Tess walked into the Harp, she felt at home. She was no foreigner there, as she stopped in least once a week.

"Tessie, you're in early," said Dave, the bartender.

"It's five o'clock somewhere." She hated it when people called her that. It reminded her of her father using "Tessie" when he was trying to explain why he'd broken yet another promise.

Dave rolled his eyes and asked her if she wanted a beer or something stronger. She opted for something stronger.

While she waited for her drink, her body secretly shook with chills, and she clenched her jaw so it wouldn't chatter. Her stomach twisted and turned. *What the hell is going on today? Have I royally pissed off the universe?* Then her thoughts turned to what was really weighing on her mind. *I haven't thought…okay, really thought, about Nick since…*the reality was Tess couldn't remember a day since she'd started dating Drew when Nick didn't somehow pop into her mind. It only took a few lyrics from a song, a picture on a sign, or, worst of all, a simple look from Drew to return Nick to her thoughts. *Oh my God! I am such a horrible person! How can I ever look Drew in the face again?* When her vodka cranberry finally came, Tess swallowed most of it in one quick gulp. Aimee joined her when she was halfway through her second.

"All right, Tess, you really need to slow down." Aimee reached for the near empty glass in Tess's hand.

"But it tastes so good, and I feel so bad, bad, bad."

"I've noticed."

"You need to tell me what I should do. I mean, you know I've always wanted to be with Nick, and now that I know he was talking about me and—"

"Not for a fact. Look, I'll give you a break on what happened with the papers. Hell, I'll give you another drink for the old lady. As for Drew—well that's just hilarious. Of course, it also sounds like you've got some work to do on—" Aimee cleared her throat— "your game, if you know what I mean."

"Whatever. What I care most about is that I've always liked Nick, and now he's actually single. But I'm not, and it would kill me if I broke Drew's heart. I just can't handle it. Aimee, please, tell me what to do."

Aimee looked like she was far away.

"Aimee? Hello? I need your help over here!"

"Hey, sorry. I was just thinking."

"Yeah, and…?"

"I think the only way you're going to get over Nick once and for all is…" Aimee hesitated. She looked like she was wrestling with what to say. Then she said, "You need to just be completely honest with him. Tell him how you feel and demand that he be just as honest with you about everything."

Tess's eyes bulged for a moment, picturing how that would go. The imaginary scenario wasn't pretty at first. She was too nervous, and Nick seemed weird, like he had acted in Drew's office. But then Tess pictured Nick smiling at her because of her honesty.

"Aimee, you are so right! It'll solve all of my problems!" Tess was feeling better under the full effect of Aimee's insights plus the vodka cranberries.

"And what problems are those, babe?" Drew asked, suddenly appearing next to Tess at the bar. He slid his arm around her waist and then gave her the kind of kiss she had wanted earlier. Now, however, it felt uncomfortable and awkward.

"What are you doing here?" Tess was relieved to no longer be kissing Drew. "I thought you were studying."

"I was, but then I thought of you sitting at a bar alone, with all these single guys around, and I just…" His voice trailed off.

Tess forced a giggle. "You're so chivalrous, coming to save a damsel in distress!"

"So, you're not still upset about earlier?"

Tess hesitated. She looked to Aimee for reassurance, but she was involved in a staring contest with a stud a few barstools away. "Oh, I'm fine now." She paused, turned to her drink, and gulped down the rest of it.

"Aww, babe—"

"Don't call me babe." She suddenly felt smothered by his affection.

Drew looked stunned by her dismissal. "But I always call you babe. I thought you liked it."

"Well, I don't."

Drew stepped back. "You still are pissed that I blew you off earlier."

"Oh, so you were blowing me off?"

Drew rolled his eyes and took a deep breath. "That's not what I meant."

"Tess! Hey," Aimee said, half whispering, half shouting. Her eyes were locked on the guy down the bar. "Don't look yet." Tess turned around. "No! I said not yet! What do you think of that guy down there?" Tess waited for Aimee to give her the go to turn around. "Well, go on! Look!" As Tess searched, Aimee said, "The one with the high cheekbones, wearing a dark-blue dress shirt."

"Ew. That's Shawn Levine from Freshman Stats. The guy who grabbed your hair and said he wanted to have sex with it."

"Shoot. Really? How come all the freaks get hot?"

"He didn't. It's the bad lighting."

"Damn, you guys are harsh," Drew chimed in. Aimee and Tess both looked at him blankly, as if to say, "Oh, you're still here?"

"He said he wanted to have sex with my hair," Aimee said in a scornful tone.

"What? You can't blame the guy. You do have great hair."
Drew twirled a piece around his finger. Tess glared at him. Aimee
looked over her shoulder and made eye contact with a girl who was
still giving her the death stare. The girl had moved closer.

"*Juste le fait qu'il est ici énervait,*" Tess said, a signal indicating
her want for privacy. She and Aimee developed it back in high
school, when Tess didn't want her mother or sister eavesdropping
on their phone calls.

"Tess, I'm not doing this right now," Aimee said. Tess was
three drinks in and far too out of shape to speak French.

"I know, but like, *j'ai besoin de parler avec toi,* like now!"

"Fine, *d'accord,* okay. What is it?"

"*En Français, si vous plaît.*" Aimee rolled her eyes and
attempted to respond in French. It didn't really work. But it wasn't
Aimee's fault. Tess was too drunk, too consumed with irritation
that Drew had showed up, and all too giddy about Nick. The coded
conversation that followed was mostly in English, with French
sprinkled in.

"Right, so I'm going to go see him on Thursday. What should I
wear?"

"You know he's standing right next to you." Aimee referred to
Drew.

"Oh *mon Dieu*, Aimee. I don't care right now. He said himself
there may have been someone else. What if it was me he was
talking about?" Tess asked, referring to Drew's earlier report that
there was someone other than his girlfriend in Nick's life last
semester.

Drew must have realized the conversation, though fast, and as a result, hard to follow, was not in his favor. "What was you?" he asked, trying to get into the conversation. Tess looked at him with a blank face and then returned to talking to Aimee. Drew's frustration became visible. He walked to an open spot at the bar to get another drink.

"Okay, enough, Tess. This is crazy. You're talking about getting with another guy right in front of your current boyfriend. Do you have any idea how messed up this is?"

"What? He's not here right now."

"Christ, Tess." Aimee finished her drink. "I'm out of booze, and at least one of us has to drive us home."

"Okay. I'm sorry, but haven't you ever liked someone so much that no matter how hard you tried to forget him you just couldn't?" Tess let that sink in. "Aimee, I've tried. I've tried so hard. Remember that day I went out with Drew for the first time? Well, just before that I was on my way to see Nick. Call it a moment of weakness. I hadn't talked to him in, like, forever. Anyway, just before I got to Herter, Drew stopped me and asked me out, and I said yes. And now look...we're boyfriend and girlfriend. So see, I am trying, like really trying, to get over Nick, but then today happened, and look at me. I don't know what it is, but I just can't get over him."

"But if you knew all of this, why have you let things go on so long with Drew?"

"I guess because I'm still waiting, hoping that I will wake up tomorrow or the next day and be like, 'Nick who?'"

"This certainly is some drama that you've gotten yourself into?"

"I didn't mean to, though! That's got to count for something."

"The road to hell is always paved with good intentions."

"So what do I do?" There was urgency in her eyes.

Despite all of her craziness, recklessness, and thoughtless ideas, she really was just doing what she thought was best. It was kind of cute and sad at the same time how honestly clueless she was. In so many ways, she was just a lost puppy dog.

"Okay, first I think you need to decide who you want to be with, Nick or Drew. And then go from there."

"But isn't it obvious who I want to be with?"

"Okay, yes, it is. So the only thing you can do is be honest and go talk to Nick. And I mean *honest*, Tess. None of your beating-around-the-bush kind of honest."

Tess knew Aimee was right. The last time Tess went to have an honest conversation with Nick, she wound up nearly kissing him seconds before he told her he had a girlfriend. *Honest. Yes. I can do honest*, she thought.

"But don't do anything until you talk to Drew. You can't leave Drew hanging. It's all or nothing. You can't have both."

"Where is Drew, by the way?"

Aimee searched the bar. "Maybe he went to the bathroom?"

"Good idea." Tess jumped off her stool. "Be right back."

"Hey, Dave." Aimee flagged down the bartender. "I'll take the bill."

"Together or separate?"

Aimee took a deep breath. "Together."

"Damn, Aimee, where were you when I was in college?" Dave wiped his hand before taking her credit card.

"Hmm. Let's see…how about not even born yet, Dave."

"Hey, come on! I'm only thirty-two."

"And I'm only twenty-two. But hey, I'm flattered. How about asking again in a few years—maybe when my vision starts to go so I don't have to look at all those gray hairs on your head?"

"Funny, Aimee. Real funny. You definitely know how to make a guy feel good!" Dave walked away to settle the check.

Weaving through the packed crowd, Tess spotted Drew just outside the bathrooms. She smiled and waved at him, but he didn't respond. He looked like he was talking to someone. He was sporting his cunning smile—the one she noticed just before things got steamy between them. Tess's blood began to boil. She pushed harder through the crowd. *What now?* For a moment, she lost him. When she found him again, she was right in front of him. The reason for his scurrilous smile was clear: a woman's leg wrapped around his waist, her arms twisted in his.

"Well, how about that? Isn't this some shit!" Tess said, cold and hard. The woman looked like an Amazon. Drew's face was buried in her chest. Tess looked them up and down several times while she waited for them to untangle themselves.

"Tess. Damn it. This isn't. Well, it is…"

"Save it, Drew. I'm not an idiot. You and this Amazon have

made it pretty clear."

"Oh, hell no, Andrew. Is this that little redhead you were telling me about?" the Amazon said in a thick Southern accent.

"You know about me?"

"Tess, this is Clio. My girlfriend from Atlanta. She flew in early." Drew looked like his proverbial tail was tightly between his legs.

"You're kidding me, right? Girlfriend? *I'm* your girlfriend, Drew! Holy shit! How long has this been going on?"

Drew began to answer, but Tess cut him off. "No. Shut up. I don't want to know. It all makes sense now. No wonder you only wanted to stay at my place. No wonder your eyes dart around every public place we enter. Does she go here too? Holy shit. Wow. Are you for real right now?"

"Tess, you need to calm down," Drew said. People were staring, but Tess didn't care.

"Don't tell *me* to calm down! You don't even have the nerve to tell me you have another girlfriend. Jesus, Drew, were you ever going to tell me? Didn't you think it might be something worth mentioning, say, I don't know, back in December? No, wait. Why the hell does she know about me?"

"Look here, you little firecracker," the Amazon said. "Drew and I go way back. We've had some bumps, like this *final* break, but they've been straightened out. So run along home and do your crying somewheres else."

Tess was shocked and stunned. It was as if she were living a page out of the *Beverly Hills 90210* script. This couldn't possibly be real. Just half an hour ago everything was fine. They had a tiff. She and Drew had lots of little fights. Sometimes she thought they picked them to have an excuse for make-up sex. She suddenly regretted not going to work after all.

Then a few tears streamed down her cheeks against her will.

She felt her heart breaking right there in front of him, and there was nothing anyone could do to stop it. She couldn't breathe or move, yet all she wanted to do was run.

"Aimee! Aimee!" Tess said, once able to push her way back to her seat at the bar. "Aimee, where are you?"

"Oh my God! Tess, are you okay?"

"Take me home. I've got to get out of here." Tess didn't even notice Shawn or the reunion she was disrupting. She focused all her energy on putting her hat and jacket on.

"Hey, I'm really sorry about this, but I've got to go," Aimee said to Shawn.

"Go. Go. Your friend clearly needs you," Shawn said as Tess pulled Aimee away.

"Great seeing you again. Call me," Aimee shouted back, putting her jacket on as they navigated through the crowd.

Once outside, Tess ran for Aimee's car and nearly ripped off the locked handle of the passenger side door.

"Tess, slow down!" Aimee called. She walked as fast as she could, digging for her keys. The second the car was unlocked they slid inside. "Okay, okay, okay. Take a deep breath." Aimee started the engine. With hunched shoulders, her hands between her legs, Tess silently begged the engine to heat up faster. "Tess, I can't hear you breathing. You need to breathe."

Tess followed orders and inhaled as much cold air as her lungs could stand.

"Good. Breathe in. Nice and deep." For several minutes, Aimee talked Tess through deep breathing until Tess seemed calmer. "Okay, so what on earth happened in there?"

"The world hates me and wants me dead."

"It may seem like that," Aimee said sympathetically. "But what actually happened?"

"Drew has a girlfriend."

"Yeah, you."

"No, *I'm* the other woman." Tess put her frozen hands against the vents. The engine was finally pushing out hot air. "Apparently, he and *Clio* have been together for, like, ever and were on a break when Drew and I met, or something like that. I don't know. When I went to find Drew, I found him and Clio sucking face by the bathrooms. She said she knew about me."

"Well, that was unexpected," Aimee said, more to herself than Tess. "Hey, what did she look like?"

"What? Why?"

"Come on, what did she look like?"

"I don't know. She was tall, like scary tall. Honestly, she looked like an Amazon."

"Did she have crazy big black hair? And eyes that looked like they were burning you?"

"Yeah…how did you know? Oh, Aimee, did you know about this and not tell me?"

"No! God, no! Earlier tonight, a woman who fits that description kept staring at me. It was totally creepy. Apparently, she was actually staring at you."

"I'm such an idiot. How did I not know? I should've known. How could he do this to me? He's *my* boyfriend."

Aimee was quiet for a long time. Her silence made Tess's anxiety increase.

"What? How are you so quiet?"

"Well, I mean the whole reason you went out tonight was because you just realized you still had feelings for someone else. So…"

"So what? I'm not allowed to be hurt by this? That's real nice, Aimee."

"No. I never said that."

"Yes, I have feelings for someone else, but you know what? I did everything I could to change that. I even started to think I could be in love with Drew. I mean, I could have just gone to Nick the moment I heard he was talking about me. I could have thrown myself at him, but no. I didn't. I was going to tell Drew everything, to show him that I do, *did*, respect him. In fact, I was going to tell him as soon as I found him." Tess paused. Her gaze was fixed on the bar's entrance. "I feel so humiliated."

"Damn, I can't believe Drew's out of the picture now. He was just so great."

When Aimee remarked that Drew was out of the picture, everything felt so…final, so official. How could the breakup already be so final? It was only ten minutes old. "I want to go home."

"On our way," Aimee said, putting the car in reverse.

The ride back to their apartment was long. They were frequently cut off or behind slow pokes or dodging animals that darted into the road. The normal ten-minute ride took nearly twenty. Aimee's nerves were pretty fried by the time she pulled into her designated parking spot. Meanwhile, Tess hadn't noticed a thing. She was too lost in herself. She was full of rage, ready to kill something, but so worn out she didn't have the energy. She was empty. Whether it was from all the vodka or all the heartbreak, she couldn't tell.

Moving from the car to the door, Tess tripped over a stubborn pile of snow. Instead of barking at it, as she normally would have done, she simply passed over it like a ghost, hollow and lifeless.

"Whoa, Tess, are you okay?"

Tess didn't respond.

Inside, Tess methodically took off her boots and placed them by door. She hung her jacket on the coat rack next to her boots and placed her purse on the dining room table. She brushed her teeth, rinsed her face, and then slipped into her bedroom. Aimee knocked on her door several times but got no answer.

Tess didn't want to talk. What was there to say? That she deserved this? That this was what she got for knowingly dating someone while having feelings for another?

Chapter 18

The next morning, Tess's radio alarm went off at 7:00 a.m., as usual, to the tunes on the local pop station. Hitting the snooze button, she buried her face in her pillows again. But she was awake, no matter how much she tried to force herself to fall back to sleep. The three-star hangover that was rolling in kept her awake.

Tess tried to sit up but fell back down. Staying perfectly still definitely felt best, except for the fact that her throat felt like the Sahara Desert. *Water. I need water.* The throbbing headache, unsteady stomach, and overwhelming thirst had her mildly paralyzed. After another eight minutes, the Spice Girls were chanting, and she rolled upright. The room began to spin, but only temporarily. As the room settled, her bladder sent a strong message that it was definitely time to go.

Aimee had just left the bathroom after showering. Tess sprinted in and ran straight back out, gagging from all the flowery-scented soaps and shampoos.

"Damn, Tess, are you okay?"

"Phew. Ah, yeah. Almost lost it for a second."

"You can say that again."

Tess's stomach wouldn't allow her into the bathroom right away, despite her bladder's pleas for relief. Unaware, she began to do the pee-pee dance.

"Geez, Tess, just go! Leave the door open. If you puke, just turn to the left and do it in the sink. I don't want you messing up the rug."

Before Aimee finished talking, Tess disappeared.

When she came back out, she fell onto the plush love seat that was only twenty feet away from the bathroom door. Her eyes were puffy, nearly swollen shut, and her lips dry and cracked. Her hair was matted in the back and stringy in the front.

"I want to die."

"Because of the hangover or Drew?" Aimee asked. She wore a sweater and jeans, a towel wrapped around her head.

"Hangover, for sure."

Aimee looked amazed. "What about Drew?"

Tess took a deep breath and slowly let it out. She found the bubble popping noise amusing. She tried to sit up straighter. The light from the windows blinded her, and her head screamed with pain. She slouched back to her original position.

"Drew…" she said, long and low. "Andrew…Drewy, Drewy, Drew…Well, that's over, I suppose."

"So that's it?"

"Yuppers."

"Seriously? Last night you were all brokenhearted. Practically on the verge. Now you're just 'whatever'?"

"Yup," Tess said, letting the "p" really pop at the end.

"Okay, you're still drunk."

Tess disagreed. She was definitely not still drunk. How could she be? There was nothing left in her stomach to make her drunk, but it didn't matter. She didn't have the energy to deny it.

"It's like that song about guys being all shady and dishonest."

"What?"

"Yeah. I never told you, but about a month ago we had this huge fight. I caught him in a lie about where he was. He said he was studying, but I found out he was at a bar. I was so pissed. Like, fire-burning-out-of-my-ears pissed."

"Why didn't you say anything?"

"Because I know how much you wanted me and Drew to be perfect. I didn't want to let you down."

"Seriously?" Aimee half laughed.

"Hey, I know how much you hate the fact that I still love Nick."

Aimee's eyebrow jumped. "Love?"

"Okay, well, not like *love*-love, but like really, really like. Like, *really* like."

"Yeah, I know," Aimee said in a dismissive tone that rubbed Tess the wrong way.

"And then he and his girlfriend broke up because she thought he was cheating."

"Who? Drew?"

"No. Nick. Come on, keep up! Anyway, when I found out, I was like, oh my God, he's been single for a lot longer than I originally thought."

Aimee sent her a look that said she still wasn't following.

"Halloween?"

"Oh, Jesus, Tess. Not this again! For the millionth time, if he wanted to ask you out he would have done it already!"

Tess scowled. Aimee was right, and she hated it when Aimee was right.

"Yeah, but what if?"

Aimee cut her off. "There are no buts. Tess, if Nick cared about you even half as much as you care about him you would be married by now. But you're not."

"We could be, though," Tess whimpered.

"Why am I even talking to you about this? It's like talking to a wall!"

"Hey, I'm not a wall!"

"Tess, I've known you long enough to know that you're going to do whatever you're going to do, no matter what I say. So go. Go. Find Nick and make him do whatever it is you want him to do. I'm certain it *won't* be worth it." Aimee rose from the couch and stormed off. "I have to go to class."

"Well, I wasn't even planning to go see Nick for at least a week! So there!" Tess retorted from the love seat. She winced at the volume of her own voice and coiled into a ball, pulling a throw blanket over her. "Today is definitely a mental health day."

The week she claimed she was going to wait to see Nick turned into two, then three, and then a whole month. Aimee's rebuke had really gotten to her. It made her sick to her stomach to think her best friend thought Tess didn't appreciate her advice. Nothing could have been farther from the truth. In more ways than she could count, Aimee was kind of like a second sister to her. Of course she respected Aimee's advice. That's why the original week turned into a month. Tess was proving to Aimee that she did care about her and the advice she gave. By not seeing Nick, she was acknowledging Aimee was right.

With the weather finally warming up, layers of clothing diminishing, Tess became really excited about graduating. A fresh start was just around the corner. *I'll go back to Boston and live in a cute little studio on Newbury Street that I'll begrudgingly share with roommates just to make rent. I'll get some job, start grad school maybe, get a boyfriend. Right, a boyfriend. I vowed to graduate with one.* Then Nick inevitably invaded her thoughts.

She wondered what he was doing. She wondered what his plans were. He was finishing his master's at the same she finished her bachelor's. *If only I had a genuine reason to go see him,* she thought. As her last week of finals began, she remembered that she had never picked up her final from his class last semester. She hoped he'd kept it. She immediately decided to go to his office. Then it hit her: Drew's office was in the same hall as Nick's.

There was no way she could see him again. They had not spoken to each other since that night in the bar with the Amazon. Seeing him again in his office, where they used to do things that only movie characters dreamed about, would just be too awkward. With going directly to Nick's office no longer an option, Tess resorted to e-mail.

To: Nick Donovan Sunday, May 8th, 2005

From: Tess Ryan

Subject: Final Exam

Hey Nick,

I know it's been a while, but I just realized that I never picked up my final exam from you last semester. Any chance we could meet up and I could get it from you?

Tess

She received the following message in response:

To: Tess Ryan Monday, May 9th, 2005

From: Nick Donovan

Subject: Re: Final Exam

Tess,

That would be fine. I'm available Wednesday afternoon around four. Can you meet at Rao's?

Best,

Nick

"Best? What the hell is that?" Tess shouted when she read the e-mail the first time. *Best* was what he used when he was being formal. *Perhaps a meet-up is a bad idea. Is he having trouble remembering who I am?* Tess was apprehensive, but part of her really did want her final exam back…and to see him one last time.

Chapter 19

Tess was pretty pleased with how she looked that Wednesday afternoon. She wore a white linen A-line skirt that fell to her knee with a cream-colored lace camisole that hugged her curves in all the right places. There was still a bit of a chill in the air, so she added a black three-quarter-sleeve cashmere cardigan. For a little flare she chose cherry-red flip-flops. She thought about wearing dressier shoes, but she didn't want to look like she was trying *that* hard.

She felt confident and worried at the same time. Knowing she looked good was one thing, but this was likely to be the last time she ever saw Nick. After all the flirting, kissing, and dreaming, this meeting at Rao's felt stressful. She couldn't help thinking that she couldn't say good-bye to him forever in just five minutes. *Please, God, let something happen!*

Rao's was bursting. The walls and tables were packed with Amherst's finest hippies and champions of fair trade coffee. Tess weaved between the other patrons, looking for Nick. Not seeing him, she pushed her way to the back room and found him sitting settled in at a four-seat table with a cup of tea and a newspaper.

"Tess, I'm glad you made it. I was starting to think you

weren't coming," he said, getting up to greet her. He attempted an awkward hug but at the last minute offered a handshake. Each laughed politely, and sat down quickly.

"Why wouldn't I show up? You know how anal retentive I am about my school work." *Oh, bad word choice.* She winced.

"Indeed, I do." He chuckled. Tess looked at him with eyes that urgently asked for her exam. He seemed to understand her silent plea and handed it over.

"There you go. See, all in one piece. Nothing to worry about."

Anticipating what he was going to say next made her fear that her thoughts were somehow oozing into his. *Oh my God, just say something already!*

"So, Tess, tell me what do you like in a guy?" he asked suddenly and very confidently.

Involuntarily, Tess's eyes opened wide. Nick had never been so straightforward before.

"Well, let's see. I like a guy who is smart, funny, kind, compassionate. Oh, and he must have one pink eye and one purple," she said.

"Different colors? Are you willing to negotiate?"

"Negotiate? Why should I have to negotiate what I like?" she said, playing along, not thinking about her actual reply.

"True, true. I'm just curious." He paused, staring at her for a moment. Then his demeanor changed from flirty to earnest. "I'm really sorry about what happened between you and Drew."

Tess's smile momentarily dropped. She was both surprised and impressed. "Thank you."

"If I'd known it was you when I first heard he was with someone besides his girlfriend, I would have given you a heads-up."

"Right, like the way you told me about yours?"

Stunned by the sting of her question, Nick leaned all the way back in his chair. He needed a moment to process. He wasn't a cheater. Hell, Liz hadn't even been a proper girlfriend. Tess didn't know that, so it didn't matter. Then he remembered how he tried to kiss her best friend. Suddenly, he wanted to explain everything, that when he went in for that kiss he had no idea Tess was the girl's best friend, that he was not himself that day, that it may have been the worst day of his whole life. Then it occurred to him that she may not even know about it and then he wondered if this was the last time he would ever see her.

Looking at her from across the table, she was more beautiful and alluring in this moment than he had ever seen her. Now that they were both on the verge of graduating, there wasn't anything to worry about. The longer he looked at her, the more at ease he felt. He then leaned forward again, elbows on the table. He decided it was best to say nothing.

"What?" Tess asked. "Why are you looking at me like that?"

He called her closer with his right index finger. Now face-to-face, Nick said in a low voice, "I've really missed this. It's great to be having a conversation with you again."

Feeling his breath on her face and hearing his pleasing words, chills ran down Tess's back. Those eyes and that smile of his were her kryptonite. They rendered her defenseless. For the next three hours, it was as if no time had passed between them. They laughed and flirted, discussing personal likes and dislikes, politics, history, environmental issues. It was like their sessions in his office, yet different. This felt more authentic. It was scary, yet intoxicating. Tess didn't want to part, but the sun was starting to set, and the sugary baked goods served would not constitute a proper dinner.

Together, they walked to the street corner. When they arrived at the corner, they learned that they had parked in opposite directions. She had to go up Main Street, and he needed to go down. Tess wanted a hug, but he gave her a handshake instead. *A handshake! A lousy handshake!* She almost called him on it, but she didn't want to ruin the moment. Tess wished him well, and he wished her the same.

Tess expected Aimee and Brie to be waiting in their apartment for her with bated breath. She had only been talking about her meet-up for the last five days. Instead, the place was empty. There was a note on the refrigerator; they were at the student union building studying for finals. Though bummed, she headed straight to campus as soon as she finished reading the note.

The bustling student union was packed with students also preparing for finals. Tess found Brie and Aimee; they'd staked out two tables. Brie listened intently as Tess gave every last detail of her afternoon with Nick. Aimee, on the other hand, could not have looked any more disinterested.

"So what do I do now? I don't want that to be the last time I see him," she concluded.

"Did either of you ask for the other's number? Did you say you would e-mail each other?" Brie asked.

"Is it bad that we didn't?"

Aimee rolled her eyes.

"What was that for, Aimee?" Tess asked. Her feelings were hurt. Her best friend really seemed to not care about what she was saying. Worse, ever since the make over, Aimee was always annoyed or uninterested in anything about Nick. Did she hate him? How could she when she's never even met him?

"That annoying Miffy girl from your discussion section is sitting next to us with a horde of lapdog-looking guys."

Tess turned around, and sure enough, there was Miffy. *Whatever*, she thought. She was graduating in a week and a half and would never see her again. Miffy was surely not someone Tess was going to miss.

"Does she even realize it's like ninety degrees outside? There is no need for two sweaters," Brie said. Aimee and Tess both looked at her and started laughing. Tess was glad that she wasn't the only one who thought Miffy's fashion sense was ridiculous.

Brie's comment made Tess feel less bitchy.

"Yes, I get it. No one likes my style. Whatever. I like it, and so do they," Miffy said, turning around. "And nothing is going to change that."

Tess thought she was going to turn back to her mangy wolf pack. Instead Miffy continued. "But God, Tess, you don't get it, do you? That guy is giving you all the signs that he's into you. Friggin' grow a pair already and just ask him out."

Tess swallowed hard. No one but Eve was ever so direct with her. "Bitch," Tess muttered in response.

Miffy gave a clipped scoff and looked Tess up and down. "For someone so smart, you really are dumb," she remarked before turning around.

Chapter 20

Tess took Miffy's advice and asked Nick out for a drink through e-mail. Two days later, on May 14, Nick and Tess met at the Toasted Owl in Northampton promptly at 9:00 p.m. Tess had considered the Harp but thought better of it. She didn't want the memories of her breakup with Drew to dampen her new opportunity. The Toasted Owl was big and clean, with lots of windows overlooking the streets of downtown Northampton— the complete opposite of the Harp. Also, none of the Harp regulars would be there to judge.

Tess hadn't said "date," but she hoped he figured out that was what she meant. When they met outside the restaurant, she noticed he hadn't brought flowers, but he wore a brown dress coat over his usual jeans and had tucked in his button-down collared shirt, which she took as a good sign. He opened the doors, chose their spot at the bar, pulled out her chair, and waited for her to sit first.

After they were settled, apple martinis and draft beer waxed the conversation, which only waned for bathroom breaks and refills. And when 2:00 a.m. rolled around, the bartender firmly placed the bill in front of them, pointing out it was time to leave.

Tess rushed to get her wallet. "I've got this," she said, sheepishly. At the same time, she felt obligated to pay out of habit with her dad, yet guilty for expecting Nick to pay even though she was the one who did the asking.

After a moment, Nick laid his right arm across her, holding onto her right hip and wallet. His touch made her weak.

"Hey man, thanks," said the bartender as Nick signed the credit card slip. Nick gave the bartender a quick smile.

"All set?" Nick asked, turning to Tess.

"Of course." She hopped off her stool and followed him to the door. Her nerves over what to do next were quickly taking over. She couldn't bear to part from him. The night was going so well. Even more amazing, he wouldn't let her pay. He was such a gentleman. Then her body began to tingle.

"Tess, you're good to drive?" he asked, holding the small of her back as he guided her down the steps onto the street. She wasn't sure why he was guiding her. She was walking perfectly fine. Nevertheless, his touch was welcome, so there was no need to complain.

"Oh, yeah. Of course." She paused figuring out how to best navigate through the awkward "how to say good-bye" stage of the date. "I'm really glad you came out tonight. It was—"

"I'm going to follow you home so I know you make it safely."

A gigantic smile crossed her face that she didn't bother trying to conceal. "Yes, sir." It took amazing self-control not to throw herself at him.

Alone in the car, Tess squealed like a prepubescent teen who had just won Backstreet Boys concert tickets. She only stopped squealing to breathe. Once mildly calmer, she talked to herself the whole time. Nick Donovan was following her home. If it meant what she thought it meant, then she was going to see him the next morning.

Her excitement expanded when she pulled in and saw an empty guest parking spot. Parking quickly, she hopped out and directed Nick to the open space. It had to be a sign from the universe telling her to go for it.

"Well, here I am, safe and sound," Tess said at the front door.

"Excellent. Mind if I use your bathroom?"

"Sure, come on in."

When he emerged from the bathroom, Nick's intentions were loud and clear; he carried his shoes and coat. He waited silently. Leaning against the exposed back of the loveseat, Tess froze with uncertainty about what to do next. Nick, on the other hand, seemed to know exactly what to do. He dropped his coat and shoes, walked over to her, circled her waist with his hands, and pulled her up against him. She gasped. His hands were warm on her hips.

They stared intensely into each other's eyes. Nick seized her hand and led her into Aimee's bedroom. Tess slipped his other hand into hers and led him to the right place.

He chuckled when he noticed her stuffed toys. Tess kicked herself for not thinking to hide them. He plopped down on her bed, grabbed a stuffed bunny, and started making it talk in a high-pitched voice. Tess grabbed it from him, gathered the others, and hid them in her closet.

"Hey! Those are my friends!" He pretended to be disappointed to see them go, but Tess didn't care. There was no way she was going to let her toys witness whatever was about to go down. With the animals safely behind closed doors, she sat down on the bed next to him. Their smiles dropped from their faces. Nick took her right hand in his left. She looked down at their touching hands. She looked up at him, beyond nervous. They smiled tentatively before he finally pulled her in for a kiss. Butterflies filled her stomach, making her weak all over. All her fantasies put together never would have added up to how amazing this kiss felt.

Gently, he cupped the side of her face in his hand and delicately kissed her lips, then her cheeks, and then down her neck. She began to sweat. Nick must have felt her temperature rise as he began unbuttoning the slinky red cardigan that Brie had insisted she wear. Following suit, Tess began unbuttoning Nick's shirt. Both shirts dropped to the bed at the same time.

"Wait, do you have protection?" he asked. She looked at him, dumbfounded. *Aren't you supposed to be in charge of that?* "Didn't think I'd need to bring anything."

Tess wasn't worried; her birth control pack rested on her bedside table. She smiled and pointed to the half-empty pack of pills. His eyes lit up. Within seconds, they were both completely naked.

"God, you are so beautiful," Nick said, his eyes meandering over her naked, quivering body. "And so damn sexy."

His slow and steady breathing ramped up. Tess shivered and tried like hell not to show it. His fingers gently caressed her body, weakening her ability to stop the goose bumps from rising. His eyes glowed with curiosity and tenderness. At the sight of his naked body her eyes were equally filled with delight.

It amazed Tess that in a mere flash they had found a rhythm that took most couples months to find. It had been a long year of waiting, wanting, yearning. Every touch, every kiss, was tender yet hungry. After all that time spent thinking, dreaming, fantasizing, her desires were at last being fulfilled. He found the spot, just below her ear, that made her cry out in ecstasy, which he then refused to leave alone. She noticed the way he trembled every time she kissed his hip flexor and wouldn't leave it be. In the wee hours of the morning, when their bodies could no longer fight off sleep, she had seen both the moon and stars more times than she could count.

Chapter 21

The next morning, Aimee left for her waitressing job at the Route 9 Diner at eight, leaving the apartment to Nick and Tess. Around nine, Tess began to stir. Her head still rested on Nick's chest, and she peeked to see if his eyes were open. They were not, but his mouth was, which made her giggle. His eyes opened wide with alarm.

"Morning," she said. She sat up, revealing her nakedness. Nick smiled, pulling her near him. He started to speak and released a cloud of nasty morning breath.

"Shhhh." Tess fought off her giggles. "Let me get you a toothbrush." She began to roll off the bed, but Nick quickly grabbed her. He planted a big wet kiss right on her mouth. Pulling free with a grin, Tess debated whether or not to cover up as she walked to the bathroom. When she looked at Nick, he seemed to be drifting back to sleep, and she decided to go in her birthday suit.

When she got back, Nick was sitting up, his back against the wall, the flat sheet barely covering him. He looked like a model for Abercrombie and Fitch.

"You're back," he said smoothly. She felt like a deer in the highlights, standing in front of him stone-cold sober and stark naked. At least he was also naked and apparently still very much in the game.

"I got you a toothbrush," she said, waving it around. Nick rose to his knees letting the sheet fall. An involuntary yelp escaped Tess's lips.

"Thanks," he said, reaching for her and pulling her body onto his. "Your body is so smooth and soft. I could touch it all day long."

She confidently kissed him square on the lips. He fell back onto the bed and carried her with him. Lying on top of him, she felt his heartbeat race. They kissed despite their mutual morning breath. Oh, how forgiving raging hormones can be! Tess rolled free, and Nick scooped her back so her head rested on his chest.

"So what are you doing today?" he asked.

"To be honest, I don't really have any plans."

"Great. I'm hungry. What do you say to making breakfast?" Simple and benign as the question was, it was exactly the kind of thing she'd dreamed of Nick saying. She actually pinched herself to be sure what was happening was not just a dream.

"Did you really just pinch yourself?"

"Oh! Ah, I thought there was a bug."

"Sure...so where's that toothbrush and where's the bathroom?"

Tess dressed while Nick brushed his teeth. She put on a ratty pair of jeans, the only clean ones left, a navy blue V-neck T-shirt, and a striped gray cardigan.

"Aww, damn it," Nick said, reentering the room.

"What?"

"You're dressed already."

"And?"

"Don't get me wrong, you look great, but personally I think you look a whole lot better without clothes."

"Duly noted. Now get dressed."

"Giving orders…oooh, that's hot, but let me show you how to get dressed with someone else in the room." He stepped into his boxers. Then gathered all of his things and then put them on within seconds. Next, he grabbed Tess and began to kiss her all over while quickly undressing her. She stalled at first. She still wasn't completely recovered from earlier, but when she felt his hot breath near her nether region, she caved and allowed him to finish.

Later, catching his breath, Nick said, "And that's how you get dressed with someone else in the room," with Tess in the crook of his arm.

"Let me get this right. You get dressed, get undressed, have sex, and then get dressed again?"

"Bingo."

"Nick, I never thought you could be so odd."

"You mean to tell me you didn't like that?"

Tess felt her cheeks burn bright red. There was no denying that she'd enjoyed the midmorning romp. As they relaxed in each other's arms, an awkwardness entered the room. Tess no longer felt comfortable under his arm and released herself. The magnitude of what had just happened was suddenly sinking in. It appeared as though Nick felt the same way. Tess watched Nick's face change.

"So...what are your plans for after graduation?" she asked, hoping he was going to say to marry her.

"Going to Ireland next week."

"That's so cool. Who are you going with?" As soon as the words came out, she regretted asking.

"Myself."

"Wow. That's brave."

"After that, I'm not sure. I figure I'll go back to Connecticut for a little while and look for a teaching job. You?"

"Awesome! You're going into teaching after all. So am I."

"No kidding? Have a job lined up yet?" He smiled and seemed a little less withdrawn. Tess, on the other hand, was overwhelmed with sadness. Her dream to be with Nick was coming true, and yet it was slipping away faster than she could catch it.

"I'm going back to New Mexico for the time being," she said carefully. "My hapless father has once again gotten himself nearly evicted from his apartment in Boston, so my bedroom is now the residence of some roommate." Just as she feared, she felt him pull farther away. "If it makes you feel any better, I really don't want to go."

Hapless father about to be evicted? This was new information.

Nick wanted to know more about it. The image of Tess's modern but stable family had just been jostled. Back in his office she had mentioned her divorced parents and that her father was in Boston, but not much else. Learning that he had been threatened with eviction multiple times was depressing and at the same time compelling. But Nick realized that of course she would share something so personal and intriguing in a situation like this. That's what Tess did. She set off little information bombs, only to step back and watch how the person reacted. He remembered her doing it all the time in his office. But he couldn't give in to his curiosity. The fact remained that she was leaving. He couldn't let himself get in any deeper with this girl than he already had.

Nick's silence was deafening.

"I made my plans thinking I would never see you again. I had no idea any of this would happen."

Rolling out of bed, Nick said, "I have to get back to grading."

Tess watched him get dressed in silence. It was slower and more painful than the first time she watched him get dressed. Her body began to ache as his body became more thoroughly covered.

"Yeah, me too. I have an essay to finish. Anne Hutchinson, here I come." She hoped to delay him a little longer. It didn't work. Once he was fully clothed, he put on his shoes and went to the door.

Standing at her front door, wrapped in what she felt would be her last hug from him, Tess felt tears well in her eyes. She blinked them away as hard as she could and continued to hope for a kiss, a sign that he wanted to see her again, but she only got a hug.

"Hey, I'll, ah, call...Be in touch with you."

Her heart sank with dread.

If ever there was a time for Tess to speak up for what she wanted, this was the moment. But all she managed to say was, "Fly safely."

Nick gave her a forlorn smile and slipped out the door.

Chapter 22

Around four thirty that afternoon, Aimee returned from work with Brie. Aimee was not nearly as anxious as Brie to hear the full report of what had happened. The whole ride over, Brie beamed with what if scenarios for Tess and Nick. It made Aimee want to hurl. At the apartment, with all of Brie's chatter and the questions flying out of their mouths, it was like a circus blowing into the apartment. Tess was on the couch eating chips and watching TV—not exactly what they thought she would be doing.

"Details! Details! We want all the details from last night!" Brie said, taking the chips away from Tess. "Leave some for next time, you know."

"No, no, you want all the details. Not me," Aimee said.

"Ouch, Aimee," Brie said.

"What? I know what happens. I don't need a play by play, okay?"

"Wow, Aimee. You're such a bitch sometimes."

"Thanks, Brie," Tess said. "Now, if you two would stop fighting, I could tell you what happened." Tess's excitement was forced and disingenuous, at least to Aimee. "Right! Okay, last night has got to be the best night of my life! Nick is the best lover on the planet. I swear!"

Biting her lower lip, Brie said, "Oh my God!"

"Well, we went to the Toasted Owl in Northampton. It was so romantic. The big windows. The anonymity. We talked and laughed so much we were the last ones out. I can't believe we closed down the bar. Then he insisted on following me home. It's not like I'm going to tell him not to. So when we got here, he asked to use the bathroom. I was like, 'Ah, yeah, okay.' He wasn't in there more than like a minute."

"Tess, that's the oldest trick in the book," Aimee said, gagging. She began to contemplate whether this was the moment to break her vow and tell Tess what happened.

"Yeah? And?"

Aimee said nothing.

"Okay, so then he comes out of the bathroom holding his shoes and jacket. And I'm thinking, holy crap, he totally wants me. Anyway, he then swept me, literally, off my feet." Tess paused, dazed and miles away, most likely picturing last night. "I saw stars last night, Brie. Stars and the moon! It was magical. I've never felt so good in all my life. Oh, and then he said I was so sexy and beautiful! Can you believe it? It was like all my dreams have finally come true! See, Aimee, I found my man."

"Okay, but you're going back to Santa Fe in like a week," Aimee said.

"What are you guys talking about?" Brie asked.

"Just this stupid bet Tess has been trying to win since the beginning of freshman year. She believes that she can make any guy she wants love her." Aimee shuttered in disgust thinking about that night at the Moan and Dove with Nick.

Brie nodded while looking at Tess.

"Maybe not true for you, Aimee, but I just know that Nick is my Dylan. I've finally found him!"

"Great. So when's the next time you're going to see each other?" Brie asked.

Tess suddenly went quiet, too quiet. "He's going to call once he's finished grading his undergrad exams," she finally said.

"Well, good. That sounds great," Brie said awkwardly.

No one looked like they were buying what Tess was selling...not even Tess. "I know, right? I can't wait for you guys to meet him!" Tess said.

Aimee knew Tess was playing a game, that they hadn't exchanged numbers. She also knew it would be a miracle if Nick called. Knowing the tremendous pain that was about to rumble in, Aimee realized now was not the time to tell her love sick friend what Nick really was like. So, reluctantly she hoped like hell he would call, for Tess's sake.

Chapter 23

A week later Tess graduated with her bachelor's but no man, at least not officially. Though she hadn't heard from Nick, she still believed he would get in touch as soon as he returned from Ireland. She reasoned that flying across an ocean was a pretty big deal. Nick's mind had to be preoccupied, especially as he was going alone on his first flight. He would call. And he said he would. What would stop him?

In the meantime, Tess busied herself with settling back into New Mexican life. Not that there was that much to actually settle. Not one thing had changed since she'd left six months ago. In fact, nothing had really changed since she and her family had arrived almost seven years ago. Well, her stepdad was still new, sort of.

Despite marrying her mother the summer between Tess's freshman and sophomore years of college, Clint remained unfamiliar to her. His affinity for rules, including curfews, as well as dinner around the table every night and playing rare music from around the world on speakers wired throughout the house, were just a few of the newer traditions Tess bucked. She missed eating when and where she pleased, as well as silence.

It was their strangeness to each other that ultimately led to the majority of their fights. Tess struggled to fit into the shifted family dynamics. She wasn't sure what role she played. For the most part she stayed in her room or at the ice rink, away from any potential run-ins. While she understood that life had moved on without her, living it was a very different experience.

It didn't take long for loneliness to set in. She and Aimee were on the phone at least three or four times a day, but that didn't make up for the lack of face-to-face contact. Her weekends consisted of counting down the minutes until Monday, when she could at least be entertained by her work as a bank teller at Bank of America. She was extremely overqualified for the job, but in a town like Santa Fe, there was little else Tess could do with her history degree. At least she was able to get the job within the first two weeks of being home.

By her third weekend in New Mexico, Tess felt like she was going to explode if she didn't have at least one night of fun. She really wanted to go out with Eve, but her sister was only eighteen, which made getting into the good bars tricky, or so Tess thought.

"Yeah, I've had this fake ID for about a year now," Eve said one Saturday afternoon in mid June. She and Tess were sitting in the backyard sipping iced tea and working on their tans. "It's a pretty good one, don't you think?"

"Impressive. How on earth did you even get this, *Juana Martinez*?"

"Shut up. It's not my fault *Juana* looks like an Irish Catholic girl. Maybe she was adopted and they changed her name."

"All that matters is that it works."

"I got into the Cowgirl a few weeks ago."

"No way. Really?"

Eve nodded her head like it was no big deal.

"Damn." Tess was in awe. "So I guess we're all set then. We should totally go there tonight."

Eve smiled and laid back in her lawn chair. "Sounds good to me. I'll call some friends. We'll make it girls' night," she said before she closed her eyes, soaking in the sun. Eve's confident and nonchalant manner made her seem way beyond eighteen.

Tess wished she could be as cool as Eve. When she was eighteen, Tess never would have been able to pass off a fake ID as a real one. Her face would give her away. Her knees would buckle and her brow would bead with sweat as she waited for the doorman's final verdict. Oh, who was she kidding? Even at a month shy of twenty-two, Tess still got nervous every time she handed over her ID, despite being legitimately legal. She was petrified of being denied entrance. But getting into the Cowgirl shouldn't be a problem. For all she knew, some of her old classmates worked there. If they recognized her, she would be served without a hitch.

By nine, Eve had assembled a gaggle of four girls as cool and mature as Eve, none of whom had a problem with ID, fake or otherwise. They were sophisticated and all about to enter college, sharing bleeding-heart goals for their futures.

"Tess, tell me how you went about picking history as your major," a girl named Milena asked. Her hair was dark and frizzy. To Tess, she looked like the kind of girl who purposely hid behind her looks and her thick, black-framed glasses.

"It was no big deal really." Her mind was flooded with memories of her early days with Nick. Even though she was already a declared history major when they met, his influence increased her love of history.

"Not a big deal?" Crissy, a wiry blonde who had yet to grow into her body, asked. "Picking the right major is crucial to solid job prospects."

"And not to mention all the networking connections the right major can lead you to," Milena said.

"Oh my God, what if I realize that a double major in ancient Asian languages and mechanical engineering is actually counterproductive to my goal of providing indigenous peoples with innovation know-how so that they can one day join the developing world?" Crissy said all of a sudden.

"Crissy, you're fine. You haven't even started college yet," Eve said. "Who knows? Maybe you'll get there and find out you want to be a circus performer."

"My God, Eve, you're such a daydreamer," Andrea said.

Clearly, Andrea is the bullish pragmatist, Tess thought.

Appearing undeterred by Andrea's remark Eve responded, "Really? Do daydreamers get awarded every scholarship they apply for? Do daydreamers enter early admission for radiology and sports medicine and sign an agreement with the University of New Mexico Hospital to work for them five years after completing medical school?"

Everyone's mouth at the table dropped, especially Tess's. Eve had just graduated from high school, and her accomplishments were shocking. Tess began to feel inadequate. "I didn't know you wanted to become a doctor," Tess said.

"Ever since I tore my ACL playing tennis freshman year I've been interested in how the body works."

"Sounds like you have everything figured out," Tess said with a gulp. Looking around the table and remembering Milena's question about picking majors, she wished her story was even half as inspiring as her sister's.

"Hey, Tess, you never answered the question. Why did you pick history?" Crissy asked. Her eyes were wide, and she looked like she genuinely wanted to know. Now Tess felt even worse. *Tell the truth or make up something better?*

"I fell in love."

"You what?" Milena asked.

"I...I fell in love with history."

"Phew! I thought you were about to say you fell in love with some guy," Andrea said. "Guys are the last thing you want holding you back."

"I know! God, I never want some guy telling me what to do or how to be," Milena said, brushing her hair back and shimmying her shoulders.

"I think girls who live their lives for guys are just sad," Crissy said.

"Right! It's like all they care about is how they look, what clothes they're wearing. All so whatever guy they like will like them back," Andrea said.

"Those girls are the worst," Milena said.

Tess felt her stomach drop as she listened to the younger girls pretty much destroy the appeal of being in love.

"Come on, you guys. Don't be bitter just because you don't fit into what society says you should," Eve said, smiling at Tess.

"I'm not bitter," Andrea said. "I just honestly think girls who live to serve men are sad and pathetic."

"You know, Andrea, wanting to look good for someone and making them feel good isn't as shallow as you're making it out to be," Tess said carefully. "I mean, you like it when people are nice to you and clean themselves up when you're around, don't you?"

Andrea gave her a look. "Wait a minute. Are you one of those girls who lives for a guy?"

Tess froze. Not everything she did during her last year of college was aimed at getting together with Nick. In fact, the whole Drew mess was aimed at not being with Nick. So no, Tess was not one of *those* girls.

"Ha! You are!" Milena said, cackling. "Oh my God, Eve, your sister is totally one of those dippy love junkie girls. Wow, you're so lucky you don't take after her!"

Eve and Tess shared a look. "In the civilized world we call people like my sister romantics and people like you mean," Eve said.

All of Eve's friends looked at her and rounded their shoulders. It looked like Eve's tongue-lashing had been received loud and clear.

"You know what, Eve? I think I'm going to call a cab and head home," Tess said.

Crissy and Andrea chuckled. Santa Fe wasn't a taxi kind of town. Remembering that, Tess asked, "Do one of you mind giving Eve a ride home later?"

"Actually, I'm feeling kind of tired too," Eve said, yawning and stretching her arms.

"No, you're not," Tess said.

Eve was already standing when she said, "I'm ready. You ready?"

Tess looked at the other girls, who didn't seem that shocked by the abrupt end to the evening. She looked at Eve and said, "Okay then. It was nice meeting all of you. I wish you all success when you start college in the fall."

Crissy, Andrea, and Milena replied with tight-lipped thank yous and quickly turned away from Tess and Eve.

In the driver's seat of their car, Tess was loaded with questions. "Did you really sign a five-year contract with UNM Hospital?"

"No way! What hospital would hire a kid right out of high school? Especially one who barely passed biology!"

"Then why did you say all that?"

"I don't know. I guess because a part of me wouldn't mind going into medicine and because those square try-hards wanted to hear it."

"Square try-hards? I thought those girls are your friends."

"Please. Those girls are just from some of my honors lit classes," Eve said. "God, Tess, I am so sorry they were so rude to you. I only invited them because I thought you would like them. They're so academic. You're so academic, always reading history and stuff. You just finished college, and I know how much you like to get into fierce battles of wit." Eve paused and looked at Tess, who was focused on the road.

"It's okay. I appreciate how you stuck up for me back there, but they are kind of right. I kind of am one of those girls."

"What? No, you're not. You're a romantic. There's nothing wrong with that."

Tess smiled. She liked hearing Eve defend her. She also wondered how her younger sister was so wise.

"So what's his name?" Eve asked, breaking the silence.

"Excuse me?"

"The guy you fell in love with, dummy!"

"Hey, I fell in love with history, not a guy." Tess fought back a smile.

"What's his name?" Eve asked again. This time her tone was more pressing, despite her smile.

"Nick."

"Wait. The same Nick, the TA you made out with at Halloween?"

Tess nodded.

"Did something else happen between you two?"

Tess nodded again wearing an even bigger smile. She was so happy to hear someone sound genuinely interested in her relationship with Nick.

"I always wondered about that," Eve said. She looked right at Tess. "Oh my God, something did happen? Tell me! Tell me what happened!"

Taking a deep breath, Tess began to tell Eve every detail about her experiences with Nick until the last time they saw each other. Eve laughed and smiled at some parts, but by the end she seemed rather serious.

"I can't believe you didn't exchange phone numbers again!" Eve said. "I just don't get you sometimes. One minute you're howling at the top of your lungs because someone took your favorite sweater without asking—" Eve cleared her throat, and Tess understood she meant herself. "The next, you're waiting at opportunity's door with your hands in your pockets, staring at the floor."

Tess didn't reply. Instead, her reaction was physical. She clenched her jaw and squeezed the steering wheel as hard as she could. It was all she could do to not howl at the top of her lungs, as Eve had described.

"Come on, Tess. It's fine. None of us are perfect. I think you just have to have more faith in yourself. That's all I was trying to say."

"Right. And how do I do that, Miss Know-it-all?"

"I don't know." Eve paused. "Do what I do. Fake it till you make it."

Tess sent Eve a confused look.

"Fake confidence until it's real. Like how I made all that stuff up about becoming a doctor. Maybe if I keep telling people I'm going to be a doctor it'll really happen."

Eve made sense. She made a lot of sense, actually. One of the reasons Tess was so drawn to Nick was his confidence. If she liked his confidence so much, she could only imagine what he would feel if she were equally as confident.

"And how did you get so wise? You're barely out of high school."

"That's easy. Between your mistakes and Mom's, I've learned loads."

Tess half laughed. "So glad we could be of service."

"So what are you going to do about Nick?"

Tess was startled by the question. She hadn't gotten to the planning stage yet. "The only thing I can do is e-mail him, I guess."

"At least you have that. It's not as personal as a phone call, but it'll be a heck of a lot easier to be confident in an e-mail. Just make sure that when you e-mail him you're honest. Tell him how you feel and what you want."

"Right," Tess said as she pulled into the driveway and put the car in park. The girls jumped out and headed to their separate rooms. It was past midnight, and exhaustion was setting in. Tess fell asleep as she wrangled with the possibilities for what she was going to say tomorrow in her e-mail to Nick.

To: Nick Donovan   Sunday, June 19th, 2005

From: Tess Ryan

Subject: Hello!

Hey Nick,

It's Tess. I am totally bursting with anticipation to hear about your trip! But of course, I know you're super busy readjusting to life in the States. I can't wait to hear all about it!

Speak to you soon,

Tess

To: Nick Donovan   Monday, July 4th, 2005

From: Tess Ryan

Subject: Happy 4th of July!

Nick,

So totally jealous that you get to have a New England cookout! Have a hot dog for me! Santa Fe really goes all out for the 4th. I've been told the fireworks here are bigger and better than Disney fireworks. We'll see about that!

Speak to you soon,

Tess

P.S. I'm not sure if you got my other e-mail. It's entirely possible it got lost by this crazy New Mexican Internet service. Anyway, I just wanted to say I had a really good time that night. I hope you did too. Okay, well, I'm still looking forward to your stories about Ireland. My

birthday is coming up on the 12th. ☺

To: Tess Ryan   Wednesday, July 13th, 2005

From: Nick Donovan

Subject: Re: Happy 4th of July!

Tess,

It's nice to hear from you. Sorry for the delay. I got your e-mails the other day. I've just been so busy I couldn't respond until now. Ireland was a blast. I saw so many things that I've never seen before. I think I'm going to move there. The fourth was good. I did have lots of hot dogs. I hope your fireworks were as big as they claimed. Hope all is well.

Best,

Nick

Best? Not that again! The salutation nearly put Tess into orbit with rage. After everything they'd shared, she was certain that they would never return to such formalities. Had he forgotten already?

To: Nick Donovan   Sunday, July 17th, 2005

From: Tess Ryan

Subject: Ireland is Amazing!

Hey Nick,

I am so happy to hear that you loved Ireland. I can't wait to see it for myself one day. Maybe you can give me some tips on where all the hot spots are? My birthday was good. Twenty-two is such a let down compared to twenty-one, but I'm sure you knew that already. Thank you for having a hot dog for me. I bet it was yummy! Other than Ireland and hot dogs, how are things in your neck of the woods?

Hope all is well,

Tess

To: Tess Ryan   Wednesday, August 24th, 2005

From: Nick Donovan

Subject: Re: Ireland is Amazing!

Tess,

It's good to hear from you. So sorry I missed your birthday. I do remember that shift from twenty-one to twenty-two. Twenty-two definitely was not as big. I've been super busy with roofing work. Great money but long hours. It will pay off in the winter when there isn't as much work. Perhaps I will do some subbing at my old high school. How are things in Arizona?

Best,

Nick

Arizona? How could anyone mix up the two states? Tess was beginning to get the hint but refused to accept it.

To: Nick Donovan   Thursday, August 25th, 2005

From: Tess Ryan

Subject: Re: Re: Ireland is Amazing!

Roofing is definitely not what I thought a master's in history led to, but, hey, I'm a bank teller. I guess we have that in common, right? New Mexico is okay. It's definitely not Arizona. I bet Arizona is nice this time of year, though. Any plans to travel while you're not roofing this winter?

Hope you're well,

Tess

To: Nick Donovan   Tuesday, November 22nd, 2005

From: Tess Ryan

Subject: Happy (Early) Thanksgiving!

Haven't heard from you in a while. Hope you haven't fallen off any roofs.

Hoping you're okay,

Tess

To: Nick Donovan   Saturday, December 24th, 2005

From: Tess Ryan

Subject: Holiday Greetings!

Nick!

Merry Christmas! Wishing you and your family a very merry holiday.

Hope to hear from you soon,

Tess

Christmas arrived and passed without a word from Nick. *Perhaps he really did fall off a roof?* Tess searched Connecticut and Massachusetts newspaper obituaries just to be sure. Luckily no Donovans were listed, Nick or otherwise. Fatal accidents ruled out, why was he not replying? Did she say something to offend him?

"Mom, why don't guys respond to email right away?" Tess asked Grace as she meandered into her mother's small but cozy home office on the evening of December 27th. The walls were covered by a mixture of her advanced degrees and seascapes of Cape Cod. The furniture consisted of a pair of classic wood-framed southwestern chairs with loud, multicolored triangles and squares. Tess plopped down onto the chair closest to the door.

"Why does anyone take so long to respond to an e-mail?" Grace said, still focused on her paperwork.

"I don't know. A lot of reasons, I guess." Tess paused. "Why hasn't Nick e-mailed me back? Is it like Aimee said the other day—with guys it's like out of sight, out of mind?"

"Oh, honey, are you still trying to get in touch with that guy?" Grace finally turned to face Tess.

"He has a name, you know." Tess stopped herself before she got too sassy. "I just don't get what I did wrong."

"You didn't do anything wrong. He's just a jerk."

"Whoa. Nick is just busy. He has to be."

"Tess, when a guy wants to be with a girl, he makes it known. He calls her. He tells his friends about her. He doesn't make her wait for a reply to an e-mail."

"What Nick and I have is different, though."

"Honey, you've really got to move on. He, for whatever reason, doesn't see things the way you do."

Tess dropped her head on the flat wooden arm of the chair and left it there despite the pain in her forehead. In some ways it felt better than listening to her mother. "Fine. So what if I do move on? Who am I going to meet here? I'm in Santa Fe, New Mexico. It's not Boston," she said without lifting her head.

"Tess, you're so dramatic. You need to open up. You never know whom you're going to meet. I met Cliff here. He isn't such a bad stepdad, right? He's taken good care of you girls. He paid for Eve's braces and part of your college. He forced us to have dinner around the table like a normal family."

"I know. Cliff's been a great addition to our family." *Minus all the fighting I get into with him*, Tess considered saying but didn't.

"See? So you never know. You just need to let life in."

Tess rolled her eyes.

"All right, fine. Don't listen to what I say. What do I know, anyway? I'm just your *mothah*," Grace said, purposely using a thick Boston accent. It gave Tess a warm feeling to hear it again. She blamed Grace's extended stay in New Mexico for it fading away. "If your heart is that set on going back east, make a plan and go. Have you heard anything about your grad school applications yet, by the way?"

"It's only December. I won't hear anything until spring at the earliest."

"Okay. Well, keep your head up. There is someone out there with your name on him. I can promise you that."

Grace gave Tess a kiss on her head and reminded her to put her empty mug in the dishwasher as she walked out of the room. Tess threw her head against the back of the chair and shrugged. *Why doesn't anyone understand?*

A week later, aimlessly clicking around the Internet, Tess checked her e-mail again hoping there would be some sign of life from Nick. But nothing, not even a return-to-sender e-mail notice. Something compelled her to write him another one, one that said everything she was really feeling but was too afraid to admit to anyone else.

To: Nick Donovan   Thursday, January 5th, 2006

From: Tess Ryan

Subject: Fuck You

Nick,

You asshole! I've e-mailed you 100 times. What the hell?...I'm pregnant...Okay, I'm not, but did that make you want to pick up the phone and actually call me? God, why do I still like you so much? I miss you...Please say you miss me too...

Tess never sent that e-mail. She read it several times. It was too raw, too vulnerable. Not the kind of thing a person said to another via e-mail. Relieved that her feelings were somewhat in the open, she let things just be.

From January to March Tess didn't send a word to or hear a word from Nick. She decided to let him make the next move and busied herself with going to the gym and stalking the mailbox for acceptance letters. On March 23rd, Northeastern, Brandeis, and Boston College sent her letters saying they all wanted her. Her ticket home had finally arrived.

Brandeis gave her the smallest financial package, which made elimination easy. Northeastern and Boston College offered her the full TA package. Both schools had beautiful campuses and everything a student could need. Northeastern was in the middle of the city. If she wanted to be downtown, she would just hop on the T and be there in five minutes. The downside to Northeastern was that student housing was in the middle of crime-ridden Mission Hill.

Boston College, on the other hand, was nestled in a leafy green corner of Brighton near her old house on Foster Street. Translation: Boston College was familiar and much nicer. As a young single female, she figured her personal safety was an important factor in choosing a place to live. Also, a degree from BC held more prestige than one from Northeastern. Remembering the trouble Nick had finding a job, she knew she needed every leg up she could get. And with that reasoning, she said yes to Boston College.

E-mailing Nick her plans was tempting, but nearly nine months had gone by without a single word from him. She toyed around with the idea of sending him a fake birth announcement to see if that would finally get a response from him. But she knew joking about pregnancy was not funny and kept her mouth shut. Of course nothing stopped her from drafting several versions of an e-mail telling him all about her grad school plans, which likewise were never sent.

Until moving day, Tess dithered over whether or not to actually e-mail Nick. She left her computer set up until the very last minute, still plugged in and waiting on the floor of her empty room. Tess was working on one of her mock e-mails when her mother called her away to the U-Haul truck.

Meanwhile, Eve was milling about the house, being a sport about helping Tess pack. She really didn't have to, but she wanted the place to herself again, and the sooner the better. She went into Tess's room checking for odds and ends and noticed her computer was still on. Humoring her curiosity, she went on the computer to find out what her sister was up to.

Outside at the U-Haul, Grace and Tess rearranged some items in the truck for a better fit. It was jam-packed, which Tess didn't think could be possible. It took about fifteen minutes to get everything fitted in just right. When her mother's phone rang she took the call, and Tess went into the house to get the computer.

When she checked her computer, she couldn't find the e-mail draft. She searched the minimized windows, but it wasn't there. She felt a pit of worry settle in her stomach. She checked the sent box. There it was. The e-mail had been sent. Tess stopped breathing. Only one person was capable of doing such a thing.

Tess clicked on the sent e-mail to see which version had gone out.

To: Nick Donovan   Saturday, July 1st, 2006

From: Tess Ryan

Subject: Surprise! Guess who? ;-)

Dear Nick,

It's been a while. How you doing? I've got some news for you. I'm moving back to Boston! I'm getting my master's at BC. I'm driving out tomorrow. I should be in town by the 6th. Let's get together. Here's my number 617-523-9842.

See ya,

Tess

Not only did Tess have absolutely no intention of sending him any e-mail, but the one Eve, and only Eve, could have sent sounded nothing like herself. Nick would know right away that she didn't write it. Then he would think she was pulling some stupid joke, that she was unbearably immature. She wanted to die.

"Eve! I'm going to kill you!" Tess shouted, on the warpath for Eve's blood.

Eve sat relaxed on the couch eating grapes and watching TV. She didn't even flinch when Tess barreled into the room.

"Eve, how could you? How could you send that e-mail to Nick?"

"You were the one writing it. I just made it sound better. Chill. I did you a favor."

"Goddamn it, Eve! As a matter of fact, I wasn't going to send him anything!"

"Then why was it open on your computer?"

"Ooooh. My. God! That doesn't matter. It's my computer. You shouldn't be on it!" Tess shouted loud enough for people on

Mars to hear.

"Whoa, chill. If anything, I helped your lovesick ass out. Who knows? Maybe he'll actually call." Eve snickered.

Tess had to remind herself that whenever they got into a fight, everything Eve said was coated in a crusty layer of bitchiness, even when she was trying to help. But in that moment, no reminder could curb Tess's rage.

"You know what, Eve? Thanks for ruining my life once again with your super-cool 'I have a boyfriend and Tess doesn't' attitude! God, I wish you were never born!" Tess screamed just as their mother walked in.

"What in the hell is going on in here?"

Tess stopped dead in her tracks. Eve remained on an even keel with the TV and grapes.

"Oh, nothing. Tess is just freaking out about me sending an e-mail to her little lover boy," Eve replied inattentively. Their mother looked at Tess long and hard. Tess knew that look. It was the *you've done it again* look. Tess hated that she was always considered the guilty one. Eve never looked guilty even though Tess could see it written all over her calm, cool, and collected face.

"Tess, could you just keep the fighting to a dull roar for one day? Do you really need to have a huge fight with your sister before you move away for good? As if this isn't hard enough. I'm breaking my back to help you fill that truck, and you're in the house fighting over a bloody e-mail," Grace said in a scornful mother's tone. "It's just an e-mail. Now pack up that damn computer and let's get out of here and find something to eat."

Tess wanted to fight back, but her mother was right. She was moving away for good. The next time she would see her mother or her sister would be for a short visit around some holiday. So she silenced her tongue between her clenched teeth—whatever it took to keep quiet. She had a long drive ahead of her and needed all her energy. She couldn't afford to waste it on her little, insensitive sister. Soon enough she would be away from her crazy family.

Hopefully she'd somehow run into Nick and be able to explain the whole e-mail thing.

The next morning Tess woke up on the couch at six ready to leave despite the aches from a bad night's sleep. The sooner she could leave the better. Shortly after Tess put the coffee on and the aroma began to fill the house, Grace, Eve, and even Cliff appeared to see her off.

Grace squeezed her daughter in front of the loaded U-Haul wearing her bathrobe and puffy blue slippers. "I'm going to miss you so much!"

"I'm going to miss you too, Mom."

"Do me one favor. Don't get involved with that Nick. He's no good for you. Remember to just keep shuffling the deck faster."

"What do you mean, 'shuffle the deck faster'?"

"You're such a beautiful, smart, and independent young woman. You don't need a guy like Nick holding you back. So when you meet someone who isn't treating you right, toss him out like you're shuffling a deck of cards."

"Got it."

"I love you, baby. Be safe, okay?" Tears streamed down Grace's face. Tess hugged her for a long time. Good-byes with Eve and Cliff followed, and after a few tears of her own, Tess climbed into the truck and went on her way.

Part Two

Chapter 24

Five days after leaving Santa Fe, Tess pulled in front of 2009 Commonwealth Avenue in Brighton, Massachusetts, on a hot and humid day, feeling like she had stumbled upon an oasis after being lost in a desert, literally and figuratively. She couldn't put the U-Haul in park fast enough before she jumped out and touched the concrete steps, but Boston being Boston, there was no parking. Tess did the mandatory circle-the-block ritual before she, like all proper Bostonians, said screw it, put the flashers on, and parked in the street.

Within the hour, the four hulking bros from Southie she'd hired had arrived. They emptied the U-Haul and set up the only furniture she brought: two bedroom sets. Grace refused to let the extra set she'd been storing since getting a new one herself and made Tess take it with her. Once it was all ready to go, Tess had to admit she was impressed by the movers' efficiency. They saved her immeasurable pain and suffering. They even offered to take the U-Haul back for her for an extra fifty bucks—an offer she didn't refuse, even if it was against the rules.

After the movers were gone, Tess wandered from room to room, exploring the apartment Aimee had picked out for them. In the living room, she ran her fingers along the exposed brick of the fireplace that was now, sadly, just for decoration. In the kitchen, she opened and closed each of the cabinets, checking dimensions and taking mental notes for where she was going to put everything. She remained in the bathroom the longest, so long that she took a seat.

The white and yellow daisy wallpaper above the half walls of 1950s pink tile and the bright yellow toilet were perplexing, charming, and hideous at the same time. Her ten-year-old-self loved it, but her twenty-two-year-old self blushed at the idea of what guests would think of it, especially guys. How on earth she was going to decorate it to say it did not belong to a Barbie-loving, stuffed-toy-hugging ten-year-old was beyond her. Even with Aimee's design know-how, it was going to be a challenge.

Feeling fatigue set in, it was around two in the afternoon, Tess left the bathroom to unpack her bed linens and make the bed before she quickly fell into it. She may not have done any heavy lifting that day, but the exhaustion from driving for five days straight had finally caught up to her. She didn't wake up until Aimee arrived after work at six thirty.

In the days that followed, Tess and Aimee seemed to live at IKEA. Aimee was a great shopper. She went in, got what she wanted, and hightailed it out of there. She was Tess's kind of shopper. Unfortunately, Aimee didn't always remember everything they needed, so what was supposed to be one trip turned into many.

"Okay, I think this is everything," Tess said, surveying the piles of boxes in the living room, which was looking a lot like a mini IKEA warehouse.

"You know, I'm looking at these piles, and I don't think we need to assemble anything. We'll just sit on the boxes. I'll call it 'warehouse chic,'" Aimee said in what seemed like an attempt to delay putting the couch, loveseat, coffee tables, end tables, dining room set, and bookshelves together.

"Come on! You're the one who said we should do it this way."

"I did?"

"Indeed. You were adamant about not having your parents buy everything." *Even though they could do so without batting an eye*, Tess thought, sighing at what lay ahead of them. "And hey, you said you wanted to show them we were adults now."

"Damn it." Aimee paused. "Fine. Give me a wrench."

"That's the spirit!"

Tess had to give Aimee credit; she knew that Aimee was not the kind of person who liked to, or ever had to, get her hands dirty. Even in kindergarten, she'd hated finger painting. When the teacher eventually forced her, Aimee's parents came flying in, demanding the teacher give her another assignment. But now Aimee put her objections aside and really tried to help construct the furniture. She opened boxes, set up piles of matching parts, and even laid out instructions.

While it all looked logical, Aimee was opening at a much faster rate than Tess was assembling. Hardware started to go missing, and couch parts were mixing with bookshelf parts. Tess began to panic when she realized what was happening.

"Stop! Aimee! Please!" Tess shouted over the blasting music Aimee had put on before they started working.

"What? Whoa! What's the matter?" Aimee replied, turning down the music.

"Don't open another box."

"Why not? I'm getting everything ready for you."

"I can see that, but everything is getting mixed up. I don't know what goes with what. So I need you to just stop."

"That's what the instructions are for. They'll tell you what you need."

Tess gave her an admonishing look. "Here, *you* read them if they're so easy to figure out." She handed the pages over to Aimee.

Aimee flipped the instructions around several times trying to figure out which was up or down, as there were no words. Her face contorted with confusion.

"See what I mean?"

"So what am I supposed to do?"

"Pick up a screwdriver and help me put this end table together."

"Which one is the screwdriver again?"

"Seriously, Aimee? You don't know what a screwdriver is?"

"Orange juice and vodka?"

"Wow," Tess said to herself, but loudly enough for Aimee to hear. "Yes, hey, how about you go get us some vodka and orange juice? While you're gone, I'll straighten this all out. By then I'm sure I'll really need a *screwdriver*."

With a grateful, conceding look, Aimee grabbed her bag and went out for booze.

"And maybe some sandwiches too," Tess called out. Alone, Tess managed to figure out what pieces went with what and got back on track. It didn't take long to realize that assembly went faster without Aimee. From then on, Tess was the sole builder, even if that meant it took several days to get it all done.

On day three of Operation Tess Builds the Furniture, Tess finished assembling the sofa. She placed that accomplishment among her top five, as it was one of the most heinous puzzles she had ever done. "Why the hell does IKEA not print words on the instructions?" she angrily mumbled to herself more than a few times.

Just as she was about to plop down and savor her victory, the phone rang.

"Hello?" Tess answered without reading the caller ID.

"Tess Ryan?" a masculine voice replied.

"This is she."

There was a long silence. "Tess, it's Nick."

Nick? Nick Donovan? Her brain froze.

"Tess? You there?"

"Yeah! Hey, Nick, how's it going?" She stumbled over her words a little.

"Good, good. How are you?"

She looked around the living room at all the packing materials and empty boxes and replied, "Steeped in IKEA furniture parts."

Nick laughed. "That must mean you're back."

"Indeed I am," she said, remembering how warm his voice made her feel.

"I'm really glad you e-mailed me," Nick said, breaking the brief silence.

At first a frown crossed her face as she remembered Eve's invasion of her privacy, but a smile won out. Ultimately, Eve's trespass had led to exactly what Tess wanted.

"So...what have you been up to? Sounds like you've been back for a while now."

"Oh, not too much. You know..." she said, staring at the unopened loveseat box with disgust. "I've been putting IKEA furniture together for three days."

"Wow, that must be a lot of IKEA furniture. Unless you're just really bad at it." She liked hearing him tease her. It felt like old times. "Are you settling in all right? Do you need any help?"

"Oh, ah, I'm good. I'm slowly but surely getting things set up. Doing it on my own for now."

"That's a shame. What kind of boyfriend sends his girlfriend to set up shop before he gets there?" Good old Nick, going straight for the jugular, or in this case Tess's heart.

"No, I don't have a boyfriend. My roommate doesn't move in until next month. At her current place, she's got a crazy roommate-landlord situation, and she can't leave until the lease is up. It's all very weird."

"I see. How about I come over tomorrow? Give you some help with all that IKEA stuff."

Tess smothered a squeal. "If you want. I mean, I guess that'd be okay," she said more cautiously. She didn't want to appear too excited.

"Great. Text me your address, and I'll come by around eleven or noon, whichever is better for you."

"Whenever's cool," she said nonchalantly. "I'll be here drowning in nuts and bolts." She regretted saying "nuts" and "drowning," but at least she included "bolts." She heard Nick chuckle.

"Great. I'll be there tomorrow to help you sort out all those *nuts*," he said, deadpan. Tess didn't know whether or not to laugh. And just like that, it was game on.

Tess didn't sleep a wink that night. She tossed and turned thinking about what it was going to be like to see him again. *Is he going to be happy to see me? Is he going to bring flowers? Am I going to get an apology? Is this the beginning of something huge? Will he still think I'm as 'damn beautiful and sexy' as he did a year ago?* The last question lingered the longest. She was terrified to see how Nick would see her after a whole year. What if she looked totally different? Was he expecting the exact same svelte twenty-one-year-old? She worried he would notice her five-pound weight gain, be disgusted, and turn around and leave forever.

Tess had set the alarm for eight, but after so little sleep, she hit the snooze button so often she didn't actually wake up until 10:50. *Crap!* Panic set in. Nick said he would be at her apartment at eleven. There was no way she could be dressed to impress in ten measly minutes. She began praying that he'd be stuck in traffic.

She threw on what she could find, a pair of jeans from the floor and a wrinkly green Care Bears T-shirt from high school that read "Feeling Lucky," with Good Luck Bear jumping for joy. Neither item was all that clean thanks to living out of boxes. She ran to the bathroom to at least put on deodorant and brush her teeth. Just as she was about to throw her hair up in a ponytail, the doorbell rang. It was only 10:55. *Damn it!* She finished her hair as she walked down the hallway. When she got to the door, she took a deep breath, her cheeks feeling flushed, and buzzed him in.

I have nothing to fear, she told herself. They had already seen each other naked. It was going to be fine. *It has to be, right?* When she opened the door, what she saw took her breath away.

Left hand in pocket, there stood Nick, in a suit and tie, a jacket draped over his left wrist. Tess took a moment to take him all in. She had never seen him look so fine, so dressed up, so mature. Looking at him, Tess felt even worse about how she looked. To his right, she saw something that looked like an overnight bag. Her left eyebrow rose involuntarily, and her lips curled into a smile.

"Hey, Tess," he said, accompanied by her favorite sweet smile of his. She smiled wider, stepped back, and let him in. "Wow, look at this place," he continued, looking all around. "You've really done well for yourself." He paused and looked right at her. "You sure there's no boyfriend coming to join you?" His tone shameless.

"Are you suggesting that a girl can't get a place like this on her own?"

He laughed as he got the message.

"So where should I put this?" He waved his duffle bag. Tess knew she looked mildly panicked when he assured her, "It's just a change of clothes."

"No, I knew that. No one puts furniture together wearing a suit and tie. You can put your things in here." She said, led him into Aimee's future room, the guest room until then. She didn't want him to think that she was inviting him to stay with her so quickly. He still had some major groveling to do.

Briefly, Nick cocked his head and looked confused. "I'll be out in a minute," he said, closing the door. Tess nervously wandered around the apartment as she waited. She would have sat down, but the couch was buried under open boxes containing the next pieces to put together.

"Okay. I'm totally confused. Is there or isn't there someone else living here?" he asked, coming up behind her a few minutes later.

"There is, just not yet. Like I said, she's moving in next month."

"Oh. Then why is her room set up like a guest room?"

"Because until then it *is* my guest room."

Nick gave her another puzzled look. *Eat your heart out,* she said with her eyes. *That's right. If you were to stay, you would stay in the guest room.*

They stood in the hallway staring at each other, finally equals. Not only was he dressed accordingly in jeans and an old local brewery T-shirt, but she was just a girl, he was just a guy. No student, no TA. She noticed that he'd neglected to put his shoes on and couldn't take his eyes off the message across her chest.

"Right, so where's that furniture you need help with?"

Tess allowed him a good ten minutes of tinkering before she offered to help. He knew what he was doing, and she liked watching him do it. As he built furniture, she fantasized. She imagined that he was building the furniture for their place. She dreamed that they were sharing the apartment, that he was the boyfriend from way off yonder who had now come to assume his rightful place.

"Do you have any water?"

"Coming right up," she said and dashed into the kitchen. Beads of sweat outlined his forehead as she handed him the bottle.

"Any chance there's an a/c somewhere in this mess?"

Tess looked around the room, wishing one would magically appear. None did. "Are you going to help, or was it your plan all along to just watch?"

"You look like you know what you're doing, so no need to get in your way."

Nick rolled his eyes and went back to work. She watched him for a little while longer and then, feeling guilty, hunkered down.

They worked steadily in near silence for a good hour. Every now and then one would ask the other for a tool or a bolt. Then they grabbed the same Allen wrench.

"Sorry," they both said, each rushing to apologize.

After a pause Nick said, "Okay this is too awkward if I don't say anything. So, I'm just going to do it," He paused, taking a deep breath. "Tess, I messed up. I know that."

Silence.

"Tess, you were my student. Then things got all weird...at Halloween." He swallowed audibly. "And then...then you and I...I..."

More silence.

"You never gave me your number."

"You never asked." Her tone was icy.

"Tess, I'm sorry. I freaked out. You said you were going back to New Mexico. What was I supposed to do?"

You were supposed to call every day. You were supposed to beg me to come back every day. You were supposed to be head over heels for me, she thought, wishing she had the confidence to say it all out loud.

"Tell me what you're thinking," he pleaded. His eyes darted across her face as if he was reading it. "I'm really sorry. I never meant to hurt you," he continued. Tess enjoyed his groveling. "Can I ever make it up to you?"

Good question. She smiled a little.

"Does that mean I can?"

She smiled wider but continued to watch his every move. His look of uncertainty quickly morphed into a look of excitement.

"Good," he said and then kissed her. His mouth was heavy, wet, and screamed for action. Despite dying for this moment for over a year, Tess could not respond in kind. She felt cold and mechanical, struggling like hell to hide it. His desire to lay her down and put something else together was all too apparent. Sensing Nick was about to make his move, Tess was all too happy to catch her elbow on the wrong side of a large screw and involuntarily jerk away from him.

"Son of a bit—" Tess grabbed her elbow.

"Whoa! Tess, are you okay?"

"Yeah. Sorry. I'm all right."

"Let me see that." He took her elbow and inspected it. "That's some serious damage you got."

Tess whipped her arm away. "What? No it's not," she said while checking it herself. The screw had only grazed her elbow. Just white skin, no blood.

Nick's eyes darkened ever so slightly. "Here, let me make it feel better." He leaned in to kiss her injury.

Before his lips could reach her, she jumped up and announced, "I have to pee," and she left for the bathroom.

Safe and alone in the bathroom, Tess took several of the deepest breaths of her life. "What is wrong with you?" she whispered disdainfully to the image in the mirror. "This is what you've always wanted. Get it together, Tess." Then she flushed the unused toilet. She quickly splashed some water on her face before heading back to the living room.

"Now, where were we?" Tess asked in a low voice, crawling toward his lap.

Pushing her away, he said prudishly, "I think you're right. Let's just focus on furniture."

"Great," Tess said, reeling backward, embarrassed.

"Hey…"

"Yeah?"

"Ah, can you pass me that bolt?"

She gave him a knowing look before passing him what he needed and left it at that. In time, normal conversation resumed intermittently while they both worked on the loveseat. He told her that before he arrived, he'd been on the Cape at a job interview for a history position at one of the big high schools down there. She was happy to hear that he felt it went well. She didn't like that Cape Cod was an hour and a half drive away, but a drive beat the hell out of a flight. He asked her about her time in New Mexico; she told him only the colorful parts. He didn't need to hear that she had zero friends outside of the bank or that she'd joined knitting circles for fun.

Four hours later they were finished, furniture and awkwardness alike.

"Not too shabby!" she exclaimed.

"Wanna set it all up once and for all?" he asked. Tess looked at his pit stains and wiped sweat from her brow. She was tired. He was tired. She just wanted to get out of her humid, sticky apartment.

"Nah, let's take a break."

"Good enough. What do you want to do now? You hungry?"

"I'm too hot to eat."

"Yeah, you are."

Tess rolled her eyes. "Let's go downtown and see what there is to see."

"Mind if I shower first?" he asked. "You can join me."

She glared at him and said, "The bathroom's down the hall on the right. Towels are in the cupboard." Nick gave her a sad face and walked into the bathroom alone.

Chapter 25

By five, Nick and Tess were out the door. They hopped on the T, got off at Copley Square, and meandered over to Newbury Street. They weaved in and out of the high-end shops before they stopped at Stephanie's on Newbury. Nick made it a date as he covered the check. *So far,* she thought, *he's sticking to his word.*

Over dessert, they decided to head to Fenway. It was July, and the chances of a Red Sox game going on were pretty high. Scalpers were usually numerous, so neither Tess nor Nick were concerned about getting seats. With the humidity dropping, they decided to walk from the restaurant. Tess led the way along Commonwealth Ave. It was a prettier and more romantic option than more cosmopolitan Newbury Street.

Her nerves fluttering like butterflies, Tess bumped into Nick every now and then, hoping he'd grab her hand. After many bumps, nothing.

"Can I ask you something?"

"Sure."

"What…?" Tess stopped, held her breath, and bit her tongue. "What do…? Ah, what's your favorite color?" She couldn't do it. *What if he can't tell me how he feels about me now?*

Nick burst out laughing. "What was so hard about that?"

"I don't know. It's kind of a lame question, and, ah, for whatever reason I've been dying to know. I felt kind of stupid asking, you know."

"Green."

"You don't say! Mine's yellow! We're right next to each other on the rainbow."

"You come up with the weirdest questions."

When they got to Fenway, they discovered the Sox were playing an away game. But as every bar in town featured the game on their big screens, they decided to head to the Bleacher Bar, the one with a garage door that opened right up to the ballpark field.

As the drinks flowed, so did Tess's confidence. Jokes were funnier, conversation was easier, and neither of them could keep their hands off the other.

"Here's to Tess," a rather tipsy Nick said. "Your birthday's in three days, and I want to be the first to wish you a very merry birthday. May twenty-three be more exciting than twenty-two." Nick took a swig of beer and kissed her on the lips. "Happy birthday, beautiful."

Fireworks burst within that kiss. Tess held onto that feeling, vowing to always remember it. She hadn't breathed a word about her birthday since the year before. His comment could only be further proof of his honest desire to set things right. It also proved that it was late, they had both had too much to drink, making it time to go home.

The stairs to the apartment posed a puzzling sobriety test. They both failed. Fumbling for her keys, Tess finally got the door open. Nick used her back as a resting post. When she moved forward, she laughed when he almost face planted.

"Not cool, Miss Ryan, not cool," he said with a tipsy smile. "So what now?" He was clearly in no shape to drive, and she wouldn't rest if she sent him away.

"I've got a bottle of Pinot Grigio that's been waiting to be opened, if you want?" Tess said, walking up the stairs.

"Perfect! I love myself a little white wine before bed."

Before bed? Tess froze in front of her bedroom. Meanwhile, Nick continued to the kitchen. Suddenly there was a loud crash in the kitchen. She ran in like a first responder.

A glass bowl of cherries had shattered into a million pieces all over the floor. She saw no blood, but Nick looked like a scared seven-year-old. She was relieved he wasn't injured, and Tess didn't mind about the bowl. She hated cherries, and they were Aimee's anyway. Nick apologized profusely. She swept it up and assured him that it was no big deal. "Lucky you didn't break the bottle of wine," she remarked. To be safe, Tess found the opener and did the honors.

She poured two glasses beyond the polite-serving size and led Nick into the living room. They both stopped. It was not the same living room they had left earlier. Aimee must have stopped by; the furniture had been arranged and the trash removed.

They both plopped down on the couch and let out sighs of relief. Then, looking straight ahead, Nick took a big gulp of his wine, placed the less-full glass on the coffee table, and pressed his lips on Tess's.

Suddenly Asia's song "Heat of the Moment" blared in Tess's head, entreating her to just let go. Her heart palpated, and she began to sweat. Within moments their shirts, along with their shoes, were left behind on the living room floor. Crossing the threshold between the living room and hallway, Nick picked her up. Naturally, Tess wrapped her legs around his waist and didn't miss a single kiss.

Nick navigated the obstacle course of boxes through her bedroom, some open, some closed, then glided her body down onto her pillow-covered bed. His hands were agile explorers, roving over every nook and cranny of her body. His fingers slipped under her bra, caressing every inch underneath it. He unhooked it and shimmied the lacy unmentionable off, two very high points revealing her excitement.

"Mmm-hmm, sure am feeling lucky now," Nick said while kissing her bare breasts. Shots of elation soared though her body. Things were well on their way when Tess suddenly stopped. Nick grunted in displeasure.

"Is this the right thing to do?"

"Mmm-hmm," he murmured, kissing her neck and shoulders.

"But how do you know? What if it's wrong and, and we don't—"

"Shhhh. Everything's fine," he said between breaths and

kisses. Fully believing him, Tess gave Nick the lead and followed his command. He was as light and gentle as last time, yet more aggressive with more conviction.

"Hmm, you're a little softer than I remember."

"Excuse me?" she asked in disbelief. *What nerve,* she thought. It was true; despite all her hours in the gym, she had gained a few. She blamed it on all the rich New Mexican cooking, but he hadn't seemed to mind when he'd carried her all the way down the hall.

"A little softer here and here," he said, poking and grabbing at her naked body.

God, please *kill me!* She scrambled for the sheets but Nick stopped her. He started kissing all the parts he'd just grabbed.

"Shhh, no, no, I really like it."

He was making her blood boil in every possible way. She could have killed him, but she liked it too much. He made her feel alive in ways no one else did. It was good; it was bad. It was hot; it was cold. It was a total rush. *If he doesn't put his mouth where I'm throbbing right now, he will be very sorry very soon,* Tess thought and proceeded to fulfill what she perceived to be his desires as well as her own. *So much for the guest room.*

When the clock struck nine the next morning, Nick emerged from the sea of pillows that he had buried himself under. His hair was matted and greasy, but still sexy. Tess chuckled; his disheveled state was because of her. She felt like a dog that had marked its territory. Nick, eyes closed, reached for her arm. Once he found it, he nestled under it, resting his head on her chest.

"Morning," he said, oozing sleepiness.

"Morning." Then out of nowhere, as she watched him snooze, wave of calm swept over her, telling her things were different this time. Rather than question where it came from, she wondered if all the pain from the past had been just a trial. The universe was just testing her true desire to be with this guy. Yet she couldn't help but wonder: *Have I passed the test?*

Chapter 26

All morning, Tess looked for signs. At breakfast, she asked if he thought eggs Benedict would be better than the $9.99 eggs and bacon special. Without a second thought, he told her to go with the eggs Benedict, a pricier $11.99. Then when the bill came, again he wouldn't let her touch it. This was something she wouldn't mind getting used to. By afternoon, when the sun was high and it was time to get back to putting her apartment together, Nick had kissed her four times in public and held her hand while they strolled from her apartment to the restaurant and back again. Surely, the test was over. Nick was doing all the things that she had fantasized.

Around three, Nick mentioned that despite not wanting to go, he had to.

"I don't even know where you're living now. Are you still in Connecticut?" Tess asked as Nick put his duffle bag on the passenger seat of his black Honda Civic.

"Allston."

"Allston?"

"Yeah, some of my buddies and I are subletting a place for the summer, over on Price Road."

"Really? That's like ten minutes from here." She couldn't believe her luck in moving into an apartment so close to his.

"You don't say. I've been applying for jobs all over the place, so it's been a good central location."

Tess began to smile uncontrollably. Her summer had just switched from a ten to a twenty.

"Wait, did you know that we were that close all along?"

"Yeah." He smirked.

"And you were going to tell me this when?" She smacked his chest playfully. In response, he pulled her in and planted a taunting kiss on her that he ended all too soon.

"You're a smart girl. I knew you'd figure it out," he said, settling into his car. He leaned against the seat. "Hey, I'm really glad I came over. It was great seeing you again."

Unsure if it was because of his words or his tone, Tess was suddenly struck by an awful sinking feeling.

"I have your number now," he continued. "So I'll call you later," he said with a smile and a kiss on her cheek as she leaned through the driver's side window. She faked a smile, said, "See ya," and refused to let her worries show. She didn't know why or how, but she couldn't kick the feeling that she might never hear from him again.

Back inside, she did her best to unpack and not think about him, but she couldn't stop watching the clock and checking her phone for missed calls.

"It's cool," Tess told herself over and over. "It's only been three hours and forty-eight minutes. I'm just being paranoid.

He'll call...right?"

Seven o'clock rolled by. Nothing on her phone but several texts from Aimee inquiring about her progress with the apartment. Tess informed her of all the milestones but said nothing about Nick or his assistance with the assembly. Fearing the worst, she figured telling Aimee would complicate more than help. Seven thirty came and went in silence. Seven forty-five. Eight o'clock arrived, by which time she was good and ready to finish that bottle of Pinot Grigio and forget that Nick ever existed.

At seven past eight her phone rang.

"Tess, hey, it's Nick. How's it going?" He was out of breath. Tears filled her eyes, whether from relief or anger she wasn't sure.

"Nick, hi. I knew it was you. Caller ID."

"Oh, right. What are you up to?"

She thought about saying, "About to drink your memory death," but instead remarked, "Not a whole lot. Still unpacking."

"Any chance you can take a break and come out for a drink? I'm at Great Scott on Comm. Ave in Allston." He was only a fifteen-minute T ride away, not a huge deal, but it was starting to get dark. By day, Allston was a trendy neighborhood full of used clothing stores, greasy spoon cafes, and dying record stores for college kids, but by night it became the epicenter of wannabe dive bars that prided themselves on hosting most of the Boston College douchebags who couldn't score at any of the nicer bars in the area. Ten bucks for a cab would get her there in half the time, and she wouldn't have to worry about creeps on the T.

Ultimately, she decided to go. He'd called and asked, which

was what she wanted. Donning a fresh coat of makeup and a slinky green halter dress, off she went.

Packed with Allston's finest punk rockers, college preps, and twenty-something artist types made it difficult to find Nick. Tess made several passes around the bar before she found him. He was center stage, a guitar slung over his back. It looked as though he and the band were packing up to leave.

"You didn't tell me you were playing," she said, impressed, surprised, and a little turned on.

"We were opening for some other band. It was nothing big." Even so, she thought it was cool. She remembered wanting to see him perform back at UMass after she learned he played the bass guitar. "Hey, order a drink. I've got to swing by my place with the guys to drop off our stuff. I'll be back in like twenty, thirty minutes tops." Nick kissed her cheek and was out of sight before she could respond.

"What the hell?" Tess said to the faceless crowd. Pissed but unwilling to waste the cab fare, she sidled up to the bar and ordered an Irish Trash Can. The peach schnapps encouraged her to think about how sweet Nick had been, and the Red Bull told her it was all happening fast, like a light switch that had been flipped from off to on. She didn't have any complaints, of course. Nick being attentive and sweet, calling her just to hang out, was exactly what she wanted. *But why did he suddenly leave as soon as I arrived? Am I pushing him too far too fast?* In barely twenty-four hours, they had progressed from not speaking for over a year to what looked like a tried and true couple. But she wasn't pushing at all. He was the one who said he would call later. He was the one who'd invited her out. Yet the question of his hasty departure lingered.

When Tess sensed that twenty minutes had gone by, she pulled out her phone to check the time. It was half past nine. He had been gone for nearly an hour and there she was, sitting at a grimy Allston bar alone, listening to a crappy band, waiting for a guy. *How much more pathetic can I get?* Her head advised her to run away, but her heart told her to hold on just a little longer. Going with her heart she ordered another Irish Trash Can.

"Any girl who can order a Trash Can is my kind of woman," a tall blond male who looked barely twenty-one said into Tess's left ear. She gave the guy one look, noticed his baby face and crooked teeth, and turned her back on him. "Come on, girl, I'm trying to give you a compliment."

"Excuse me?" She whipped around to face him.

"Damn, look at that hole in your dress. What else can you show me?" the scumbag asked, eyeing her neckline.

"Get away, loser," Tess said, looking him dead in the eye.

"Whoa! I'm not a loser!"

Tess hesitated before turning around. This was not the first time a newbie to the bar scene had hit on her. She knew full well the best method was to just ignore him, but annoyed and a bit drunk, she decided to let off some steam.

"Oh yeah? Your mom teach you to talk to women like that?"

The guy said nothing. "Yeah? Didn't think so. Now shoo!" Tess waved him off.

The kid was clearly too drunk to understand what she'd said, but at the very least he realized she was insulting him.

"Whoa, you like need a Midol or something. Go get laid for once," the kid said before moseying over to his next target.

"Asshole!" Tess shouted after him.

Seconds later he returned. "What did you just call me?" His face was uncomfortably close to hers. She could smell his bad breath as well as see all the blood vessels in his eyes.

"Hey, man. How you doing? We all good here?" Nick said calmly and plainly, as he suddenly inserted himself between the kid and Tess. The kid moved right into Nick's face. From the crazy look in his eyes, Tess could tell the kid would have definitely punched Nick had Nick not met his stare and held it for an uncomfortable amount of time. Finally, the kid backed off, not saying a word. Nick watched him until he was a sufficient distance away and then asked Tess, "What was that about?"

She squealed and threw her arms around him. "That was so cool!"

"Right, right, but what happened?" he asked again, lifting her arms off.

"Oh, just some drunk kid who wanted to get my dress off."

"He told you to take off your dress?" He looked her up and down.

"Well, not exactly in those words, but that's what he meant." Her stomach tightened, fearing she said something wrong.

"You're right. What an asshole." He paused, staring at the empty keyhole on her chest. "But the kid's right, that dress is very...what word should I use? Tantalizing? Titillating?"

Tess burst out laughing at his choice of words. Leave it to Nick to use academic vocabulary in a dive bar. It was just one more reason she was so taken with him. Not to mention that he had just become her knight is garage band armor. *Could he be more perfect?* she wondered as she let him send that scandalous little dress to the floor after they returned to her place. After his chivalry and a mind-numbing combination of Irish Trash Cans and draft beers, all was forgiven. And who was she kidding? Secretly, she relished the strife of the "will he, won't he?" uncertainty.

Chapter 27

The intensity of their first forty-eight hours continued through the remainder of the month and into August. The only bumps in the road began just before Aimee moved in. Tess, knowing Aimee was not a fan of Nick, had kept the new relationship a secret for as long as she could. It wasn't that she was ashamed, as Nick suggested; it was that their relationship was still so fragile and new she didn't want Aimee's negative opinions to dampen it. But secrets have their way of coming out.

All was revealed after Aimee walked in on Nick using the bathroom one morning a week before she officially moved in. She was there before work looking for a fabric swatch she thought she had left there.

"Oh, wow! So sorry about that," Aimee said, quickly shutting the bathroom door. She turned on her heels and flew down the hall to Tess's room. "Tess! I need to talk to you, like right now talk to you," she announced as she entered Tess's room.

"Damn it, Aimee. I'm not even dressed!" Tess, naked,

scrambled for her robe.

Aimee dismissed Tess's nudity. "Tess, who is that man relieving himself in our bathroom?" Her tone was calm but piercing.

"What? Oh my God!" Tess said, realizing what was happening. "What are you doing here? Why aren't you at work?"

With a curt smile, Aimee said, "I go in late on Wednesdays? Now, who is that guy in our bathroom?"

Before Tess could answer, the very naked guest walked in. Not shy and very curious, Aimee completed an up-and-down look-over. When she realized who he was, her heart skipped a beat. She couldn't disguise her recognition as a look of horror crossed her face.

Nick shot Tess a panicked look. She got up and stood in front him. "Aimee, this is Nick. Nick Donovan." She handed him his pants, which she'd picked up on the way over.

Aimee gulped. He was the last person she thought she would ever see in her apartment, and naked at that. Not knowing what else to do, she bowed her head and went to the living room.

"I am sooo sorry."

"I thought you said she's not moving until this weekend."

"She's not."

"But she's here, with a key," Nick paused. Guilt writhed

through his bloodstream. He started to feel sick. "I'm going back to my place."

"No, wait. Please don't leave like this. Aimee's really a nice person. She just doesn't do surprises well."

Nick frowned then kissed her rigidly and left.

From the living room, Aimee watched Tess chase after Nick. When Tess joined her a few moments later, her tone was bone chilling cold. "Are you fucking insane? Nick Donovan? How long has this shit been going on?"

"Whoa! Stop it, Aimee. What the hell?"

"No you stop it, Tess. Do you have any idea how stupid you're being?"

"Well, he's gone. So thanks to you probably not anymore." Tess settled onto the couch and looked prepared for an onslaught.

"Tess, he's a user. You know that. How can you let him back into your life? He's just going to hurt you again."

"But he isn't though."

"Oh yeah? How long have you guys been, you know, together?" Aimee's tone was harsh and critical.

"About a month, almost a month and a half," Tess said cautiously. "Look, he's been very attentive. Almost too attentive. He calls everyday. Sometimes several. We see each other nearly as much. He's really changed Aimee."

"That's such crap. And how long do you think that's really

going to last? How long until you become his doormat? You
know he's that kind of guy!"

"God, Aimee! I can't take this from you. You only want to
rain on my parade don't you. You just can't stand the fact that
I'm right. Fairytale love is possible!"

Jesus, Aimee couldn't take it anymore. Now was the moment.
Tess needed to know that Nick tried to kiss her. Gathering
courage, Aimee said, "Look Tess there's something I have to tell
you about Ni—"

Tess put her hand up in front of her face. "No. I won't hear it.
Nick isn't the scumbag that you somehow think he is. So he's
made some mistakes. Haven't we all? It's not like you're always
the nicest girlfriend, we both know that." Tess paused.
"Whatever it is, save it. I'm sure it's just another ploy to get me
away from him."

Aimee was at a loss for words. If only Tess knew that the high
holy Nick Donovan was the kind of guy who went around kissing
basically anything that moved, Aimee was sure Tess wouldn't be
so quick to defend the loser. But based on her over zealous
reaction, there was no possible way she could tell Tess the truth.
Tess was so delusional she wouldn't believe her anyway. She
would probably then go on to end their thirteen-year friendship.
Since Aimee couldn't bear that thought she was forced to swallow
her pride and just move forward.

Chapter 28

Before Tess had the chance to get the word out about her relationship, Nick accepted the teaching job on Cape Cod and found an apartment in Plymouth, a town famously rich in history just outside the Cape. It was about time he found a job that utilized his degrees. He was not at all sad to say good-bye to construction work, ramen noodles, and lawn mower beer. Amid the commotion of moving, he realized he needed a bed. Lucky for him, with Aimee moving in, Tess was forced to find a new home for her guest bed. Never one to miss an opportunity, he claimed the bed as his.

The day Nick and his old roommate, Will, collected the bed began just like any other day.

"Hey, guys!" Tess said warmly when she opened the door around two that afternoon. She wasn't wearing anything Nick hadn't seen before, but something about her made him take notice. She wore a strapless knee-length black dress that cinched her waist, creating the perfect hourglass shape. Her hair was in a loose braid that draped comfortably on her left shoulder. Her skin looked soft and dewy thanks to the mid-August humidity, and her feet were bare. *It must be the bare feet*, he told himself.

The bareness of her feet reminded him of other parts of her body when bare. Noticing his inappropriate thoughts made him suddenly tense.

Tess went to kiss Nick hello as she normally did, but he managed to pull away before she hit her target. He stood there, nervous and distant. She responded with an icy stare.

"Hi. I'm Will. It's nice to meet you," Will said, extending his hand and interrupting the awkward moment.

"Hi. I'm Tess, just in case Nick forgot to mention it."

Purposely ignoring her, Nick headed straight for the guest room and got the ball rolling. The bed was out of the apartment in less than fifteen minutes. Tess appeared hurt by his distance.

During their goodnight call, he'd been tender and sweet, telling her how much he was going to miss her. *Quit being such a dick*, he told himself, but he couldn't do it. Being rude was simpler. So much simpler. He would get anger from Tess instead of tears, and he just couldn't do tears while his friend waited for him.

"Hey, Will, do you want some water or anything?" Tess asked after the guys had come back upstairs.

"Thanks, that'd be great," Will said. Tess went into the kitchen and returned with two sweaty, cold bottles of water. Nick gave Tess a look. It should have been an apology, but he just couldn't. Tess distributed the water, and each guy promptly guzzled.

"All right. Well, we've got to hit the road if we want to beat the traffic," Nick said.

"Oh. Ah, okay." Tess looked caught off guard. Will also looked surprised.

"You know that Cape traffic. It's awful at rush hour," Nick said. He went into the kitchen and deposited his empty water bottle. Tess followed him, leaving Will in the hallway to fend for himself.

"Tess, look, before you get all bent out of shape, I just really need to beat the traffic. I still need to go back to Connecticut and pick up another load of stuff." He used a convincing and plausible tone. All the more reason Tess shouldn't be mad. He watched her mull his words over in her mind.

"No, no, that's fine. I just thought…"

Nick saw trepidation written all over her face. He wondered what she was thinking. In some ways he felt like they were back at UMass all over again, standing in her apartment by the front door. *Am I going to call? Does she call me? Is this it?* Despite having each other's numbers, they had never talked about what the move would mean for them.

Nick being so cold and distant was killing her. The past month and a half had been the best month and a half of her life. She had been his guest of honor at each of his shows, but that was kept a secret so none of the other band members would think she was trying to Yoko Ono the group. They'd savored lazy mornings full of physical passion that she thought only happened in movies, and her long awaited fantasies were now reality.

Her time with Nick was her proof that fairy-tale romance was real and possible. In fact, all the pain from the past had made the present so much more riveting. Tess compared the past and present to the surprise and delight of watching an epic hero survive the belly of the beast and land at that hope-inducing turning point. This past month and a half was the turning point she had been waiting for, but just like the epic hero's journey, Tess realized, they still had some tests to conquer. His move to the Cape had to be one such test.

Nick looked at her forlorn face. He suddenly reached for her hand, pulling her body into his, and kissed her hard. Tess put everything she had into that kiss. If she could do nothing else to keep him close, she would at least leave her mark.

Tess heard the door shut and got the hint. Will must have left for his truck.

"I'll call you tonight, when I settle, if it's not too late." He kissed her again, but this time long and tenderly. Then he left.

That night, Tess stayed up waiting for his call until eleven thirty, which was as long as her body could hold out. The next morning, blurry-eyed and half awake, the first thing she did was reach for her phone. Finding a missed call and voicemail from Nick made her grin. Listening to Nick's voice was such a relief. She didn't even really hear what he said; she was just happy that he'd fulfilled his promise. Without thinking, she called him back right away. After only two rings, the call went to voicemail. She shrugged and then left a message for him to call her back. Several days passed before they reached each other's live voices.

The days that followed were rough. Her body trembled, craving Nick's embrace. Her mind couldn't focus on anything but what he might be doing. It didn't help that every time she called, his voicemail answered. Each time Nick called, she was either in the shower, at the gym, or on campus preparing for school. The weeklong phone tag felt like an eternity. Had they been better versed in the new fad of text messaging it wouldn't have been so bad, but that regular practice was still several months in their future.

When they did finally connect, she said over and over how much she missed him, and they agreed to see each other every weekend, which worked well at first. Then, despite their best efforts, things changed when the school year officially began.

Every weekend quickly became every other. Nick said he needed time to acclimate. He explained that he had no idea that the lesson planning, grading, and behavior management would take up as much time as it did. Back when he was a student teacher, his cooperating teacher had warned him about how little time Nick would have to himself once he got his own classroom, but he'd shrugged it off, convinced the seasoned pro was trying to scare him. But apparently not. He was so much busier than he thought he would be. Tess agreed to give him more space, to his obvious, huge relief. He reminded her that she too needed to get focused. Grad school was serious. There was no room for messing around like when she was an undergrad, he warned.

Between visits, she thought about Nick constantly. She went to bed and woke up thinking about him. She wondered what he was doing, where he was going. She wanted to see him all the time, the way it was over the summer. The less she heard from him, the more she needed him.

She must have checked her phone every fifteen minutes, at least. Aimee told her she needed to calm down. Tess disagreed and made up a story about weak cell reception on the Cape that meant she needed to always be on the lookout for his calls.

By November, he was only calling a couple of times a week. At most, she saw him once a month. Things were definitely not the way Tess neither expected nor wanted. She couldn't stop feeling the end was near. She saw it happen to her friends all the time. Whenever a guy decided he didn't want to see one of her friends anymore, he would slowly start pulling away until there was no contact at all. Usually, it happened after one of her friends tried to define the relationship. But it occurred to her that they hadn't had *that* conversation yet, the one where each party stakes his and her claim and the girl hopes that they come out of it calling each other boyfriend and girlfriend.

Upon this realization, Tess told herself she needed to get a grip. That conversation was coming. He would initiate it when the time was right. He was simply too busy. Plus, if Tess had learned anything from her friends, she wasn't about to start hinting if Nick wasn't ready. Feeling mildly better, Tess was confident about her decision to wait. The moment was coming. Nick wasn't the kind of guy to not have *that* conversation.

Chapter 29

Now December, Nick feeling more comfortable in his classroom, opened up more time for his personal life. With Christmas fast approaching and having put off his holiday shopping, he invited Tess down for the weekend before Christmas vacation.

With the seasonal decorations merrily displayed on street lamps, business signs, and homes alike, a mood of wonder and romance surrounded them. Nick chose to begin the evening with dinner at a fancy Italian restaurant. There were no prices on the menu, which was in Italian. Tess thought, *Ooh la la.* Afterward, they strolled around downtown Plymouth, hand in hand. The wreaths and Christmas lights lit up the brick buildings and sidewalks, making the streets feel cozy despite the freezing temperature.

Being close again reminded Nick of what he'd been missing. He also got the sense that Tess was feeling the same way. Staring into her eyes proved that the distance between them had only been geographic. They would overcome the distance. It was just a matter of time. They'd make it work. And Christmas was the perfect vehicle to get that ball rolling.

"Oh, my. Nick, I can't accept this. Where did...? Why?" Tess said, almost falling to the floor when she opened the black little box he handed her when they returned to his apartment.

"Slow down, it's only white sapphire, but all those little stones on the part the chain goes through, the saleslady said those are real diamonds."

"But why? How?" Tess began to look more content. Inside was a beautiful pendant necklace. It was a perfect, clear oval-shaped gemstone, set in four sterling silver prongs. On top sat a sterling silver X outlined with small diamond chips.

"While we were walking, I noticed your eyes light up every time we passed a jewelry window. It reminded me of the story you told me, back at UMass, about how you were promised a diamond necklace for your thirteenth birthday but never got it because of some crazy, complicated story." He paused, looking at her. She was still staring at the pendant. "Anyway, I know how much you wished you'd had that necklace and I wanted to get you something to take its place."

Tears welled in her eyes. She blinked them away, but her eyes were still a little glassy when she looked at him and asked him to help her put it on.

"Wow. Looks great," Nick said tenderly when she returned from the bathroom mirror displaying it for him.

"I know, right?" Tess was beaming. "Everything about it is perfect: the sparkle, the length, everything!" Even though this wasn't a formal conversation about their status, Tess considered the necklace Nick's way of finally marking his territory. Who needed words when a guy gave a girl jewelry?

The next day, when it came time for Tess to leave, she had to force herself to go, hyperfocusing on the need to get her own work done. She joked that Nick should do it for her. He laughed and said there wasn't enough money in the world to get him to do that again. As they hugged good-bye, Tess felt the way she had over the summer. Everything was fine—more than fine. Nick had given her jewelry. He wasn't going anywhere.

Chapter 30

Knowing things were just fine with Nick, Tess struggled to stay focused on wrapping up the semester. All she thought about was the next time she would see him. She debated asking him to Christmas dinner but nixed that idea. She didn't want to risk the taint her father and his crazy girlfriend of the month would inevitably place on their relationship. Years of experience taught her that going was tense and awkward; it would be unfair to subject an innocent bystander to such torture. And inviting herself to his parents' would be rude. As a result, the next time they could get together was New Year's Eve, at which point Tess realized it was time for her to tell him how she felt.

Despite her original decision to wait until he brought it up, the necklace had been a game changer. Though the conversation hadn't come with the necklace, it was still a strong statement, and she felt she should respond in kind. She pictured it. *He'll take me to some fancy place like the Top of the Hub. The glint of the city lights below will make me sparkle like the necklace. He will tell me how much he cares about me, how much he wants me in his life, and not just on weekends. I'll light up and say I feel the very same way.* But due to bad weather and the crappy tires on his Civic, they were forced to ring in the New Year separately.

The following weekend, the clouds cleared, and Nick arrived on Tess's doorstep exactly an hour and a half after his school's Friday dismissal bell. Tess's stomach flopped with joy to see him so early.

"For me?"

"Still wearing the necklace, I see."

Tess's face lit up. "This rose is beautiful," she said, taking in its wonderful scent.

"You're welcome."

Surely something special is happening. A single red rose is never random, Tess thought.

Unable to afford Tess's five-star fantasy, which she hadn't told him about anyway, Nick took her to the North End for hot chocolate and a pastry. Later, as they strolled down the narrow sidewalks, hand-in-hand he said, "I have a story for you." He smiled. "Remember the last time you came down?"

Tess nodded. She pictured the cuteness of all the little shops, especially the jewelry store, where she imagined Nick buying her necklace.

"Apparently, a few of my students saw us together." He paused. "Anyway, the following Monday in class, they asked me who you were." He laughed. "And I didn't know what to tell them."

"What do you mean, you didn't know what to tell them?" Tess asked impatiently. "They're students. They don't need—"

"Hang on, I'm getting there. I told them I would talk to you and get back to them on that," he said. He gripped her hand tighter. She could tell that he was looking for something. *Is he about to say what I think he's going to say?* The eagerness in his eyes made her smile but then jet her eyes away quickly.

"So, Miss Tessalie Ryan, what is this that's going on between us? Who are you to me?" There was hopefulness in his serious question. It was the kind of tone used in all those Hallmark movies Tess watched as a guilty pleasure. Even though this seemed to be the question she had been longing for, she suddenly couldn't speak. She'd rehearsed her answer so many times. She had imagined so many responses. Of all moments to be tongue tied, why now? No, not now! All she could do was smile and nod.

Watching her stand there silently with an embarrassed look on her face, Nick's nerves turned into anger. He began to wonder if Tess was just playing games. It wasn't as though he asked her a hard question. He was certain that she would say "girlfriend," at the very least. How surprisingly wrong he'd been. He snapped his hand away and quickened his pace, leaving her to catch up.

The drive back to Tess's apartment was deafeningly silent. Nick's eyes were locked on the road and hers on the passing surroundings. As the car roared, Tess berated herself. *Why, Tess? Why? You fucking idiot. Just say how you feel for once!* She wanted nothing more than for Nick to call her his girlfriend. It had been her wish for two and a half years. *What the hell went wrong?* She'd been so determined to share how she felt. Each time she tried to reach for him, he pulled his hand away, causing her to retreat. After her forth attempt, all of a sudden her own repressed anger from the past burst to the surface.

She'd had no idea she was still so mad. It had lain dormant behind the flowers, the dinners, the sapphire necklace. But in this moment, none of that negated the pain he'd originally caused her. He still hadn't *really* apologized for it. She needed to feel like they could talk about it, but she didn't feel like they could. She still had too many questions that she needed answered. Why had he been so okay with Halloween? Didn't he feel like a total creep? Why didn't he ask for her number? Why did it take him so damn long to respond to her e-mails? The questions were an invisible dark cloud that hung over her. And yet, a huge part of her was still desperate to officially be his girlfriend, making it all so complicated.

When they arrived in front of Tess's apartment, Nick threw his car in park on the street instead of going to his spot in the back. He got out and marched to her apartment but was stopped by the locked front door, forcing him to wait for Tess and the key. He kept his back to her while he waited. Once the door was open, without saying a word, he flew into the bedroom, past Aimee, who happened to be raiding Tess's closet, grabbed his things, and headed back to his car.

"You're not even going to say good-bye?" Tess managed to

finally say as she followed him down the stairs.

"What's the difference? You'd probably just smile and nod." He paused, looking sharply into her eyes. "I'm done. I am so done with this—and with you!"

Tess shuddered at what she saw reflected back in his eyes. *What the hell kind of answer is that?* Tess would have done anything to turn back the hands of time so that she could give him a different answer.

As she watched Nick walk ahead of her, a little voice inside her head screamed for attention. She had heard that voice many times before, and once again told it to shut up and go away. Now was the not time.

"What are you talking about, 'done with *this?'" she asked now on the sidewalk.

Nick suddenly whipped around, startling her. He chuckled mechanically, then said, "Let me ask you something. Is this a game to you? Do you enjoy getting me all worked up about the distance between us, telling me how much you miss me, wishing I had more free time for *you?*" Tess tried to respond, but Nick didn't let her. "It sure as hell seems like it, because after all we've been through, all this time we've known each other, I can't believe you don't know what you want."

"It's not that easy, though."

"You either want me or you don't!"

"That's not fair. That's not even what you asked me earlier. God, Nick. That's why it isn't as easy as you think. From the very beginning you've been hot and cold. I still don't know where your head is at with me." She took a deep breath. "And how can you sleep with me and then barely respond to my e-mails, much less call me?"

"You know what, Tess?" he said. "It's just that I..." He looked into her eyes, searching. Then his eyes fixed on her chest, on the necklace. "Whatever, Tess. I'll see you when I see you." He looked her in the eyes once more. Tess noticed a change; this time his eyes were rounder and glassy. He gestured toward his Honda, stopped as if to speak but didn't.

"Wait! Nick, don't go! Nick! Don't leave!" Tess screamed as she watched him speed away. "Not like this!"

After almost half an hour, Aimee checked the front window and jumped when she noticed that Tess was still standing outside in the icy fifteen degrees. She ran down with a blanket and wrapped Tess in it before she guided her frozen body up the stairs.

Tess thawed out on the couch while Aimee made tea. Tess's head felt cold and hollow. She thought nothing, felt nothing. Nick was gone. She had truly failed this time. He didn't love her the way she thought he would. Something deep in her heart of hearts told her he wasn't coming back. If she weren't so cold, tears would have run down her cheeks.

Aimee brought the tea. She sat next to Tess and talked. Her words were muffled and cloudy. Tess did her best to look like she was listening, though she wasn't. By midnight, Aimee had passed out on the couch. Tess sat, still wrapped in the blanket, holding a full mug of cold tea. She got up and draped the blanket over Aimee before she headed to her room and collapsed on her bed.

Chapter 31

The next morning, Tess woke up with a pounding headache after a terrible night's sleep. She tossed and turned all night, trying to keep up with her racing thoughts about what had just happened. Disappointment, sadness, and disbelief didn't even begin to describe what she was feeling. Panic was the most prevalent. She picked up her phone, praying to see a voicemail, a text, anything. *Nothing.*

"Jesus, what have I done?" She looked around her room at all the things she had collected during their time together: a misprinted T-shirt for his band, a pair of shot glasses they stole from the Hong Kong bar the night they won trivia, the NY Jets hat he loved that she managed to steal from him, the picture a stranger took of them on the swan boats at Boston Common last summer. Seeing him smile, cheek-to-cheek next to her was just too much. She couldn't hold in the pain any longer and began to sob.

Aimee came rushing in a few minutes later.

"He's gone, Aimee. Really gone this time."

"I'm so sorry, Tess," Aimee said, holding her friend.

"And when we were on the street, he wouldn't even listen to

me when I was finally able to talk to him. He was so mad. I was so scared, Aimee. And I was confused. And I didn't know what was happening. One minute he was all lovey-dovey, asking me what we were doing, and then—"

"What happened? Did you tell him you love him?"

"What? No! Why in the hell would I do that?"

"Sorry. Go on."

"God, I really screwed up," Tess said, a little more coherently. "Hell, I wish I had said I loved him. At least that would have been better than what I actually said."

"What did you actually say?"

"Nothing. I said nothing. I just smiled and nodded when he asked me what we were to each other. God, I could kill myself right now!" Tess thrashed a pillow to the floor. "He was all I've ever wanted. Then, when I finally had the chance to make him mine, I blew it. I'm such an idiot."

Aimee thought quietly. "Is that it? He left like a bat out of hell because you didn't answer a question?"

Tess nodded.

Aimee's eyes momentarily flared with anger then she abruptly said, "Hey, it's okay. Everything's going to be just fine. He was probably just frustrated and needs some time to cool off. I mean, it's not like you had an easy start. He'll maybe call as soon as he's calmer."

Tess gave her a weak smile, hoping her friend was right. Aimee passed her the box of tissues from the night stand. Tess wiped her face and blew her nose. "And if he doesn't? If it really is over?"

"Then I'll make good on my original offer to rip off his prize piece and slap him in the face with it." The girls chuckled. "Either way, though, Tess, you're going to be fine. I hope for your sake he calls, but if not, then I get my wing woman back, and we'll paint this town like it's never been painted before. I promise."

"Do you think I should call him? Text him?"

"Not right now. Give him some time. Maybe in a couple of days—"

"A couple of days!"

"Yes, a couple of days, Tess. Then give him a call. You don't want to push him right now."

Tess knew Aimee was right, but that didn't make her dislike her advice any less. At least Aimee's tone was soothing instead of judgmental as it had been for the last few months. So Tess waited, but after three full days of silence, Tess was losing her mind. On the one hand, she didn't want to push. On the other, she needed answers, even if they confirmed that they were, in fact, over.

By the end of the day, she had called three times, only leaving a message after the second. "Hey, Nick, it's me, Tess. Just wanted to check in. See how you're doing. Give me a call when you get this."

After that she called him once a day, sometimes leaving a message, sometimes not.

"Hey, it's me again. Just wanted to talk. I really hate the way we left things the other day, so call me when you can, okay?"

"I know you're fine, but I'm worried. Give me a call, just to let me know you're alive," she said in her last voicemail.

After a full week of not hearing from him, she began sending text messages.

January 15th: Hey there! Haven't heard from you in a while. Just want to make sure you haven't fallen off the face of the earth or anything. Call me. Tess ☺

January 18th: You won't believe what happened on the T today! Call me! Can't wait to tell you all about it!

January 19th: Fine. I get it, you're mad. I never meant to upset you. I was just blindsided. Will you please just call me so we can talk about this?

January 25th: Hello?

No response.

Her heart hurt in ways she didn't know were possible. She reached out to her father, but as usual, he was nowhere to be found. Aimee did her best to comfort Tess, telling her not to dwell on the past. She even forced Tess to go out with her as often as possible but each night out, successful or not, led Tess to the same place: her computer.

Retreating into the cyberworld she found refuge. Placing a few words into the Google search bar, she surfed endlessly for anything Nick Donovan: a picture, a newspaper article. Though impossible, she fantasized about finding a secret message hailing her back to him. She spent hours looking but found nothing. After she accepted that there weren't any cyberlinks to Nick, she looked up images of Plymouth. Seeing pictures of where they'd created such sweet memories was her way of feeling close to him.

Looking at those Google images gave her a warm, nostalgic feeling that enveloped her, making her feel safe. She longed for what she saw in those images. They were what she had once hoped to experience, but now she would never take another autumn stroll, hand-in-hand, down the brick sidewalks of downtown Plymouth. She would never know what it would be like to wake up together every summer Saturday to the smell of saltwater and the sound of city dwellers stampeding to the beach and then laughing, because they knew the ocean would still be there after Labor Day. Never again would she be encapsulated in the safety of Nick's arms on a beach during a winter nor'easter.

The nostalgic ache was so strong it was kind of enjoyable, like the satisfaction of pressing a bruise. Sometimes when Tess was struck really hard by this feeling, her heart clung to it like it was hope for the future. *Perhaps he feels what I'm feeling. Maybe there is a chance we can go back to where we were?*

Nick was the reason she was getting a master's degree in history instead of education, as she'd originally planned. Eventually they would both be history teachers. She remembered that at UMass he'd said he wanted to be married, to have kids. So did she. During one office visit, he declared his desire to travel the world, to see what it had to offer. So did she. But of course they never said they wanted to do those things with each other. And that was a fact that Tess refused to face.

Chapter 32

By April, Tess had gone out on at least fifteen dates, but none of the men merited a second thought. This guy was too tall; that guy was too fat. One guy was too needy, one too dull. Without fail, with each new date Tess discovered some sort of deal breaker. Aimee was appalled when Tess declared a date was too nice. Aimee begged her to give the nice guys at least a second chance. She said nice guys always needed a couple of false starts before their true charm came through.

"Fine, then. Tell me what I need to do to finally get over him once and for all, Mom," Tess begged one rainy mid-April afternoon. She was snuggled in blankets tucked into the sofa, phone to her ear and a cup of hot chocolate by her side. "I'll admit I'm getting sick of wasting time thinking about him. So tell me, what's my problem?"

"You can't just flip a switch, honey."

"But that's what you're all telling me to do. And that's what guys do. I'm sure that's what Nick's done."

"Well, you're not a guy, and I'm telling you to work on it. I know it doesn't happen overnight."

"Mom, are you now telling me not to get over Nick? I thought you hated him." Tess couldn't figure out why her mother did not have a foolproof remedy ready for her. Based on the number of relationships she had as a youth, surely she should know something.

"Tess, I don't hate the guy. I don't even know him, but what I do know is I don't like how he's treated you. I think he's bad news. If I had my way, you would be over him already."

"Then tell me how!"

"Do you remember what I told you the morning you left Santa Fe?" Grace paused. "Remember I told you to shuffle the deck faster? Well, that's what you've got to do now."

"Be with as many guys as I can?"

"No, not *be* with as many guys. Date, go out—meet as many different guys as you can. Just see what's out there. If, after a while, you find someone special, then you'll see that Nick doesn't matter anymore."

"Really? That's it?"

"Well, it's a start."

"I can do that. Aimee and I meet guys all the time. I'm sure I'll meet someone."

"Great. Now just don't *be* with as many guys as so many of you young girls do today, okay?"

"What's that supposed to mean?"

"I just don't want your heart broken, that's all. What I mean is, deep down you're far too sensitive to just sleep with guys and then move on to the next. You need a nice guy who wants you for who you are, inside and out. At times, I fear the rampant oversexualization that is all over the place is really ruining young people's relationships these days. Back when I was your age, there

AUDREY DILLION 275

was a protocol to follow. Everyone knew where you stood based on that protocol."

"Whoa, Mom, slow down. I think you're way overthinking modern relationships. And remember, you burned your bras for women's lib. So it's your fault so many young people are freewheeling and fancy-free, as you've said in the past."

"Tess, it's okay to want more than just sex. Don't give guys what they want because you think it'll make them want to be your boyfriend. Hey, why don't you try one of those online websites that sets you up with dates? I hear they can be good screeners."

"Oh my God, no, Mom! We've been over this. That's for desperate people."

"Oh, stop it. No, it's not. All the young people are doing it now."

"Whatever. I'm a young person, and I've never thought about it."

"Well, think about it. How else are you going to shuffle the deck faster with your busy schedule?" Grace had a point.

"Fine. Whatever. I'll see what Aimee says about it."

"All right. I have to get going. I'll speak to you later. I love you. Remember to keep shuffling that deck."

Over the next couple of weeks, Tess considered her mother's advice. *What does Mom know about online dating? She's old and married.* But as the weeks passed, Tess's sadness became angry loneliness, at which point her curiosity about the world wide web of dating got the better of her.

Chapter 33

By the end of the second day she was listed on match.com, Tess was blown away by the plethora of guys wanting to explore her interest in long walks on the beach and underwater basket weaving. It was especially intriguing to her because her interests were so clearly fake. Her inbox was flooded with messages, offering a wide variety of romantic dates. Her favorite was a night at some guy's karate studio followed by a couple of rounds at a shooting range. "Sorry, guns and violence don't equal romance, buddy," Tess said, quickly clicking delete on that one. It didn't take long for her to click through the throngs to realize none of the guys were cute; they were all forty-somethings on the prowl for young, dumb meat. She may have been young, but she wasn't dumb. She also realized that if she was going to actually get anything out of her $29.99 subscription fee, she needed to take her profile a little more seriously.

"The online dating world," Aimee said, "is like a cyber bar, only you can't be sure both parties are equally drunk at the same time.

Just know that you're going to see a lot of gross dudes on there. I like to laugh and put their pictures on hotornot.com." Aimee sat across from Tess at a table they shared at Dunkin Donuts early Saturday morning. She had become quite an expert of the online world of dating since she'd joined seven months ago.

"Aimee, that's so mean! Ugly guys need love too."

"Next, whatever you do, don't let the guys know where you live. You can never truly be sure if they're freaks or not. All dates must be in a public place."

"What if I really like a guy, though, and he seems legit?"

"Don't do it, Tess. Trust me. A girl at work took a guy home once, and she was not the same person the next day."

"I don't believe that. She probably had the best sex of her life that night."

"No, she was messed up after that. Her hair was all nasty, her clothes rumpled. She became totally jumpy...like all the time jumpy. She was never that way before. It was weird."

"Okay, whatever. I wouldn't go home with a guy on the first date anyway. You know that. Okay, well, not a full home run on the first date, but a little hands and whatnot never hurt."

Aimee's eyebrow peaked into a sharp triangle. "We'll see about that. Internet dating has weird and unknown powers. Anyway, the most important rule of online dating is...well, the two most important rules are that you never pay and you never give up your address."

"Duly noted."

Taking Aimee's advice seriously, Tess didn't go on her first match.com date for nearly a month and a half. But being a single, somewhat lonely, but primarily broke grad student in Boston was starting to take its toll.

Even Aimee was impressed with Tess's sudden ingenuity. Not only did Tess use online dating to possibly find a mate, she began to use it to get dinner and fun for free. Each night of the week she lined up a date. In addition, she scheduled an eighth just in case one got sick. The plan garnered her so much success that at one point she had to purchase a little red date book to note key information about each date: name, physical points of interest, and employment status. Otherwise, she would sit at the dinner table without a clue about whom she was eating with. Through this process she got to meet some real characters. The first was a professional shopper named Tucker.

ProShopper4Love, 31, Abercrombie model look-alike seeking his match

Tess met Tucker on a Tuesday evening at the Prudential Center. He was a tall blond with honey-brown eyes. He wore an untucked sky-blue dress shirt and khakis. It looked as though he had just left the office.

"How long have you been a professional shopper? That sounds so exciting!" Tess was genuinely intrigued. The fact that they were sitting on real leather bar stools at Towne Stove and Spirits had nothing to do with her excitement. Nor did the two glasses of wine play into her excitement either.

"Believe it or not, about two years now. I can't believe it myself. I'm pretty sure I have the floor plan of every store in Boston memorized."

"I think I'd love your job! Do you get to keep all the stuff you buy?"

"Usually no. Skirts and tube tops just don't seem to fit me right."

Tess giggled. "Then why do it?"

"Well, the pay is great. The work is easy. Can't beat the hours, and on the off chance I do like something, the majority of the sweet little old ladies I shop for tell me to just treat myself. I think they sometimes think I'm their grandson or something." Tucker's eyes gleamed into Tess's.

Goosebumps ran down her spine. *Perhaps online dating isn't so bad after all.*

"And what is it you do to pay the bills again?"

"I'm getting my masters in history to become a social studies teacher."

"Aw, so you are like a do-gooder and stuff. I like it. It's cute."

"Watch it. I'm no do-gooder. I can still break the rules. I just have to be home by midnight."

"Or what? You turn into a pumpkin?"

Chemistry was definitely brewing. He was easy to talk to and his witty flirtation couldn't be ignored.

Their fourth date, which was only two weeks after their first, began with dinner at Tess's place and didn't end until the next morning with breakfast and two very satisfied appetites. Totally swept up in the rush of a new relationship Tess stopped dillydallying at second base and gave Tucker a home run. Although they had only known each other for a short time, Tess felt like Tucker was someone special.

Shortly after taking their relationship to the next level, Tucker invited Tess along on a work assignment at the upscale Chestnut Hill Mall. On that particular assignment, he was on the clock looking for a young lady's fashion outfit.

Knowing women's fashion a bit better than Tucker, Tess thoroughly enjoyed the expedition. She tried on many of the summer season's trends, modeling all the hot ones.

"How about this one?" Tess twirled around in a chiffon skirt just outside her dressing room at Banana Republic.

"Do that again. I want to see how high it goes."

Tess twirled again without thinking about it. When she stopped, Tucker was standing directly behind her.

"Yes, that'll do," Tucker whispered, gently pushing her back into the dressing room. With her back against the wall, Tucker took full advantage of the small privacy the dressing room afforded them.

"Guess you like the skirt." Tess cleared her throat. Tucker's face was so close to hers it looked like he had just one eye. He kissed her again while his hands made their rounds over her body.

"Not in here, you little creep," Tess whispered, smiling but shoving him out of the dressing room.

"Yeah, yeah."

Tess came out in several other outfits. Each was as satisfying as the first. Then she emerged in a see-through chiffon shirt and curve-hugging tube skirt.

"Well. Hello there, good lookin'." Eyes locked on the sight before him, Tucker let himself back into the room without an invitation and took Tess by surprise. "You are so friggin' hot," he said, pulling the clothes off her as fast as he could. She felt his excitement press against her. Her skin sizzled with every kiss, every touch. Enjoying the rush, Tess urged him on until he found the zipper. Feeling his warmth against her own hot skin was suddenly all too real and she had a change of heart. The tight quarters and thin walls were too much. She saw flashes of the *Boston Globe* headlines: *Teacher in Training Shacking Up Like a High School Student.*

"Seriously, get out! Not in the store!"

Begrudgingly, Tucker tucked himself back together and left. *Jesus,* Tess thought. *That was way too close.* At the same time, she regretted kicking him out. In reality, that kind of thing probably happened all the time. Hell, it probably wasn't the first time Tucker ever did it in a dressing room, being in malls so much. And what a story it would have made for her friends had she gone all the way. It had enough sex, sin, and notoriety to be a Hollywood headliner. But now it was time to get dressed and pick an outfit. *Next time,* she thought with a smirk. As she recalled Tucker's reaction to each outfit, she decided to recommend the last one.

"And your total is $179.98," the androgynous clerk said,

deadpan. Tess was busy looking through the jewelry several feet away. Tucker winked at the clerk and turned to Tess.

"Ah, Tess? Tess, the clerk needs your attention for a moment," he said, moving a distance away from the clerk.

"Who, me?"

Tucker nodded.

"Hi, is everything all right?"

"Your total is $179.98. Will that be cash or charge?"

Tess looked at Tucker. His hands could not have been farther away from his wallet. "Give me just a second."

"Hey, Tucker, can I speak to you for a moment?"

"Sure. What's up?" They stepped farther away from the register.

"So, ah, are you going to take care of this? I mean, you're the one who needs to buy a woman's outfit."

"What do I need a woman's outfit for?"

Tess got the feeling he was playing dumb on purpose. "I thought you said you needed to buy an outfit for Gretchen's granddaughter's birthday present. Did I miss something?"

"I do, but I don't want to buy that one. It's way too sleazy."

Now Tess knew Tucker was purposely punishing her for denying him in the dressing room.

Tess gave him a hard stare. After reading his face, she took a deep breath and went back to the cash register.

"It will be charge," Tess said, handing over a nearly maxed-out credit card. As the clerk ran the card, Tess crossed her fingers as well as every other crossable body part. *Please let the charge go through,* she prayed.

"Sign inside the box when it comes on the screen." Relieved, she picked up the stylus and did as she was told. The clerk handed her a small brown paper bag that didn't seem to show off just how expensive the contents were and went back to folding shirts.

"You're going to look so hot in that outfit," Tucker said with dark eyes. "I hope you didn't buy it just for me."

She oozed sarcasm. "Course not, silly. I so clearly bought it for my future students."

"You're a bad, bad teacher in training." Tucker kissed her cheek and placed his arm around her.

"Right."

Tess never wore that outfit for Tucker. She also did not hear from him again, despite sending him numerous text messages and voicemails, at which point she took the clothes back. Her credit card thanked her profusely as she left the store.

Tess couldn't deny she was bummed. She had really liked Tucker. He was funny and smart, hot as hell, and really sweet, well when he wanted to be. She thought he could have been it. Plus, how cool would it have been to be known as Tess and Tucker?

Duncan324, 34, Don't judge a book by its cover. Read me from front to back

Tess's next big date, the man who introduced himself as

Duncan, sported an English accent and professor attire: sport coat, collared shirt, and jeans. He brought her to a little hole-in-the-wall Thai restaurant in Cleveland Circle on a nice Thursday evening in July. His skin tone and hair clearly indicated that his heritage was from India. From certain angles he looked a lot like the actor Kal Penn, one of Tess's favorite celebrity crushes.

The primary light in the restaurant came from the dozens of tropical fish tanks that lined the walls and even separated tables. An electric lantern on each table also spread dim light. Tess may not have been able to see her food all that well, but what she could see was the chiseled outline of a strong jaw and the intriguing eyes on the other side of the table.

"You know, for every Thai place here, there's an Indian shop back home in merry old England. Truly miss it. Sometimes I think I want to go back just for a good curry. You like Indian by any chance?" Duncan's accent was smooth and creamy.

"Curry and I don't really get along that well."

"That's a shame, truly."

When the food arrived, temporarily suspending conversation, Tess noticed that Duncan was already working on his third glass of wine.

"This has got to be the best Pad Thai I have ever eaten, like, in my whole entire life."

Tess raised an eyebrow. She'd never heard a Brit use "like" the way Americans did. "So, Duncan, I take it you've been in the States a while now?"

"Duncan? Who's Duncan?" He looked truly confused. So was

Tess.

"Okay, time for more food and less drink." Tess pulled his fourth glass of wine away from him.

"Oh, right, that's me. Ha ha." His accent was suddenly more American. "So, yeah, I moved here, ah, five, no ten years ago. There were like no jobs back home, so, I, ah, moved to the city." *Again with the "like."*

"The city? I thought you said you were from London. How could a city like London have no jobs?"

"Oh, Jason, you're so stupid. You did that last time too," he said to himself. Continuing in a thicker and then weaker British accent, he said, "Right, right. I meant the city of Boston. Everyone in America likes a British guy? More money, more women. Am I right?"

"You need water, okay, Duncan?"

"Who the hell is this Duncan guy? Is he your boyfriend or something?"

"Okay, remind me what your name is again?"

"Mike Cappolini. Damn, how can you forget a name like Cappolini?" He chuckled.

"So you're not Duncan Bingsley then?"

"Jesus Christ, I am starting to think you're crazy. I've told you my name's Markus Verma like ten times." By now, the British accent was completely gone, just like the actor sitting across the table. Tess impatiently waited for the water to arrive. While she could appreciate first date white lies, engaging alternate personas was completely unacceptable. When the water finally came, she made up her mind to leave.

"Well D—, Mi—whatever your name is, I appreciate the meal, but I've got to feed my seventeen cats now." *Seventeen. Really, Tess?*

"Wait a second, the date's not over. We haven't gone to my place yet."

"I know, I know. Next time, I promise."

"Okay. Good, next time is right. You can go now."

Tess collected her purse and stood when her date suddenly grabbed her hand and unbalanced her. She wobbled and almost fell against the table next to them.

"Wait, give me a kiss."

"A kiss?"

His lips were already puckered. Tess quickly gave him a peck on the forehead.

"I'll see you next time babe."

"Yes, next time it is."

For a moment, she thought she wasn't going to make it out. She feared he would abduct her and then become national news. She thanked her lucky stars that she had the sense to leave and made sure to never let that kind of thing happen again. This date, the first time she walked out on someone, had been particularly eye-opening. Part of her felt guilty for abandoning that poor intoxicated guy like that, but he definitely was a creep. What if he was some serial killer? Tess couldn't risk finding out. Later, when she shared the experience with Aimee, Aimee told her she did the right thing.

After the fiasco with Duncan, or whatever his name was, Tess was a little weary and decided on an official break from her electronic matchmaker. She canceled nearly an entire week's worth of dates. It felt good for a little while, but then the loneliness and fear of missed opportunities overcame her.

Not comfortable with the online dating platform just yet, Tess purchased two tickets for a harbor cruise featuring a Guns N' Roses cover band for the following Friday night. Tess wasn't the biggest Guns N' Roses fan, but she knew lots of guys were. Plus, these things were known to have lots of singles aboard.

The area around the cash bar on the no-frills cruise ship was covered with cheap red Astroturf. All the walls were bare white plastic. The primary decorations were the die-hard fans. Big hair, ratty T-shirts, and leather pants were everywhere. The average age, much to Tess's dismay, was close to forty-five. She quickly sensed her male prospects might be limited, but that wasn't her only reason for being there. She was there to have a good time with Aimee and blow off a little steam.

"I don't even know why I come on these things anymore," a masculine voice said behind Tess in the line for drinks. "This is my fourth cruise."

"Fourth cruise, eh?" Tess turned around. "I'd say you just like all the big hair and tight pants."

"And so what if I do?" The deep voice belonged to a handsome blond.

"Then I would say…" Tess didn't finish because it was her turn to order at the bar. "I'd like two vodka cranberries, please."

"Two?"

"That'll be fourteen dollars," the bartender said.

Before Tess could take out her wallet, the good-looking stranger had paid for the drinks.

"Oh, no, you didn't need to pay for those. Here's the fourteen dollars."

"It's my pleasure, especially for such a pretty face."

"You're ridiculous," Tess said, returning the twenty to her pocket.

"Ah, thanks for the compliment?"

Tess didn't know what to do next. She also had no clue as to why she called him ridiculous. He was only trying to hit on her. *Great, I screwed up again.* She looked down at her hands, full of drinks. She looked back at him and then turned to find Aimee.

"Hey, hey—slow down. I'm sorry. I didn't mean to offend. My name's Jason. It's a pleasure to meet you." Jason offered his hand. Tess looked down and remained still.

Suddenly, Aimee appeared alongside them. Tess instantly felt relief, but when she noticed Aimee inspecting the fine specimen in front of her, she felt jealousy flare. He seemed instantly struck by Aimee's golden hair and svelte physique, as if he'd been mesmerized by a spell.

"Well, well, well, Tess, who is this? Aren't you going to introduce me?" Aimee said without looking at her. She seemed to be under a spell as well.

"I'm Jason Williams. And you are?"

"Aimee, Aimee Babineaux."

"I got you a drink. It's a vodka cranberry," Jason said, lifting a glass out of Tess's hand and passing it over.

"You must be psychic! This is my favorite!" Aimee accepted the drink and put the skinny straw in her mouth.

Tess rolled her eyes. "Yeah. Hey, guys, I'm still here." She waved a little wave.

Jason's eyes did not leave Aimee's. Tess had become invisible. She waved her arm in front of Aimee to get a reaction. She got nothing but maid of honor duties two years later at the nuptials of Aimee Babineaux and Jason Williams.

For the rest of the booze cruise, Tess spent her time watching Aimee fall for a guy she decided was a total jerk. At least that's what she told herself. He had totally and technically hit on her first. What had made him change his mind so quickly would elude her for years. In the meantime, Tess couldn't help but feel jealous. Jason was much more of a jerk than Nick. Nice guys didn't flirt with one girl and then fall for her best friend right in front of her. Feeling totally defeated, with little hope remaining, Tess bemoaned her fate. Her search for true love would never end. But dating had become a preoccupation she just couldn't quit. Not long after the cruise, Tess jumped back onto match.com.

*DollaDollaBillsDollface, 28, financier on the rise, let me show you
what's up!*

Jim's mini potbelly preceded him. From behind, he looked as
if he didn't carry an ounce of extra fat anywhere. He was too
young for such a shape. Despite being certain that he'd have heart
problems down the road, Tess went out with him anyway, having
significantly lowered her standards. Luckily, he was self-assured
and fully understood who he was, which Tess found very
attractive. He also had a killer sense of humor. After their first
date Tess's stomach muscles ached for a couple of days from
constantly being in stitches.

Having convinced her to go on a third date, Jim asked her out
for a Friday lunch at Kingfish Hall in Quincy Market. Kingfish
Hall, known for its perfect summer patio and broiled scallops,
was good enough for Tess. Even if Jim proved to be a
disappointment, at least she knew the meal wouldn't be. Coming
from the office, he arrived in a navy blue suit and steel-gray tie.
His dapper look was intriguing enough to make his belly
practically disappear.

The patio bustled with other hungry lunch-goers lapping up
the warm rays and chattering away with their companions. By the
time the appetizers arrived, Tess's eyes were watering from
laughter. Jim was doing spot-on impressions of English accents
from around the world: England, Australia, India, and even
Jamaica. By this point, other people were starting to stare because
once he got going, Jim's voice carried. When the meal arrived,
the food quieted them both down, and the stares ended.

Just before the check came, the sun shifted behind a cloud. Tess got a funny feeling. When the waiter placed the check on the table, Jim reached for it without question.

"Hmm. Well, well what do we have here?"

"Is something wrong?"

"No, no. Just shocked, that's all."

Her funny feeling grew.

"This is just the most expensive lunch I have ever had to pay for," he blurted. Tess quickly looked around to see if his audience had heard that. They appeared to have missed it. "But that's okay, because you're worth every penny of the seventy-eight dollars and nineteen cents, and not a dime more," he said with a smug smile.

Tess sat back puzzled. *Did he really just say that?* When the magnitude of his comment fully set in, she said, "Wow. Thank you so very much for defining my value in terms of dollars and cents," and got up from the table. "I hope you take those cents that I'm not worth and spend them on a girl who likes cheap pricks!"

Now, that the audience heard.

Tess didn't bother making a proper exit through the restaurant. Instead, she swiftly stepped over the white chain in her floppy skirt and heels and made a straight line for the Government Center T stop. No one was going to equate her value as a person with a lunch bill and continue to enjoy her company.

"I'm telling you, I nearly threw up my scallops all over him," she told Aimee later, after work.

"What a d-bag. I can't believe he said that!"

"Seriously. There's no way I'm ever speaking to him again. If only I could've seen his face when everyone was clapping for me as I walked away."

"Wait, people clapped for you?"

"Okay, I imagined that part, but I'm pretty sure he felt like an ass sitting there after I walked out on him," Tess mused as they continued to make fun of the situation for the rest of the night.

In the days and weeks after Kingfish Hall, Jim called incessantly. Tess's voicemail box was filled with apologies and pleas for another chance. Finally, she decided the madness needed to stop.

"Tess, thank you so much for picking up."

"Hi, Jim. What can I do for you?"

"I just wanted to tell you how very sorry I am. I never meant to say what I did. It just came out all wrong. I thought you would think it was funny. It was supposed to be joke."

"On what planet would a comment like that be funny?"

"Look, I'm here on my hands and knees trying to get you to accept my apology." *Interesting image.* She stayed silent. "Let me take you to Ninth on Park. It'll be great. You can order whatever you want. Drinks. Apps. Hell, order one of everything if you want." He paused. "Tess, I just want, need, to see you again."

She wondered where his desperation came from. It was only their third date. "Jim, that's sweet, but no. You and I just see the world differently. It was getting to know you. I wish you the best of luck. Please don't call me again."

Jim huffed and puffed. She let him whine like a child for about a minute. Then she politely told him that she was hanging up, and did. Seconds later Aimee burst into her room.

"You go, girl! I heard the whole conversation through the door."

"No you weren't?"

"At first I was, but I couldn't really hear everything so I got a glass. You know, like in the movies. It really does work. Clear as a bell. So, wow, that guy really did put a dollar value on you?"

"'Tis true."

"What a tool. I'm so proud of you! Finally some of that pre-Nick spunk is coming back!"

Aimee's comment was mildly insulting, but Tess let it go. It was more fun reveling in how good hanging up on Jim felt than to fight with Aimee. At twenty-eight years old, he really should have known better. As Aimee said, Tess was finally starting to "get it." Finally, she began to see through some of the garbage that people tossed on others, even if in the name of humor.

Her date with Jim was ultimately the last straw. She was exhausted. With her last year of graduate school starting in just weeks, Tess no longer had the time or patience to deal with dating. *So much for that six-month guarantee,* she thought. *A better guarantee would have been "Daters beware: like a guy and he won't like you. Dislike a guy and he won't go away."* That became Tess's disclaimer. On August 19, Tess deactivated her account.

By the end of what Tess liked to call her "dating escapades," she'd added five notches to her proverbial bedpost, for a grand total of eight. Despite not being altogether comfortable with her number, it was something she couldn't change. Instead of berating herself, she learned to accept it and work through the feelings of fear and loneliness rather than seek a new guy to fill those voids. She felt better able to recognize and listen to her red flag alerts. All those dates—the good, the bad, and the ugly—empowered her to tell guys what she really thought right there in the moment. Each man had given her insights into herself that she truly would not have discovered any other way. She now knew how to get any guy's attention, no matter how hot he was. She learned to tell the difference between the guy who was in the market for just one thing and the guy who was willing to put in more effort to get that one thing. Ultimately, Tess realized that should a man be out there for her, online dating was *not* the way she was going to meet him.

The best benefit of the change was that thoughts of Nick had been largely vanquished. When she went on a lame date, each time her desire for him diminished. Of course her drive to be a better graduate student than he was secretly spurred her on, which was a good thing. Her thesis paper on what she nicknamed "the diplomatic love triangle" between England, France, and Ireland, beginning with the Irish rebellion of 1798, wasn't going to finish itself.

It was a long final year. She pretty much holed up in the library, only coming out for food and sleep. She officially put dating on hold and learned that being single wasn't all bad when all her hard work paid off. She graduated with high honors and the frame of mind she needed to get a job and step out into the "real" world.

Part Three

Chapter 34

Tuesday, September 2, 2008

Sitting in her car, parked in her first professionally assigned spot, on her first day of teaching social studies at Evergreen High School in East Boston, Tess took a deep breath and prayed for the best. Evergreen High was known for its rough-and-tumble students as well as a high faculty turnover rate.

"Come on, Tess. You can do this." Then she noticed another teacher pull into the spot next to her. His scowling face told her he must be one of the veteran teachers. His frown quickly turned into a warm smile as soon as he caught Tess looking at him. She waved and smiled back. His presence prompted her to get out and proceed through the metal detectors and into her classroom.

Having spent the previous week setting up and decorating, Tess at least appeared ready. She certainly didn't feel ready, even though all of her course materials were printed, classroom rules and expectations were displayed throughout the room on various posters, and all her extra pens and pencils were full of ink or sharpened.

"Settling in okay?" Elaine Craft asked as she floated into the room. Elaine was Tess's assigned mentor. She was a twenty-four-year veteran of social studies. Astoundingly, all her years were earned at Evergreen High. After meeting over the summer a few times, they had already developed a friendly rapport.

"I think so. What do you think? Too much on the walls or not enough?"

Elaine took a quick look around. "It looks fine. Frankly, most of the kids don't even look at the walls until test time, when they're looking for the answers."

Tess chuckled a little.

"Now, remember today is the day in which you must make one student in each class your bitch."

Tess wondered if Elaine was serious or not. "Come again?"

"Yes, you heard me right. The first day of school is always make-a-bitch day. If you don't, classroom management will be impossible. Trust me on this one."

"And how does one do that exactly?"

"It's simple. You get on a kid's case for breaking the easiest of rules until you have to throw him or her out. It shows the rest of the class you mean business. I do it every year. Works like a charm."

"I'll keep that in mind."

"Good. I will leave you to it then."

Surveying the room, Tess sat back in her special-order teacher chair and thought about what Elaine had said. At first she laughed. It was absolutely ridiculous to make a kid her "bitch." *Me, Tess Ryan, make someone bend to my will? Ha! Like I could ever do that.* Yet as she sat there regarding what she had accomplished in just a week's time, it made more and more sense.

She had made it to twenty-five without the complications of getting hooked on drugs, having a baby, or not finishing college. She had not just a bachelor's degree but a master's as well, and she'd done it all on her own. At UMass, she couldn't go home for the weekend and have her laundry done for her. Though her father was a two-hour ride away in Boston, more often than not he was too busy scraping by to invite her over. It was the same story when Tess was in graduate school, despite being only a ten-minute train ride away.

Of course, she could make someone her bitch. She was Miss Tessalie Claire Ryan, survivor of divorced parents, multiple and sometimes lonely cross-country moves, Nick Donovan, graduate school, and even some dicey online dates. *High school kids will be nothing*, she thought. She smiled confidently and headed to the hallway to greet her first class.

By sixth period, Tess was tired but feeling good. She followed Elaine's advice and succeeded in letting the students in her previous classes know that she wasn't going to take any crap from anyone, especially her four bitches: Vernez, Josh, Gage, and Savannah. Heading into the second-to-last class of the day, Tess was fearless—at least until she met Ronnie DeCarlo.

A junior in her sixth-period US History class, Ronnie was a

hard read right away. One minute he was the devil incarnate, the next an angel. Tess never had any warning as to which version of Ronnie she was going to get. He also came with an individual education plan, known as an IEP, that looked about ten feet thick. It was a legally binding document that instructed his teachers as to what his learning disabilities were and how to make learning easiest for him.

Being a new teacher, Tess was curious and frightened by such documents, especially one as imposing as Ronnie's. This document said that Tess had to give him exorbitant praise any time he did something right. It didn't take long for the IEP to translate into a pass for Ronnie to not be held accountable for his actions as well as allow him to be lazy and disrespectful.

The nightmare that became the norm for sixth period was all Ronnie's work. If Tess got the class quiet, Ronnie riled everyone up. If Tess attempted a class discussion, Ronnie dragged everyone off topic. If Ronnie wasn't the center of attention, he found a way to become so. It only took a few weeks before Tess felt like she had already been through the wringer.

One day in November, Ronnie was actually quiet and on task. Tess had assigned a group activity in which each student had a clear and precise role. All the groups were producing and learning, even Ronnie's. Tess humored herself into thinking that there was hope for the class.

Fifteen minutes later, Ronnie began wandering from group to group, harassing the cute girls, pulling their hair, sneaking up behind them. Following special education protocol, Tess gave him several reminders to return to his own group, each lasting two minutes at best. Toward the middle of class, two girls asked Tess if they could work in the hallway. Trusting the girls, Tess granted their wish.

Barely five minutes later Tess heard, "Ronnie, stop! Stop! Ronnie, don't do it!" from one of the girls in the hallway. Tess flew out of the room. Ronnie was standing over the screaming girl, who was sitting on an adjacent stairwell, with a twisted water bottle, ready to launch the cap at her. By the expression on the girl's face she was clearly frightened.

"Ronnie, give me the water bottle and back away from Cheryl." Tess's tone was calm but firm.

"I didn't touch her, I didn't touch her!" he said, getting in Tess's face, physically threatening her. His stare ripped through her like a knife.

"Ronnie, give me the water bottle and back away," she said in the same firm, passionless voice. At this point, Tess considered the possibility of Ronnie hitting her. If he did, he would surely be out of her class for good.

"Miss Ryan, I didn't touch her. I didn't touch her," Ronnie said mildly, a little calmer, when he finally gave up the water bottle.

"Ronnie, go to the office."

"Are you fucking kidding me right now? This is bullshit! I didn't even fucking touch her," he yelled, storming back into the classroom. "She's such a bitch. Kicking me out when I didn't even do anything." Tess heard him announce to the students in the classroom. She bristled at his foul language and was tempted to call him on it, but she decided that getting into a screaming match with a sixteen-year-old wasn't the most important issue at the moment.

"Cheryl, are you all right?"

"I'm fine, Miss Ryan. Ronnie was just playing around. He wasn't really going to hit me."

Tess couldn't believe Cheryl just defended the guy who could have physically harmed her. It suddenly occurred to Tess that thanks to girls like Cheryl, defending such bad behavior, it was no wonder males practically got away with murder. This was a teachable moment not only for Ronnie.

"You know, Cheryl, you don't have to let boys treat you like that if you want them to like you." Tess paused, reading Cheryl's face. It was mostly blank. "You know guys like girls more if they respect themselves."

"Are you saying I don't respect myself, Miss Ryan?" Cheryl's expression now defensive.

"No, no, that's not what I'm saying at all. I just wanted—"

"I've known Ronnie since like forever. That's how we play here in Eastie. You'd know that if you were from around here, rich girl." Cheryl's hard stare gave Tess the chills.

"All right then." Tess stared at the girls for a moment before walking back to the classroom. She felt like a failure but also somewhat offended. She *was* from here—well, Brighton, which was notably less crime-ridden and slightly more affluent. Even so, she knew what it was like to struggle. Then something dawned on her: her own past with men.

The revelation shook Tess to her core. As if standing in the middle of a three hundred and sixty-degree room, all the times she allowed bad behavior flashed before her eyes. The newish guy, James, she had been seeing over the summer who she actually hadn't heard from in several weeks and who only called her after nine at night. Tucker at Banana Republic...the drunk at the Thai place...Nick...Oh God, Nick.

"Miss Ryan? Hello? Miss Ryan?" a female student called after she and the rest of the class had waited several minutes in silence for Tess to tell them what to do next.

"Hmm? Oh! Yes, right," Tess said, returning to the present. As she looked at her students with their bright eyes and quizzical faces, her cheeks flushed from embarrassment.

Although she attempted to salvage what she could of the lesson, Tess's attempt was in vain. The kids were no longer focused and neither was she. Finally, after ten topsy-turvy minutes, she gave the class the rest of the period to work on homework.

That night, Tess tossed and turned. She was unable to stop thinking about Cheryl defending Ronnie. She also couldn't stop thinking about allowing so much bad behavior from the men in her own past. She really should have pummeled Robbie Powell back in kindergarten after he kissed her, pushed her over, and then ran away laughing. Had she beaten him up it would have sent a message to the rest of the world: Don't mess with Tess. But alas, she just laid there stiff as a board, in shock, hoping nobody saw anything. Some redhead she could claim to be.

"Oh, God, stop it, Tess!" she shouted into the dark room. It was 3:36 in the morning, and she was drenched in sweat from her restlessness. "Get hold of yourself. That was then. This is now. You're an adult now. You know what you won't stand for, so just follow through. You're a redhead, for chrissake! You're supposed to be hot-tempered and feisty!" She was right. It would actually be good for her to speak up. Really, what were people going to do? Give her a dirty look? Yell back? Surely she could take that. She was an Irish Bostonian after all. It was finally time she acted like it.

The next day at school, Tess really should have stayed home, but she couldn't risk appearing like a weak first-year teacher, unable to handle bad behavior from one child. In the teachers' room, she was still fuming.

"If only I could just…that little jerk's…" Tess mumbled to her salad.

"Abusing your salad again, I see," Elaine said.

"Oh, yeah. Sorry," Tess said, returning to reality.

"Everything all right?"

"Yeah. Fine, thanks."

"Did something happen with that fellow you were seeing?"

"Who, James? No. I haven't heard from him in weeks. Guys

just seem to drop like flies around me. Ha!"

Elaine was silent, appearing unsure of what to say next. "Seeing anyone new, then?"

"Single and ready to mingle." Tess chuckled again, enjoying her little rhyme. She knew it wasn't funny, but she couldn't risk another interrogation about why she was still single.

"And how is your little friend Ronnie DeCarlo?"

"Oh, the usual. Attempting to physically harm any and everyone around him."

"Whaa? When was this?"

Other teachers in the room appeared to tune into their conversation.

"Yesterday. Girls screaming and Ronnie all up in my face swearing at me—it was great."

"What did you do?"

"Sent him to the office." Tess took a bite of salad. Then continued, "He won't receive any consequences, though. Just the other day he was hopping from desk to desk purposely knocking down student projects that were hanging from the ceiling. Not a single consequence for that."

"Oh, Miss Ryan, you're making that up!" Mrs. Cranston, a science teacher, cried from one of the couches.

"Cross my heart and hope to die, I'm not telling a lie."

"What did admin do?" Elaine asked.

"Like I said, nothing."

"Nothing? I find that hard to believe," Mrs. Cranston said.

"Nothing." Tess paused, staring at Mrs. Cranston's confused

face. "They gave him a slap on the wrist and told him not to do it again."

Elaine sat back, agape. "What the hell's going on in this place? That's insane! It's like the patients are running the asylum. When I first started teaching here—God, almost twenty-five years ago—stuff like that would never happen. Kids were expelled for looking at teachers funny. My God! Did you call the parent?"

"Uh-huh. Guidance, Ronnie's assistant principal, the president. Don't you worry. I completed all the documentation we're supposed to. CYA, as you say." Tess grinned at Elaine. Elaine smiled back.

"CYA? What's that?" Mr. LaDuke, a math teacher, asked.

"CYA, Martin, means cover your ass," Tess growled back. Martin LaDuke was the dullest, least imaginative person Tess had ever had the displeasure of working with. He also never called other teachers by their first name, which matched his naturally uptight nature.

"That's so inappropriate, Miss Ryan!"

"Why do you think I said CYA instead?" Tess growled again. She couldn't stand his constantly annoying rigidity. Though he was a brilliant math teacher, he had no sense of humor.

"Someone's got her panties in a bit of a twist, eh?" Mrs. Phillips, a snide English teacher, said.

"Excuse me, Mrs. Phillips?" Tess said. "Did you have a question?"

Mrs. Phillips looked at Tess for a moment without responding. Instead, she whispered to Mrs. Cranston, loudly enough for Tess to hear, "I bet if things had worked out with that James fellow, she wouldn't be nearly as frustrated all the time." Mrs. Cranston giggled, looked at Tess, and then jetted her eyes away. It was bad enough that Tess pitied herself for being single, but knowing her colleagues thought it was okay to do the same exacerbated her feelings of inadequacy.

"Thank you for mentioning that, Mrs. Phillips. I'll be sure to start sleeping around. Don't want to be too frustrated at work, do I now? Perhaps I'll start with your husband."

Mrs. Phillips looked shocked. By the look of it, no one had ever dissed her back like that. Tess looked at Elaine and promptly left the teachers' room.

Who was she kidding? Yes, Ronnie DeCarlo got under her skin. If she had the opportunity to vaporize him, she would. But when she considered what Mrs. Phillips had said, Tess couldn't disagree. Maybe if she did have someone special to come home to, brats like Ronnie DeCarlo wouldn't drive her to abuse her defenseless salads or explode into flames like she just did in the teachers' room.

Chapter 35

When Tess got home, she opened a fresh bottle of white wine, poured herself a glass, set the glass in the fridge, and walked into the empty living room carrying the rest. With the lights on and TV off, the only sound in the apartment was Tess swallowing straight from the bottle. The glass in the refrigerator was to cure the hangover the next morning. Letting the wine send the day's events farther and farther away, Tess grabbed a photo album from her bookshelf.

UMass 2001–2005

The first five pages of the album were a collage of the good old days. "Aw, we were so young!" Tess said to the pictures. "Oh, wait. What? Aimee, what on earth were you doing there?" Apparently Aimee's attempt at jumping a fence in her graduation robe had been caught on film. Tess laughed as she remembered the moment.

Her laughter stopped when she remembered being so certain that senior year was her year. That she was going to graduate with a boyfriend who would, by now, be her husband. "Such a stupid little fool, Tess. Stupid…little…fool." With another large gulp, she swallowed more wine and a growing lump in her throat as she turned the page.

Brie's Wedding 2006

"Brie, Brie, sweet Brie, you finally found your prince. And see, what did I tell you? You didn't need to lose a pound." Tess patted the top of Brie's head in a picture. "God, what is wrong with me! I'm half the size of Brie, and even she's married! I am so doomed. I'm never going to get married."

Boston College Graduation May 2008

An overwhelmingly bright sun bleached most of the BC graduation pictures. Tess and her family looked more like glowing orbs than humans. Tess remembered that day. She was so happy, looking forward to actually being paid to be at school. As she looked closely at a photo of herself alone, she noticed a guy standing behind her who looked very familiar.

"That can't be…? He wasn't there. Wait, is Nick?"

Her mini investigation proved that the guy in the photo was, in fact, not Nick. Why would it have been? They had been detached from one another's lives for a year and a half by then. Nostalgia brewed as she continued looking through her album.

Aimee's Wedding July 2008

Aimee made such a beautiful bride just a few months earlier. She was statuesque, with perfectly round accents in all the right places. God, the bride was happy that day. To think that if Tess hadn't made a stink about those vodka cranberries on that booze cruise, Jason and Aimee would never have met. Tess smirked and swigged some more wine, remembering that Jason had hit on her first.

"Damn it, I wish I was married! Why can't I get the pretty dress and have all those people ooh and aah at me?" Tess paused. "Oh, right, because of you, Mr. Nick. You didn't want to marry me!" The wine was clearly coloring her memories.

Tess turned the page and looked at a picture of her and a rather good-looking man. His arm was around her. He wasn't a groomsman, but the smile on Tess's face meant she was definitely enjoying his company.

"What was his name? He's so hot!" Tess stared into the mystery man's blue eyes. "Tim! That's right, it was Tim! Oh God, Tess and Tim—that would never have worked. I hate those couple names, like Jack and Jill. Tess and Tucker...ew. Oh, but Tim, you were so hot. Why did I let you go? Hmm, I wonder if you're still single?" Tess closed the album and sat motionless. Then a memory filled her mind.

It was just before Aimee got engaged to Jason in early 2007. It was a blustery March day and Aimee invited Tess out for coffee.

"So what's Jason's excuse this week?" Tess asked, referencing Aimee's naked finger.

"Oh, the usual. He's got a headache. It's raining."

"How can you be so cool about it? I'd be flipping out, like, every day."

"He's what I want, and if I'm what he wants then he'll ask. If he doesn't ask by the time I want him to, then I guess I'll hit the road," Aimee said confidently, in a way that told Tess she meant it. Tess couldn't figure out how a girl could live with someone for nearly a year and not have a ring on her finger. "Plus, I found the box."

Tess lost her breath for a moment. "That's such great news!" Immediately she was happy and jealous, feeling even more undesirable. "You must be so excited! Do you think it's going to happen soon? Does he know that you know?"

"Whoa, whoa! I just found it last night. And of course I'm excited! I hate to admit this, but I'm also a little bit relieved."

"You know, I remember when Nick was going to ask me— okay, when I *thought* he was going to ask me. I remember how amazing it was when he gave me that box," she said, referring to the necklace box, trying to convince both Aimee and herself.

"Tess, Nick was never going to ask you to marry him."

Tess recoiled. Aimee had always been honest with her, but never so sharp.

"You don't know that."

"Tess, it has been over a year."

Tess was silent. Then said, "Easy for you to say. You're friggin' engaged! I don't even know why we're talking about this. We haven't talked about Nick in forever."

"That's not true. Just yesterday you were talking about some conversation you two had in his office at UMass. Yeah, UMass, like years-ago UMass. I'm really worried about you. It's not healthy to hang on to someone like this."

Tess rolled her eyes. Aimee was a broken record.

"You know what, Tess? Fine. Enjoy your fantasy about Nick. Go on and dream about how he'll never call you again. How he'll never see you again." Aimee was heated. Tears flooded Tess's eyes. "Tess, he's gone, and he's never coming back."

Tess cried openly in response to Aimee's final words. She wasn't crying because it was news. Everything Aimee said was something Tess had thought herself a millions times. It just sounded so much worse when she heard it out loud.

"You don't know that," Tess said, swallowing hard before she made a dramatic exit from the cafe.

A few days later, Aimee apologized, explaining that was not why she'd wanted to go out for coffee. She felt horrible that things had spun out of control. Really, she'd just wanted to ask if Tess was interested in any of Jason's single friends.

Back in the present, tears rolled down Tess's cheeks once again. Desperate to squash the rest of her tears, she took a big gulp from the bottle. It spilled too quickly for her throat to accommodate, and she began to choke. As she thumped her chest, Tess noticed something under her hand. It was the white sapphire necklace Nick had given her in what felt like a lifetime ago.

Tess stopped choking immediately. Of all the nights for this to happen, why was it happening on a night she felt so single? It was a sign. It had to be. Nothing made it clearer that he was more than just an ex-boyfriend. He had to be her soul-mate. The timing just wasn't right yet. Perhaps now was finally the right time? For the rest of the night, Tess did the only thing that made her feel a little less single, which was to reminisce about the good times with Nick and think of the best way to get back in touch.

Chapter 36

The next day, Saturday, Tess woke up with a bell ringer of a headache but also with a resolution to get back out there. Despite wanting to find Nick right away, she knew she was out of practice when it came to dating. She thought it would be best to go on a few dates with other men first. That way she would get her jitters out and appear that much more desirable to Nick when they did finally reconnect.

She believed the best place to start was the Isabella Stewart Gardner Museum. She remembered that it was a place her mother often took her and Eve as children after Hugh had made her feel particularly horrible and ugly for simply asking him to contribute to his family.

Born in 1840, Isabella Stewart Gardner had a remarkable eye for art and a keen sense of interior design. She knew exactly how to highlight every piece in a room in the most effective way. Grace had once told Tess that sitting in those vast rooms of enduring art had revived her inner beauty, as if she were wrapped in a warm winter blanket after a cold day of sledding. Tess hoped her visit would do the same for her.

"One admission, please."

"Just one?" the grizzled ticket woman asked.

"Just one."

"All right then. That'll be fifteen dollars for one solo admission."

Tess found the woman's words odd. As she looked around the museum, she noticed that it was littered with couples. Tess took a deep breath and handed over fifteen single dollars. The woman chuckled as she counted each one.

"There you are. We close at five. Thank you for coming."

The sign to the right of the cash register clarified everything. It was a two-for-one weekend deal. Tess could not have felt more alone at that moment; she considered going home. *Whatever*, she thought. *Stay strong. Maybe my guy is there, in the Gothic Room, waiting for me.*

The Gothic Room was her favorite. The large open space catapulted her back to a dark and mysterious time. Fear and curiosity ran through her simultaneously. She wanted to run and hide, all the while feeling safe in that room. Perhaps it was because this was the room where John S. Sargent had been an artist-in-residence. Tess felt his energy, as if he were still painting next to her, even though he'd last been there nearly one hundred years ago. Tess found a spot to sit and began doodling in a notebook she found buried in her purse.

"Tess Ryan? Is that really you?" a familiar voice asked.

"Who's asking?" she replied, playfully not lifting her eyes from the page, just as a focused artist might. She could feel a man loom right in front of her, forcing her to look up.

"So it really is you," Nick Donovan said.

Tess was momentarily paralyzed. How was it that just last night she was thinking about him and now he was here, in the flesh, standing in front of her? She must have been dreaming.

"Nick? What are you doing here?"

"Just thought it would be something nice to do." He looked down at her notepad and then back at her face. A curious look crossed his face. "I would never have thought I'd run into you like this." His smile instantly forced her eyes down to his left hand. She was surprised at what she saw and couldn't stop herself from smiling. It was bare.

"Want a seat?"

They sat in awkward silence for a little while.

"So what's new?"

"Ah, well, teaching at Evergreen. It's my first year."

"No kidding? Tough school, I hear."

"It has its moments, that's for sure."

"Good for you," he said, followed by a conscious pause. They began smiling at each other as they had all those years ago.

"You look good, Tess."

"Thanks." He looked good too. He barely looked a minute older than the last time she'd seen him. A little tired maybe, but that was to be expected. Something in his appearance told her life had molded him in a good way.

"So how long has it been since I last saw you?" He paused. "A while, right?"

"Something like that." It had been exactly one year, ten

months, and a few days.

"What have you been up to all this time? Getting your first teaching job, yes, but what else?" His questions were calm and comfortable, despite how obvious it was that he was fishing for information.

"You know, living the dream. Taking in the sights."

Nick's laughter had a relaxing effect. "There's the Tess I remember. Always cagey, yet intriguing." She turned and looked him squarely in the face, about to pounce.

"Excuse me?" *What the hell is that supposed to mean?*

"Come on, you know what I mean. You've always had this incredibly intriguing, yet guarded, way about you," he paused. Then added carefully, "It's hot."

Staring at him, she tried to picture herself as *cagey*, an adjective she would never have selected to describe herself. In her mind, *candid* and *sweet* were more apt. Then she remembered the night they broke up. Her expression became more somber as the memory played through her mind. *Oh my God, cagey* is *appropriate*, Tess thought. Then she began to chuckle.

"What's so funny?"

"Oh, nothing."

"Right."

"Okay, okay. I was just thinking about what you said. You might be onto something."

"How so?"

"I was thinking about the last time I saw you. We were fighting. You were so mad because I wouldn't answer a question.

I think you may be onto something about me, Mr. Donovan." Everything suddenly shifted into perspective for her. *Be less cagey and get more of what you want.* But for some unknown reason Nick wasn't laughing. His body became stiff. She placed her hand on his forearm in hope of relaxing him.

"Thank you."

Nick looked down at her hand on his arm. "Ah, you're welcome?"

They looked each other straight in the eyes, as if they were going to kiss.

"Nick? Nick! There you are. I've been looking all over this weird place for you. Can we go now? It's so creepy here," said a young blonde wearing a skirt so short it would make a streetwalker feel lewd.

"Jen, hey, there you are."

Tess quickly removed her hand from his arm.

"Who's she?" Jen asked.

Nick quickly rose from his seat and stood next to the squawking parrot-like girl. "Oh, yeah. Jen, this is Tess. Tess, this is Jen."

Jen's thorough up-and-down made Tess feel like she was under a microscope. Once Jen appeared to have had made her final judgment, she cocked her head to the side and shrugged her shoulders. "Nicky, can we go? This place gives me the willies."

"Sure. Just give me a minute."

"Whatever. I'm going to the car."

"Wow," Tess said, watching Jen walk away. "Not her thing, I

take it."

"Guess not."

"So, Jen's your plus-one?"

"Jen? Ah, yeah, something like that."

"Well, it's a good thing you guys got the couples' discount today."

"Ha ha. Right." Nick paused. "So, ah, are you here with anyone?"

"Just me, myself, and I."

"Nice to see you're really taking advantage of the discount."

Ouch. Thanks, Nick. Way to drive the knife in and twist it. Then his cell phone started screaming.

"Jen's lost. She needs help finding the exit. Hey it was really nice to see you again, Tess."

"She can't find the exit?"

"Yeah, being on the third floor is a little confusing for her."

"Right. Well, go save your *friend.*"

"Yes. Thanks." He waited, staring at Tess for a moment. When she went back to doodling, he took a deep breath and let her be.

The doodling only lasted until Nick was safely out of sight. Once he was definitely gone, Tess sat back and used every fiber of her self-control to not lose it. Never in a million years would she have thought Nick would be with such an ignorant, sleazy, whiny brat. The girl couldn't have been more than twenty years old. It was insane to Tess that someone could be freaked out by so much beautiful art. *And how did she not remember she was on the third floor? Nick couldn't possibly be with a girl like that.* But any way she tried to spin it, finding out that Nick had someone felt like salt on the open wound that was her heart.

Chapter 37

Thanksgiving, which arrived just a couple of weeks after Nick and Tess ran into each other, was the time Aimee and Jason, Tess, and Hugh, along with his woman of the hour, gathered at Tess's apartment and played nice in exchange for food. Now that Aimee had married Jason, Tess had been compelled to get her own place, a small one-bedroom apartment. It was cozy, and everyone was happy to sit around a folding table, in folding chairs, in the middle of her living room. Like the previous years they had shared, Tess was thankful for Aimee's presence. If she weren't there, Tess would certainly have had words with a few of Hugh's pseudo girlfriends.

Thanksgiving 2008 was no different. This one's name was Gina. She had an obnoxious laugh and a reprehensible flare for everything trashy, from clothing to makeup and, of course, hair dye. But trashy seemed to be all her father could handle when it came to women. Their lack of sophistication usually meant they lacked the ability to stay committed, which suited him just fine.

Gina began the conversation as everyone sat down to dinner. "And Tess, your father has told me so much about you. You're a teacher. How respectable! He also tells me you have a great guy in your life. What's his name again?" She looked at Hugh for the answer. Tess smirked and couldn't wait to hear what name Hugh had given the imaginary boyfriend this year. Tess was used to Hugh making her appear like the perfect child he so often claimed he'd raised all by himself. "Nick! That's it. Speaking of which, where is he? I would have thought he would be here."

Tess glared at her father. *Does he know I ran into him a couple of weeks ago? Is he taking out some of his rage at my mother, brought on by Gina, onto me,* Tess wondered.

"Really, Dad? Of all names you could choose, you choose *Nick*? Christ, thanks a lot, Dad," Tess said and went to her room.

"Oh, Hugh, did they break up? Why didn't you say anything? That was so cruel," Gina cried.

"Don't worry, Gina, Tess is fine. A bit dramatic, but fine." Aimee paused. "Nick's just the one that got away—you know how that is."

"Oh no, should I go talk to her? I'm so sorry. Had I known I wouldn't have said anything."

"It's okay. I'll go check on her."

Tess was facedown on her bed with a big fluffy stuffed toy under each arm. Aimee closed the bedroom door loudly enough for Tess to know that she was there without startling her.

"Hey, Tessie, are you okay?" Aimee asked gently from the end of the bed.

"Don't call me *Tessie*." Her face still buried in pillows.

"I'll only stop calling you Tessie if you sit up and tell me what's wrong, *Tessie*."

"God, I hate you!" Tess said, springing erect. Her face was red from crying and breathing in her own recycled breath.

"I know. I love you too. Now what's going on? Gina actually doesn't seem that bad. She scolded your dad, and she wanted to come in and apologize."

"Really? That's so nice." Tess paused. "I'm the one who should apologize. It has nothing to do with Gina. Hell, not even with my dad for once."

"Well, then, what is it?"

"I ran into Nick a couple of weeks ago, when I went to the Gardner Museum."

"Seriously? Why didn't you tell me?"

"Because he was with this moronic blonde—"

"Watch it!"

"Sorry, but she was a moron, and her hair was blonde. She couldn't find the exit from the third floor."

"Ooh, yeah. That's pretty bad."

"Anyway, for whatever reason, he's with her. *Her!* Aimee, what's wrong with me? Why can't I find anybody? Is there something I don't know?"

Aimee put her arm around Tess. "There's nothing wrong with you, Tess. These things take time, you know."

"Right. Like with you and Jason, or Brie and Mark. Hell, even my two-timing father always has a girlfriend. Something's got to be wrong with me."

"Tess, trust me. There's nothing wrong with you. You'll find someone when you're ready. I just know it."

"What do you mean by *ready*?"

"You have to be ready for it."

"But I've been ready since I was, like, ten."

"Remember when I met Jason? I was just along for the cruise. I didn't think I was going to meet anyone."

"You always meet someone, Aimee, even when snot is exploding from your face."

"Oh, that's so not true!"

"Remember that guy Eli at the drugstore, when you had bronchitis last year?"

Aimee had to think for a minute. "Oh yeah! Okay, well, that was just a freak occurrence."

"Whatever. He would've taken you home anyway, ring and all."

"The point is, Tess...when I met Jason, I was just looking to have a good time. I didn't have any expectations."

Suddenly interrupting, Tess's phone rang. Her palms suddenly were slick with sweat. Only one person could cause that reaction. *How is it even possible that he is calling at this very moment? Don't answer it. Let him sweat it out,* she told herself. *What is he doing? It's Thanksgiving. He has a girlfriend. Don't answer, Tess! Do not answer!*

"Hello." *Crap.*

"Hi, Tess. It's Nick. How are you?"

"Well, thanks. You?"

"Fine, fine." Just then it was clear they had both run out of things to say. "Yeah, so I'm calling to apologize."

"Apologize for what?"

"For leaving so abruptly...at the museum."

"Don't worry about it."

"Well, still. I'm sorry."

Tess grinned uncontrollably. Hearing his voice issue an apology was magnificent. "Was that all?"

"I think so?"

"You think so, eh? Well, how about you call me back if something else comes up, okay?"

"Sounds good."

"Great. Well, I'll talk to you later."

"Great. I'll talk to you later too."

Tess lowered her phone to her lap and let out a prepubescent girl squeal through a mile-wide grin.

Aimee gave her a perturbed look. "There's no way. How? Why would he be calling you now?" Aimee didn't look pleased. Then Tess's phone rang again.

"Look, I'm sorry," Nick said. "And I just wanted to tell you that it was really nice to see you again."

Tess's smile became brighter. "It was nice to see you too."

Aimee cocked her head to the side with a look of confusion when she heard Tess agree that it was nice to see him again too. She must have been able to hear him through the phone. Tess shooed Aimee away, but she didn't budge.

"How's your Thanksgiving going?"

"Great. I'm hosting. I assume you're busy with family too."

After a brief silence Nick said, "Hey, would you like to go out for a cup of coffee? Just two old f—"

"How about tomorrow afternoon?"

"—riends getting...Wait, what?"

"I'm free tomorrow."

Aimee flapped her arms and said no as loudly as she could without making a sound. Tess turned her back on her.

"Really? Okay, great. How does two at that little place in Brookline we used to go to sound? What was it called? Christina's?"

Tess's heart exploded with excitement. Christina's was their café cuddling spot. She remembered that they used to walk in there out the rain, arm-in-arm, and burrow into a warm corner with mugs of hot chocolate or tea. Sometimes she would read a book or the newspaper. Other times, she would simply people-watch. Nick, on the other hand, always read the newspaper, starting with the sports section.

"Christina's sounds great," she said. After working out the logistics, Tess hung up, and sat there frozen in la-la land.

"That better be some other Nick."

"He wants to get coffee at Christina's tomorrow."

"Nick Donovan? You've got to be kidding me!"

"That's right. *My* Nick Donovan," Tess answered dreamily, worlds away in a torrid fantasy.

"Oh, God. You're not going to go, right?" Of course Tess was going. It was written all over her face. "Promise me you won't go?"

Tess laid her hand on her chest, patting the now clean and shiny necklace she put back on just that morning. "Aimee, I've got to go! What if that Jen chick was just a blind date? What if she is just a friend?"

"Trust me, Tess, you don't want to go back down that road again."

Tess wasn't in the mood to repeat this old conversation again. She signaled that the conversation was over by wiping her face and readjusting her hair and top before she returned to the table.

"Sorry, Gina. That was Nick on the phone just now. He won't be able to leave his family tonight, so we're going to get together tomorrow."

"Since when were you with Nick?" Jason asked.

"Since we've been together, Jason. Now shut up and eat some more green beans."

"Tess, is there something going on that, as your father, I should know about?" Hugh leaned closer to his daughter.

"Oh, nothing, Dad. Just a change of plans, that's all."

"I can't believe you, Tess," Aimee said as she rejoined the table. "Gina, Nick was—"

"The guy I met in college and have been with ever since," Tess said. Tess was playing up the fantasy.

Gina nodded, trying to follow.

"Tess, it's okay to be single. You don't have to hide it," Hugh said. Leave it to Hugh to not tell anyone when he was changing his story. And just like that, Tess's charade was over. "Think about all the time I spent single before I found my wonderful Gina."

"You can't be serious. Dad, you were with Sheila right up until you met Gina." Tess didn't hesitate before throwing a jab back at her father.

"Hugh, is that true?" Gina looked like she was one word from detonating.

"Well, ah, not exactly. We broke up, but we were, ah, just figuring things out when you came along. Once I met you, it was Sheila who?"

Gina was clearly unconvinced. She stood and stormed off to the bathroom. Instead of following her, Hugh happily turned to his mashed potatoes.

"Good one, Dad."

"She'll get over it," Hugh said without looking up. "Tessie, these are great mashed potatoes. Wonderful, wonderful, wonderful."

"And here's to another eventful evening with the Ryans," Jason said. Both Aimee and Tess gave him the stink eye.

"Tess, I know you're dying to be with someone, but Nick isn't that someone. Trust me," Aimee said. "Don't you remember all the times he let you down and broke your heart?"

"And how do you know, Aimee? It's not as though I have guys lining up to go out with me. Hell, once Jason saw you, it was like Tess who?" Tess had never uttered a word about Jason's initial attraction to her in public before, and now, apparently shocked, Jason choked on the beer he had sipped. "Whatever. Everyone tells me to get over Nick, just let him go. Okay, fine, but tell me how. How do I get over someone I have loved since I first saw him?"

The room fell silent. Tess looked at each guest's face. Hugh was busy eating, completely oblivious to the world around him. Jason followed Hugh's lead, and Aimee met Tess's gaze. Aimee held it until Tess finally broke the silence. "I'm not feeling well. I think I'm going to go lie down. Help yourselves to whatever you want for leftovers. Tupperware is in the third drawer below the silverware."

From there, Tess left her own party and went to her room for the rest of the night to dream of Nick. *To hell with what everyone thinks!*

Chapter 38

The next day, hell-bent on filling the void and proving everyone wrong, Tess focused only on the positive. She no longer cared if Nick was single or not. Once and for all, she was going to make him love her, no matter what.

Nick had hinted about picking Tess up, but she didn't like the idea of sitting in a car with him so early in their reunion. He wasn't allowed to have any sort of advantage just yet. At the very least, she wanted the playing field to be even.

Arriving first, Tess noticed the waiting line right away. It practically looped around the block. If her memory served her right, this had to be the first time Christina's was so packed. Back when she and Nick were regulars there were always open tables. Tess couldn't help but wonder what changed. Then as her thoughts ran away from her, a feeling of dread washed over. Was this a sign that they weren't meant to get back together? Was the universe saving her from future embarrassment? Just as she was about to launch into a full on tizzy, several couples vacated their tables. Feeling slightly relieved, Tess smiled and told herself at least one table would open up by the time Nick joined her.

Speaking of which, where was he? Looking at the time on her

cell phone, and seeing no missed calls or texts from his truly, Tess learned he was already fifteen minutes late.

Fighting trepidation and doubt, Tess silently debated what to do. Call? No. She would look far too eager. Text? No, he would think her rude, being that he was most likely still driving and all. Or was he? Oh no, was he blowing her off, already?

Feeling the prick of tears behind her eyes, Tess fixed her gaze on the painting of bursting strawberries hanging just above the cash register. Her mind still raced, but her heart wouldn't allow her to leave. *Just a little longer,* she thought. She stood frozen in the middle of the entryway, studying the painting. After another five minutes there was a tap on her shoulder.

Without hesitation, Tess threw her arms around him saying, "You made it! I was starting to worry!" With the embrace over, Tess noticed an odd look on Nick's face, causing her to think the hug was too much. *So much for playing it cool,* she thought.

"Hmm. Interesting…what was that for?"

Crap. Old habits die hard? Sensing an unequal lack of enthusiasm, she began to feel the urgency to justify herself and say, "Sorry about that. I was just so scared you'd ditched me once again, and, and…" but Tess stopped it. Instead she said, "What? I'm not allowed to worry about you? I mean you are twenty minutes late and you could've called, like you've done—"

Nick interrupted her. "I'm here now aren't I?" He gave her a reassuring smile. "Now stop worrying and let's get out of here."

"But you picked this place? I don't mind waiting a little longer."

"I see, but the thing is I can't wait. I'm starving. Plus, I never really liked the food here that much anyway."

This was news to her. She had distinct memories of him gushing about their chocolate hazelnut crepes despite the fact that it was such a girlie thing to eat. "Right. What are you in the mood for then?"

"Something easy. No fuss. How about pizza?"

Pizza? He drove an hour and a half for plain old pizza? Tess got a funny feeling but pushed it away. Now was not the time to be impertinent. Reluctantly, she said, "If that's what you'd like." But that funny feeling refused to be ignored. "You know, on second thought, there's a Thai place just down the street that I think would be better."

"Thai?" Nick looked like he was considering it. "Yeah, I could do Thai. Lead the way."

Having finished a delightful meal, much more satisfying than pizza, and now waiting for the check, the conversation fell still by what Tess felt needed to be said but that she and Nick had done a great job equally avoiding. It was as if an elephant were sitting at the table next to them and neither of them dared to say a word about it.

"All right, someone needs to just say it." Nick began. He waited until Tess met his gaze. "It's been too long, and the way things were left between us, wasn't great."

Finally, there it was, the elephant. "Me too. All the craziness, the misunderstandings. I had no clue what I was doing," Tess said so fast the words spewed out. Nick laughed a hearty chuckle. Tess delighted in hearing his laugh again. Staring into each other's eyes, they shared a warm silence.

Moments later, the waitress dropped the check between them. Wanting to prove her maturity, Tess reached for it. She got there first, but only by a few seconds. Feeling his hand upon hers, she froze. Shock waves of electricity flowed all the way up her arm. His hand was just as warm and strong as it had always been.

"Well, well, well," Nick said.

"Well...," she managed. Throwing his hands in the air, Nick surrendered. In the end, Tess wished that he had paid. If he had, it would have meant they were on a date.

They walked slowly back to Nick's car. Nick spotted it before Tess did, which she knew because he began playing with his keys. It was a quirk she remembered from the past. *Is he in a hurry to leave? Did I miss something?* Her mind swirled with thoughts of what she could possibly have done wrong, other than what happened at Christina's earlier. She was trying her hardest not to revert into that idiotic, lovestruck puppy that she had once been with him. She couldn't let all her personal growth go down the tubes. *Stay strong, Tess, stay strong,* she told herself. *I didn't do anything wrong. If he has a problem, it's his—not mine.*

Nick was noticeably quiet when they reached his car. Before Tess could sort out a reason for that, her back was against the driver's side door and Nick's lips were firmly planted on hers.

Resist and push him away or give in and kiss him back? It felt so good, so familiar, and so right. She gave in and kissed him back, but only for a nanosecond.

"What the hell, Nick!" she said, shoving him away.

"What?" He looked totally confused.

"What do you think you're doing?"

"Oh! Oh, God, you have a boyfriend?"

She waited a bit. Watching him squirm was intriguing.

"No boyfriend."

"Then why did you push me off?"

So much for all or nothing. She didn't know why but something told her to do it. Tess folded her arms with a bewildered look. This was all too similar to that night in January. She had to say something. Anything. "What about Jen?" Nick fell silent and leaned on the car next to his. "I knew it. She *is* your girlfriend. Your silence says it all. God, Nick."

Suddenly feeling caught red handed, Nick hesitated. "How does she always see through me," he asked silently. While wondering, he found himself wanting to tell her exactly how things were, but he knew she wouldn't understand. It was complicated. He was single...well, sort of. There were several women in his life, none of whom he was that serious about. Jen was just one of them. The problem was he liked different things about all of them. He often thought if he could take the different parts and put them into one woman, he would have...Tess?

After a long silence, he responded. "Tess, I'm not attached.

Yes, there are a few women I spend time with, but I'm not committed to any of them." Nick looked ready to duck and cover after the rare moment of honesty.

Tess was silent. She was clearly thinking about what he had just said. "I'm sorry you distrust women so much. You must be terribly lonely." He felt her stare at him, as if searching for an opening. As if she wanted to tell him everything was all right, that not all women were whatever he feared, but she didn't say anything.

"I'd better get going. Don't want to get stuck in traffic. Can I give you a ride?"

Tess took a deep breath. "Thanks, but I'm going to walk."

"It's really no trouble."

"It's so nice out for the end of November. I don't want to miss the opportunity."

"If you say so."

"Hey, drive safe."

Nick gave her a weird smile and then was off.

Once out of sight, Tess called a cab. It wasn't actually that nice out and the walk to her apartment would have taken over an hour. She wished she had driven instead of taken the T.

In the cab everything began to sink in: the kiss, the *multiple* girlfriends, his uneasiness after her hug. She didn't know what to make of it all. Did Nick want her back, or did he want just another notch? Did she even want him back? Why was he so weird about the hug? It was just a hug. And that easy no fuss comment continued to plague her. Why did she get such a horrible feeling when he said it? He was just talking about pizza, right?

Chapter 39

Nick called Tess as soon as he got home, but the call went directly to voicemail. He left a message, confident she would call back within the hour. Hours passed, and his phone remained silent. At nine Nick left the following message. "Hey Tess, Nick again. Ah, hmm. I don't know if you're purposely not answering or if your phone died, but could you call me when you get this?"

When Tess was in grad school, Nick never had to wait more than an hour for her to call back. *Maybe she doesn't want anything to do with me?* He had never felt this kind of anxiety over a woman. It made him do things he never would have considered in the past, like join Facebook.

As an extremely private person, he had never found Facebook appealing. Several times during the profile-building process he almost gave up, concerned about the security of his information. He never wanted any of his students, past, present or future, to find him. But when he thought of Tess, he got back on track.

Much to his disappointment, Tess was nowhere to be found. He thought that was odd. He remembered seeing her on Facebook regularly. He searched by name, school, location, even her e-mail address. Nothing. Nick threw his hands up and abandoned his account.

That night his mind just wouldn't let him sleep. One line kept playing over and over in his mind: "You must be terribly lonely." With a sharp turn from his left side to his right, he shouted, "No! I'm not lonely! Well, I'm not *that* lonely..." He rubbed his face with both hands. Behind his closed eyes, the image of Tess's concerned eyes pierced his heart. "Okay, so I'm lonely. Yeah, I've got a few women. So what? None of them are like Tess." Nick continued talking to himself. "Tess just gets me. I don't have to be someone I'm not when I'm with her."

Hearing his true feelings out in the open calmed his mind. He felt as if a heavy weight had been lifted. He was officially finished with all the women he was seeing, especially Jen. No more calls, no more text messages. If they tried to reach him, he just wouldn't answer.

Then something occurred to him. Another option to get in touch with her was to actually go to her apartment in person, but he remembered that she'd moved. He had no idea where she lived and thus was at a loss, until he remembered Aimee. He had met her at her office a few times with Tess before the three of them used to head to Red Sox games.

He remembered the power of Aimee's influence over Tess. He hoped she would be on his side and help him find Tess. It wouldn't be easy by any means, but he had to at least try.

Thursday after work, Nick raced to Boston. When he arrived at

565 Boylston Street, he was relieved to see Aimee's shop sign. It had been updated and was a little nicer than the last time he saw it: Babs Designs and Sews, Inc. It was clear that in the years since graduating from UMass, Aimee had turned her design skills and eye for trends, as well as her parents' financial support, into a healthy fashion business.

Walking into the shop, he tucked in his shirt and straightened his tie, stowing the bouquet of roses meant for Tess under his arm as he did so. He'd use the flowers as bait to persuade Aimee to talk, if necessary. He caught the eye of several women who were either shoppers or employees—he wasn't sure which—and quickly darted his eyes away.

"What do we have here? Nick Donovan in the flesh," Aimee called out, entering the swanky showroom from the back. She wore pointy high heels that put her at eye level with him. Her tight bun and crisp black suit intimidated him. It didn't help that the look on her face said loud and clear that he was absolutely the last person on earth she wanted to see. He gulped and thought of his goal. He held the bouquet out to her.

"Aimee! Hi. It's good to see you!"

"What on God's good earth are *you* doing here?" She ignored the roses and the people around her who were staring.

"Can we take this somewhere more private?"

"Fine." Aimee led him into her office and shut the door behind him. "All right, Nick, why the hell are you here? What are you pulling this time? You and I both know that she—"

"I'm not pulling anything. I just really need to get in touch with her." Aimee's right eyebrow lifted. "I've called several times and texted her, and she hasn't responded. You know that's not like her. I need to know if she's okay."

"She's fine. If she wanted to talk to you, she'd call you back. Looks like she's finally come to her senses. Praise the Lord." Aimee raised her hands as if to pray.

"Look, I get it. You don't like me very much, but what happened between Tess and me was a long time ago. We're different people now."

Nick could tell Aimee wasn't buying a word he said. She leaned against her desk and crossed her arms. "Why? Why now? As you said, it's been years."

"You're right, but as I'm sure she told you, we ran into each other recently. Since then, I haven't been able to stop thinking about her."

"Wow, that's riveting. I really feel for you. I watched a movie with Leonardo DiCaprio, and a week later I'm still thinking about *him*. God, he is just so dreamy. Hey, maybe I'll fly out to LA and bring his agent some roses and then we'll be together forever too!"

Nick struggled to keep his cool. *Aimee is a real bitch.* "Aimee, it's not like that. Trust me. You've got to help me out. Will you call her and tell her that I'm here? Tell her I'll wait for her or go anywhere she wants to meet."

Aimee didn't bat an eye. She stood in front of him, immovable as a stone wall.

"Come on, Aimee, you're a woman. You know what being

head over heels for someone is like. What it's like to beg, borrow, and steal for that person."

"I remember I used to have to fantasies of some guy making grand sweeping gestures, just as you're trying to do now. I remember even being a little jealous when I found out Tess's little crush on you was reciprocated, but you know what, Nick? I know what kind of guy you really are. Don't you think for a minute I haven't forgotten about that night at the Moan and Dove."

Nick felt his face flush but he remained resolute. Aimee was being so difficult he didn't feel she deserved an explanation. "I'm going to find Tess and make this right, with or without your help," he said forcefully. The air was thick with tension. Aimee's demeanor was stoic, but he could tell she was angry.

Then without warning, Tess walked through the door.

"What the hell is this?" The panic in Tess's voice filled the office. Her eyes locked on the red roses. Suddenly all the years of Aimee discouraging her relationship began to make sense: she and Nick were having an affair. Tess swallowed hard telling herself this wasn't actually happening. She noticed Aimee glare at Nick. He quickly handed the roses to Tess.

"Tess, these are for you."

She took the flowers mechanically.

Looking at the clock, Aimee said, "Crap, I forgot we were meeting for yoga."

"You're okay," Nick said to Tess, relieved. "When you didn't call me back, I got worried. So I found Aimee's shop and pleaded for your address. I was—"

"Wait? You came all this way on a school night just for me? I don't know what to say." Tess suddenly focused a thousand-watt smile on him. "My God, I'm so sorry I didn't call you back. School has just been insane. Oh, I can't believe you came all the way up here to see if I was okay." Tess inhaled her roses. "That's so sweet."

Nick sent Aimee a victorious glare.

"Tess, can I talk to you for a minute? Alone," Aimee said. She stared coldly at Nick. He got the hint and left the room. "Tess, don't do this again. Please, for the love of all things holy, don't do this again."

"Aimee, he just drove an hour and a half to come see if I was okay. He brought red roses! I owe him a conversation at least."

"Tess, you don't owe him anything! He is sucking you in. He's using you. He doesn't care about anything except his ego."

"Really? What does he ego gain by coming here?"

Aimee suddenly stood up, shaking her shoulders. It looked like she was gearing up for something big. Then she said, "Nick kissed me."

"He what?"

"Nick kissed me at the Moan and Dove back in college. Well, tried anyway. I put my hand over my mouth and then slapped him."

"You're making that up. That's not even possible. Why? How would you two be at the Moan and Dove together?"

"It's true. Ask him."

"God Aimee, you just won't let me be happy with the guy of my dreams will you?"

Tess's mind was spinning. Aimee wouldn't do that to her. They were best friends. Remembering that Nick was waiting for her, she knew going out with him was not an opportunity she could afford to squander. After several long moments of silence, Tess prepared to leave.

"Tess, I swear—if you start seeing him again, our friendship is over," Aimee said to the back of Tess's head. Tess didn't turn around. She left the office, clinging to the hope that her dear friend was once and for all totally wrong about Nick.

Chapter 40

Of all times to be tongue tied, this had to be one of the worst. At least this time it wasn't because her mind was blank. Quite the opposite actually. Her head swirled with questions. Had he really kissed her? Had Aimee seduced him the whole time she was after him? Did they hook up when she was at BC? How did they even connect in the first place? Why did they connect?

"Hey, Tess. Are you okay? You've barely said a word or touched your wine since we sat down ten minutes ago." Nick pushed her glass closer to her. They were at Joe's All American Bar and Grill. Tess didn't move. "I thought you were happy to see me? Did I upset you already?"

"Did you actually kiss Aimee?"

Nick threw his head back with a deep breath, then said, "So she just told you?"

"Answer the question."

"That was years ago Tess. What does it matter now?"

"She's my best friend, was my best friend. I don't know! How could you do that to me?" Tess felt her ability to not cry weaken. Her lower lip quivered.

"Hey, hey. I didn't even know she knew you. I only learned

that after she slapped me." Nick reached for her hand. She pulled away. Taking the hint, Nick proceeded to explain what happened that night.

"At least you have the same story. But what I don't understand is why on Earth you kissed her. It's not like it was a date."

Nick sat back. He rubbed the back of his neck in what looked like distress.

"Well? What was so bad Nick? Did you fail a class? Were getting evicted?"

Bracing himself, he said, "That day I received a letter from my ex fiancé—"

"You were engaged!"

"Briefly. Yes. It was just after I finished undergrad. It was all very fast. I should've known it wasn't going to work out."

Rendered speechless, Tess had a sinking feeling that there was more to come and took a large gulp of wine.

"Anyway, I hadn't talked to her in two years. Then out of no where this letter shows up. I was in complete shock. There was no way anything she said was true," he paused and stared at Tess. "She'd said she had a baby and that it was mine..."

"Holy shit! You have a kid?"

"Keep your voice down. And no, he's not mine. The night before she ended our engagement, she slept with some other guy named Ben. Based on the kid's birthday, he's definitely Ben's, not mine."

"That doesn't mean anything. He could still be yours."

"Jesus Tess, what kind of man do you think I am? Do you really think if there was any chance the kid was mine I wouldn't take care of it?" Nick's words stung. Of course he wasn't the kind of guy who would skip out on a child that he helped create.

"You're right. I'm sorry. This is all just so much to take in."

"So now you see my mind was completely messed up that night?"

"God, half an hour ago I thought you were just a ah..." She didn't know what to call their past. "And now I find out you were engaged to a woman who thinks you're the father of her child. I feel like I have no idea who you are. Why didn't you tell me any of this?"

"How could I?"

He had a point. If he had, she probably would have labeled him damaged goods and moved on. She could barely deal with her own baggage, much less an ex fiancé and love child. Nick's confidence that the kid wasn't his reassured her. Focusing on that, Tess realized at their ages, there was bound to be some bruises. So if she were to stick to her proclamation to once and for all make him love her she would have to make some allowances.

After a rather long silence and a deep breath, Tess asked, "Are you hungry? Want some dinner?"

"I think that's a good idea."

They put the heavy conversation on hold while they figured out food. Just after it arrived, Tess picked up where they left off, well sort of. "Well, that was heavy."

"You can say that again."

"I appreciate you being so honest."

"And I'm sorry I didn't tell you sooner."

Tess hesitated more for herself, then said, "So we're good?"

"We're good."

"Great. Then I have to ask you. What brought you to Boston tonight?"

Nick was slow to start. "Well, after I saw you last week, I realized you were right. I am lonely and I've denied it for a long time. Sure I was heartbroken after my fiancé left me. Then I met you. You just got me so much so it made me break rules. Then I let the fear of getting caught get in the way of how I truly felt about you." Nick paused. "Anyway, when I ran into you at the museum, it got me thinking. There has to be a reason why you and I keep reuniting."

"Okay, who put you up to this?"

"No one put me up to anything. It's the truth. I know it sounds phony and ridiculous, especially in this moment, but you were a student. We shouldn't have ever been together, but we were. What if that's precisely why we should be together? Hell, Tess, you're, believe it or not, the only girl I want be with."

"All right, for real. Who's paying you?"

"Nobody, Tess. You've got to believe me."

"If that's so true, why did you just let me go?"

"Because...because I...let me ask you something."

Tess nodded.

"Why are you here? Why aren't you married with five kids by

now?"

That caught her off guard. How could she answer? She asked herself the same thing every day.

"You can't deny it either. Something is meant to happen between us. We just needed time grow up. I see you're still wearing the necklace."

Tess grabbed the pendant as a couple of tears escaped down her cheek.

"No, no, no, Tess, don't cry. I think we have something really unique here. It'd be insane not to explore it." Nick moved to her side of the booth. He wrapped his arm around her shoulders.

"So, what do we do now?" Tess asked, wiping away the tears.

"Whatever we want to do, I guess."

"Great! Let's get out of here."

"Good idea."

After dinner, they strolled through Boston Common, reminiscing and reconnecting. When the temperature began to drop, Tess accepted Nick's offer of a ride home.

"Wow, nice place. You've done well."

"Thanks. I'm pretty happy with it."

"Uh-huh." The look in his eyes meant only one thing.

"You feeling okay over there?"

"You look hot." He stepped closer, tugging at her sweater. "You should take this off."

Tess knew exactly how he was feeling. All she had to do was

say yes.

"And if I'm not?"

"I'll warm you up," Nick said, taking her in his arms. His kiss was full of desire. Tess couldn't resist. In moments their clothes were on the floor, and they were doing what her body had been missing for far too long.

She was amazed at his memory of her body. He evoked all of her hot spots and even managed to find a few new ones between her inner thigh and hip flexors. She hadn't forgotten his hot buttons either. When her lips gently kissed his happy trail, his body quivered.

After several hours of thoroughly enjoying his company, Tess was ready for sleep. Nick, equally satisfied, rolled out of bed and started dressing.

"What are you doing?" Tess asked. "Where are you going?"

"It's a school night. I have to get back."

"But we just—"

"Don't worry, you'll see me again. Trust me. After a touch like that," he said, kissing her teasingly, "I don't think I'll ever be able to leave again."

But you're leaving right now, she thought. "Yeah. Ah, okay. So how do we do this?"

"What do you mean? We just did it."

"No, I mean *us,*" she said confidently.

"Oh, right. Don't worry about it. I want to see you again. Very much, in fact. I presume you want to see me too, after the way you did that little thing you did." His smile was devilish. "Trust me, we'll call each other. I have a feeling it's going to be really great this time around." He tied his shoes. "I'm off. I'll call you tomorrow."

Though his words were right, Tess's feelings weren't. Anxiety, regret, and plain old fear overwhelmed her. *What if he doesn't call?* That familiar old tape played in her head. "This is now. That was then. We've grown up, and when adults say they're going to call, they call," Tess said out loud.

Nick gave her a funny look. After a moment, he smiled again and opened the door.

When it closed behind him, Tess said aloud to the empty room, "Just breathe, Tess. He'll call. And if he doesn't, you'll kill him yourself."

He called the next day, and the following day, and the day after that.

It was hard to start a relationship during the holidays, especially to restart an old one, but Tess reminded herself daily that she was in control. She could end this at any point. She wasn't putting up with any of his shenanigans this time around.

Chapter 41

After three months of genuine dating and knock-your-socks-off sex, Tess was flying high. She and Nick talked every day. They saw each other every weekend; he drove to Boston two or three nights a week. Everything was perfect. He really had changed, and so far only for the better. Yet she felt like a piece of her was missing. That piece was Aimee.

Each time something wonderful happened, Aimee was the first person Tess wanted to call and share the good news with, but they hadn't spoken since she walked out of Aimee's office three months ago. Unable to keep the news inside any longer, Tess attempted to reach out to her mother, but the call went to voicemail.

"Hi, Mom. It's Tess. Just checking in. I have some news. Give me a call whenever you're free. Okay. Love you. Bye."

Tess tried Brie next. Same result.

She needed to tell someone or she was going to burst. Eve was next on list.

"Hey, Eve, how's it going?"

"Oh my God, Tess, I'm so glad you called!"

"Of course you're glad. I'm your one and only sister, after all."

"Yeah, whatever. Hey, did you talk to Mom already? Did she tell you?"

"Tell me what?"

"Oh, good, she hasn't told you. Okay, are you sitting down?"

Tess rolled her eyes. "This better not be a pregnancy joke again, Eve."

"Gimme a break! I outgrew that forever ago. Are you ready for this?"

"Out with it already."

"Rick asked me to marry him! I'm so happy. I can't believe it! The rock is so big!"

"Nope. Mom *definitely* didn't tell me that. Congratulations," she said, thinking, *Great. Another one is engaged before me.* "So tell me, how did he propose? Was it all romantic and cute?"

"Oh, Tess, it was just magical..."

Tess stopped listening. She was truly happy for her sister, but that didn't change the fact that she felt super single all of sudden, even though Nick was back in the picture.

"Oh, Tess, you should've seen me! I was sobbing like a baby. I totally stained my shirt with mascara!"

"Eve, that sounds really so wonderful." Tess was clueless about what was so wonderful. "He did a really great job. You're a very lucky girl."

"Me, the lucky one? Sure, but don't forget that he's even luckier for getting me. Ha ha!" *Oh, that Eve—never one to miss an opportunity for self-promotion. But she's happy, let the girl enjoy her moment,* Tess told herself. Even so, it still hurt. Tess was now officially the last one to get married and, worse, was only sort of with a guy who had yet to prove dependable for the long haul.

"So, Tessalie Claire Ryan, will you be my maid of honor?"

"Of course I will, Eve. I would be honored."

"Thank you! Thank you! Planning the wedding is going to be so much fun. Well, some will be tough, with you being so far away, but we'll make it work. You might just have to take me dress shopping down Newbury Street!"

"That'd be great, Eve," Tess said, picturing her little sister buying a wedding dress first. *Ouch.*

"Shoot! There's Mom. Hang on."

"Okay. Tell her I said hi."

Eve was back in a flash. "I'm back. Sorry. Mom is in overdrive. I think she's had this wedding planned for months already."

"Well, it's not exactly unexpected." *And now I know why she didn't answer my call a few minutes ago.*

"True, we are living in sin. Ha! Anyway, enough about me. How are you? I haven't heard from you in a few weeks. What's going on up there?"

Eve's engagement took the wind out of Tess's story. Her twenty-two-year-old little sister was getting married and she, soon to be twenty-six, was calling to tell her about an ex from a million years ago who was finally being nice to her. It seemed so insignificant by comparison. She debated holding on to the story until there was something more concrete to report.

"Oh, not too much. Things are a little crazier than usual at school, but whatever. Aimee and I haven't seen or spoken to each other in months, and I'm seeing Nick again."

The phone went silent.

"Hello? Eve? Are you still there?"

"Yeah, I'm still here. What happened between you and Aimee?"

"Wait, you don't want to hear about Nick?"

"No. Not really." Eve paused. "Tell me, what happened between you and Aimee. That's important."

"It's a funny story actually. The two are directly related. But I'll give you the quick *Reader's Digest* version. I ran into Nick a few months back. A couple of weeks after that, he showed up at Aimee's shop looking for me. Everyone got all emotional. Turns out Nick tried to kiss Aimee when we were in college because his ex fiancé lied and said her kid was his. It's not. Long story. Anyway, then Aimee said if I got back together with him, our friendship was over. Nick and I have been seeing each other ever since," Tess rattled off before finally stopping to breathe.

"Whoa. I don't even know where to start."

"But Nick is a totally different guy now. Anything I want, he does. Anything I need, he gives me."

"You and Aimee have been friends for, like, ever. Is Nick really a worthy replacement?"

"Nick could never replace Aimee. Whatever, she'll be fine. Aimee'll come around. We'll talk about it, and everything will be fine." Tess wondered whether she was trying to convince herself or Eve.

"Be careful, Tess. I know you and I haven't always seen eye-to-eye, but you're my sister. I'm leery about any guy who treated you so badly, especially one you feel so strongly about. God, he really tried to kiss Aimee? What a creep."

"He didn't know we even knew each other at the time."

"Still, but whatever. You should really consider the impact of your actions."

"I know, but he hasn't hurt me once since we got back together."

"Have you talked to Mom about this yet?"

"No. I don't need her approval."

"No, you don't, but maybe she has some good advice."

"Gee, thanks, Eve. I'm so sick of everyone being so against me and Nick! He truly is nothing like he used to be."

"Hey, whoa, I'm not telling you not to date him. You're a grown woman. But just know a lot of people care about you, and we don't want this guy to take advantage of you again. That's all."

"I appreciate that, Eve, but I think it's like Nick said. Why do we keep running into each other? It's like we are meant to be."

"He didn't really say that."

"He most certainly did. I started crying a little, and he just wrapped his arms around me and let me cry. Guys who don't want to be with a girl don't do that, especially in public."

"Use your head, not just your heart. Promise me that?"

"I promise. Hey, will you do me a favor? Don't tell Mom? I want to be the one to tell her."

"Your secret's safe with me. I won't tell anyone."

"Thanks, Eve. I'm glad you understand."

"You're welcome. You're my sister. I love you. All I want is to see you happy."

Holding back a sudden lump in her throat, Tess said, "All right. Well, stop yapping with your ridiculous big sister and go plan that wedding of yours!"

"Oh, I will. I will. I'll call you in a few days."

"Awesome. Hey, wait a minute. Have you told Dad?"

"Not yet."

"Are you going to?"

"Yeah, I guess. Why?"

"Because he's Dad. He kind of has to walk you down the aisle. Don't you think you should give him a heads up?"

"I guess...Come on, I've only been engaged for like eighteen hours. I haven't even told my friends yet."

"Okay. Well, I'll let you get to it then. Just don't forget to tell him on purpose. He's your dad, after all."

"Uh-huh, right. I'll call you later."

Tess hung up and leaned back on the sofa. Being both happy and jealous of her sister getting married felt yucky. She wanted to be happy for Eve, but she just couldn't. Then, as she so often did, Tess let her mind slip into fantasies of her wedding to Nick.

Chapter 42

Inspired by Eve's engagement, Tess managed to get Nick to agree to taking turns staying over at each other's places on Sunday nights. His willingness was a sure sign that things were moving in the right direction. When it was her turn to stay over in Plymouth, Tess hated getting up early for what could be an hour and a half commute, but she had no other choice.

"No, no, no, nooooo," Tess moaned, slapping Nick's alarm clock half to death on her third Monday morning there. It was four. "Don't make me go."

Nick rolled over and tucked Tess under his arm.

"That's better," she said, falling back asleep. *Waaaahhhh! Waaaahhhhh,* the alarm clock screamed, just as their breaths fell into the same rhythm. Tess rolled out of bed and landed on the cold, hard floor.

"Ouch!" Nick was out cold. "Good to know you won't wake up in an emergency, Nick."

Her bum sore, she stood up and went to take a shower. After she was dressed and ready, she shrugged, reluctant to pack everything she'd brought yet again. It would be much easier to just leave it all there. She smiled at the thought of Nick's place becoming a second home. "Slow down there, Miss Ryan," Tess said to herself as she tossed her toiletries into a plastic bag. "I doubt he's even thought about that."

All of a sudden, Nick was in the bathroom lifting the toilet seat. He seemed to still be asleep.

"Whoa! Nick, wait till I leave!" Tess warned, her voice shrill. Nick looked at her with a blank smile.

"You're here?"

"I am here." She wondered how he could have forgotten that.

"Cool." He took her face in his hands and planted a big sleepy kiss on her mouth. Tess enjoyed the sudden passion. Then Nick prepared to relieve himself. She squealed again and left the room.

A few minutes later, when Tess was putting on her coat, Nick reached her side.

"Leaving so soon?"

"I have to."

"No. Don't go. Stay a few more minutes."

"I'd love to, but I can't get caught in traffic."

Nick kissed her again. "It's okay, you won't be late."

"I'll call you tonight," Tess said, proud of herself for resisting.

Tess felt like I love you was appropriate, but only got good-bye. Lately there had been many moments when Tess could have said it or she thought he certainly might have said it. *It will happen soon enough,* Tess told herself, walking to her car in the ice-cold February air. *Guys just need more time to say "I love you."* Of course, if he didn't say it soon it would definitely be an issue.

To her surprise and disappointment, traffic was a breeze. Had she known, she would have been able to drive into work with an early-morning afterglow. Instead, Tess arrived at work at six fifteen. Normally, she arrived a little later. It felt eerie. Only a few rooms were lit, and a dropped pin could have been heard from any corner of the school. Taking full advantage of the extra time, she got a jump start on her tedious behavior progress reports, particularly Ronnie's.

The kid was still a pain. He possessed an uncanny ability to be in the right place at the right time for any and all trouble. Despite a mile-long list of major indiscretions, Ronnie remained in Tess's class. How he had lasted for five and a half months without a single consequence boggled her mind.

Even as a first-year teacher, she realized the way the administration handled this kid was wrong. What had happened to adults running the school? In any case, at this point his bad behavior seemed normal. At least Valentine's Day was coming soon, along with February vacation. Surely, all the pink and red hearts on the walls, the constant reminders of the Valentine's Day dance, and the impending time off, should put Ronnie in a better mood. They definitely put Tess in a better mood.

That year the lovers' holiday fell on a Saturday, so celebrations at school took place on Friday the thirteenth. Despite having to deal with Ronnie on a superstitious day before a lovely one, Tess could not have been in a better mood for her first Valentine's Day with Nick. She couldn't wait to see what plans he had in store. Ronnie, being Ronnie, instantly picked up on her good mood and went above and beyond to ruin it.

Her back facing the class, Tess stood at the board writing notes. She should have known something was up when the entire class remained uncharacteristically quiet, even Ronnie. Giving the class the benefit of the doubt, Tess spent a few extra moments on the notes.

Tess turned back to her class, and in a flash her face was red, her expression horrified. The class roared with laughter.

Ronnie stood there, looking smug. He had shoved his right hand down the front of his pants, unzipped the zipper, and stuck one of his fingers through the zipper, as if it were his penis. He waggled it at her.

Disgusted and annoyed, Tess immediately sent the offender out of the room. Inside she simultaneously panicked over how much trouble she was going to be in with the administration over this one. She knew they would somehow make it her fault. They would probably tell her that she shouldn't have turned her back to the class to write notes on the board. Picturing the disappointment on her bosses' faces made her tremble with fear. She was certain she wasn't going to be asked back next year. She was going to go down in history as the worst first-year teacher ever. The thought made her sick to her stomach.

The second school let out, Tess wasted no time documenting everything. For the umpteenth time, she called Ronnie's mother, the assistant principal, the principal, and every parent in the class, in case someone complained. She also sent an e-mail to the school psychologist, again begging for an evaluation as soon as possible. Because of all the extra phone calls and paperwork, Tess left work much later than she had planned.

After her miserable day and getting home late, she struggled to let it all go, even after she discovered that Nick was already there, waiting in the cold.

"I am so sorry I'm so late. I was held up at work, and then there was tons of traffic. I got here as quick as I could," Tess said, assuming a fake smile. Seeing him with his sweet smile shrank the crappiness of her day a little bit. She rushed to open the building door and get him out of the cold, her smile was a little more sincere.

Nick stopped her halfway up the stairs to kiss her. "Happy Valentine's Day."

"Why, Happy Valentine's Day to you too," she said, a little dazed. Inside, Nick presented her with two dozen red roses, which normally she would have noticed right away. But her mind was still stalking the problem with Ronnie, like a terrier with a snake. She set the flowers on the coffee table and went to her room to change into something more comfortable.

"Yoga pants? I made reservations at 75 Chestnut."

"I'm sure you can move them to tomorrow or something."

"Actually, I can't. I tried."

That piqued her curiosity. Why would he try to change the

reservation? Was he only here out of obligation?

"Okay, let me sit for a few minutes. Then we'll go."

"The reservation is for five. It's already four."

Tess forced herself up from the wonderfully comfortable couch she had just plopped onto and went to change. She came out wearing a pair of jeans and a red sweater.

"Jeans? Come on Tess."

"What's wrong with jeans?"

"Tess, it's Valentine's Day. You must have something dressier?"

She shrugged and went back to her closet. Nick followed her.

"Tess, what's wrong?"

Half naked, Tess turned around and said, "A kid sexually harassed my whole class today."

"How is that even possible? Are you sure you didn't misinterpret something?"

"Because it's Ronnie friggin' DeCarlo. Who knows how he pulls off half the crap he does, but he does."

"Hey, hey, I'm not the enemy here."

"I'm sorry. It's just…well, I've told you, his IEP basically says he can do whatever he wants. That's why I was, yet again, late. And I'm sorry for that, really. I should've called, but I was consumed with the fact that the administration only gave him, yet again, another warning. He's due back in my class on Monday when we come back from break."

"You're documenting everything, right?" Nick said in a tone that made it sound like she was more experienced than she was.

"Of course."

"Well, then you have nothing to worry about. I'm sure the kid is a ticking time bomb. He's going to do something that'll get him expelled soon enough. Then you won't have to worry about him."

"But it's February, and he's still in my class. He makes it so chaotic. I can't teach. What about all the other kids in the class who want to learn?"

"I don't know what to tell you. I'm not your administrator. If I were, I would've kicked that kid out a long time ago. In the meantime, you just have to think of him as an annoying kid," he said in a tone that Tess could only take as dismissive. She felt herself become distant. He continued. "Look around you. I'm here. It's Friday night. It's almost Valentine's Day. We're free for a whole week! Forget about him. Let's go celebrate." He kissed her tenderly. "Now get dressed," he ordered with a tap on her rear.

At the restaurant, most thoughts of work vanished. Tess's only lingering angst was from the way Nick had dismissed her crappy day and insisted on going out for a good time. She totally understood his sentiment, which *was* distracting, but what she really needed was for him to support her and tell her everyone she worked with was an asshole and to hell with them all, especially Ronnie.

"And how about dessert?" the bubbly waitress asked.

"Dessert?" Nick asked.

"I'll have a coffee, please," Tess told the waitress.

"I guess I'll have the same."

The waitress bounced away.

"Coffee? What are you, old now? Need more energy for later?" Nick asked, implying something lascivious.

"After the day I've had...," Tess looked at Nick's eager face. "Fine, let's get this party started."

Nick settled the bill, and they were off to prove Tess was not yet old.

They landed at 21st Amendment near Beacon Hill, a hodgepodge of politicians and common folk known for spirited discourse over Boston's finest draft beers, spirits, and wines. With so many people there, Tess felt even more pressure to look alive and full of energy, even though she just wanted to go to bed. After three too many shots of tequila and an unknown number of apple martinis, Tess had more than exceeded her limit at which point they finally called it a night. They caught a cab and crashed the moment they got to Tess's place. At least Tess did. She was too drunk for any Valentine's Day boom-boom-pow, thoroughly disappointing Nick. Whatever, it was his fault. He was the one that forced her out.

Chapter 43

The next morning, now officially on February break, Tess was packing so she could spend the weekend in New York—well, Jersey City—with Brie. Dragging his heels, Nick made Tess almost miss her train.

"I know you want me to stay, but as I've all ready told you, Brie and I planned this weekend before you and I even ran into each other at the museum," Tess said, repacking the things Nick was taking out of her travel case. "Hey, if you don't knock it off..."

"What? You'll never see me again?"

"Thinking about it."

"But it's break. You can't run away to New York on me. Plus, today is actually Valentine's Day, and, well, we didn't, you know, last night. And I know you don't want to leave me here alone on a day like today, do you?"

Tess stopped for a moment. The warm sunlight floating through the window strengthened Nick's point.

"I know. I know! But I can't let Brie down. She finally has a weekend away from her kid."

"Kids, shmids, who needs them?" Nick grabbed Tess and

kissed her neck. She relented momentarily. "Okay, okay. Stop. I have to get to the train."

"I'll drive you." Nick kept kissing her.

"To New York?"

"Wherever you need."

"Really?"

"Just come over here."

Tess noticed the devilish look in his eyes. He was focused on one thing, and it wasn't driving to New York.

"Nick, I want to stay. I really do, but I have to go."

Nick sat on the bed, defeated.

"Don't give me that look. You're not going to guilt me into staying. I can't. I won't. Not this time."

"Fine. I'll just stay here then and wait."

Tess finally finished packing her bag. "No, you won't."

"Why not? It's not like I'm going to ruin the place. I am house broken, you know. How about I stay here and have dinner waiting for you tomorrow night?"

"I'm not getting back until Monday around midnight. You know that."

"So it'll be breakfast. Whatever. It's not like I have anywhere to go on Monday."

Tess weighed the pros and cons. "Fine, but you have to drive me to the train right now. There is no way I'm going to make it if you don't."

Luckily, Tess made her train just in time. Once settled in her seat, she thought about Nick's tenacity. It was so sweet and made her feel so wanted. *See Aimee, he is a good guy.* Then panic flared. She left in such a hurry she didn't realize how vulnerable she had just made herself. *Why was he so adamant about staying? What would he even do in a girl's apartment all weekend by himself? Was he up to something? Did he have this plan all along?* She pictured Nick rummaging through her stuff and having a change of heart about her. *No, stop it Tess, he's not that kind of guy.* Plus, it's not like he would find anything *that* embarrassing. Just some old stuffed toys, which he's seen, some bad pictures, oh and every single memento from their past together. *It's fine. He'll just laugh, think it's cute. Hell, maybe even another sign.* Then it occurred to her that by him staying in her apartment without her was a major sign of his comfort level. Not to mention his level of commitment, which gave her stomach butterflies.

If only Aimee could see it. She would be so impressed. How desperately Tess wanted to call her, but she was in the quiet car. Text? No, there was no way Tess could explain all that had happened in the last few months via text. Hopefully, after a weekend with Brie, a line of communication could be opened.

Chapter 44

Tess always loved going to New York. She completely bought into the overly romanticized version of the metropolis she enjoyed on TV shows like *Sex and the City*. The beautiful people were hotter, the cab drivers were scarier, the cost of everything was higher, but it was all worth it; it was New York City. Thanks to *Sex and the City*, Tess believed New York was the place where dreams came true. From time to time, she'd thought about moving to New York and wondered what would have happened if she and Nick lived there. Perhaps they would now be on round happily-ever-after instead of unclear round three.

Brie arrived at the Jersey City train station just as Tess's train was pulling in. Tess expected to see Brie's old, beat-up Toyota Corolla. She had been driving that old clunker since college and even joked about being buried in it because she loved it so much.

"Nice ride, Mom," Tess said, referring to the new minivan.

"Shut up. It's practical. Now we can take everything we need. Plenty of room to spread out. No more being cramped."

"Wait a second. Does this mean what I think it means? Are you pregnant again?"

"Oh my God, is it that obvious? I'm not even showing yet.

Did Mark tell you?"

"Really? Who the hell just chooses one of these super-cool mommy-mobiles?"

"I'm due in August."

"Oh, congratulations, Brie!" Tess hugged her friend from the passenger seat.

"Thank you. We're really happy."

"So happy you forgot to tell me we won't be drinking this weekend. Boo!" Tess stuck out her tongue.

"I know, I know. I'm sorry! But hey, you and Aimee can drink for me." Brie inhaled sharply.

"Aimee?"

"She's watching Chloe back at the house," she said, releasing her breath.

"Oh."

"I invited her down."

Tess nodded silently. Half of her was thrilled; the other half was scared.

"Tess, it kills me that you guys aren't talking. I had to do something."

"No, it's okay, Brie. I appreciate the sentiment. I'm just not sure she's going to be too happy to see me. Does she know I'm coming?"

"Of course she does. I told her just before I left to pick you up."

"Ha! So you duped us both. Gotta hand it to you, *Mom*. Never saw it coming."

"So you're not mad?"

"Was she mad?"

"Don't worry about a thing. Everything'll work out. You guys have been friends far too long to let a silly fight over a guy come between you."

They didn't talk the rest of the ride back to Brie's house. Tess needed to collect her thoughts, in case she was facing a fight. Conflict resolution was still an area where she needed improvement. Brie appeared as though she had something to say but didn't know how.

Finally at 4:22 p.m., Brie and Tess stomped through the door, armed with multiple bags from Target.

"What's all that?"

"Just some stuff for the baby. I thought I would take advantage of your help and get a couple of things before Tess arrived," Brie replied. Aimee shot her a death glare.

"Hi, Aimee," Tess said from behind Brie.

"Tess," Aimee said, curtly.

"It's a nice surprise to see you here."

"Surprise is an understatement."

"Aimee, remember what we talked about," Brie chimed in.

Brie was so meant to be a mother, Tess thought. "Did Brie tell you she and Mark are having another baby?" Tess asked with an upbeat tone.

"Another baby? Well, well, Brie, aren't you just full of surprises today."

"Okay, Aimee, what's with you? You've never been like this!" Tess said, surprising herself with her sudden assertiveness.

"I'm fine. Just great. Everything's fine with me. How about *you*?"

"I can see you're still upset."

"Oh, I'm not upset at all. I don't know what you're talking about."

Tess could tell Aimee was lying through her teeth and wondered how long Aimee was going to play this charade.

"Aimee, whenever you get mad, you start twisting your nose, like you're doing right now."

"Okay. I'm not doing this." Aimee stood abruptly. "Thanks for the coffee, Brie. I'll call you later." Aimee moved toward the door.

"Aimee Jean Babineaux, get back here," Tess said.

Aimee must have thought it was Mama Brie scolding her as she looked rather surprised to turn around and see that it was Tess.

"Don't walk out on me like that!" Tess paused. "I can't take it."

Aimee folded her arms and looked everywhere but at Tess.

"Aimee, I miss you." Tess paused again. "I can't tell you how many times I've wanted to pick up the phone and call you. You're my best friend. I need you in my life, especially now that Nick's back in it."

Aimee looked from Brie to Tess. She swayed back and forth before she assumed her seat at the kitchen table.

"I'm afraid he's taken you away for good this time. I mean, the last time you guys were together he was all you talked about, the only person you hung out with. I can't do that again," Aimee said. "And he's just not a nice guy."

"I had no idea I was doing that. I never meant to ditch you. But I can honestly tell you things are different now. I'm the one calling the shots. In fact, he almost got me to not come down here today, but I said no, my friends are more important. To hell with Valentine's Day."

"Oh right, it's Valentine's Day...I totally forgot," Brie said. "Thank God I keep a stash of cards." She chuckled to herself. No one else laughed. "Do something nice for Jason, Aimee?"

"Huh? Yeah, it's just a Hallmark holiday." Aimee turned back to Tess. "So..."

"Whatever. Don't believe me. The point is, I'm not wrapped around his finger."

"There's no way I can believe that. How can you be so stupid? Did you not hear me when I said he tried to kiss me! You're my best friend. I know how much he means to you. Why would I just make up something like that?"

"Jesus, Mary, and Joseph. Here it comes," Brie said.

"Want to know why he *almost* kissed you Aimee?"

Aimee sat back in her chair and crossed her arms.

"That day he got a letter from his ex fiancé, yeah he was engaged. Took me a while to get used to that, but anyway, his ex told him she had a kid and that it was his. He was so confused that day, he didn't know what he was doing."

"Huh," Aimee paused, looking like she remembered something. "Well, isn't that great. You're dating a deadbeat dad too."

"Am not. The kid's not his. The night before she dumped him she slept with someone else. It's his kid, not Nick's."

"And you believe that crap?"

"If I didn't, you really think I'd stay with him?"

A silence grew. Each looked as if they were mulling over what had just been said. Brie appeared to be the most anxious to move one when she said, "See, Aimee, I told you everything was fine," several minutes later.

"If you say so," Aimee replied less defensively, though she was clearly ambivalent about letting the argument go.

"So does that mean you'll answer the phone when I call?"

Not able to hide a smile, Aimee said, "I guess."

"Great! I think this went way better than I thought it would! Let's go have some fun!" Brie said.

"Ah, what about Chloe?"

"Oh, right." It was funny to see how quickly Brie forgot about her responsibilities when her old friends were around. "We'll just wait until Mark gets home at six, then."

With everything finally settled, the girls had a great time. They hopped around bars, danced in a few clubs, and nursed Tess back to health from her killer hangover. It was like they were back in college—except that Brie wasn't drinking and Aimee wasn't chatting up any studs.

"I'd be happy to give you a ride instead of you taking the train. We can jam to the radio, have chocolate shakes, French fries. Like old times," Aimee offered when it was time to leave Sunday evening.

"I already bought my train ticket…Nick's picking me up."

"Can't you just call him and tell him not to?"

"But he's waiting in my apartment."

"I knew it! You *are* wrapped around his finger."

"Excuse me?"

"Whatever, Tess. Go be with your little boyfriend," Aimee said, getting into her car. She shut the driver's door and drove off without another word.

Just as Tess had feared, Aimee was not over her feelings. She began to worry that the rift between them was to great to overcome. Had she really ruined her best friendship?

Chapter 45

In addition to casting a shadow of doubt on reconciliation on their friendship, Aimee cast a shadow of doubt on Tess's relationship with Nick. The train pulled into South Station just after 12:00 a.m. and Tess was full of trepidation. *Is he going to be waiting as promised?*

"Hello, there, beautiful. Welcome back," Nick said, welcoming her into his arms with a kiss.

"Why, hello."

"How was the weekend?"

"Exhausting."

"Uh-oh. Do I really want to know?"

Tess wanted to tell him, but not just yet. "I'm starving."

"Got it. Let's go home."

Chills ran down Tess's back at the sweet sound of the familiar words coming from *his* mouth.

At her place, everything was exactly as she left it, except for the bed, which had been made. *How sweet,* she thought. Tess dropped her bag and changed into her pajamas. Nick was in the kitchen preparing scrambled eggs, toast, and that cardboard-like veggie sausage she liked so much.

"Wow, veggie sausage!" Tess said, entering the kitchen. "Thank you."

"Tell me how the weekend went. It couldn't have been that bad."

Tess buttered her toast and took a few bites before she answered. "Let's just say that it wasn't the weekend I thought it was going to be. These eggs are awesome, by the way."

"See. You should've stayed here."

"Actually, no. It was good that I went. Aimee was there."

"Oh."

"Don't get the wrong idea. It wasn't like that. Well, at first it was tense, but we had it out. I'm quite proud of myself, actually. I was confident, and when she tried, I didn't let her walk away. I don't know what came over me. It was cool, though. Anyway, for a while, it was like nothing had ever gone wrong. But when I declined to ride back with her, she got all bent out of shape, saying that I'm wrapped around your finger again."

"Knew it. Still a bitch."

"Excuse me?" Tess didn't want to believe Nick had just said that.

"Aimee's still a bitch from what I can see. Who is she to mess around in your business?"

"Nick, she isn't a bitch. She's my best friend."

"Is she, though? Making you choose between her and me? A friend doesn't do that, especially a best friend."

Nick had a point. The truth stung deep, too deep. Tess struggled to hear one of the most important people in her life be called a bitch.

"But that's easy for me to say. You chose me. Clearly the better choice." Nick leaned across the table and kissed Tess's cheek.

Tess should have been happy but she lost her appetite and pushed her plate away.

"Is something wrong with the food?"

"Not at all. I'm just full."

"But you've only eaten half a piece of toast and one sausage patty thing."

"Traveling makes my stomach all wonky. I fill up quick. I'm fine. Really."

Nick gave her a funny look but gestured for her plate. She gave it up without question.

"Okay then, time for bed." Tess watched Nick shovel the rest of her food down his throat, cardboard sausages included.

"But don't you want to, you know…?"

"I need sleep," Tess said, carefully.

"Well then, okay." Nick kissed Tess on the forehead instead of the mouth and let her go to bed without him.

But Tess couldn't sleep. Her thoughts focused on Nick's comments about Aimee. Part of her agreed with him. Aimee was being a bitch. Tess wouldn't end their friendship because she didn't like some guy Aimee was dating. Tess could have ended things when she stole Jason right from under her nose, but she didn't. She was the bigger person. But Tess was floored that Nick had insulted someone so important to her. It was disrespectful.

No matter how much she disliked one of his friends, she would never disrespect Nick with the same disregard. Although she would never admit to disliking any of his friends for fear of upsetting him and pushing him away. Suddenly, Tess heard the TV shut off and Nick shuffle around in the kitchen. Shortly after, Nick crawled into bed.

He immediately began kissing her cheek and then her neck. Despite the intrigue, Tess pretended to be asleep. She knew if she had sex with him, she would be condoning his bad behavior, something she was determined not to do. Yet if she denied him, he would know she was mad, which would lead to a fight, which was something else she was determined not to do. Then a sneeze snuck up on Tess and refused to be a quiet one.

"Oh, so you are awake."

"No, I'm not." Tess rolled over, but Nick hung onto her tightly. He continued to seduce her with his hands and lips. Tess did all that she could to resist. Then he reached her sweet spot just behind her ear. She went down in flames.

"Morning," a groggy Nick said the next morning around eleven.

"Morning." Tess was ever so appreciative of her extra-plush pillow-top mattress. As she lay there dozing, she felt like she was resting on clouds.

"Whoa, it's eleven o'clock!" Nick said, sitting up. "Shit! Why did you let me sleep so long?"

"What?"

Nick's rough tone jolted Tess awake. She rolled over and tried to look at him squarely in the face. Her eyes were still out of focus.

"I've got to head back to my place and get a couple of things done."

"Like what?"

"You know, stuff...laundry."

"Um, okay."

"If I get everything done, I'll call you. You can come down."

"Oh." Tess waited for him to say something more. He didn't.

Nick got out of bed and slipped into the bathroom. He came back, brushing his teeth.

"Nick, that's so gross! That's my toothbrush!"

"Mine now."

"Is that so?" Tess asked, unable to withhold a smile. Lines like that made it very hard for her to stay mad at him.

"Uh-huh."

"Well, why don't I just come down with you today?"

"Fine, but could you get moving?"

"Can I shower first?"

"How about a shower at my place?"

"Why are you in such a rush?"

"I'm not. I'm not. I just want to get back to my stuff, you know. I mean, I have been here all weekend."

Tess thought it was odd that Nick wanted to get back to his place so badly. He had only been away for a couple of days. It's not like he had a cat to feed. Nevertheless, Nick and Tess got out the door and on the road in record time.

Tess saw Nick's his old friend, Will, at Nick's door just as they pulled into the driveway. It didn't take Tess long to realize why Nick had been in a rush. She wondered why he didn't just tell her he had plans.

"It's Tess, right?" Will asked as they got comfortable in the living room. He sat in the middle of the loveseat; Tess sat on the end of the sofa farthest from him.

"Good memory."

"It's hard to forget the face of a girl who gives a guy a bed."

Tess smiled, not getting the reference. A few seconds later when she did, the smile dropped from her face. She wasn't sure if Will had just called her a tramp or not.

"Right, so…are you and Nick doing this like for real now?"

Tess looked at Nick for reassurance. She had no idea how to respond. But he was too busy setting out napkins and plates on the coffee table to notice her need. *Has he said anything to Will? What does Nick call me? Girlfriend, friend…booty call?*

"I still think it's hilarious that you bagged him as an undergrad!" Will said, breaking the silence.

Hilarious? Courageous, yes, a little reckless, sure, but hilarious? No. "I take it you knew him at UMass?" Tess asked, holding her annoyance back.

"Of course I did," Will said, as if it were common knowledge.

"We were roommates." Her stomach tightened. She began to wonder how much he knew.

Nick came in carrying cold beers that he passed around. Tess smiled timidly at Nick. Wondering if he'd talked about their first night of passion to all of his friends made her feel both relieved and panicked.

"Aww, Nick," Tess said, trying to be as positive as she could.

"What's with you?" Nick asked, giving her a funny look.

"Oh, yeah. Nothing."

Nick looked at Will, who ticked his eyebrows but said nothing.

"Am I missing something?"

Tess and Will shared a look. Will spoke first. "Just talking about how you guys met."

"Man, I told you that in confidence."

"What does it matter now, dude? That was like forever ago. I mean, you're together now, aren't you?"

Tess held her breath, nervous about what Nick might say next.

"That's beside the point. I told you not to say anything."

"Come on, it's kind of cool how you two got together. It's the stuff of after-school specials and such." Tess started to like Will. He turned out to be more supportive than she'd originally thought. The ring on his left ring finger also suggested he might be a good influence on Nick.

Nick stared at Will for what seemed like an eternity. Tess wished she could know what he was thinking. Her heart sank. Where was all this hostility and distance coming from? Did this mean he didn't really mean anything he said when they reunited several months ago? But then a smile appeared when he looked at her.

"Yeah, you're right. It is cool," Nick said. He grabbed her hand and was about to kiss her when Will interrupted him.

"Ah, dude, this is why we said no wives or girlfriends!"

"Excuse me?" Tess felt the proverbial rug being ripped from under her. Nick looked stunned.

"Girlfriend?" Nick's head cocked to the side as if he were considering the situation.

"Boyfriend?" Tess countered with a cute smile.

Nick's eyes darkened and narrowed.

"Girlfriend, yeah." Nick said with a contented smile. He turned to Will. "Dude, it's my place. I can kiss my girlfriend any time I want."

"Oh, yeah, three pointer! All right!" Will shouted. His focus on the game proved he was finished with the sentimental moment. Tess and Nick, on the other hand, collided and fell into a place Tess had never thought they would discover so casually.

Tess had always imagined this moment would have more grandeur. She'd envisioned soft light, rose petals, a fountain, and singing birds. Sitting on the couch with a beer and a friend in front of a Celtics game could not have been farther from her ideal setting. But it was finally out there in the open: Tess Ryan and Nick Donovan were officially girlfriend and boyfriend. It had only taken nearly four years.

Chapter 46

Although Tess and Nick were enjoying the new definition of their relationship, Aimee was not. Several days after it became Facebook official, Aimee found it while surfing the site, avoiding a mound of paperwork. The story dominated her newsfeed. In the time it had been up, thirty people had liked it and twenty-two had commented with congratulations—including Brie and Eve.

"What the…is going on in this world? Tess, I can't even…" Aimee muttered to the computer. Dozens of happy-couple pictures were strewn over both pages, rendering Aimee speechless. The small amount of the air left in her lungs escaped when she saw the picture of Nick kissing Tess's cheek. Tess's eyes were sparkling, and rays of light burst from her smile. The worst part was the fact that it was *his* profile picture. Aimee sat back in her chair staring at the photo.

"Hi, Sarah, something's come up. Can you let anyone who needs me know that I'll be out of the office for the rest of the day?"

"Sure thing."

"Great. Thanks." Aimee hung up and left the office. It was just after two on a Tuesday afternoon. Consumed by indignation,

Aimee didn't stop to think if Tess would be home. After a never-ending thirty-eight-minute T ride to 1697 Commonwealth Avenue, Aimee was in luck.

"Aimee? Hi. What are you doing here? Is everything all right? Are you okay?" Not having seen or spoken to Aimee since her visit to Brie's house, Tess looked shocked.

"I just had to see you in the flesh. Make sure you were okay."

"What are you talking about?"

It was clearly difficult for Aimee to answer. "I was on Facebook today, and..."

"You saw my updated status." Tess crossed her arms.

"Oh God, it really is official," Aimee said, more to herself than Tess. Tess looked calm and quiet. It was eerie. Aimee thought Tess would've been rattling off a million justifications by now. The silence unsettled her. "You've never been this relaxed and calm before. What has he done to you?"

"Okay. Yup. I see you're still bent out of shape. Whatever, Aimee." Tess turned to shut the door.

"Tess, wait."

Tess turned around.

"I know I've been acting childish about this whole thing. I just didn't think it was real. I guess I thought it was somehow just one of your fantasies. When I saw it on Facebook, as dumb as that is, I had to know for real. My brain can't comprehend this."

"Is that it?" Tess was obviously irritated.

"What else am I supposed to say?"

"I'm so tired of this! You know, I've accepted all the crap, and yes I am referring to the kiss, and I've moved on. You really need to do the same. God, I didn't think you were serious when you said our friendship would end because of Nick. Turns out I was wrong."

"Tess, don't say that!" The memory of how they met suddenly filled Aimee's mind's eye.

On a cold, blustery afternoon at the bus stop in February 1993, Tess's zipper refused to cooperate.

"You stupid, stupid zipper! Come on, just go in the little..." Tess focused for a minute. No, it wouldn't cooperate. "Son of bitch! I hate you, you stupid—"

Kids stared. Aimee was one of them. But unlike the other kids, Aimee walked toward Tess, who simmered like a pot about to boil.

Aimee bravely approached. "You know, saying bad words like that isn't going to get your jacket zipped any faster."

Tess didn't even look at her. "Oh, yeah? Well, I bet if I told you to go to hell that would make you go away faster."

"Here, let me help you," Aimee said, unaffected. She grasped the bottom edges of the jacket in her small ten-year-old hands.

Tess shoved her away. "I can do it myself, thank you very much."

Aimee was not deterred. "Will you stop moving for a second?" Her forceful tone stopped Tess dead in her tracks.

Aimee fiddled with the zipper for a moment and then smiled. "See? It's zipped. You can stop going crazy now."

Tess looked down at her zipped jacket and then stared at Aimee.

"I'm Aimee Babineaux. What's your name?"

"Babin what?"

"Babineaux."

Tess laughed and snorted. "That's a funny name."

"Oh yeah? What's your name then?"

"Tessalie Ryan."

Aimee burst into giggles. "Ha ha! You've got a boy's name!"

"No, I don't! It's a last name!"

But Aimee continued to giggle. Tess looked like she was about to swat her, but quickly Aimee's giggles infected her. Tess began to laugh too. Both girls stood in the cold and indulged in a giggle fit. In fact, they laughed so intensely they forgot about the buses. Their buses came and went unaware to them. When Aimee realized none of the people she recognized from her bus were still waiting, she stopped laughing.

"Oh, no! Oh, no! I think I missed my bus," Aimee said. Tess looked around. "What am I going to do? My parents don't get home until six, and that's after all the drivers have gone home for the day."

"Drivers?"

"The people who drive me and my family around."

"Then why do you take the bus? Why don't they pick you up from school?"

"Because my parents say they want me to be like the other kids. They don't want to spoil me and all that stuff."

A funny look crossed Tess's face, and she started to chuckle.

"What?"

"Your skirt's tucked into your tights. I can see your underwear."

Aimee whipped around as fast as she could. Her hands roamed her backside, pulling and flattening, double-checking that everything was covered.

"Come on. We can walk to my house and you can call your parents from there," Tess offered.

"Do you live far away?"

"It's like a block from here."

"Really? Why do you take a bus then?"

"I just like to get on buses and see where they take me."

Aimee's mouth twisted in confusion.

"It's not like I do it all the time. I only do it on the days my dad forgets to pick me up."

Aimee smiled.

"Are you coming or what? It's not going to get any warmer out here," Tess said as she started to walk home. "Fine. Stay out here and freeze. It's your funeral."

"Hey, wait, it's getting dark. You shouldn't walk by yourself."

"So you're like my mom now?" Tess asked once Aimee was at her side again.

"Someone needs to watch out for you. You couldn't even zip your jacket!"

Back in the present, standing on Tess's doorstep, Aimee felt a smile lift her cheeks. Every time she thought about that day, she smiled. From the moment they'd met, she and Tess were each other's number-one lookout.

"Really? Where the hell have you been the last four months of my life?" Tess asked. She was definitely not smiling.

"What if he hurts you again? It's like your zipper and my skirt. Since day one we've had each other's backs."

Tess paused for a moment. "I don't know. I'd be hurt I guess, but—"

"You'll be devastated, and I'm the one who'll have to pick up the pieces and—"

"Yes, I'd be hurt for a while, but then I'd be okay," Tess said confidently, staring hard at Aimee. "I'm really happy right now, and I'm too old to miss any opportunity."

"You're not old. You're only twenty-five. And I know how happy you are. I saw the pictures on Facebook."

Tess smiled. "Aimee, I miss you like crazy."

"I miss you too. I'm so sorry."

"Don't be sorry. Be my friend. I need your support more than anything."

Aimee threw her arms around Tess and promised to be more herself again.

"Shouldn't you be heading back to work now?"

"Probably, but I told Sarah that I'd be out for the rest of the afternoon."

"In that case, want to come in and make fun of soap operas

with me? I've got *Days of Our Lives* on my DVR."

"Is this what you do with your afternoons?"

Tess nodded a guilty looking but strong yes.

"I definitely picked the wrong career."

As they goofed on the soap opera drama, Tess caught Aimee up on everything that happened with Nick since December. With Aimee's acceptance, though not an approval, once again everything seemed right with the world.

Chapter 47

A few weeks later, during lunch at school, Tess said, "Elaine, I don't think I can go to sixth period."

"Just send the little bugger out then."

"I know, but then admin will get on me, saying I can't control my class, which is the truth. Except that when Ronnie's gone, it's a great class."

"Tess, you have an obligation to give those other twenty-five kids an education. It's your job to do whatever you have to do to create an environment for them to learn in. If Ronnie interferes with that, then…well, get rid of him. That's what I'd do."

"And admin hasn't jumped down your throat?"

"As long as it's all documented, you're fine."

"Ha, no kidding." Tess began thinking of the pages upon pages of notes where she had detailed his horrible behavior and the countless phone calls home. She had all the proof she needed. "Well, then, bye-bye, Ronnie," she said, feeling reenergized. "Nick said the same thing. Thank you, Elaine. I needed that."

"Speaking of Nick, are you guys still getting along?"

"Sure are." Tess glowed. "It's a Nick weekend."

"Didn't he just come up? I thought you only saw each other

every other weekend?"

"I mean I'm going to his place."

"How long have you guys been doing this now?"

"Ah, it's April second, right? So just over four months."

"Have you guys thought about moving in together?"

Tess blushed a little. She had been secretly thinking about that since they'd reconnected. Elaine noticed Tess was daydreaming.

"I'll take that as a yes."

"I don't know if he has, though. Isn't four months kind of soon to be talking about that?"

"Well, you did say that you met in college. I presume you've dated on and off since then? It's not like you discount the previous time you've been together."

"In that case we've been together for over a year."

"That's it?"

"Is that bad?"

"I just thought it was longer. I mean from the way you talk about him, and it's not like you were in college just yesterday..." Elaine's voice trailed off. "Anyway, if you think this relationship is the one, I'd consider finding a place to share."

Tess's imagination flashed with fantasies like a lit-up pinball machine. Hearing someone encourage her to be with Nick was a nice change. It didn't matter that Elaine didn't know about all the crap Nick had put her through over the years. They were on the right track now, and that's all that mattered.

The bell rang, reminding Tess it was time to get back to work.

"Just keep swimming; just keep swimming," Elaine sang to

Tess as they left the teacher's room. The start of sixth period was the worst part of Tess's day.

Keeping Tess on her toes, Ronnie kept his antics down to a duller roar that day. That's not to say he didn't act up, but at least he didn't involve every student. Instead he only bothered the students sitting closest to him.

Working with Ronnie was a roller coast ride that Tess kept hoping would end. She really hoped Nick was right about Ronnie eventually doing something catastrophic. On the really bad days she considered egging him on enough so he'd punch her, but the thought of a black eye or a broken tooth ended the fantasy.

On the brighter side, it was April, and April meant the possibility of nicer weather. But more importantly, the light waiting at the end-of-the-school-year tunnel started to shine. Tess began thinking more about Elaine's comment on moving in with Nick. She decided this was the weekend to bring it up. Excited and nervous, Tess practiced everything she was going to say as she drove down a few days later.

As if fate were playing a role, Nick and Tess were housebound when a late season nor'easter decided to roll in for the whole weekend. *So much for nice April weather,* she thought. The rain and snow swirled around Nick's apartment without any sign of letting up. Nick had heeded the advice of the weatherman and stocked his kitchen with hearty soul-warming foods: grilled cheese, tomato soup, mashed potatoes. Although Tess would have loved to be out and about in fresh air, being homebound with Nick was a worthy alternative. It created the perfect opportunity to talk about moving in together.

"Looks like we're inside for the weekend," Tess said, peering out the window.

"That's what the weather guys said." Nick sat on couch, reading yesterday's newspaper.

"What should we do? I'm kind of restless."

"Anything you like."

"Well, if you had a fireplace, I'd build a fire and we'd roast marshmallows."

Nick lowered the newspaper. "Roast marshmallows?"

"Hey, it was just an idea. And yes, I realize you don't have a fireplace. Come on, you must have some ideas."

"I've got all the *It's Always Sunny* seasons on DVD."

"What do you have for games?"

"Cards, Battleship, Scrabble, Monopoly."

"Monopoly sucks with just two people. How about Scrabble? I bet I can beat you with my eyes closed."

"Is that so?" Nick said, finally putting down the paper.

"There's only one way to find out, isn't there?"

Nick smiled and set up the Scrabble board. To prove her Scrabble acuity, Tess let Nick go first. She and her mother had played for years. When Tess was in grad school, she discovered tons of online Scrabble games to maintain her skills. It was safe to say that she was a bit of a Scrabble shark. There was no way Nick would beat her.

"You absolutely cheated!" Tess said.

"Maybe I did, maybe I didn't. How are you going to prove it?" Nick paused. "You could always challenge some of my words, but if you're wrong, then you lose by even more."

"If *I'm* right, then you not only lose your points, you lose your dignity!" Tess looked down at the Scrabble dictionary. It was begging her to pick it up, but she left it alone. She couldn't risk the humiliation of being wrong.

"Fine, you win this one, but I swear it will be the only one!"

Nick chuckled and sat back, relishing his victory.

"So what's next?" Her appetite to fill the silence was insatiable.

Nick looked at the clock. It was only three, and they were both still in their pajamas.

"I'm going to hop in the shower."

Without thinking, she cleaned up. Their relationship had cooled a bit. They were at the point where it was okay to shower alone and they were comfortable being in separate rooms. Once Tess finished putting away the game, she settled into the couch and picked up where Nick left off with the newspaper.

In the shower, Nick said, "Oh, damn it," to his empty shampoo bottle. "Stupid nor'easter." He noticed Tess's nearly full bottle of shampoo. "Hey, Tess?" he shouted. "Tess, can I use some of your shampoo? I'm out."

A few moments later Tess was in the bathroom.

"Did you say something? I couldn't really hear you."

"I'm out of shampoo. Can I use some of yours?"

"Of course. Take what you need."

Familiar with the floral scent of her shampoo, Nick conservatively squeezed out just a dab. It smelled great on Tess, but he wasn't so sure about it for himself. As he rubbed the shampoo through his hair, he thought about how convenient it was to have someone else's shampoo around, which got him thinking that it may be time she kept some of her things there permanently.

Later, when Nick and Tess were watching an *It's Always Sunny in Philadelphia* marathon, Tess floated somewhere between awake and asleep. Noticing her twilight state, Nick got up carefully and then covered her in a soft throw blanket.

"Hmm, what's this?"

"Your throw blanket."

"This isn't mine. I didn't bring it."

"I know. I got it for you a while ago because you always fall asleep on the couch."

"Really? Thanks."

"Tess, what do you think about leaving a few of your things here? Nothing big, but like some pjs and shower stuff?"

Tess was now fully awake. "Are you serious?"

"Why not? I mean, I used your shampoo. It'd be kind of cool if you kept some of your stuff here."

Tess tingled all over. "I think that'd be really nice." Tess paused. *Here is my moment,* she thought. *Remember. It's all about communication. How can he give you what you want if you don't ask?* she heard her mother's voice say in the back of her mind. "Have you ever thought about moving to the South Shore, like around Weymouth or Braintree?"

"Ha. No. I would never live in Braintree."

"Oh."

"What? Why?"

"Oh, just..." Tess took a deep breath, prepared to speak her mind, but then bit her tongue and held her breath instead.

"Just what? Are you thinking of moving there?"

"God, no! Ha ha," she said, letting all her air and anxiety out. "I just heard some people talking about it at work. That's all."

Nick nodded, his expression revealed that he knew what Tess was really talking about. "You sure? Because I don't think that's why you brought it up?"

Tess didn't know what to say and sat there feeling vulnerable.

"And...Weymouth and Braintree are in the exact middle of our apartments."

"Wait, what?" How did he know that? Had he been thinking about this too?

"I'm not an idiot, Tess. The distance is getting...long."

"Are you saying what I think you're saying?"

Nick lowered his head with a chuckle. "Look, I think what we have going here is great, but I don't think I, we, are there yet. Moving in together is a big step. We haven't even met each other's families."

"But you just asked me to leave my stuff here. You bought me a blanket!"

"I know, I know, but moving in is a process. It shouldn't be rushed. It has to start slowly. You know leaving stuff at each other's places first."

Tess didn't like the mixed messages. How the hell did he know how the process should go? Look at how well his engagement worked out.

"Hey, don't frown. I'm not saying we won't live together, but it's only been four months. Don't you think that's kind of soon?"

Tears welled in her eyes. She swallowed them away and nodded her agreement. Of course that didn't stop the tension from growing between them as they continued watching *It's Always Sunny.* She felt defeated and couldn't risk further embarrassment by asking when they might move in together. While it was a relief that he saved her from bringing it, her hope to hear him say that he had already been looking for a place, that he even had a lease ready to sign, had been crushed. At least he didn't say never.

Chapter 48

Overwhelmed by their failed conversation about sharing space, Tess became more distant than she ever had been before. With Tess back in Boston, they still called each other, but the distance left little room for more than five-minute conversations about the weather or local sports. Tess's anxiety increased. She couldn't help but spend most of her time thinking about what remained unspoken. She couldn't stand not knowing when Nick would be ready, but she was too scared to ask him.

Even so she knew she couldn't devote all her time to her personal life. She had a career and couldn't neglect her responsibilities, no matter how enticing the idea was, particularly her struggles with managing Ronnie. The truth was simply that she didn't have the time to think about anything more than survival whenever that kid was nearby. It had become a war: Ronnie versus Miss Ryan for supreme ruler of her classroom. Each day was a contest to see which side the rest of the class would support. On the days when Tess had the class on her side, Ronnie's tactics became that much stronger.

Then on Thursday, April 9, the rules of the game suddenly changed. Ronnie appeared to surrender. He was quiet. He didn't disturb anyone, not even the kids sitting next to him. Tess was not the only one who was off balance as a result. Everyone waited with bated breath for Ronnie to spring into action.

"Okay, Ronnie, stop playing. You're not fooling anyone," his classmate Beana suddenly remarked. The comment didn't seem to register in Ronnie's mind. He continued doodling on his notebook as if no one else were around. Markus, the guy who sat to Ronnie's right, lifted Ronnie's hood from his ear as if searching for headphones, the popular contraband. But Ronnie's ears were empty. Even more surprising, Ronnie didn't whack Markus's hand away. Something was definitely up. Tess got the class focused on reading and quietly went over to Ronnie.

Crouching down to eye level, Tess said, "Hey, Ronnie, are you feeling okay? I'm worried about you." Ronnie didn't move. "Ronnie? Ronnie, can you hear me?" The doodler kept on doodling. "Ronnie, I want to help you," Tess said, trying to sound as if she meant it.

The rest of the class, though pretending to work, was focused on the teacher and Ronnie. Tess waited for something, anything—a look, a movement, a word, or even a breath that indicated he could hear her. Nothing. Then all of a sudden, Ronnie pierced Tess with the most nefarious look she had ever seen from a student or anyone else for that matter. She jerked back and almost fell over, her breath catching. As quickly as he'd turned on her, Ronnie returned to his art, without a word.

When Tess stood, the students appeared eager to see her next move. To their surprise she did nothing. She knew that whatever was going on was not a prank. Only time would reveal what was involved. Tess decided to utilize the rare quiet and actually get some teaching done.

Tess knew she had to document Ronnie's eerie behavior, even if it was the opposite of what his IEP required. The IEP was very clear about what to note and what not to note. For that reason, she did not document his silence in the computer system. She was too worried that it would raise a red flag and come back on her. Instead, she used an old-fashioned notebook. Afterward, she tucked it into a locked drawer for safekeeping.

Days turned into weeks, and Ronnie maintained his silence. The students benefited and finally learned a few things. Tess was relieved but very leery. Even the fact that she had somehow managed to be asked back next year did little to calm her fears. Elaine identified it as first-year jitters, which wouldn't go away for at least three or four more years. Tess appreciated her mentor's support, but it wasn't jitters. Every time she thought about teaching, her mind went straight to Ronnie.

The change in Ronnie's behavior was suspiciously abrupt. Tess had the sense that something big was coming. So each day she noted each thing he did and didn't do in her notebook. She expected the other shoe to drop at any minute, when the crazy Ronnie would reappear. Because of the anxiety at school and the ongoing awkwardness with Nick, at the end of each day Tess felt like a pressure cooker about to burst.

When the stress in her life got the better of her, she decided to lean on Aimee. They lived only a mile apart, so on a cloudy but warm day Tess walked over. The clouds looked too high to actually do anything, so Tess left her umbrella behind. But as luck would have it, it started to pour. Trying to avoid becoming completely drenched, Tess ran the remaining half-mile.

"I'll get you something dry to wear and a towel," Aimee said the moment she saw Tess, sopping wet and shivering, on her doorstep. Her clothes stuck to her like plastic wrap. With gratitude, Tess accepted the dry clothes and hot shower.

"All right, let me at that ice cream," Tess said, as she entered the living room looking refreshed by the hot water. Aimee grinned and went to the kitchen, soon returning with two pints and two spoons.

"So what's up? Everything okay?"

"I wish I was living someone else's life. Oh my God, this is so good! What is it? Is it a new flavor?"

"Tess, it's half baked."

"Oh." Half baked was her favorite. "I don't think I've had any since Nick and I got back together."

Aimee rolled her eyes.

"What? I'm just watching my figure! Damn, I don't even remember the last time I put on my skates. What like three years ago?"

"Anyway...how's school? Is that kid still giving you crap?"

"Actually, it's weird. Since April started, he's been absolutely silent. No one can get him to talk, not even his buddies."

"Did something happen at home?"

"Not that I know of. If something did, I'd think his teachers would have been notified."

"Well, then he's probably on drugs," Aimee said, stuffing a particularly large scoop of ice cream in her mouth.

"Nah. Drugs would make him even crazier."

"Have you done anything about the new behavior?"

"Why would I? He's quiet. He's finally letting me teach." Tess paused to swallow more ice cream. "But I'm keeping records, if that's what you're asking."

"Good. I don't want to see you lose your job over some nutcase."

"Neither do I."

Aimee turned on the TV. She flipped the channels for a while trying to find something interesting. Reruns of *Beverly Hills 90210* happened to be on the soap opera channel. Aimee began snickering right away.

"What? What's so funny?"

"This is the exact same episode we were watching when you vowed to find a guy just like Dylan McKay! Ha! It was the summer before eighth grade. Do you remember that?"

Of course Tess remembered. "I did *not* make such a stupid vow...did I?"

"You sure did. You were obsessed with Dylan McKay. Every day that summer you said something about how you were going to marry him."

"Oh my God. No I didn't!" Tess paused, mildly mortified at her thirteen-year-old self's taste. "Okay, so maybe I did, but whatever. It's not like I've kept *that* vow going all these years later."

Aimee looked Tess squarely in the face with complete disbelief. Who was Tess kidding? She knew that vow was just the beginning of what would later become the bet she made in college, which became what made her get up in the morning. It was what drove her straight back into Nick's arms time after time.

"So how's Nick?"

"He's great. Really good."

"Things are going well then?"

"Good. Really good," Tess lied. Aimee just knew it. "Actually, I wanted to tell you that we've started talking about moving in together," she said, still lying. She couldn't stop.

"Wow. Really?"

"Yeah, he asked me to start leaving my stuff at his place. Oh, and he bought a throw blanket for his couch just for me, since I always fall asleep on the couch."

"Well, that's sweet."

"We talked about moving to either Weymouth or Braintree. I hear the schools are pretty good in either town."

"Wait. Braintree? From what I know about Nick, he would never live in Braintree. He's way too Connecticut for that."

Tess looked at the floor. "Well, right. That's why Weymouth is an option too. We just need to visit both places and see what's there."

"Who would have thought? Brenda just might tame Dylan after all. Now, if you guys are planning on moving in together, does that mean you've met each other's families and all that stuff?"

"I've met a couple of his friends. I really like his friend Will. I think he's a good influence. He's married."

"How about Nick's parents? Does he have any siblings?"

"He has a couple of sisters."

"Interesting. How about your dad? Have you told your dad that you're going to be moving in with a guy?"

"Whoa, Aimee, what is this? The Inquisition?"

"Not at all. I just remember that before Jason and I moved in together, we were both already parts of each other's family."

"I see." Tess looked panicked and pensive.

"Well, if he hasn't met your dad yet, I'd be happy to host a little informal early-season cookout. I'll invite some other friends so it's less intimidating, just in case your dad is more than Nick can handle. Oh, and Nick can invite whomever too."

"You'd do that for me?"

"Why not? I haven't hung out with you guys as a couple. And I think it's super important for your dad to know who his daughter is sleeping with."

"Gross, Aimee! You didn't have to put it like that."

"What? You guys sleep next to each other, don't you? You're the one with the dirty mind."

"Sure, okay. Whatever." Tess smiled. "This is going to be awesome. Thank you so much, Aimee. I'll call my dad later and invite him. Nick'll love the idea too. I just know it!"

Chapter 49

All the weathermen agreed; the first Saturday in May would be the best weekend to kick off the cookout season. Tess set about tracking down Hugh, which, surprisingly, didn't take as long as usual. Hugh was delighted to be invited and promised to be there with bells on. Tess told him to leave the bells at home and wear a clean shirt.

With Hugh taken care of, Tess focused on selling the party to Nick. Fearing that he'd think she was putting the pressure on to move in, she decided to purposely leave out the fact that her father was going to be there until that morning.

"It really means a lot to me that you're coming to Aimee's cookout. I know she isn't your favorite," Tess said from Nick's sofa as she brushed her wet hair. Nick was ready to take his turn in the shower.

"It's no big deal. There'll be other people there. It'll be easy to avoid her."

"Right." Was it really that hard for him to at least pretend to be nice to her best friend? "Plus my dad will be there. He's really looking forward to meeting you," she said quickly.

Nick froze. "Your dad? I thought you didn't really talk to

him?"

"Well, I don't talk to him all the time, but he lives in Boston too, so I see him from time to time. Thanksgiving, Christmas, my birthday."

"Then why is he coming today? It's not any of those holidays."

"Because he wants to meet you. Trust me, it's no big deal. Really. If anything, he's just a space cadet. That's why I don't see him that much. He's kind of hard to pin down."

"Yeah." Nick paused. "I'm getting in the shower."

Alone, she almost cried. Nick's response was not at all what she expected. Her mind reeled with reasons why he'd reacted that way. Granted they weren't ready to move in at that moment, but wasn't meeting parents a step toward that? He may not have said he wanted to meet her family, but he didn't say he didn't want to either. She was utterly confused.

"Don't you dare cry, Tess. Not today. We're just in a funk. We haven't always been on the same page, but then we get back there. We'll do it again. Plus, Nick's shy. Everything's going to be fine," she told herself. "Just be cool. He's going to have to meet Dad sooner or later. Be light, be gay. It'll all be fine."

Now that he was going to meet Tess's father, Nick felt obligated to shave. He opened the medicine cabinet expecting to find his razor in its usual spot, but it wasn't.

"Where the hell is it?" He began pulling all sorts of girlie products—blackhead remover, teeth whitening strips, and hair ties—off the shelves. He couldn't believe how much stuff Tess had left. Most of it he had never even seen her use. "What is all this crap? Where the hell did you put my razor?" he said to the medicine cabinet. When the cabinet was half empty, Nick stormed into the living room.

"What the hell have you done in there? It's like a friggin' chick's bathroom." His cheeks were red and his eyes beady.

As soon as she heard his voice, Tess looked like she was about to jump out of her skin. He'd never yelled at her like that before. She stood right away wearing a remorseful face.

"I'm sorry. I didn't think it was that much."

"Christ, Tess, I can't even find my razor! This is my apartment. My stuff comes first."

Tess's eyes turned glassy. She made a beeline for the bathroom. Nick followed.

"See. It's right there on the top shelf," Tess said, pointing to the razor. The only other thing on that shelf was shaving cream; his stuff was all there in plain sight.

"When I said 'leave some things here,' I didn't mean move in," he said, mildly less angry.

"Nick, I'm sorry. If I'd known, I, I…"

While Nick stared at her with a look Tess could only interpret as sheer anger, something inside her brain clicked. She suddenly felt her face flame, and the pit in her stomach burned with her own anger.

"No," she said. Nick cocked his head with a confused look. Tess took a deep breath and walked closer to him. He took several steps backward into the bathroom. "No, Nick. You're not going to talk to me that way. You're a grown man. Since it appears you knew exactly how much stuff you were comfortable with me leaving, you should have said so from the beginning. And grown men don't yell at their girlfriends like impish children." She brushed past him as she left the bathroom.

In the living room, Tess momentarily paced back and forth shaking her arms. Her whole body tingled. She was proud of herself for actually standing up to him. What had come over her was a mystery, but that didn't matter. The point was she'd done it. Replaying it in her mind, she realized she could have been softer, but what she'd said was perfect. *Finally putting that redhead temper to good use.*

The ride to Aimee's was quiet. Even though he sat in the driver's seat next to her, Nick seemed miles away. His silence made Tess nervous. After half an hour of silence, all the confidence she had felt at his apartment became muddied with anxiety. Was he going to be this distant with her at the party? Suddenly the cookout was the last place she wanted to go. *God, I am going to look like a fool!* she thought. She almost texted Aimee to tell her they weren't coming.

"I'm sorry I yelled earlier," Nick said, breaking the standoff.

"Thank you." Tess breathed a sigh of relief. She could tell he was softening.

"It's just that meeting your dad isn't something I expected."

"I'm so sorry. I should've told you."

"Meeting parents is a big deal, and like moving in, I'm not sure we're at that point yet."

"Oh, no. Yeah, I get it. I'm sorry. I should've talked to you about it first."

"Look, I'm not saying I don't want to meet your family and whatever. I just need more time. I can't, don't want to rush things."

"That's totally cool. Yeah, I agree. Let's not rush it."

"I knew you'd understand." He grabbed her hand and rubbed it with his thumb. "Now tell me more about your dad. What's he like?"

For the rest of the ride, Nick seemed to want to learn as much about her dad as possible. His questions calmed Tess's anxiety a bit. The day may have started rough, but everything would turn out just fine.

Chapter 50

Aimee's place was jumping by the time they arrived. She had invited all their mutual friends as well as some of Jason's friends. Seeing so many people put Tess at ease. Even Hugh had arrived before Tess. From the look of it, things could not have been more promising had she organized the cookout herself.

"There's me girl!" Hugh said, coming over with a beer in hand. "I was starting to think I got stood up."

"Hi, Dad," Tess said with an abashed tone. *Well, if I had stood you up, I could say I'd learned how from the best,* she was tempted to say, but she bit her tongue. And just like that, anger toward Hugh came bubbling to the surface, as it always did when she first saw him.

"Hey, no problem, Tessie. No need to get all bent out of shape."

"God, Dad I'm not—"

Aimee arrived just in time to save Tess from screaming.

"Nick, Tess, I'm so glad you guys made it! Nick, I see you've met Hugh, Tess's father," Aimee said. Tess softened in her presence. She surely would've blown up if Aimee had appeared just one second later.

"Actually, we haven't been formally introduced yet," Nick replied. "Tess?"

"Dad, this is Nick. Nick, this is my dad, Hugh."

"It's a pleasure to finally meet you. I've heard quite a lot about you."

"Geez, thanks," Hugh gave Tess a look.

"Only good stuff, of course!"

"Great. You guys seem to be getting along. Help yourselves to whatever you want. Soda, beer, wine—whatever you want. Tess, you know where everything is anyway. Jason's got the grill going, so let him know what you'd like and he'll throw it on for you," Aimee said before leaving to attend to her other guests. "Tess, I'll catch up with you later."

"So, ah, Tess tells me you're a painter. That's gotta be nice," Nick began. "Is your work in any galleries?"

"Galleries? I've had to paint more houses than canvases, if you know what I mean. People just aren't buying art like they used to. Gotta do something to pay the rent."

"House painting?"

"Summer is the high time. In fact, I could be on a job right now, but I couldn't turn down my little Tessalie and her party." Tess wished she could crawl under a rock and die. "I hear you're a history teacher like Tess?"

"We teach at different schools, but yes, I'm a history teacher as well." There was a mild air of pretension in his voice.

"That's great. Really great. I have the utmost respect for teachers. And I'm not saying that because of my daughter. I really believe they're the key to the future. Forget all that technology crap."

"I hear ya."

"Sure, all these computer outfits are making lots of money, but what happens if the power goes out? How are people going to know what do to?" Hugh took a swig of beer. "Teachers, that's what'll happen. They're the only ones who know how to keep this damn planet running."

Nick chuckled. Despite how outdated Hugh's argument was it was still charming. Plus, he shared Hugh's feelings about technological reliance. It was reassuring to hear someone outside the realm of education say it.

"Well, it looks like you guys are all set. Nick, do you want me to get you something to drink?" Tess said. Both men turned to her as if suddenly realizing she was there.

"A beer would be great."

When she returned, she handed a beer to Nick, completed a quick inspection of the situation, must have deemed it fine, and told Nick she was off to find Aimee.

"She's a great girl, you know," Hugh said in a clearly fatherly tone. Nick felt himself stiffen. This was not where Nick wanted the conversation to go. He scanned the backyard for Tess, feeling uncomfortable.

"She certainly is."

"So smart. So kind. Will do anything for you. Then *boom*! Like a bullet, she's suddenly breathing fire and ready to kill you."

"Wait, I'm not the only one who's experienced that?" Nick asked, remembering the morning.

"Hell, no. It's freaky as hell, right? She musta got that from her mother. I sure as shit don't have that kind of emotional range."

"Wow. I thought I was the only one freaked out by that."

"Nah, man, it's a woman thing. They're all like that really. See that woman over there? That's Gina. We've been seeing each other for a while now. She practically lives with me. It's all right and stuff, but man, when she gets all moody and shit, I disappear."

Nick found himself liking Hugh. They spoke the same language. Knowing Tess's father was as independent as he was, Nick no longer felt as bad about the earlier bathroom incident.

"What's your deal, kid? Relax. I'm not going to bite or anything. Well, if you try to steal my food I might get a little touchy."

Really? You'd have more of a problem with me over food than hurting your daughter? Nick began to relax. "Thanks for the tip." Nick paused. "Tess didn't tell me I was going to meet you until this morning."

"No kidding? That's definitely like the shit her mother would pull. Sorry, man. Here, have another beer." Hugh passed Nick his own.

"I'm good, thanks." Nick pointed to the one in his hand.

Hugh nodded. "Women. Can't live with 'em. Can't live without 'em."

"Cheers to that!" Nick clanked bottles with Hugh.

From across the yard, Tess could see they were hitting it off. Her relief released her anxiety, and she momentarily went limp. "Aimee, will you look at them? They look like they're having a great time! I cannot thank you enough for putting all of this together."

"You guys seem happy, like legit happy. I'm glad it's working out."

"Thanks. This means a lot." And it really did. Before the party Tess was thinking they were heading to Splitsville. After seeing Nick with Hugh, she wasn't so worried.

The cookout broke up around the time the mosquitoes came out seeking dinner. Once Aimee's backyard was mostly put back together, Nick and Tess said their good-byes. Nick drove back to Tess's place.

"Why are we going to my place?"

"I figured I would drop you off so you don't have to drive tomorrow." Nick seemed distant in his response.

"But my car is at your place."

"Oh, that's right. My bad." Nick tried to play innocent, but Tess observed his instant frustration. He clicked the indicator on when they approached the next southbound exit.

"Are you all right?"

Nick hesitated. "Of course," he finally said. "Your dad's pretty cool. It's a shame you don't see him more."

"Hmm, weird. Definitely not how I'd describe him. What did you talk about?"

"Just stuff. You know, a little of this, a little of that."

"That's descriptive."

"Come on, we're guys. We talk about whatever. Nothing really. It was cool. I liked him."

"If you say so. I'm sure he liked you too."

"If it's cool with you, I'd be happy to invite him along on some of our outings."

"You want to hang out with my dad?"

"Sure, why not?"

"Because he's old. He's my dad. You guys couldn't possibly have that much to talk about."

"Your dad knows more than you think."

Yeah, he knows a lot of bullshit, Tess thought. "I guess I can give you his number so you guys can make playdates." Hearing the words out loud, Tess instantly regretted saying them. Nick, on the other hand, laughed.

Realizing Nick wasn't going to share her opinion of her father, Tess went quiet. She forced herself to bottle up what she really wanted to say, which was that she felt unappreciated and passed over for, of all people in the world, her father.

When they arrived, Nick said, "You're going to head home tonight then?" He looked through the day's mail he'd picked up on the way in to the apartment.

"Excuse me?"

"You want to go back tonight, right?"

"We just drove for an hour and a half. I don't really want to drive back again."

"You sure?"

"Do you not want me to stay?"

"You can if you want. I just thought you might want your space. It was kind of a stressful day, after all."

Nick had to be projecting.

"Got it. Let me just get the rest of my stuff." She really wanted to stay, but at this point she was too tired to start what could become another fight.

"I don't mind if you leave the stuff here. Come get it tomorrow or whatever."

Tomorrow? What is going on with him? He was hot and cold, worse than a water heater on the fritz. *Does he or doesn't he want me here?* He knew she couldn't stand that much driving in such a short period of time.

"Yeah, something like that."

They kissed good-bye coldly and automatically. She really didn't want to leave, but she told herself Nick just needed some space. After a little while, he'd surely return to his sweeter self. She drove off in the name of repairing their relationship.

Chapter 51

After the lively weekend, being back at school seemed like a vacation. Even sixth period felt more relaxing as Ronnie continued to doodle quietly. Tess still hadn't figured out why. She almost called his mother to find out if something major had happened, but she really didn't have the energy. Every phone call with the woman had turned into an impromptu therapy session, with Mrs. DeCarlo divulging secrets about her childhood that had nothing to do with her son. There really was no need for that, in Tess's opinion.

The new, quiet version of Ronnie meant the class could actually watch a film without a disaster. Tess was more than ready for the break that showing a movie afforded her. Still needing to make up for all the lost instruction from Ronnie's previous disruptions, and it now being May, Tess played the movie *Cinderella Man* to open another perspective on the Great Depression to her class. The class would need two days to watch it. The first day went off without a hitch. The majority of the students claimed to love it. Even Ronnie seemed engaged.

The next afternoon, there was a familiar buzz in the room that Tess hadn't sensed since March. She looked around, concluding the students were just eager to get the movie started. Then Tess noticed that Ronnie was more talkative than he had been in months, but by no means was he carrying on as he had in the past. At first, Tess didn't worry; everyone was talking excitedly. *Perhaps* Cinderella Man *is reaching him,* Tess hoped. However, Ronnie continued talking to three guys next to him after the movie started.

"Gentlemen, that'll be enough."

"Boys, do I need to separate you?" Tess said a few minutes later.

The three boys stopped talking immediately. Ronnie, on the other hand, continued as if she didn't exist. Tess approached him quietly to avoid disturbing the students who were absorbed in the film.

"Ronnie, I need you to move your seat to the other side of the room," she said passionlessly, firmly.

Just as Ronnie froze, Tess felt a sinister feeling roll in. She asked him again to move. He looked at Tess, holding her gaze and assumed a twisted smirk. The anticipation over what was going to happen next was palpable. Ronnie turned to talk to his friends again.

"Ronnie, I'm not going to ask again. You need to move your seat, or I'm going to call your assistant principal and have him personally move you."

Without warning, Ronnie roared to his feet, lifting his desk. "Fine, you nagging bitch, I'll move my seat." He whipped it across Tess's body as hard as he could. When she didn't fall right away, he continued swiping it against her. With each blow her consciousness slipped farther and farther away until she dropped, barely conscious. Then he threw the desk so hard, the force sent it through the window, shattering it, with shards of glass flying all over the place. Ronnie stood over Tess with a demonic look of pride on his face.

Mr. Gargiullo heard the commotion from next door and rushed in. The first thing he saw was Tess on the floor surrounded by shards of glass. *Cinderella Man* was still playing on the screen at the front of the room. There was a hole the size of a desk in the window. Every student looked petrified except Ronnie. Mr. Gargiullo immediately called for backup. The school went into lockdown. The swarm of police officers pushed students back so the EMTs could maneuver Tess onto a stretcher and into the waiting ambulance. Ronnie was escorted from the building in handcuffs.

Tess began to come around at six that evening. In a semiconscious state, her eyes closed, she pictured her father, mother, and sister all smiling with a bright, warm light behind them. She wondered if she had entered heaven. Seeing them all together and looking happy made Tess feel at peace. Soon that soft, comforting light sharpened and grew dark.

Images of her classroom filtered in. It looked different. She recognized it as her room, but she felt like it was the first time she had been in it. Everything was quiet. Sunlight glinted off fragments of glass. She noticed blood, lots of blood. *What happened? Is everyone okay? My hands are bloody. My leg hurts terribly!* Tess whimpered. The scene of Ronnie's attack flooded back, playing over and over. Every blow was more painful than the last. Worst of all was the wild rage in Ronnie's eyes. He was like an untamed beast just released from a cage. Tears rolled down her cheeks. Tess whipped her head back and forth, as if avoiding the attacker.

"Tess! Tess? Hey, shhhh, it's okay. I'm here. It's me, Aimee. You're safe." Aimee soothingly stroked Tess's head, comforting her. Tess opened her eyes and looked all around her. She first noticed the insipid green walls and blazing fluorescent lights, but they triggered no clues about where she was. All the knobs and switches on the numerous machines were unfamiliar and scary. Then the distinct hospital smell hit her, instantly informing her about where she was.

From down the hall came the voices of a couple of Boston Police Department officers, followed by voices Tess recognized as her students.

"Holy hell, my body hurts." Tess mumbled as she tried to sit up.

"Hey, hey, hey, just relax. No need to sit up." Aimee gently held her down. She found the switch on the bed that lifted the top of it. "That's better. You comfortable? Can I get you anything?"

"Can I have something for the pain?"

Aimee left to find the doctor. "He'll be here in a minute," she announced when she returned. Aimee grabbed Tess's hand again and smiled. Knowing her friend was there made Tess's head feel a little better.

"Thank God you're okay. I was so worried when Elaine called and said you'd been assaulted by a student." Genuine concern shone in her eyes. "God, Tess, you've got to find another school. It's just not safe."

"Did you call my mom? Where's my dad?"

"I talked to your mom. She's looking into flights right now." Aimee paused. "The hospital's still trying to get a hold of your dad. I've been calling him too."

Sadness welled in Tess's eyes when she heard her dad was MIA. Tess asked, "Nick? Where's Nick?"

Aimee hesitated. "I texted him, but he hasn't texted back."

Tess looked at Aimee with a blank expression.

"Hey, Tess, you're okay now. You're safe. I'm sure Nick and your dad will be here as soon as they can." Tess moaned. "Hey, hey, no more tears. It's time to be brave. You know you are, deep down. You're going to be just fine. And hey, two of the hottest cops I've ever seen are about to come in here. That's something to smile about."

Tess did smile; a cute man in a uniform was never something to frown over.

"You even have that hot reporter from Channel 5 Fox News, Brett Connolly, waiting to interview you! He is even hotter in real life."

"Fox News? Why are they here?"

"I hate to have to tell you this, Tess, but you're breaking news.

'Teacher Assaulted with Desk'. It's all over the place."

"Great, just what I need." Tess had never yearned to be famous. If she had to be featured in a headline, she hoped it would be for some contribution to society, not as a first-year teacher beat up by a student.

Suddenly, like a bullet, Nick barreled in.

"I got here as soon as I could. Are you okay? Are you in a lot of pain?" Nick brushed past Aimee to approach Tess.

Tess winced when he kissed her head. "Much better now."

"You're comfortable. Good. That's really good." Nick turned to Aimee. "Hey, thanks. I tried to leave as soon as I got your text, but there was no one to cover my classes. And traffic was a mess. There was an accident and—"

"You're here now." Aimee's tone put a stop to his rambling.

"Do you remember what happened?" Nick asked, turning back to Tess. Her face was blank. "That's okay. I'm sure it'll come back." Nick looked overwhelmed at the sight of Tess helplessly lying in a hospital bed. He shared a concerned look with Aimee.

This was a side of Nick that Tess had never seen before. His display of panicked worry made her feel desirable in the way she had been waiting for since they had first met.

"Hey, I need to tell you something."

His urgent tone changed the mood in the room. He looked like he was about to share something huge. His shoulders stiffed and he held his breath. Aimee gave Tess a tender smile and left the two of them alone. Tess started thinking, *Here they come, the three little words I have been so anxiously waiting to hear.* She was so excited she almost forgot her pain.

"I like...ah, I think that—" Nick stopped and looked around the room. "What I mean is I don't want...God, this shouldn't be so hard to say."

"It's okay, you can say it. I bet I already know what you're going to say."

Nick hesitated a little more and then finally blurted, "Tess, I really like you," just as Tess said, "I love you too."

The smile on her face dropped to a frown. Nick looked confused but continued. "So please promise me that you won't let this happen again."

She didn't think it was possible, but somehow the physical pain throughout her body paled in comparison to the hurt and shock her heart suddenly felt. How in the world could she make sure another student didn't beat her up? Nick was acting like she had asked Ronnie to beat her up. But the fact that he didn't tell her he loved her shocked her the most.

Before she could worry about that, a young and fetching male doctor entered the room. *Is the universe giving me the consolation prize of hot men to tend to me in my time of need?*

"Hi, there. I'm Doctor Charlie Pierce. How are you feeling?" the hot doctor asked. Aimee followed him in, silently smiling and pointing both index fingers to show how hot he was.

Tess chuckled at Aimee before responding, "Like I've been hit by a truck."

"I would think so. It's not every day that a teacher gets pummeled by a desk. Now I'm going to ask you a few questions, okay? Some of them may seem silly, but I need you to answer them seriously. Between you and me," the doctor said, leaning flirtatiously close, "if you don't, they'll put me in detention." He paused long enough for Tess to smile and nod.

"All right, here we go. First, what's your name?"

"Tess."

"Tess what?"

"Ryan. Tess Ryan."

"Like, Bond, James Bond. I like it." He chuckled. "Good. And how old are you?"

"You know it's not very nice to ask a lady how old she is before you buy her dinner." The flirtation between doctor and patient did not go unnoticed by anyone in the room.

"Duly noted. Now the date?"

"Wow, you really do want to know how old I am. I'm flattered, but my boyfriend's standing right next to you." Nick rolled his eyes, but Tess didn't notice. Had he said he loved her she might not have responded so playfully to the dapper doctor.

"No, no," the hot doctor chuckled again. "What is the date, as in day and month?"

"Oh, May 8th."

"And the year?"

"2009."

"Good. Last one. Can you tell me approximately what time it is?"

"About five, six, seven, maybe?"

"Perfect. All right, Tess, I'm going to tell you what you've got going on. You endured mild trauma to your midsection, arms, and neck. Both your femur and tibia are broken. Because both were broken we had to go in there and surgically insert screws here and here." The doctor pointed to the spots on her cast where the screws were placed in her leg underneath. "To properly align the bones. Luckily, they were clean breaks so they should heal up nicely, which is a good thing. You'll need to be off your feet for at least six to eight weeks."

Tess choked a little at the idea of being off her feet for so long. "How am I going to teach sitting down?"

"I know. It sounds like an eternity, but I'm afraid you may not be going back this year. But from the looks of it you've got a lot of support here. I'm sure someone can take you in, make sure you stay off that leg." The doctor's tone was leading and his eyes vividly intense. He looked at Aimee and then Nick, as if waiting to see who would step up and take his bait. Catching on to what the doctor was doing, Tess looked at Nick in earnest. She wanted him to be the one to come forward.

The moment was short, but tense. Aimee and Nick shared a look. Aimee shrugged and opened her mouth to speak but Nick's voice was heard first. "Tess will be staying with me," Nick said directly to the doctor. Tess couldn't stop the smile that crossed her face, although she winced again in pain from the cuts and scrapes on her cheeks.

"Great, now that arrangements have been made, I think you should get some rest. In a couple of days, you'll be good to go home. Until then, I want to keep you here for observation. Make sure there aren't any complications with infection or from that knock on the head."

Tess held the doctor's gaze. He was very intriguing. It was as if he knew her needs without having to say a word, and she was rather curious to find out if he was legitimately flirting with her. Maybe that was just how he acted with all his busted up patients. Then her face went blank because her brain was in overdrive processing everything he'd just told her. "And now I'm part bionic. Lovely," Tess said after the long pause. Aimee failed to stifle a chuckle.

"Only the finest girls are. Keep that spunk. You'll need it."

Tess smiled. "Hey, doc, my body really hurts. Can I have something for it?"

"Sure, I'll send the nurse."

"Thank you."

"You've been through a lot." He paused, looking at her endearingly. "Let me know if you don't feel relief soon and I'll see what I can do about getting you the good stuff."

Then the doctor vanished around the curtain. Looks of relief, the kind expressed when the end of a life-threatening event had finally come, filled the room.

"So, Ronnie DeCarlo finally took me down, eh?"

"Apparently," Nick said. His eyes were still a little glossy, and his cheeks were redder than usual.

"I'm glad you're here," Tess said to Nick. He squeezed her hand and kissed her on her head. "Hey, Aimee, have you gotten in touch with my dad yet?"

"Not yet," Aimee said softly. Tess looked at Nick for a brief second; perhaps he knew where Hugh was. Nick shook his head.

When the nurse returned with medication, she was followed by the police officers Aimee had mentioned. Before anything was said, Tess swallowed the medication.

"Good evening, Miss Ryan. I'm Officer O'Reilly, and this is Officer Mendez. We would like to ask you a few questions, if that's okay."

"Seriously? Can't you see she's not ready," Nick said.

"Excuse me? Who are you?" Officer O'Reilly asked.

"I'm Nick Donovan, her boyfriend." He leaned over to look at Officer Mendez's notepad. "It would be better to ask her questions tomorrow. She needs her rest." Nick flashed a smug smile.

"Yeah, look, buddy, I see what you're doing here, but it's just a couple a questions. Won't take long," Officer O'Reilly said. He looked Nick up and down. "All we need to know is what she remembers."

The three men turned to Tess. She felt pressured to pick a side.

"I, ah, I only remember asking my student Ronnie DeCarlo to move his seat. He was talking during a film. Then, ah, I really don't remember. All I know is I was in my classroom and now I'm here." Tess took Nick's side. He was right. She wasn't ready to talk about it.

Officer O'Reilly and Officer Mendez shared an unreadable look.

"Okay, Miss Ryan, do you mind if we come by later on or give you a call to ask you what you remember?" Officer Mendez asked.

"That'd be fine."

The officers turned to leave.

"Thank you, officers, for your understanding," Nick said in a victorious tone.

They both smiled curtly and left.

"Man, what dicks. They couldn't wait even a day."

"Nick, it's fine. I'm fine. No need to get all worked up about it. They're just doing their job."

Aimee scowled at him.

"Ooh, yeah, okay! That's the stuff. Ahhhh, this is the good stuff! Love that doctor. Oh yeah, nice and lightheaded." Tess smiled without wincing.

"Right. Time to sleep. Sleep as long as you need, Tess. I'll be here when you wake up."

"Nick, you'll stay with me too?"

Nick looked at Aimee and then Tess. "Of course I'll stay. I just have to make some sub plans." Nick paused. "Make some for you too?"

"You're the best, best, *bestest*!"

"Covering the Depression, right?"

"Exactamundo!"

He smiled, kissed Tess on the forehead, and went off. Tess fell asleep shortly thereafter. Aimee remained, reading *Better Homes and Gardens*.

Grace was able to get a flight the same day Tess was attacked. Aimee graciously picked her up from the airport at midnight.

"Aimee, sweetheart, it is so good to see you. You look amazing."

"Same to you Grace. I'm just so happy you were able to get a fly so soon. It'll really help Tess."

"How is she? Is she okay?"

"She was sleeping when I left. I assume she'll still be that way when we get back."

"I'm still in shock," Grace paused looking out the window as Aimee drove through her old stomping grounds.

"It's okay we all are."

Aimee gripped the steering wheel tighter. Grace gave her a knowing look and returned her gaze to the passing scenery.

"Nick's been real great though. He came as soon as he could. Then as she fell asleep he left to make her lesson plans for the substitute."

A curious smile crossed Grace's face. "Is that so. Well, that makes me happy. He's taking care of her then?"

"From what I can tell. I think he's finally grown up. In fact, he met Hugh the other day at a cookout at my place."

"Interesting...So they're meeting parents and the like now..." Grace paused, looking lost in thought. "Thank you Aimee for telling me that. I really do worry about Tess and her taste in men. Of course, I blame myself for a lot of that. God, I hope she doesn't become the girl who said yes, like me, simply because I didn't think I was good enough to say no." Grace looked at Aimee who looked a little uncomfortable. "Aw, Christ listen to me blather on about my past. Sorry dear. The important thing is that I know she has you looking out for her."

"She's like a sister to me. You know that."

Grace reached over and gave Aimee's hand a squeeze.

"Almost there, Grace."

Grace smiled and rested her head on the seat's head rest until it was time to go in.

Just as Aimee had figured, Tess was still sleeping when they returned. Even so, Grace rushed to her daughter's side and took her hand.

"Hi baby. It's Mom. I'm here now. Thank God you're okay." Grace softly kissed Tess's forehead. Aimee pulled the large comfy chair up to the bed for Grace to sit. Once comfortable, Grace thanked Aimee for being there and told her to go home and get some rest.

The following morning Grace was woken to the sound of Hugh's thick Irish brogue calling out for Tess like a mad man.

"Christ, Hugh keep your voice down! It's only six o'clock in the morning," Grace said the moment Hugh appeared in the doorway.

Hugh looked stunned. "Oh. Why hello Grace." His volume and tone were much softer.

"Hugh."

"How is she? I got 'ere as quick as I could."

"Lets go out in the hall."

Hugh followed without a fight.

"How are ya Grace? You're looking good? That Santa Fe sun treating ya well, then?"

"Indeed."

An awkward silence grew between them.

"She's okay then? Going to make a full recovery?"

Grace nodded, fighting back tears. Not tears from seeing her ex-husband, but for the fact that he had changed so little. He was still the same old out of touch Hugh. Grace was overwhelmed with guilt.

"And how are you? Doing okay?" she asked.

"Okay as I ever am. Can't complain."

"Where were you Hugh?"

"What do you mean, 'where was I?' I was here in Boston."

"Exactly. Jesus, I was here before you and I had to fly across the country. So tell me, where were you? What was so much more important than your daughter that it took you over twelve hours to get here?" She paused. "What was her name? Did you even bother to ask before you rolled out of bed and took your jolly old time getting here?"

Hugh looked up and down the hospital corridor, first left, then right. "Oh yeah, well where's Eve huh? If it's such a big deal that the whole damn family has a reunion, where the hell is she?

Grace scoffed. "I guess you didn't hear the news. She's

engaged."

"And how's that stopping her from comin' 'ere, for her sister?"

"Wow. Not even a congratulations? Not even a flicker of interest that your youngest is getting married?"

"What? How was I supposed to know Evie's got herself engaged?"

"Gee, I don't know Hugh. You could try calling them once in a while. Remember every now and again you are in fact a father." Grace's voice was soft yet cutting.

"Eh, I love me daughters very much. Never once have I stopped loving them."

"Of course you do. Got a funny way of showing it though."

Hugh had no response. He lowered his shoulders with a forlorn face. Grace gave him a curt smile as she tapped his shoulder and went back to Tess's bedside.

Grace stayed for a full week. She and Hugh managed to figure out a suitable visiting schedule that minimized run-ins with each other. At night, she stayed with Aimee, happy to spend some quality time with the girl she often considered her third daughter. Grace also had the pleasure of getting to know Nick. She found him pleasant and respectful. Grace appeared relieved to see him there tending to Tess just as Aimee said.

Chapter 52

Tess wound up in the hospital for two weeks. She was infection free, but the physical therapy was long, and progress was slower than she wanted, which worried doctors. When she prevailed and was finally released, she hobbled straight back to school, despite pleas from both the hospital staff and Nick. She needed to know what had happened with Ronnie. *Has he been removed from school? Is this the catastrophic event I was hoping for?*

"Miss Ryan, what a surprise! Come in, come in," her principal, Mr. Wilkes, said, welcoming her into his office. "So, how are you feeling?"

"Better than the last time I was here."

"You look good." The tension between teacher and administrator was strong and awkward.

Tess blushed, looking down at her white-plastered leg. "How have things been going here? Is Ronnie still in my class?"

"Tess, you know as well as I do that is irrelevant. There're four weeks left in the year." Mr. Wilkes stopped and repositioned himself at his desk. "Now, I *can* tell you that the investigation is ongoing. Some other events have come to light. I'm not sure when we'll have an answer for you as to why this happened, but when I do, I'll be sure to let you know."

"I appreciate that. And to think that I thought he was making a turnaround."

"There is another matter that I need to discuss with you." As Mr. Wilkes's words entered the room, an apprehensive silence followed. "The window. When we looked into having it replaced, the district found that you are responsible for paying for the damages."

Tess choked a little. *What did he just say? Is he serious?* Of course he was; he was the principal. For a moment, Tess was about to accept the verdict, but then she remembered what Aimee said in the hospital: *be brave.*

"You're joking, right?"

"Not in the slightest, Miss Ryan."

"How am I liable for it? I'm not the one who broke it."

"We, meaning myself and the special education coordinator, looked at your behavior notes, and there is nothing there to indicate that this event should've happened. Based on what's in there, it appears you simply stopped fulfilling that portion of his IEP."

Tess leaned back in disbelief. "Jonathan, if I may," Tess began, attempting to sit upright. She had never called the principal by his first name. It felt both awkward and empowering. "Ronnie's IEP very clearly states to note only disruptive behaviors in his weekly progress report. Since April ninth, he has not had a single disruptive behavior besides this specific event."

"Miss Ryan, how long have you been teaching here?"

"This is my first year."

"That's right. Now, I'm surprised that as a first-year teacher you made the assumption to stop recording any behavior. Didn't they teach you during your preparation program that all behavior is a symptom of something and should be written down?"

No. She never took a teacher preparation program. She got a master's degree in her content area, which caught the hiring team's attention during her interview. "But the IEP clearly states to only note negative behaviors. I was doing my job. I was following his IEP." Tess remembered her personal notebook for tracking Ronnie's behavior since April 9. "As a matter of fact, Jonathan, I've been keeping track of all of his behaviors."

"Is that so? Where is it then? I can't see it in the computer system." He clicked the mouse of his computer while looking at the screen as if he was looking at the file.

"That's because it's not in the computer system. Since it was not what the IEP asked for, I noted behaviors in a notebook that's locked in my desk upstairs. If you like, I can go get it right now."

Looking at her cast, Mr. Wilkes said, "That won't be necessary, Miss Ryan. The fact is you should've seen this coming. Since it's not formally documented in our system, I'm left no other choice than to hold you responsible for the repairs."

"Are you accusing me of incompetence?"

Mr. Wilkes looked stunned. He choked on the words he was about to say. "The DeCarlos are not in a position to pay for the damages."

"Of course they're not," Tess said. "What about restitution?

The student works off the damage in service to the school."

"I am well aware of the definition of restitution, Miss Ryan. Thank you." He looked her up and down. She felt slimy and violated.

"Mr. Wilkes, I can't afford to pay for a new window."

"The payroll office will make biweekly deductions until the $746 is paid off."

"No, no, no. I didn't agree to that. You can't force me to pay for something that I didn't break." Everything Mr. Wilkes was saying had to be illegal in some way. An employer could not just take out wages without consent. *If I taught somewhere else, this surely wouldn't be happening,* she thought.

"Sorry, Miss Ryan, but you don't have a choice. Now look, take as much time as you need. Come back only when you're ready, even if that means not until next year."

His cold words were unnerving. Tess thought what he was actually saying was he would keep her on payroll until next year, when he could formally fire her. Totally numb, Tess superficially thanked Mr. Wilkes for his time and hobbled on the still-unfamiliar crutches back to the car where Nick was waiting for her.

Chapter 53

"What a complete asshole!" Tess shouted as Nick drove out of the parking lot.

"Tess, you need to calm down."

"Oh my God. I can't believe the school is saying this is all my fault. My fault! And Ronnie. Jesus, flippin'...Ronnie isn't even being held responsible for the window!"

"So the school's not going to fix it."

"Nick, really? Where am I going to find seven hundred and fifty bucks?" Tess took a moment to catch her breath. She noticed Nick was sitting as far away from her as he could in the driver's seat. "I can't fricking believe this. He's such an asshole."

"Honestly, though, Tess, how could you not report his behaviors? Wasn't he one of the kids who had weekly progress reports?"

"He was, yes, and I did keep records. I just didn't put them into the computer. I kept them in a notebook that's locked in my desk."

"Oh, Tess."

"What? You can't say I didn't do my job. His IEP instructs me not to list anything in the progress report that isn't among specific behaviors. For over a month now, he hasn't been doing anything that I was required to record, so I didn't note anything there."

"Tess, I understand where you're coming from, but you must know that all behavior is progress. You really should've put it into the computer."

"Oh my God, you're siding with the administration?"

"Tess, I'm not picking sides. All I'm saying is you should've recorded all of it."

"Yeah, okay. Right...no one's side. So does this mean you think I should have to pay for the repairs too?"

"Well, you didn't do part of your job..."

"I can't believe you just said that!"

"Tess, don't be like that. So what? You made a mistake. Pay for it and move on."

Since Nick clearly wasn't going to take her side, she stopped talking. She was sick of fighting. She was sick of the feeling that their relationship wasn't going the way she wanted it to go. Nick might have been there for her physically, but there was something missing on an emotional level. What that was exactly, she wasn't sure. Unable to put her finger on it, she raged internally about what was currently so upsetting. *And why isn't anyone talking about the fact that I was brutally attacked at work? I could've died! Why isn't anyone talking about that? Me? My safety! Doesn't anyone care?*

For the rest of the ride they didn't speak. Nick played with the radio a few times, but he eventually gave up on a pop station Tess usually liked.

It was just past noon when they arrived at her apartment. Living on the third floor in a building without an elevator was something Tess had never thought about until she was standing in front of it in a cast, on crutches. Still mad at Nick, she tried to make it up the stairs without his help. It was an epic fail. She could barely manage a step without losing her balance.

Without warning, Nick picked her up and, slinging her over his shoulder, carefully carried her up the winding stairs. At first she resisted, but it didn't take long for her to realize it really was the quickest way. And she really had to pee.

As she hung over his shoulder, she discovered it was impossible to be mad at him anymore. Even though they had been fighting, in her time of need he'd gone above and beyond to take her where she needed to be. Suddenly picking her up was the final sign she needed during their long and bumpy relationship. She'd always known the man she would marry would be able to pick her up and carry her around, and here Nick was doing just that. Of course they would fight from time to time. They were only human.

But a dark thought entered her mind. *Why didn't he do this before now? Why did it take a brutal beatdown for him to take care of me the way he should have all along?* Something inside Tess changed. It was scary, and she fought it off, but she couldn't ignore it.

"I'll go get your crutches," Nick said, as he gently lowered Tess onto the couch. He smiled a wistful smile before running back downstairs. *Does he sense the change?*

Alone in her apartment, Tess made an effort to ignore the strange thoughts she had been ignoring for far too long. *This is not the time to explore them,* she told herself. Later, after everything was settled, she would face what she had been denying for years.

When Nick returned, he handed her the crutches and flopped onto the couch. "I need a drink," Tess announced. She waited for Nick to rise. Comfortably settled on the couch, he looked at her in a way that said he wasn't moving. With a sigh, she rose to her feet with the help of the crutches and hobbled to the refrigerator. She heard Nick turn the TV on. Annoyed, she managed to pour half a glass of wine while she balanced on the crutches. When she returned to the living room without spilling a drop, Tess sat on the loveseat.

"You know, I would have gotten that for you."

"Really?" *Then why didn't you?*

"Truly," he said with a charming smile that caught her off guard. He was being sweet, and she figured she should respond in kind. It was only fair.

"It was really nice of you to carry me up the stairs."

"No problem. But you owe me a complete back massage once that leg is healed."

Tess smiled sheepishly, disguising her renewed annoyance. She felt awkward and uncomfortable. No longer interested in the wine, she said, "I think I'm going to go lie down. Wake me in an hour or so?"

"Yeah, sure. Okay." He quickly glanced at her. The glint in his eyes made her shudder. He was there physically but not emotionally.

Although she was annoyed and frustrated with him, she still desperately wanted him to sweep her up in his arms and tell her how much he loved her. *Why hasn't he said it? Does it even register in his head that I said it?* She had spoken The Words two weeks ago, and he hadn't even mentioned it. *Why won't he just say it?*

The nap did little to silence her doubts. For the rest of the day and into the night, they didn't talk much. He was becoming a stranger in her apartment who happened to know his way around it. What they did say was concrete and had a purpose: "What do you want for dinner?" or "Could you pass the salt?"

When they retired to the living room after dinner, Tess sat on the loveseat, not feeling comfortable enough to sit next to him while he chose the couch. Neither said anything about their choices, despite clearly feeling the tension. They shared limp smiles and carried on as if everything was normal. Tess needed to know what he was feeling. *Is his mind racing as much as mine?* she asked herself over and over. *Does he not feel this weirdness?* Unable to bear the awkwardness anymore, Tess went to bed just after eight. She would have gone sooner, but she'd been waiting for him to say something first.

Inside her room, Tess felt like she was going to burst. She could no longer ignore what she was feeling. She felt like she couldn't catch her breath or a break. Since Ronnie had broken her leg, life was sending one bad thing after another. And now things with Nick were at the worst point ever.

Anxiety washed over her as she considered the future of the relationship. *Is this uncomfortable distance between us a sign? Does it mean he wants it to end? It can't, not now, not ever.* She had worked hard to reach this point. Their relationship wasn't perfect, but whose was? He was her intellectual soul mate. He inspired her to be the most intelligent person she could be. He made her want to explore the world. Their conversations were sometimes enough to give her an orgasm without any contact. How would she ever find that in someone else?

As her thoughts flowed, so did tears. She thought about the last four, almost five, years of her life with, and at times without, Nick. *God, how I liked him! All those butterflies in my stomach every time he was nearby. I was secretly in a competition with him for intellectual superiority. Oh, and that stupid swan e-mail! Halloween...the shock and euphoria of kissing him the first time, without disguises. He was the perfect boyfriend that summer before grad school. The sex! Oh boy, the sex...*She found herself smiling about all the good parts. *Yeah, the sex he had with me before graduation with barely a word afterward. He didn't call me or e-*

mail me...Freaking out about meeting my parents. I constantly worried about whether or not he was going to call or if he still wanted to see me the next day.

"I'm not that kind of girl! I don't live my life for guys!" she paused. "Oh my God...Eve's friends were right. I *am* truly that girl," she said out loud, realizing just how much she'd let her relationship with Nick define her identity, both in- and outside of their actual time together. At last, Tess was listening to that little voice in the back of her mind she had been silencing for years. The voice she'd fought vehemently a dozen times: after Halloween, after graduation, while they'd put furniture together, the night he left her on the sidewalk in the cold, and especially the night he left just after they'd reconnected. She'd ignored the voice because she was in love with Nick, just not the one currently watching her TV.

With a lump she felt in her throat, Tess understood that the Nick she loved was the fantasy version, the one who could play the lead love interest in any Hallmark movie, the one who somehow always knew the perfect thing to say and when to say it. She began to feel guilty about dragging the real Nick, whoever he was, through her insane fantasy. "No, I'm not doing this anymore," Tess vowed and drifted off to sleep.

The following morning Tess woke to the sound of Nick's phone alarm, feeling more rejuvenated, broken leg and all. After a brief battle with the cast to get out of bed, the first thing she did was find an empty box. Nick was in the middle of his usual morning routine when Tess began hopping around, against doctor's orders, collecting his things.

"Hey, what are you doing?" She heard mild panic in his voice.

"Just taking care of things." She dismissively continued to fill the box.

"But that's all my stuff?"

"Good eye there, detective."

"Tess, will you stop? You're weirding me out."

"Nick, can I ask you something?"

"Uh, yeah?"

"Do you love me?"

Nick looked at Tess in the mirror and stopped tying his tie. "Are you still mad about what happened with your principal yesterday?"

Tess laughed.

"How is that funny?"

"I ask you if you love me and you ask me if I'm still mad at my boss."

"How am I supposed to answer that? You totally blindsided me."

"With a simple yes or no."

"All right. Ask me again."

Tess laughed. She had her answer. She didn't need to ask, but watching him sweat was enjoyable.

"Fine. Do you love me?"

Nick opened his mouth to answer, but all that came out was hot air. "Tess, I haven't had my coffee yet."

"I haven't had any either, yet I know that I love you. Hell, I said it to you two weeks ago, in the hospital. Do you remember that?"

Nick tensed his shoulders. Tess saw a muscle twitch in his jaw. "Yeah...why?"

"And is there any chance you were ever going to bring that up?"

"You were hopped up on pain medicine. How was I supposed to know you were serious?"

"Wow, Nick. That's just great. Well, that confirms it for me." She saw the real Nick Donovan in front of her mirror for what felt like the first time.

"Confirms what?"

"That you don't love me."

"Wait a second. That's not fair. I never said I didn't love you."

"You didn't have to. I can feel it." Tess paused. "But that's okay. Really."

"Wait, what is happening right now? You're not breaking up with me."

Tess looked at him and said nothing. She left the bathroom to continue gathering his stuff.

"Nick, I need to take care of me. Something I'm not sure you'll ever be able to do," she called over her shoulder.

"What's that supposed to mean? I'm here now, aren't I? I've missed work so I could be here. What more do you want from me?"

"I want you to want to be here, Nick. I don't want you here because you feel obligated. And the simple fact that you're going to work today proves where your priorities are."

"Jesus Christ, Tess! I've been out of work for over two weeks! It couldn't have been a worse time of year to be out. You know that."

"Here's your stuff." Tess tossed the box on the floor by the front door. "You need to leave. I'm not doing this anymore."

"Tess, don't do this. We can work this out. We always have, haven't we? I can love you. I will love you." She saw desperation in his face but knew it wasn't about her. He was desperate for the familiarity of what they had built, the comfort, but not for her. She saw in that moment that if they ever had gotten to 'I love you', even married, it would only have been because it was time to get married, not because he wanted to marry her and that simply wasn't good enough.

"Good-bye, Nick," Tess said, closing one door and opening another.

Finally.

With a soft click of the door latch, Nick Donovan was gone once and for all. Tess stood and stared at the apartment door. She thought she would feel differently if this moment arrived. Until it actually happened, she honestly never thought it would. Nick was always the one to break it off and break her heart. She thought she would feel devastated and lost and probably cry hysterically, but she didn't. Instead, she felt clean and clear, as if she had finally showered after a two-week backpacking trip across no-man's-land.

Her good leg began to tire, so she limped over to the couch and settled herself comfortably. "Well, you did it, Miss Ryan!" Tess said aloud. "You finally saw the light. Good job, you." She smiled because she was talking to herself so freely.

Tess had finally realized that what made them last this long was not love at all. In fact, it was the farthest thing from love. It was her desire to make him love her that had kept her in the game. She realized that the more she forced it, the more she pushed it away. *Real love cannot be forced. It either happens or it doesn't.* She chuckled, which quickly turned into full-blown laughter.

Instead of Nick, or any other person, realizing her worth, Tess saw worth in herself. She was done living for a fantasy. She wanted to live in reality, where love actually existed. Tess leaned back on her couch happier than she had felt in a long time.

Looking around the room, her photo album caught her eye. She chuckled again thinking back to the last time she'd looked at it. She nearly gave up on love that night. Then she recalled the night she'd made that ridiculous bet with Aimee. She was never thrilled to lose a bet, but this time she was happy to make an exception. In losing the bet, Tess, at long last, was set free. She may not have gotten the MRS degree she wanted from college, but today was a new day, and she was finally open to whatever and whoever the day may bring. But first it was time to call Aimee and tell her the good news.

Epilogue

Two and a half months later, fully healed and cast free, Tess and
Aimee met for a late summer ice cream at J.P. Licks. Looking at
what was left of her banana split, Tess wished she hadn't eaten it
so quickly. She wanted more but didn't want to look like a fatty in
front of the cute shift manager behind the counter. Before
continuing the conversation, Tess glanced at him. She smiled
when they met eyes and he smiled back at her.

"It's weird, you know. I was certain if we ever broke up again
Nick would be the one to do it. Man, I was such a doormat with
him! You totally called it way back when. I should've listened to
you."

"Tell me something I don't know."

"Thanks. Anyway, after all that I went through, you'd think
I'd still be sobbing and depressed, even as the dumper, but I'm
not. Honestly, I feel really good."

"You say that now. It's been what? Two, three months since
you broke up?" Aimee paused, taking another bit of ice cream.
"Your feelings are likely to change."

"I have to disagree. It's been long enough now. I know if I
wanted him back I'd be chest deep in schemes to win him back,

but I'm not. In fact, I'm having a lot of fun."

"Wait what? Are you telling me you're dating someone? You little shit! How could you not tell me?" Aimee's eyes were bright with what looked like excitement and joy.

"Slow down, slow down. I'm not dating any one person in particular, but I am seeing what's out there."

"Okay, where's the real Tess Ryan? Have you seen her? How? When did all of this start?"

Tess caught the shift manager smirking at her. Getting the sense that he was watching her, her stomach got a squiggly feeling and she felt her cheeks turn a little red.

"Hey, will you stop eye fucking the kid behind the counter and answer my questions?" Aimee said, catching onto what Tess was smiling about. "Oh! Are you dating that guy? Is he even old enough to drive?"

"He's not *that* young, Aimee. And so what if I am? It's not like I'm going to marry the guy. I'm just having fun."

Aimee choked on her last spoonful of ice cream. "I am so proud of you, Tess." Tears welled in her eyes.

"And why are you the one about to cry?" Tess handed Aimee a napkin thinking she had nothing to cry about.

"Shut up. I'm not sad. I'm just so relieved that you see finally see what I've seen all along but haven't been able to say."

Tess cocked her said to the side with a confused look. "What do you mean?"

As Aimee was about to respond, the shift manager came over with another banana split.

"Compliments of the management," the attractive employee said. While standing over their little round table, Tess noticed the guy had one blue eye and one green, triggering her memory of telling Nick how her ideal man would have two different colored eyes. Though not pink and purple, the mere fact that they were different colors, she expected herself to immediately jump up and profess her undying love to this guy right on the spot. Instead she remained seated and waited to see what happened next. "I'm Nathan. I couldn't help but overhear your conversation and from the sounds of it I think I'd be safe if I told you," he turned to Tess. "That I think you should let me take you out."

Aimee sat back in her chair.

"Let me ask you something," Tess said. "How old are you?"

"Twenty-one. Why?"

"See Aimee, I told you he could drive. He can even buy me a beer."

Nathan looked uncomfortable.

"I'm sorry," Tess said, returning her attention to Nathan. "I'd like that. What's your number?" Tess pulled out her phone ready to record his digits.

"I already wrote them on that napkin there." Now he was blushing.

Tess looked at the number on the napkin. "I'm Tess. Thanks for the extra ice cream." She looked over and noticed Aimee had already started eating it.

"What? He didn't say I couldn't have any."

"Don't mind her," Tess said. Nathan exhaled with a smile.

"I'm glad you came over. I'll definitely give you a call."

They exchanged another smile before Nathan returned to work.

"You pig! That's my ice cream!" Tess took the spoon out of Aimee's hand.

"Give that back! He brought two spoons. What was I supposed to do? Watch you double fist it? That's just cruel and unusual punishment."

Tess rolled her eyes dismissively.

In a low voice Aimee asked, "So when are you going to call him?"

"I don't know."

"But you said you would definitely call him."

"I know, but, whatever, that's just what people say."

"It's going to take me forever to get used to this new you. What happened to all the true love and happily ever after, soul mate stuff?"

"Oh don't worry. I still want all of that, believe me, but I just think I need, and I do want to, make up for all the time I lost with Nick."

"So then call Nathan!"

Tess looked over her shoulder. Nathan was still looking at her, but this time instead of a confident look, the expression on his face made him look like a lovelorn puppy dog. She suddenly began to question his attractiveness. "Maybe. We'll see. Anyway, what did you mean about me finally seeing what you saw all along?"

"Just that you finally see Nick for what he really is. Now that I think about it, no wonder it took so long. It's not like you had the best example of what a good relationship should be."

Tess was utterly confused.

"I'm serious. You got a rough deal with your dad. Don't get me wrong, he's the nicest guy in the world, but the way he treats women is awful. When that's all you see, it's no surprise you'd go for guys like Nick."

Aimee's words felt like a dull rusted knife stabbed through her heart. Nick was nothing like her father. Nick was reliable, Hugh was not. Nick had a respectable career, Hugh dug in couches for rent money. She only had to remind Nick to call her. She had to tell her father to call her. They were both late in getting to the hospital…Nick thought Hugh was really wise…

"Relationships aren't supposed to be that hard, Tess. Sure, it's not a cake walk but boyfriends aren't supposed make their girlfriends work that hard to keep them. Think about it, if Nick put me through all the stuff he put you through, you'd say that same thing."

Aimee had a point, but Tess still didn't think the reason she fell so hard for Nick was because of her relationship with her father or was it? This new idea found the place in her brain where her drive to make Nick love her lived for so many years and made itself very comfortable.

Now standing, ready to leave the ice cream shop, Tess said, "Okay then, Miss Relationship Expert, tell me, how. How do I find these easy relationships?"

CPSIA information can be obtained
at www.ICGtesting.com
Printed in the USA
FFOW04n0455210217
32662FF